"Guy Adams is ei... I
haven't decided. Th... g
caught in a theme... ,
adventure, the odd ... n
you're not looking." MARK CHADBOURN

"A fearless grand adventure of escalating escapades and
escapes so hair-raising that [Adams'] deranged imagination is barely able to contain them all. I knew we
were in trouble as soon as the ostrich appeared. It's a
fearless, hurtling hell of a debut."

CHRISTOPHER FOWLER

"Playful, intriguing and a barrel of laughs, *The World
House* is a quirky, tumbling box of delights full of adorable
eccentrics on a wild, wild ride. It really knocked me in
the lobes! Great fun!" STEPHEN VOLK

"An extraordinary feat of imagination. It is wonderfully
bizarre, it is brutal, funny, disturbing and vivid throughout. It is populated by a genuinely entertaining and
believable group of characters. Guy Adams has a hit on
his hands. I want more." JAMES BARCLAY

"An audacious, joyous rollercoaster of a book, and yet
what makes it such a triumph is that even in its wildest
excesses it never loses sight of the little people. *The
World House* is a novel with lashings of heart and soul."

MARK MORRIS

ALSO BY GUY ADAMS

The Imagineer
More Than This

Deadbeat
Makes You Stronger
Dogs of Waugh
Old Bones

Kingdom
Prodigal Son

Torchwood
The House That Jack Built

The Case Notes of Sherlock Holmes
Gene Hunt's Rules of Modern Policing:
1973 Edition
Life on Mars: The Official Companion
(with Lee Thompson)

GUY ADAMS

THE WORLD HOUSE

ANGRY
ROBOT

To Diana Adams, with infinite thanks and love,
for passing her passion for story onto her son
and being unwavering in her support.

ANGRY ROBOT
A member of the Osprey Group

Lace Market House,
54-56 High Pavement,
Nottingham
NG1 1HW, UK

www.angryrobotbooks.com
Open the box

Originally published in the UK by Angry Robot 2010
First American paperback printing 2011

ISBN 978-0-85766-037-4

Printed in the United States of America

9 8 7 6 5 4 3 2 1

CHAPTER ONE

They had threatened to break his legs if he didn't find them the money owed. It wasn't an inventive threat but the best never are. What's the point of intimidation if it's not easily imagined? You want the recipient to get their head around the concepts on offer, to feel the sensation of bones splintering inside their legs like shattered lead in a dropped pencil. With a *great* threat the pain starts the minute you finish talking.

For Miles Caulfield it had done its job, his every thought filled by men with lump hammers and an eagerness to use them. Perhaps that's what had happened? He couldn't be sure. His body felt distant, something important he owned but hadn't seen in a while, like a childhood memento stashed in the attic.

It was dark, with a smell so familiar as to have been beneath his notice for a moment: the muskiness of old things. Was he in the shop then, rather than his flat above? Perhaps they had dragged him down here amongst the junk and cobwebs to check his till. To work their way through his shelves and display cabinets for something of worth. If so they needn't have bothered; the sign outside promised "the antique and collectable" but he would hardly be receiving leg-breakers at his door if any of it was valuable. It was a shop dedicated to the battered and broken, the discarded and worthless. He now realised that included the owner. Probably it always had.

So he was surrounded by the smell of old things but there was something not quite right about it. He had spent countless hours sitting amongst his own stock, flipping through a newspaper or completing a crossword. The sorts of pursuits one might involve oneself in when not distracted by the intrusion of customers. It didn't smell like this. This was real age, the sort of dust that might contain fragments of God. He tried to move again but his body was so remote to him that the simple act of twitching a limb was telekinesis. They must have done one hell of a job on him.

"They'll kill you, you know," Jeremy had said as they sat on the wooden bench teasing the ducks with the steaming contents of their takeaway containers. "It won't be quick either, I've seen enough movies, they'll make an example of you. Probably cut your dick off and stick it in your mouth."

Miles, a hunk of meat and bread turning to mush in his mouth, put the rest of his burger down and swallowed reluctantly. "Thanks for that."

"Just saying." Jeremy mixed a slurry of ketchup and mayonnaise with a pinch of fries and popped them in his mouth. "That's the kind of thing these people do."

"We're talking about Gordon Fry not Tony Soprano."

"Just think of me when you're gagging on your own bell-end."

"Fuck's sake…" Miles dumped his food in the bin and lit a cigarette to fumigate his mouth.

Jeremy gave him a dirty look, wafting the smoke away from his face. "I'm eating here, do you mind?"

Miles felt a tickle in his nostrils. In the absence of any other physical sensation he fixated on it. The feeling spread, like leaking oil, from his sinuses to his face. His cheek began to prickle against the wool of a carpet. That settled it, he definitely wasn't in the shop. His floor was bare boards, all the better to wipe up after the tourists dripped their ice creams and trailed their muddy footprints. The dust bristled in his nostrils like static. He sneezed.

"Bless you," Jeremy said, working his way through the contents of Miles' shelves. "We've known each other long enough for me to be honest, haven't we?"

Miles shrugged. "Apparently."

"This really is all crap, isn't it?" Jeremy picked up a tatty looking child's doll, one of its eyelids fluttering at him while the other stayed in place over its sun-damaged blind eye. "You have an entire shop filled with rubbish nobody wants."

"Some of it's collectable."

"Jesus, Miles, but no, it really isn't. You'd have more chance learning how to shit money than make it from this stuff."

"Remind me why we're friends again?" Miles asked.

"Because I'll always tell you the truth." Jeremy smiled, making the doll wave its chipped hand at Miles.

"Nobody's ever been friends for that. I know I haven't got any good stock, OK? If I did, I wouldn't be in this situation. All the good stuff went ages ago."

Jeremy shoved the doll back on a shelf, causing a few items to tumble to the floor.

"Careful!" Miles shouted. "It may be crap but it's all I've got."

He walked over to pick the items up, ducking beneath the arms of a shop-window dummy who modelled a German steel helmet on her flaking bald head.

"Sorry." Jeremy, contrite at last, stooped down to help. "This is quite nice," he said, holding up a rectangular wooden box. "Where's it from?"

Miles, still angry at his friend, pointed at the Chinese writing burned into the pale wood. "Sweden, where do you think?"

Jeremy rolled his eyes. "No need to be sarcastic. Knowing you it's from one of the takeaways in town. How much do you want for it?"

"I don't want your money," Miles snapped, snatching the box off him. "I still have some pride left."

"That's all you'll have soon. Much use it'll be."

Miles sat down on the floor, energy deflated, his arms filled with worthless junk. "About as much as the rest of this shite, I imagine."

Jeremy sat down next to him. "I'd lend you the money if I had it, you know that."

"Then you'd be an idiot." Miles dropped the stock, the box falling into his lap. "I'd only gamble it away."

"Really?" Jeremy looked at him. "Even now, with the threat of a pair of broken legs – or worse – you'd blow it all if I gave it to you?"

Miles turned the box over in his hands. "In a heartbeat."

He promised himself it was the dust in his eyes making them water, not the memory of that conversation. Inch by inch his nerves were reporting in. His left thumb twitched. A spasm trickled along his arm. Immediately he tried duplicating the sensation. For a moment it was beyond him, but then he began to flex the muscle in the ball of his thumb. He would have grinned were his mouth not so numb. Soon his whole hand was twitching at the end of the wrist. There was hope yet.

"You haven't given up?" Fry had asked as Miles stepped into the bar. He gestured to the barmaid to pour him another glass of wine but didn't offer Miles a drink. "I fucking hope not, there's no fun – or profit for that matter – in my debtors just offering their necks up for the noose. Where's the sport in that, eh?"

"I need more time," Miles replied, inching towards the barstool next to Fry but not quite daring to sit on it.

"Oh Christ," Fry sighed, scooping peanuts from a ramekin on the bar, "you're going to be a fucking cliché." He popped the nuts into his mouth, slapping his fingers together to knock away the salt. "Please, save me from the 'more time' conversation. I really haven't the energy for it. It's been a long day. I just want to work my way through this wine and then find some blonde cunt to treat like shit for a few hours. Is that so much to ask?"

Miles opened his mouth to speak but Fry held up a finger to stop him. Miles watched the bar lighting bounce off the grains of salt stuck to Fry's manicured nail. He had the ludicrous notion of licking them off.

"If you were about to say, 'I can get the money,'" Fry continued, "then you should be warned that my response would have been to smash the stem of this wine glass and put your fucking eyes out with it. It's an even bigger cliche than 'I need more time'. Jesus…" he took a sip of his wine "…feel like I've wandered into an episode of fucking *Minder* or something. You can't have any more time and I sincerely hope you can get me my money as I'll turn you into a spastic if you don't." He beckoned the waitress over. "Get this twat a ten-quid chip for the tables," he told her before turning back to face Miles. "Take the tenner, piss it up against the wall – just to show I'm not an unfriendly sort of fucker – and then come back tomorrow with my money or I'll smash your kneecaps, all right? It's perfectly simple: cause and effect, black and white, you pay or we hurt you."

The barmaid returned with the gaming chip. Fry took it off her and tossed it to Miles. "There you go. From small acorns great big pissing fortunes grow – you might even win me my fucking money back."

Miles stood there for a moment, wanting to fling the chip back at Fry and be the bigger man. He was still imagining what that might feel like when he handed it over to the croupier on the blackjack table and took the cards she dealt.

He had one good hand but the other still refused to move. That was OK. If he could get the feeling back in one then logically it would return in the other. He scratched at the carpet. It was deep and expensive but matted with dust. Any money here was old and long undisturbed. His neck loosened and he found he was able to rub his face on the pile, a friction burn developing in his cheek. There was a noise from somewhere to his right and he clenched his hand, automatically preparing to defend himself. It came again: the rustling of feathers.

After he had played (and lost) his ten pound chip, he spent the last few quid in his pocket on rolling to-bacco and cheap wine. He sat in the darkness of his shop, rolling thin cigarettes and quaffing the wine from the bottle. The amber sheen of the streetlights made everything in the shop look unfamiliar and two-dimensional. He shuffled his way through the stock, turning it over in his hands before hurling it across the room. A chipped decorative plate went first. Originally it had celebrated the Queen's Jubilee, now it rejoiced at nothing more than vented anger, shattering against the wall and showering the floorboards with china fragments. Then the child's doll that Jeremy had played with. Miles wrenched its limbs from its sockets, flinging them over his shoulder before dropping the rattling plastic skull to the floor and cracking open its smiling face with the heel of his shoe. Then a pewter tankard turned into a makeshift hammer to pound a selection of thimbles to dust in their wooden display case. He reached for the Chinese box, meaning to reduce it to splinters, but stopped as its surface rippled in the light of the streetlamps. He fumbled it in shock, dropping it to the floor. It must have been a combination of the cheap wine and lighting, but he could have sworn it had moved. He

stared at it, daring it to repeat its trick. It refused. He took a swig of wine and rolled another cigarette, staring at the box, not trusting it enough to take his eyes off it.

That rustling again as something moved past him in the darkness. He managed to windmill his arm across the floor, ignoring the pins and needles. He tried to put his weight on it to turn himself over but his palm beat uselessly at the floor, the nerves shot. He tried again, fighting against the elbow's inclination to bend uselessly. He placed his palm gently against the carpet and fought to stiffen his arm. Once convinced it would hold him, he pushed. A thin strand of saliva pulled from the corner of his mouth as he flipped successfully on to his back. He wiped his lips with a tingling but functional hand. He still couldn't see anything so he flexed his fingers again and burrowed in his jeans pocket for a cigarette lighter. He snagged his fingers on the disposable lighter's flintwheel just as he sensed something draw close. He heard footfalls on the carpet, felt the vibration of its weight through the boards. There was a slight displacement of air as something leaned over him. Pulling the lighter from a nest of loose change and pocket fluff he spun the wheel and found himself staring into the black eyes of an ostrich.

The delusion, if that's what it had been, had taken all the energy out of Miles' anger so he took the box upstairs to stare at in some degree of comfort. The wine was done but in a twist of good fortune he found half a bottle of cheap-shit calvados in the kitchen cupboard. He'd bought it when trying to impress a date by his ability to cook. It burned all the way down his throat, whether with alcohol or regret was impossible to tell.

He placed the box on the stained coffee table in the lounge, turned on all the lights and sat down on the carpet to roll another cigarette. While he packed strands of tobacco, tangled as pubic hair, into the centre of his cigarette paper he tried to remember where he had bought the box. After a while the auctions and house clearances had a habit of blending together. An endless parade of tatty banana-boxed "treasures", things once precious reduced to funky-smelling trinkets wrapped in decades-old newspaper. He had a vague memory of a house near Coventry, the stink of a dying man's piss, and ticks in the upholstery. Hadn't there been a whole chest filled with decorative boxes? The spoils of a youth in the navy? He picked up the Chinese box, meaning to open it. The lid wouldn't shift; possibly the wood was warped or the hinges rusted. Now the box was so close to his face he became aware of a noise, a gentle ticking from inside it. He held it next to his ear and listened. It was a precise but unrhythmic clicking, not clockwork, more the sort of noise a beetle might make. He turned the box over in his hands, shaking it and rubbing his thumbs along its edges. The ticking grew louder. Suddenly, something sharp stung his palm and he dropped the box. Rubbing at the sore flesh on his hand he watched a red weal, like an insect bite, begin to develop.

He pulled his mobile out of his pocket and called Jeremy. The phone rang out a few times before his friend's voice groaned into the receiver. "Miles? Bloody hell... do you know what time it is?"

When his friend spoke, the box stopped its noise, as if shy.

"No," Miles admitted, glancing at his watch. He'd lost a few hours somewhere along the line: it was nearly two in the morning. "Sorry... didn't realise it had got so late. Listen, that box…"

"Are you drinking?"

"Of course I am, what else is there to do in my current situation? I'd be eating heroin like toffee if I had any. You know the box you were looking at? The Chinese one?"

"Please tell me you didn't wake me up to sell me antiques."

"Don't be stupid, there's something…" How to pin it down without sounding mad? "There's something weird about it. When I was looking at it I thought it changed shape. Now it's ticking."

"You really have been drinking, haven't you?"

"Jesus!" Miles' exasperation made him clench his teeth "It's not the bloody wine, all right? I'm pissed but I'm not hallucinating… There's something seriously weird going on."

"I'll tell you what's weird," Jeremy replied. Miles could hear him getting out of bed and turning on a light. "That's the fact that you've got a bunch of thugs waiting to pay you a visit and you're just sat in your flat messing about with stock. If you can't find the money – and of course you can't – then get out of there, for fuck's sake. Come round here, or even better get yourself to a train station and bugger off somewhere. What about that friend of yours in London? Gary something… go and kip on his floor for a few weeks."

"And then what?"

"I don't bloody know!" Jeremy's voice distorted in Miles' ear. "Stay there, I suppose! Anything's better than just sitting around waiting for them to come knocking on your door."

"Don't worry about it," Miles muttered, hanging up. A few seconds later Jeremy rang back but Miles ignored it.

He wouldn't run, though he couldn't have told Jeremy why, not without sounding pathetic. He had just sunk too low. Movement, thought, self-preservation… they all required energy, they needed him to care. Right now, the only thing he could sum up any enthusiasm for was this damned box. It began ticking again.

"What are you about?" he muttered. A throbbing pulse of drunkenness surged through his head as he moved, his brain bobbing like a boat in a storm. He nudged the box with his foot, nervousness vanishing alongside the last few crumbs of his giving a shit. He rubbed at the mark on his palm but it didn't hurt. He sat down on the floor, his back against the nicotine-stained paintwork that he had promised himself he would touch up for the last three years.

The box flipped over and landed on its base. Miles stared at it, unsure how to respond. The ticking continued to grow in volume, an angry jazz rimshot that made his left eyelid twitch.

The ostrich cricked its neck, startled by the fire from the lighter, and there was a dry, tearing noise like a baguette being broken in half. A cloud of dust sprinkled from its throat and it opened its beak with the creak of a pair of rusted garden shears. The heat from the flame singed Miles' thumb and he let the light go out. Panicking in darkness all the more dense for the flame's absence, he blew on his thumb and spun the flint wheel, desperate to reignite it, sparks leaping into the dark and vanishing quickly. Finally, the flame lit and the ancient bird gave a startled squawk. It reared its head back and, with another cry, thrust it forward, stabbing at Miles' hand. Now, without thinking about it, Miles found he was able to move a little more, the upper part of his body rolling to one side as he tried to avoid the angry pecking. The beak punched the small of his back as he pulled himself out of the way, his legs dragging uselessly behind him. He lashed back with his right arm, catching the bird on the side of its head with his fist. The bird gave another squawk and retreated in a rustle of feathers. Miles kept pulling himself along the carpet, clouds of dust stinging his eyes. A dull throb pulsed in his lower back from where the bird had hit him. His hand smacked against a wooden pole. He ran his fingers up and down it, feeling its bulges and contours. It was a table leg, stout enough to be Regency (the absurdity of his trying to date the thing by touch, given his current situation, was not lost on him but it was hard to break the habit of a lifetime). He pulled himself past it, rolling on to his back and feeling the underside of the table above. Hopefully it might offer some protection. The ostrich was trotting to and fro some distance away; he could hear its scaly feet pounding the old carpet. It wasn't alone – the whole room seemed to be coming to life: there was creaking and hissing; a sound like someone tapping on a window; a shuffling of something large pulling itself along the floor; a low growl... The scent of age was growing stronger too, sweet and dusty, making him want to sneeze or vomit, perhaps both. Something jumped on to the table he could hear its claws tapping as it walked along the wood. *Tap... tap... tap...*

He woke to a knocking on the door and, for a second, thought the sound must be coming from the box. He was still sat in the corner of his room, unaware of the moment when he had lost consciousness. Daylight shone through the windows, making him squint. The knocking came again, echoing along the stairwell that led from his flat to street-level. His door wasn't used to visitors and there was only one man he could imagine eager for his company (or, more precisely, his wallet). Surely he still had a few hours to find the money? He checked his watch as the knocking came a third time, staring at its hostile face and the late afternoon it swore he had woken into. The person at his door ran out of patience and started rattling at the lock.

Now that the threat was solidifying, becoming an actuality rather than an abstract, he realised he hadn't been scared at all. Fear, *real* fear, was the surge of nausea he felt right now, curdling the cheap red wine in his stomach and turning his lower jaw to jelly. How could he have imagined that he could just sit here and take what had been promised to him? Getting to his feet he slammed a hand to the wall to steady himself as his legs buckled and his stomach ejected the previous night's self-pitying booze in an arc across the paintwork. There was no time for cleanliness and he ran through to the kitchen and his back door. The rear of the flat boasted a wooden balcony with a row of steps that would see him in the delivery area behind the building; from there it was a short jog to the street.

The person at the front door was working the lock. Miles could hear the careful investigation of metal on metal as the tumblers were forced to roll over and let the intruder in. He pulled at the handle of the back door, spitting some of the filth from his mouth in anger as he realised it was locked. He yanked the kitchen drawers open, hunting for the key. He found it, still wearing the rental agency address tag on a length of old, thick string. He shoved it into the lock. He heard the front door open behind him as the key turned, heavy feet beginning to ascend the stairs. The back door was stiff and the wood cried out as he wrenched it open. If he could just get on to the street he had some hope of giving his pursuers the slip. Surely they would be wary of attacking him in plain sight?

"Don't be a dickhead," Gordon Fry said, standing on the balcony just outside Miles' door. "Give us a bit of fucking credit, yeah?"

The feeling of safety offered by the table began to wane. Miles couldn't begin to imagine what was pacing up and down above him but the sound of its claws, tapping and scratching on the polished wood, was all he needed to know to be afraid. The growling was getting closer too, though the animal must surely be sick as the noise was too harsh to come from a healthy throat. Perhaps it was also lame; certainly it was dragging itself rather than walking towards him. There were more birds, tuneless whistles and squawks and the occasional whoosh of air as they flew past the table, stirring the dust with the beating of their wings. Sometimes the noise would stop with a dull thud as they found the perimeter of the room, beaks pounding into wood-panelling like inaccurately thrown pub darts. There was a dry rattle, a maraca shaken in the dark.

Miles, terrified of snakes, found a cold sweat beginning to form on his forehead as he imagined its dry belly curling its way along the greasy carpet. He held the lighter in his hand and wondered whether to strike it. He couldn't decide whether it might attract the creatures or scare them off. He rubbed his thumb indecisively along the flint wheel as the noises drew nearer…

After so long insisting he wasn't going to run, it now seemed he couldn't stop. It was completely pointless, of course; he could hardly lose them in a one-bedroom flat. Fry knew this and took his time stepping into the kitchen, closing and locking the door behind him, casually poking through a couple of the cupboards out of sheer nosiness. The two men that he had brought with him – who had proven so adept at forcing locked doors – also knew their quarry was going nowhere. They followed Miles into the lounge as casually as if they had been invited, perhaps to discuss Our Beneficent Lord or the benefits of solar panelling as an alternative energy source. Miles wasn't fooled by their nonchalance, nor did he think for one minute that the heavy-looking canvas bag that one of the men dropped on to the sofa contained promotional literature. There was the chink of metal against metal as the objects inside the bag tumbled together. It was a deceptively prim noise, like the tapping of champagne glasses during a wedding toast.

The men had the sort of bland appearance that was only found in the true professional: long wool overcoats, pink muscular heads razored baby-arse smooth. They showed no sense of eagerness for the task ahead but no concern either. Miles, on the other hand, was so concerned that he was close to losing all physical control. He was shaking violently as he watched Fry enter the room nibbling on a chocolate biscuit he'd found in the kitchen. His legs desperately wanted him to run and he didn't altogether disagree, just had no idea where or how. Fry, noticing the purple spray of wine-laced vomit that bruised the wall in the corner of the room, grimaced and threw what was left of the biscuit on the floor.

"Heavy night, was it?" he asked. "If it weren't for the fact that you were trying to fuck off over the back wall I'd hope it was in celebration of getting me my money."

Accepting there was no way he would walk out of the room, Miles started trying to talk his way out instead. His jaw was shaking so much with nerves that he couldn't get his words out straight. Fry punching him in the face didn't help.

"Think how I feel," Fry said, the small amount of feigned civility he had offered gone, "coming all the way over here, only to hear the bad – if not altogether surprising – news that I'm deeply out of pocket." His cheeks were reddening as he got angrier, pounding his shiny leather shoes into Miles' legs and belly. "Hardly fucking fair, is it? I lend you some money, you don't pay it back and now I'm supposed to be the bad man for taking it out on you. Well, *fuck you!*" He gave him one more kick to the arse, sending a wave of pain through the base of Miles' spine. "Thieving fucker."

Miles was hunched, foetal, trying to protect himself from Fry's kicks – though, Lord knows, in a few moments he would likely look back on them as the gentlest of kisses. Despite the fear, despite the sight of one of the bald men unzipping the canvas bag and pulling out a pair of wooden blocks, despite Fry wiping at his spittle-covered chin with his coat sleeve and looking sorely tempted to resume his attack, despite all that… Miles became aware that the wooden box was ticking again. He twisted his head to look at it, his interest, once again, somewhat inappropriate to his circumstances.

Fry certainly felt snubbed, stepping over Miles to snatch the box from the floor. "Worth something, is it?" he asked, shaking the box in his hands, maybe to silence the ticking. Miles found himself scared to see the box manhandled in such a fashion, though he knew he was due for heavier treatment.

"Fucking *fucker!*" Fry shouted, verbose as ever, slamming his hand to his mouth as if to shove the words back down his throat. Miles glimpsed a trickle of blood on the man's lips and realised he'd caught himself on the box. "Cunting thing," Fry mumbled, sucking his wound. He threw the box at Miles, who instinctively grabbed it.

And promptly vanished.

Miles gritted his teeth, waiting to feel the gentle curl of the rattlesnake against the soles of his feet. The floor vibrated with the pounding of the ostrich, and he heard a whistle of air and a rattle from the snake that suddenly went distant as it was snatched in the bird's mouth. Miles bent double with relief, his stomach churning. Above his head, the clawed creature began hopping up and down and yapping. This made Miles feel doubly relieved. He was damned if he was going to cower in fear of what sounded like an asthmatic terrier. Emboldened, he spun the lighter's flintwheel and screamed at the sight of a tiger's wide-open mouth a foot or so from him. The big cat growled and again Miles had a moment to wonder what was wrong with the animal that it could sound so ruptured. With a reflex action he shoved the lighter towards it and was startled to see that it froze as the light of the flame drew close. Its wide-open

jaw, its sharp fangs… utterly still, like a paused piece
of film footage. Suddenly aware how close his fist
was to the animal's mouth, Miles moved it away a
few inches. As he did so the tiger came back to life,
freezing again as he returned the lighter to where it
had been. So… as long as he held the flame right to
its eyes the animal wouldn't move. Right… of
course… not a safety tip he had ever picked up from
wildlife documentaries but he couldn't argue with
the evidence. He held the lighter as close as he dared,
his thumb beginning to burn.

He could hear the ostrich running towards the
table but didn't dare shift his attention away from
the tiger and its shiny yet dead eyes. The flame of the
lighter danced secondhand in its pupils. His thumb
grew hotter but he reasoned that the pain of a
burned thumb was nothing compared to having the
whole hand bitten off. There was a flicker of movement from his right that he hoped wasn't the ostrich
wanting to pick another fight. Surely nothing was
likely to advance while the tiger stood so close? His
thumb continued to singe. There was movement
again and the… Wait – how could he see anything
anyway? He turned his head slightly, enough to see
the room taking shape around him as gas lamps in
the walls glowed brighter while he watched. His
thumb slipped off the lighter and the flame died. The
tiger, with a fresh growl, hurled itself at him only to
slump almost instantly, its fangs fixed around the
arm he had raised to defend himself. It was a rug,
which explained why it had sounded so lame in the

darkness, though not how it could have come to life with hunger on its mind. He threw it to one side and crawled out from under the table, getting shakily to his feet.

Gripping the edge of the table to steady himself, he looked around what appeared to be a Victorian-style billiard room. The space was filled with stuffed creatures. The ostrich frozen mid-step, stiff rattlesnake held in its beak. A deer rearing up on withered back legs. The creature he had heard above him was nothing more intimidating than a raccoon, its tail threadbare, a hole where one of its eyes had tumbled from its dry socket. There were deep scratches in the table surface, and cobwebs that had hung between a set of crystal decanters had been torn apart, caught in the raccoon's ears and raised paws.

Miles walked over to a case fixed on the wall. The glass was cracked from the pounding of the fat, flightless bird within. Its beak still poked from the white-ice of broken glass.

He moved around the room and saw tarantulas that had been marching in formation across the baize of the billiard table; distorted heads of horned game that had been howling noiselessly, their voice-boxes lost to the taxidermist's trash bin; a small iguana, half-peeled with age and damp, mouth clamped on the cold and empty egg of a pheasant; a peacock, with tail furled and head cocked to one side, appearing almost as curious as Miles about its surroundings. Saddest of all, a large black bear, no longer forced into a majestic or threatening stance, curled in the corner of the room, a single heavy paw covering its eyes.

He ran over to the far side of the room, grabbed the heavy glass knocker and turned it in both hands, desperate to get out. The door swung open, bringing him face to face with a short woman wearing an old-fashioned bobbed hairstyle and nothing else. There was a pause as each took in the presence of the other and then the woman screamed. Miles found his adrenalin spent. It's not that a man can't panic in front of a naked woman – he can and frequently does – more that he mustn't let it show.

"It's all right!" he insisted, "I won't hurt you."

To his credit, he sounded perfectly genuine but she kicked him square in the balls anyway, just to be sure.

CHAPTER TWO

Was there anything more sensual in life than "Sultry Sunset" pushed through the sweat and cigarette smoke of the Cotton Club from the bell of Johnny Hodges' saxophone? If there was, Penelope Simons (of the Boston Simonses, naturally) had yet to experience it. Though that might change in a few hours if everything went according to plan and Chester was willing. And God knows, Chester *was* willing. He broke out in sweats and a stutter just from being in the same room. He would never admit it, of course, his family background was as puritanical as Penelope's. One only had to look at his mother, a brittle, cold creature, wool-wrapped and masked in permanent disapproval, to wonder how he had ever been conceived in the first place. Back in his parents' youth they would at least have been allowed a drink stiff enough to encourage the condition elsewhere.

"I've never slept with a coloured," Dolores purred. She washed this deliberately contentious comment down with a mouthful of orange juice cut with a dash of home-brewed liquor. Dolores didn't believe in prohibition – of anything – and always carried a small bottle of "liquid pep" in her purse. Penelope, though not opposed to the principle of drinking, was far too nervous to share. She doubted she'd ever be thirsty enough to risk blindness.

"Give you time, darling," Penelope replied, taking a mouthful of her own drink and pulling a cigarette from her purse.

"My constant worry," Dolores replied, passing Penelope a book of matches but never taking her eyes off the saxophonist. "So little time, so many to do."

Penelope cackled, the cigarette quivering between her lips before the sight of a proffered flame stilled it. "Thank you," she told the waiter, but he was already gone, pushing his way through the tables towards the bar. "Good service," she muttered.

"Absolutely," Dolores replied. "That's what we need!"

The pair of them burst into hysterics, Duke Ellington's band covering their laughter as it sprang to life *en masse*.

Dolores was scandalous, but that was why Penelope enjoyed her company. If one didn't have the nerve to be scandalous oneself then seeking it out secondhand was the next best thing. A modicum of the fun with none of the risk.

"Good evening, ladies." Chester had arrived and was shifting from one foot to the other, at a loss how to present himself. Eventually he settled for putting his hands behind his back and inclining himself towards the table in a slight bow. Penelope thought it made him look like a waiter but would never tell him so. She jumped to her feet to put him out of his misery, kissed him on the cheek and guided him towards a chair. The nervous sweat had appeared and he mopped at his forehead with his handkerchief. "Hellish hot, don't you think?" he muttered before remembering himself and addressing Penelope directly. "May I say you're looking stunning this evening, Penelope?"

"Of course you may!" She laughed, giving a little shimmy in her seat. "Sequins and lamé, darling, I wouldn't be seen in anything else!"

The need to vomit had passed but Miles decided it was safer to stay on the floor. They were in a long corridor, its décor as dated as the room he had just left, with deep-red paintwork and cornicing. The naked woman was bent over in an attempt to conceal herself. She dripped water as she inched towards a pair of heavy curtains that framed a Roman bust at the end of the corridor. Had she just stepped out of the shower? Her left eye sported a bruise and her lower lip was fatter than it should be; someone had picked a fight with her recently, that was for sure. But then, having had his reproductive organs shunted to just below his lungs, he remained open-minded as to whether he might sympathise.

"I'm not looking," he said, holding up his head to show his eyes were closed. He heard the tearing of velvet and the rattle of argumentative hooks. "Wouldn't it be easier just to go to your room and grab a gown?" he asked. "Seems a shame to take it out on the furnishings."

"I don't have a room," she replied. "Where's Chester?"

"Chester? I don't really know… somewhere up north."

"What are you talking about? Isn't this his house?"

"Oh." Miles didn't really know how to reply to that. "Maybe… thought you meant the town. Look…" He risked a peek. She was wrapped in the curtain now but keeping her distance. "I know this is going to sound ridiculous but I don't actually know how I got here, had some sort of blackout I suppose, woke up in that room, completely out of it." He shifted awkwardly on his knees. "Delusional, I guess, I thought the stuffed animals were…" He looked at her and decided not to admit what he had been about to say; the last thing he wanted to do was sound even madder. "Well, doesn't matter, I was disorientated, could hardly move. Anyway, the lights came on and I made to leave, which is when I bumped into you. I'm obviously trespassing and I'm only too happy to go."

"That makes two of us then," she replied.

"He's so sweet," said Penelope, watching Chester negotiate his way back from the cloakroom. He caught his foot on a chair leg and nearly fell into a table of laughing women. This made them laugh all the more and his pale face turned crimson. He tried to keep hold of the coats in one arm and straighten his oiled hair with the other. "Excuse me," he muttered, moving away as quickly as he could.

"The car's outside," he announced, once back at the safety of their table. He draped the coats on his empty chair so he could lift them off individually and help the ladies don them.

"Why, thank you, kind sir," said Dolores, fluttering her eyelashes at him as he draped her fox stole around her neck.

"Not at all," Chester replied, giving a slight bow of his head, formal as ever.

Penelope turned to receive her own shawl and stroked the back of his hand while it was within reach at her shoulder. "Thank you, Chester." He squeezed her fingers by way of response.

Stepping on to the Harlem street there was a crispness to the air that even the jazz filtering faintly out of the club was unable to thaw.

"Over there." Chester gestured towards a black DeSoto and extended his arm for Penelope to hold.

His driver climbed out and held the back door open. He was a giant of a man who looked ready to pop the silver buttons off his chauffeur's jacket at the very next breath. Dolores clambered to the far side, the leather seat giving a sigh of surprised air as she dropped on to it roughly. She was drunk, Penelope realised, glancing at Chester to see if he had noticed. If he had, he made no sign of it. He was so polite he would likely not comment even if she were vomiting over the upholstery. She sat down next to her friend, lowering herself so gently she could only be over-compensating. Chester followed, sitting down a little awkwardly, Penelope thought, probably wary of the close physical contact. The driver closed the door behind them with a gentle click. He grinned at Penelope through the window, which she thought somewhat strange; certainly she wouldn't encourage the help to be so expressive. It was disconcerting.

"Nice car," Dolores said. 'I've known smaller apartments."

Penelope was pleased to see Chester smile. "It is roomy, isn't it?"

"This is just stupid." The fear Miles had felt when first waking up had been stifled for a while. The human mind can't tolerate relentless panic – it's tiring and unconstructive – and is only too happy to fart justificatory nonsense as long as doing so gets things moving. That said, there is only so much impossibility a human being can stomach. "The corridor just never ends."

Penelope was becoming more withdrawn. The bruise around her eye had darkened noticeably, proof of its freshness. She refused to tell him how she'd come by it and he'd given up asking. In fact he had given up conversation altogether but there was only so long they could ignore the obvious: no matter how far they walked, the end of the corridor drew no closer. The illusion only seemed to work ahead of them; when he glanced over his shoulder, the alcove where Penelope had torn the curtain free of its rail was so distant it was impossible to see it clearly. It made his stomach churn, horizontal vertigo.

"It's just not possible," he muttered.

"Obviously it is," Penelope whispered, pulling her curtain around her. "We're looking at it."

Miles did his best to bite down on his irritation. "You know what I mean." The corridor had no shortage of rooms. Every fifteen feet or so they passed a heavy wooden door. Miles moved to the closest. "We need to start checking the rooms," he said, turning the handle. "Maybe there'll be a window or something, somebody we can ask."

"Ask about the impossible corridor, yes, let's do that." Penelope's voice was quiet and flat. Miles was worried that she was going into shock.

He reached for the door handle.

Penelope freely admitted her lack of knowledge of the city's geography. She experienced New York internally: from club to fashion store to gallery to restaurant, shuttled between them by a succession of taxicabs. When you loved designer shoes as much as she did, you understood they were not for walking in. It therefore took her a few minutes to suspect that Chester's driver was following a strange route to Dolores' house. The dark brownstones of Harlem were long behind them, replaced by an industrial landscape, chimneys and pipes, soot-covered brick and high fencing.

"Where are we?" she asked Chester as the car pulled into a warehousing area for one of the factories.

"My father's plant," he answered, rubbing his palms dry on the legs of his trousers.

"What for?" Dolores asked, her words slurred. She peered through the window at the dark building outside. "All you big families blend into one, steelworks to chicken plants, I can never remember who's who. What do you guys do?'

"Whatever we want," Chester replied, leaning past Penelope to slam Dolores' face into the window. The shove was hard enough to make her friend's nose pop, spitting a spray of blood on the glass.

For a moment, as the door handle turned smoothly on its bolt, Miles had an almost overwhelming urge to remove his hand and run. It was irrational, of course – at least that's what he told himself. He had just spooked himself before: taxidermy wasn't predatory and one simply couldn't get eaten by a rug. No.

(But why is the corridor so damned long?)

He hadn't the first idea how to explain his circumstances but at least he was better off here than in the company of Fry and his impromptu surgeons.

(Don't be so sure of that, this place… bristles… there's something so, so wrong with it.)

Penelope was at his shoulder, forgetting for the moment that she didn't trust him. He could see from her face that she felt it too. Like excess ozone before a storm, there was an atmosphere that didn't sit right.

He opened the door...

...to find a bedroom of moderate size, a little os-tentatious but not life-threatening. There was a wood-framed bed with lace drapes, a solid-looking dresser whose mirror showed him his own nervous face, and a large set of French windows that must lead to a balcony (unless the architect liked to en-courage guests to walk out into thin air).

"Anticlimax," he muttered, stepping into the room.

Penelope crossed to the wardrobe, hoping to find spare clothes. She opened the doors and sighed at the emptiness they revealed.

Miles went straight to the window, wanting an idea of the outside geography. He stood in front of the dark glass, seeing nothing but his own reflection. "Too dark," he said, though Penelope wasn't listen-ing; she was hunting through drawers. Miles took hold of the handle of the French windows and then snatched his hand back with a small yelp as a shock ran up his arm. "Static or something," he said, reach-ing for it again more tentatively. He touched the handle carefully but it was fine this time. He opened the door and stepped outside into complete dark-ness. No stars, no lights, nothing. Leaning over the stone balustrade he saw no sign of the ground. It was if the world stopped the minute you reached the house's edge.

The events in the back of the car wouldn't sit clearly in Penelope's mind. Chester had hit her, she knew that; she could feel the throbbing on the side of her head where his fist had smacked her in the temple. She suspected that she had passed out at that point, for certainly there was nothing between that and her next memory: the feeling of the door-panelling cold on her cheek and the sound of tearing fabric. At that point she couldn't say whether it was her clothes being torn or Dolores'. She could hear her friend moaning, a wet, bubbling sound, delirium and fear pushed through a broken mouth. She had a feeling that she had tried to reach for the door handle – either that or Chester had kicked her in the kidneys for fun. It was possible: it seemed clear that there was no behaviour too unconscionable for him. There was another gap in her memory at this point, a jump-cut to the sound of Chester grunting and a high-pitched giggling that she could only assume was the driver. She remembered the man's strange grin as he had closed the door and a terrible sense of stupidity grew in her, a certainty that she should have seen this coming, should have known something was wrong. But then horrible things like this just didn't happen to people like Penelope. It was this thought that followed her into unconsciousness but it offered no comfort. The next thing she knew, Chester was talking.

"…about world-shaping," he was saying, "the willingness to make changes, both moral and physical. You can't build without breaking boundaries. The things I've seen…" There was a wistful quality to his voice, a gentility that one might expect in a discussion of a view or landscape painting, or perhaps a piece of gentle pastoral music. She turned her head to look at him but couldn't tell if the blood on his face was hers or Dolores'. She hoped it was the blood of her friend and the guilt that followed that thought stung almost as much as the bruise on the side of her head.

Chester was still talking. "This is not it. This is not the limit. There are worlds on top of worlds, on top of worlds…" He was holding up a wooden box – a cigar box perhaps? "I just want to explore." He looked at her. "You'll help me, won't you, Penelope?" He punched her in the face, his expression the calmest she had ever seen it. Gone was the nervous socialite, the awkward would-be lover. She had found what made Chester comfortable, what made him utterly at ease in his own skin. She'd always known she could bring him out of his shell.

"There's no breeze." Penelope had appeared at the French windows and her voice made Miles jump. He had been thinking the same thing, that the air here didn't feel right. It was empty, breathable but tasteless.

"There's nothing," he replied but even as he said it he knew it wasn't true. There *was* something out here, he could sense it if not see it. It was an animal instinct. There was no noise, no obvious clue to a presence, yet he knew it was there as surely as if he were staring at it.

"Get back inside," Penelope said. Did she feel it too?

Whatever it was, this thing in the dark, it began to push towards them.

Miles was more scared now than he had been with Gordon Fry on his doorstep, though unable to say precisely why. It was as if the invisible force heading toward him were fear itself, and the closer it came, the more Miles was unable to move. Closer, closer, closer…

When Penelope woke again she was mortified to see she had been stripped. She drew herself as far away from Chester as the space in the car would allow, which was not far. Dolores was gone and it took a few moments of hearing the noises from the driver's compartment to guess where. Her friend was silent; the driver was not.

"You're awake," Chester said, as gentle as a man greeting a wife from a night's sleep. He was playing with the box, turning it over in his hands, rubbing his fingers along the edges. "This is breathtaking," he said, though she couldn't be sure whether he was referring to the box or the general situation. The car was shaking from the exertions of the driver and Penelope knew she was fast approaching the point when it would be too late to save herself. She needed to fight now and live or die by her efforts. Chester sighed, staring at the box held out in front of him, perched on the tips of his fingers. "Don't worry," he said, "I won't abuse you." He inclined his head towards the driving cabin. "Not like that. Henryk has his tastes. I pander to them but they are not my own." Had she been feeling braver Penelope might well have asked him why, if that were the case, he had felt the need to remove her clothes. It was a pointless question; she knew hollow words when she heard them. "I want something altogether more spiritual from you," he continued, "though I can't pretend it won't hurt." He held the box towards her. "There is a box, and inside that box is a door, and beyond that door…" He smiled. "I'm getting ahead of myself. The problem is that the door is locked. I want you to help me unlock it."

"With pleasure, Chester," Penelope said, punching him as hard as she could between his legs. If his tastes were so noble she wouldn't be damaging anything he intended to use. Chester bent forward, dropping the box. Penelope grabbed it, wrestled with the door handle and pushed the heavy black door open. She was aware that Henryk had paused in his ministrations; she could see his face through the glass partition. He wasn't grinning any more.

She stepped out of the car. Chester's hand tugged a pinch of hair from her scalp as he snatched at her. Her feet complained at the grit of the road but if cut soles were the only injury ahead she'd consider herself lucky.

She expected to hear the sound of pursuing feet but when the engine turned over she realised that chasing her on foot was the last thing they would do. She ran down a gap between a storage shed and a churning drainage gully. The water rushed past and she wondered if escape might be found by jumping in. The decision was taken from her. Tripping over a pipe that led from the shed into the gulley, she went head-first into the rushing water. For a moment the box seemed to twist in her hands, as if tugged free, then there was nothing, no water, no car, *nothing*…

Then she woke up.

"Come on!" Penelope shouted, pulling Miles back through the doorway and sprawling on to his arse. She slammed the French windows shut and, though there was still nothing to see, she felt the door bow inward as if something had collided with it from the other side. She let go of the handle as a surge of static nipped at her palms, and backed away from the door, hoping that whatever was outside stayed there.

"I don't know what was wrong with me," Miles said. "I just couldn't move."

"Can you now?" Penelope asked.

"Yes, I'm fine." Miles got to his feet.

"Then let's get out of here."

CHAPTER THREE

Only flies could pretend to savour the Valencian midday heat. Everything else kept to the shade, dozing through siesta-time as the clock crept towards the threat of more work. Curtains of humidity draped themselves across the streets in such thick layers it was almost impossible to force yourself through them. It was a day that sapped effort, a day to be endured from the comfort of an armchair or the cool shade of a bar. Certainly it was not a day for running, but then Kesara, as always, had little choice.

Kesara was good at running, having done a considerable amount of it during her twelve years. She had run when she left home – of course she had, her father was likely too drunk to chase her but only a fool would take the risk – and she had never really stopped. Travelling north along the coast she had run just because she could, betraying a childhood of captivity and oppression with lungfuls of sea air and the urge to see how fast your legs could carry you.

Once she had reached Valencia, and sat at the port
dangling her hot feet in the sea, she realised she
would have to stop running eventually. The thought
made her sad. Still, the port was busy enough for a
young girl to hide and there was enough spillage
from the crates to fill her belly. It would be foolish
not to stay. On that first night she had dined on
overripe Nispero, peeling the oval orange fruit,
sucking their sweet flesh and then throwing the
dark stones into the waves. She had slept on a
mound of potent-smelling fish nets, her guts
painfully loose from too much fruit. Despite her discomfort, it was the best night's sleep she had ever
had. Now, a couple of months later, she still enjoyed
bedding down wherever the mood took her and eating whatever fell her way. She was never happier
than when watching the sea, every crashing wave a
symbol of freedom.

Today that freedom was at risk, and all because of
the smell of chicken.

The bird had sat on the kitchen sideboard, sweating translucent steam from the collar of its crisp
golden jacket. The meeting house was used as a bar-
racks for the Republican army. Kesara had seen the
soldiers smoke cigarettes in its doorway, undressing
the girls with their eyes as they walked by. Even if
she had not seen them hanging around she would
have guessed by the smell. It wafted from every
window but the kitchen, where nothing lingered
but the sweet smell of roasted meat — the stink of
well-worn army boots and sheets so stiff they might

snap in a firm grip. Men were smelly, Kesara knew that. Her father had worn his stench as a bear wears its fur, sitting in their small fishing cottage burying the waves of whisky sweat and unwashed clothes beneath endless mouthfuls of cigarette smoke. While he was at home on the water, he rarely allowed it to touch him in the name of hygiene.

The chicken was being left to cool. Kesara had no idea where the cook had gone or when they might return but if she climbed through the window that meat could be hers. The risk of a beating was no risk at all. Her skin had received enough blows over the years to be almost immune.

She reached for the sill, finding a couple of holes in the masonry for her toes, and forced herself up and through the part-open window. Once hanging inside, she let her momentum pull her down on to the cool kitchen-floor tiles. Advancing on the chicken she realised that it was too hot to pick up with her bare hands. She walked carefully towards the kitchen door and stuck her head into the small corridor beyond. She could hear lots of snoring coming from the dormitory, like pigs in prayer. A few feet from the kitchen was a large laundry trolley. She tiptoed over to it and yanked a yellowing pillowcase from the bundle inside. She could use it as a sack, drop the chicken inside and carry it over her shoulder.

She stepped back into the kitchen and used a carving fork to hook the roasted bird into the pillowcase. That done, she dashed towards the window. The bang of a pair of double doors, from just along the corridor outside, sent her heartbeat into her throat. She dropped her legs over the sill and spun around to drop to the street below. Her feet hit the cobbles just as the face of the cook appeared at the window, bellowing a stream of obscenities at her from purple cheeks. A pair of soldiers appeared from the front of the building, flicked their cigarettes into the street and ran towards her.

Kesara ran, the hot air parting for her as she darted through the winding side-streets, changing direction at random, hoping to lose her pursuers through confusion as well as speed. The hot chicken swung behind her, planting hot, greasy kisses on the small of her back as the fat leaked into the fabric of the pillowcase. As fast as she was, the soldiers kept pace with her. She didn't turn to look – that would slow her down – but the sound of their heavy boots loomed over her as surely as the smell of roasted poultry. She was lucky that the streets were nearly empty, and the soldiers' cries for someone to stop her found nobody with the energy or interest to carry them out. She had planned to aim for the docks but her attempts to disorientate her pursuers had been no less effective on herself. The streets around her were unfamiliar. She needed to change tack.

She turned a corner and ran straight through the open front door of a house. Her eyes struggled with the sudden gloom, but she saw the old owner well enough, the woman struggling to her feet with a cry as Kesara ran straight past her into the central atrium. With no space for gardens, the townhouses all possessed roof terraces accessed by a set of steps leading from an open central courtyard. It was clear from the chipped tiles along the stairway that the old lady hadn't visited her roof in some while but Kesara didn't have time to worry if it were still structurally sound.

She emerged into daylight, aware that the cries of the old lady were sure to draw the soldiers. She ran to the edge of the terrace, clamped the pillowcase between her teeth and jumped to the sun terrace of the house next door. The terracotta tiles were baked hot by the sun but she moved quickly enough not to burn her soles. She leaped from one roof to the next, continuing to make her way along the tops of the houses.

One of the soldiers appeared on the old lady's terrace and shouted in her direction but he was too concerned whether the roof tiles would take his weight to follow her. Glancing over the edge of the building she could see his friend in the street below. She gasped as he unslung his rifle from his shoulder. Surely they wouldn't shoot her for the sake of a chicken? But what was Kesara to know of the Republican state of mind? On the losing end of a civil war, tired and frustrated by heat and lack of supplies, the young soldier was damned if he was going to lose his dinner just because some light-fingered wretch fancied a bite of it.

The shot clipped the edge of the roof and Kesara yelped as a fragment of tile cut a thin line across her forehead. The shooter's friend began shouting again, though whether it was at her or his fellow soldier Kesara was too scared to tell. Another shot cut its way past her and she ran towards the rear of the roof terrace. The jump across the street was much farther than she would have liked but her fear of being shot was the greater concern and she took to the air with barely a thought. She sailed over the cobbled street, chicken still swinging in its pillowcase as it dangled from her hand. She crashed into the railings of the opposite house's balcony, her knees slamming into the iron bars, her arms hooking over their edge. The chicken popped between her body and the railings, distorting in a spray of yanked bone and compressed meat. A legbone stabbed her in the ribs as she pulled herself on to the balcony and ran across the terrace. She skidded to a halt behind a large potted cactus and peered through its sharp arms at the roof opposite. The other soldier was nowhere to be seen, the angle of the roof having stood between him and her. He couldn't have seen where she'd gone. Unless they chose to search for her house by house, she had given them the slip. The cactus stood in the far corner of the terrace, the rectangular pot affording a well-hidden niche between it and the wall. She settled herself in the gap wanting to get her breath back and give her bruised feet a rest. Suddenly there were footsteps heading towards her, the soles of leather sandals slapping the steps that led up from the house below.

"I heard something," a voice said, a young man with a strange accent. He spoke the words as if they were uncomfortable in his mouth. A foreigner then. She had heard many different voices in her time at the docks though she couldn't place the countries they were from.

"We are quite alone," his companion replied in relaxed Valenciano, "but please suit yourself."

Kesara drew herself tightly into a ball, desperately hoping that she was completely hidden. The foreigner paced across the roof terrace.

"Likely it was a cat," said the Spaniard. "The city is lousy with them." He laughed and Kesara was reminded of her father by the tobacco hoarseness of the sound. "At least it keeps the rats down, eh?"

"Maybe." Though the foreigner sounded unconvinced he had stopped pacing and, judging by the sound of his voice, was looking over the balcony at the street below. Kesara wondered if he could see any soldiers.

"So, my friend," the Spaniard said, though the sneer in his voice made it clear to Kesara that he was no friend at all, "what is it that I can do for you? You have not travelled all the way from America to hunt strays, am I right?"

So, the stranger was American. Kesara had never met one before; they stayed away at the moment because of the war. They had no desire to see their boats bombed or their goods impounded. Kesara couldn't say she blamed them.

"I am hunting for a box," he said. "Something that used to belong to my family but was lost, stolen in fact by a rather treacherous woman."

"Are they not all treacherous, señor?" The Spaniard laughed. "I have never trusted one my whole life. It is her you wish me to find?"

"No, she lost it almost as soon as she laid her hands on it."

"Treacherous and clumsy, eh? A terrible combination."

"She is of no importance, I traced the box here. It was recently sold to a local gentleman, Jésus Garcia."

"Garcia? You know who he is?"

"One of your rather self-important Republicans, why?"

"I don't want you thinking your request will be cheap." Again the Spaniard laughed. "If you wish me to retrieve something from Garcia then there will need to be... what is it you Americans call it? Danger pay?"

"You will be extremely well paid if you can bring me the box. Don't concern yourself with that." There was the rustling of paper and for a moment Kesara imagined money changing hands. Then the American spoke again: "This is a sketch of the box in question. As you can see it is nothing special, a small, rectangular wooden box. The wood is light in colour, decorated in Chinese characters. Its value lies purely in its personal connection with my family – it was stolen from us and we wish it back. We are very wealthy, Señor Jimenez. These things are not problematical to us."

Jimenez made a noise that was not quite a laugh and not quite a cough, the sort of noise an unpleasant man might make after seeing a stray dog run over. "Please, señor, there is no need for this… theatre. The object is of extreme value otherwise you would not be calling on me to retrieve it for you. I care not, it is all business to me. I will retrieve this box and I will give it to you; that is the service you are requesting and it is one I shall deliver, for a suitably high price."

"You will forgive my caution, Jimenez. I have done business with many thieves and it is always best to be cautious. You are quite right that the box is of value and that I merely sought to dissuade you from setting your own sights on it as a prize. A mistake. Let us clarify our business: you will steal the box and you will deliver it to me. For this I will pay you five thousand American dollars. If you attempt to keep the box, or sell it to another client, I will use that money to ensure you die painfully at the hands of the best cutthroats it can afford."

This time Jimenez did laugh. "For five thousand you could employ Franco himself, I think!" His tone lost its humour. "Enough of this. I will not be threatened in my own house. The box will be yours and there is no more to be said on the matter."

The American gave a small grunt and there was another rustling of paper. "A thousand upfront, no more. That should cover a down-payment on the hiring of house-breakers. We will meet tonight, by my boat. Shall we say midnight?" With that he moved past Kesara's hiding place and back down the stairs. She caught a glimpse of him; he was younger than she had imagined, his face soft and pudgy, reddening above the lapels of his linen suit, the oil dripping from his hair to mix with sweat on his forehead. "I'll see my own way out."

A few moments later and the sound of the front door closing signalled the American's departure. There was the striking of a match and the creeping odour of cigar smoke. "I do not like you, American," Jimenez muttered. "A man should not be insulted in his own house. But I will fetch you your box and then spend your money. Just mark that you do not offend me further with your tongue or likely I will cut it from your mouth."

He moved past Kesara's hiding place and, shortly after, followed the American on to the street. Kesara was alone.

She climbed out from behind the cactus, lifting her grease-stained blouse from where it had stuck to the skin of her belly. Five thousand dollars? That sort of money was impossible to imagine! Think of what she could do with such a fortune. She looked into the pillowcase and screwed up her nose at the mangled mess of flesh and bone inside. Five thousand dollars could buy a house filled with chickens; she would eat them until she was sick if she so wished. She pulled out a soft piece of breast meat and chewed it on while imagining the sort of house she might buy. The meat was good, but not worth being shot at. Five thousand dollars? Now *that* was worth taking risks for.

Later, she walked along the mammoth quay at the port, weaving in and out of the gathered workers, sailors and the pendulous swings of the cranes. She needed to decide whether she was really going to steal the box. Once Jimenez had left she had run to the edge of his balcony, meaning to catch sight of the American and, hopefully, follow him to his boat. He stood out in his foreign suit, looking like a character from a movie, not a real person. She marked the street he was walking down before running cautiously through the house – she was sure it was empty but there was no harm in being careful – and heading after him. The soldiers were forgotten in this new excitement, but there was no sign of them as she made her way to the port, keeping a close eye on the American all the way. He wasn't like some of the foreigners she had seen around the city; the ones with money walked slowly everywhere, staring at every new building and church as if they didn't have homes or God where they came from. Perhaps they didn't; she hadn't travelled enough to say. This man kept his eyes low, looking at nothing but the road as he made his way back towards the sea.

Valencia's port was huge, almost another city in itself; one made of package crates and rope, towering, rusted vessels and a populace of wind-blown, cursing men. Away from the commercial area, there was a marina where private vessels could be moored. This was where the American headed. Kesara watched him walk along the small jetty to a pleasure yacht of which her father would certainly have disapproved. Occasionally these pristine vessels would sail past their old home in Moraira and he would spit towards the lapping waves. "Boats like that," he would say, "are overgrown lifeboats, saving people from a sea they have no knowledge of. Be better if the whole lot stayed on dry land and left the water for those of us who know what to do with it."

Perhaps the American didn't know what to do on the ocean but Kesara was sure he could buy the knowledge of those who did. And what was wrong with that? Given a choice between her father's honest poverty, a life dictated by the ebb of the sea and the flow of cheap brandy, and the life of the American, a life of choices and the money to make them, she knew which she wanted. And what were her chances of a better life living on the street? She felt no shame about sleeping under the stars, savoured every breath of freedom it offered, but she wasn't stupid, she knew that her lot could only get worse. So why not risk it? Here she had been offered a chance to change her life beyond recognition. Maybe the American would even take her away on that "overgrown lifeboat", show her new shorelines and new possibilities.

But how to go about it?

All she knew was the current owner's name, Jésus Garcia. She had no interest in the politics of the city; if it didn't affect her belly it was no business of hers. She was aware that the Republican government, forever on the run from the Nationalist forces, had been based here until recently – that was why there were so many soldiers here, to protect these important men and the ships that brought them food and guns. But who was this Garcia? And why was his connection to the government enough to give Jimenez cause for concern? Did any of it really matter? All she needed was his address and then she would see what she would see. She needed help and there was only one place she knew to get it: she would go to see Pablo.

Pablo was the son of a freighter captain and a couple of years older than Kesara. He rarely sailed with his father – something he moaned about so often that Kesara did anything she could think of to avoid the subject – but would often help on board when the ship was moored. He would scrub the decks, sew nets, all the boring jobs. He wore his bitterness like a heavy jacket; it made him hunch his shoulders and sweat with anger as he worked in the morning sunshine. Kesara didn't trust him – it wasn't personal: she didn't trust anyone – but she recognised a little of herself in him. Perhaps he would one day run away from his father as she had, though she doubted it.

"It's all right for you," he grumbled as she sat down next to him on the quayside. He was fixing a hole in one of his father's lobster pots, his thin fingers working the wicker automatically as he stared out beyond the ships and cranes to an empty blue sky. "You don't have to work for your food."

"No," she said with a smile, "I just steal it." Her stomach was uncomfortably full from the chicken she had eaten earlier and she felt a little guilty, not for stealing it but rather for not saving some to offer to Pablo. By the time she had decided to come and see him the bird had been nothing but bones.

"And proud of it, apparently." He put the basket down and checked along the quayside to make sure his father was nowhere in sight. He pulled a bent cigarette from his pocket and lit it with a match.

"I'm not proud," she said, "just honest. I don't steal much, just enough to keep me going." The chicken rumbled in her belly as if to accuse her of lying.

"I'm not bothered really," Pablo admitted with a half smile. "Steal what you like. I've just had a bad morning."

"Your father?"

"No, for once, just everything else." Pablo quickly threw his cigarette away and picked up the lobster pot again. Kesara couldn't see anybody watching them but bowed to his sharp senses in the matter.

"You heard of a man called Jésus Garcia?" she asked, deciding that it was better to hide her interest by being upfront.

"Of course, he's the bastard that deals in weapons for the Republic, his men are always down here conducting their deals and acting like they own the place. Why do you ask?"

"No reason really. I heard someone mention him…"

"Who? You shouldn't be hanging around people that discuss Garcia."

"He was nobody, just an American, down at the marina."

"An American? Since when do you speak English?"

"I don't, he was speaking Spanish…" Kesara wasn't making a very good job of this – whatever she said seemed to interest Pablo even more.

"A Spanish-speaking American down at the marina was talking to you about Garcia?"

"No, he wasn't talking to me… he was…" An idea suddenly occurred to her. "He was arguing with another man about who lives in that big place overlooking the marina."

"The Ramirez house?"

"I don't know, probably, the expensive place… the American was insisting that this Jésus Garcia lived there. He was willing to bet money on it."

"Then he would have lost. Garcia has that walled villa near the cathedral."

Kesara tried to think of it. "The one with the little bell-tower?"

"Yeah, people joke that he was jealous of the cathedral bells so had one built of his own."

"I know it."

"What did the American want with Garcia anyway?"

"No idea…" Kesara tried her best to sound as if she really meant it, adding: "None of my business, is it?"

"No, it isn't, and make sure it stays that way. You don't want to start getting mixed up with people like that."

They talked about other things for a short while – only as a further attempt on Kesara's part to hide her true interest – before, finally, Pablo's father shouted to him from the prow of his fishing boat and the boy was forced back to work. Kesara was relieved. She wanted to go and have a look at Garcia's house.

It was a building she had seen many times but paid no attention to. After all, what importance did it have for her? A rich man's house was neither here nor there to Kesara; she wasn't welcome there and had better things to do with her days than look on things she couldn't afford. Now it was entirely different. In her imagination she hoped she might soon be able to afford a house just like it. Of course five thousand dollars wouldn't even begin to pay for a house like this but Kesara wasn't to know that. Anything over a few hundred pesetas was beyond her ability to imagine; there was "very little" money and then there was "more than you could ever dream of", nothing in between.

The house was surrounded by a high white-plastered wall above which poked the bell-tower and the large blue-domed roof of the main house. Just below the dome was a small balcony window that revealed Garcia to Kesara as she watched from the steps of the cathedral. He stepped out through the dark archway, wrapped in a silk gown that was so soft and colourful it looked to Kesara like a woman's dress. He was smoking a cigar, watching the city come back to life after its siesta. A slender hand appeared at his shoulder, its long feminine nails painted a deep Rioja red. Garcia gave the sort of smile Kesara had seen fat men offer a heavily laden dining table and for a moment she thought he meant to bite the proffered fingers, chew them off one by one like shapely asparagus stalks. He kept his teeth sheathed, kissing the hand and taking it in his, holding it against his shoulder as if to carry its owner on his back. Kesara watched the woman emerge into the late-afternoon light and at first glance decided that she had found the face she wanted to grow up into. Then, as the soft light began to pick out flaws, Kesara realised that nobody – least of all the woman herself – would wish themselves into this skin. She was beautiful, yes, but it was a beauty painted over an inner ugliness. The eyes were not as happy as the smile pretended to be, and the woman's slender shoulders were hunched as if prepared to bear the greatest weight one could imagine. Kesara thought that weight was probably the companionship of the man standing next to her.

Garcia pulled the woman in front of him and kissed her neck like a man chewing on a chicken drumstick. His piggy little hands rumpled the silk of

her nightdress, pushing her breasts face upwards towards the sun. She sagged in his embrace, her face
empty and devoid of passion. But then Garcia's un-
subtle devouring was nothing to do with passion
either, even Kesara could see that; it was about *possession*. He was offering this young conquest up to
the eyes of the town and making sure all who saw
them knew only too well that he had taken all he
could want from the woman and would do so again
and again until he tired of her. His hand dropped
briefly between the woman's legs before retreating
to follow its laughing master back into the darkness
of the house. The woman held her position for
awhile, her fingers gripping the wrought iron of the
railing as she leaned forward, perhaps imagining
what it might be like to topple over and away from
the life she had found herself in. Kesara – no
stranger to running away from oppression – hoped
she might free herself from the man. But not today,
it would seem, for the woman followed Garcia back
into the house and Kesara found herself staring up
at an empty window.

She shifted on the hard stone steps, massaging
some life into her buttocks. Now it wasn't just the
money that had her itching to scale the wall; now
she wanted to take the box simply because it be-
longed to the pig she had seen on the balcony. It
would do him good to lose something.

The afternoon light crept towards evening, the
sun losing its harshness and settling a hazy glow
across the streets that made them appear wrapped

in plastic. Kesara sat with her nerves for company, watching the house and trying to decide how to get inside. She walked around it a couple of times, hoping to get an idea of what lay beyond the wall. The bricks stretched too high to give her anything but a glimpse of the house roof, the tower and the tips of the most mature fruit trees. A sprawling bougainvillea clutched the external wall and, as wary as Kesara was of tearing herself to shreds on its thorns, she could see no better way of sneaking into the garden.

Walking back to the front of the house she panicked as the front gate opened and Garcia exited. He walked towards her, the woman from the balcony holding on to his arm. Kesara did all she could do to vanish into the background, sitting down in the dirt and holding out her grubby little hands for coins. Garcia walked straight past. Nothing was more invisible in this city than a beggar, there were so many of them.

Kesara realised this was her chance; she knew Garcia wasn't in the building and she had a way in, however uncomfortable. She ran around to the rear of the building and began to climb the bougainvillea. She was careful not to let the thorns bite into her hands or feet but they transferred their attention to her clothes, tugging and tearing at the fabric of her skirt and blouse. She reached the top of the wall, peered over to make sure the garden beyond was empty, then dropped down to the dry soil of a flower bed. To her right was the lazy gurgle of a

water feature: a small cherub appearing to throttle
a goose, water gushing from the unconcerned bird's
beak and stirring a pond of koi carp. Kesara watched
the fat fish glide pointlessly in their small world and
had a momentary urge to fish them out to rest on
the sun-baked gravel that lined the pond. They
would die, of course, but maybe that was better
than moving redundantly in a world that was only
a couple of times as big as themselves.

There was a swimming pool, something that
seemed utterly alien and pointless to Kesara – if you
wanted to swim, the sea was no distance away. To
move up and down in this oversized bath… well,
that was as unfulfilling as the lives of the carp. Beyond the pool a large covered terrace was draped
with the burgeoning fruit of grapevines. A large dining table in the centre was surrounded by statuary,
a selection of stone nymphs whose gritty breasts
poked out from the demure yet ineffectual swathes
of cloth draped over their exaggerated curves.

Kesara suddenly realised the house might not be
completely empty. Somewhere as large as this likely
had staff, and all it would take was for one of them
to glance out of a rear window and see her gawping
amongst the garden furniture. She ran towards one
of the vine-wrapped alcoves and stood close against
the cream-coloured stone. The only thing to do was
to get to the house as quickly as she could. Bending
almost double she ran towards a pair of glazed double doors, using the table and then the various
potted plants for cover as she went.

She crouched to one side of the doors, quickly popping her head around so that she could peer through the glass and see if anyone was inside. The doors led to an indoor courtyard, walls covered in paintings and tapestries. No doubt when Garcia was entertaining he would open the doors and let his guests mingle between the gardens and his expensive works of art. He was a man who would enjoy showing off. She tried the handle and heard a panicked moan build involuntarily in her throat as the door opened. Now it was real. Now it was breaking into a man's house. A koi carp straying from its pond. She slipped around the open door and stepped inside.

Two women laughed raucously in a nearby room and Kesara looked for somewhere to hide. The gallery held a wide marble staircase and she ran up it, the stone cold beneath her feet as she raced upwards. The two women were talking with the sort of freedom that only comes from having your employer out of the house for a few hours. Their voices bounced off the high white ceilings and chased Kesara up the stairs. She peered over the banister, glimpsing the black uniform of a woman in the room. The cleaner laughed again, flicking at the back of an armchair with a feather duster.

Now the stupidity of Kesara's plan – or rather her complete lack of one – began to pick at her nerves. She had no idea where Garcia might keep the box. Would it be on display? Hidden away in a bedside drawer? Sitting on a desk? Now she was inside, it

all seemed absurd and she was tempted to run out
of the double doors and back to the safety of the
port. But dreams are strong and hers were already
built on the money she hoped to She ran on up the
stairs. The landing stretched itself around a thick
Persian rug, and the spaces between the heavy
wooden doors were filled with busts and sculptures.
Kesara checked the length of the corridor in case the
box was out in the open. There was no sign of it so
she opened one of the doors and stepped into a large
and lavish bedroom. In the far wall she could see
the balcony where Garcia and the woman had stood
earlier. The bed was piled high with cushions and
thick cotton sheets, a mountain range of bedlinen
that she would have loved to roll in had she not
been so nervous. She went to the cabinets by the
side of the bed, pulling the drawers open and rifling
through them, finding some of Garcia's underwear
(she turned her nose up at that), a bible – unread
and unheeded – and a selection of watches. Deciding she might as well swing for a collection of stolen
goods as for a single item, she grabbed one of the
watches -– the smallest, its pearlescent face suspended on a black leather strap – and fixed it on her
wrist. It was a quarter to nine. Looking out of the
window, she could see the darkening sky as night
prepared to push away the blue for another day.

She moved across the room to a large dressing
table and searched through more drawers. There
were women's things this time, pearls and glistening
stones, gold chains and bracelets. Again she was

tempted to fill her pockets but a noise from downstairs stopped her. She ran back to the open door,
listening out for someone coming. All was quiet – it
was probably just the housemaid shifting furniture.
Her appetite for jewel theft had been chased away by
the panic and she left the room for the one opposite.

It was Garcia's office. At the centre was a heavy
desk inlaid with leather, its thick legs twisted in or-
nate carvings. She looked over the objects on the
surface, a marble penholder, a brass cigar cutter...
the humidor got her excited until she opened it and
realised her mistake looking at the thick rolls, piled
like sawn timber, waiting to be smoked. She tried to
check the drawers but they were locked and there
was no sign of a key. She moved over to the window
and looked down on to the roof of the covered terrace. She could climb out here, make her way down
from the terrace roof and be away, a watch on her
wrist to prove it hadn't been a wasted journey.

There was another noise from downstairs, a loud
crash followed by the tinkling applause of breaking
glass. The cleaners would be in trouble when Garcia
came home, Kesara thought. Something caught her
eye on a bookcase facing the window: amongst the
thick leather spines and document folders was a
light-brown square of wood. Her breath caught in
her mouth and she dashed across to the shelf. It was
the box, surely it was, covered in Chinese writing –
at least she thought it was Chinese, lots of curves
and squiggles; she saw them sometimes on crates of-
floaded at the port. It was acting as a prop, keeping

the books wedged against the wall so they didn't spill out. Was it possible that something so valuable was being treated in such a careless fashion? She tried to open it but her fingers couldn't discover the trick. She shook it: it was light and seemingly empty. Suddenly it gave a ticking sound and she dropped it in surprise. Stooping down to pick it up she tensed as footsteps clapped the marble stairs beyond the open door. Someone was coming!

She grabbed the box and dashed across to the window, seeing no option but to escape across the roof. As she climbed out, she heard a voice behind her. Looking back over her shoulder she found herself gazing straight at Jimenez, here to carry out his own thievery. He noticed the box in her hand and, swearing profusely, pulled a revolver from the belt of his trousers. Kesara jumped on to the tiled roof of the terrace, fighting not to drop the box as she scrabbled to keep her footing. She kept moving, coming to the end of the roof and looking over the edge for a way to descend. The pool... A bullet was fired at her for the second time that day. Her luck held as she sailed through the air before crashing into the clear water of the pool. Her skin smarted with the impact but she kept her breath, kicked with her legs and yanked herself out at the pool's edge. Dripping wet, she hoped the box was undamaged but had neither the time nor the inclination to check. The terrace was protecting her from Jimenez above but he would be downstairs in seconds. She looked all along the garden wall, at a loss as to how she could climb it from this side. She would have to try the front.

Running around the side of the house she heard the double doors at the rear clatter open. She was praying under her breath as she darted around the large urns and decorative pagodas, sure that her pursuers wouldn't fire on her once she was out on the street. The front gate was slightly ajar and she ran toward it, laughing in relief. She saw another man – one of Jimenez's friends, presumably – out of the corner of her eye but ignored him, keeping her attention fixed on the gate and the square beyond it.

"Don't!" Jimenez shouted behind her, though whether he was addressing her or his accomplice she could neither tell nor care. She ran out of the gate and into the square. Spanish squares are always filled with old men, standing around smoking cheap cigars, chatting and avoiding the women at home (who gather together in one kitchen so as to avoid all the men). Kesara pushed through a small group of them, drawn no doubt by the sound of the initial gunshot.

"Devil on your tail?" one of them asked as he spun on the cobbles to keep his balance. One of his friends laughed, opening his sagging mouth to reveal a single yellow tooth.

Kesara ran out of the square and into one of the side streets, sure that Jimenez would still be following. She had five thousand dollars of his in her hand and he was hardly likely to give it up easily. Her best hope was to get to the port as quickly as she could; once there he would never find her.

As she ran through the city streets she found she was still laughing. She knew she was being premature, she was hardly in the clear yet, but the sense of relief – to be out of that house and with the box in her hand… She had never known anything like it and the elation added speed to her legs and strength to the little soles of her feet. This is what it felt like to be really free, wind in your hair and cash in your hands. She would let nothing hold her back ever again.

"No." The old man stepped out right in front of her as she rounded a corner, sending her tumbling. "No," he said again, "not you. You're the wrong one."

Kesara didn't understand his words. He was speaking English and she knew not a word of it.

His clothes were unsuited to the heat, a long overcoat and wide-brimmed hat; he looked utterly out of place. "Give me the box," he insisted – in Spanish this time – holding out a wrinkled hand with which to take it. Kesara shook her head. She could outrun this old man any day. Hadn't she said she would let nothing stop her? She jumped to her feet and ran past him, the box in her hand.

"No!" he shouted, "I must have it!"

Not a chance, Kesara thought, this box is mine and it'll take more than you've got to take it…

A gunshot rang out in the sleepy Valencian street, a noise that Kesara didn't immediately associate with her until she saw the blood spreading across the front of her blouse. She couldn't get her head around the sight of it; it made no sense to her. Right up until the moment she died.

"Here."

Pablo finished stuffing the coils of rope into his duffel bag, and stared at the old man in the final dying light of this hot Valencian day.

"What is it?" Pablo asked, taking the wooden box the old man offered.

"Your destiny," the old man said, pointing his gun towards the young man's head.

INTERLUDE

"Can you understand me?"

"If you mean that noise you're making then, yes. I'm not mentally subnormal." The First Observer sits down, the weight of the flesh around it unwelcome and stultifying. "How can they bear to be caged like this?"

"I rather like it." Its colleague thrashes about, experiencing the body, feeling the centre of gravity shift as it moves. "They consume this as well, you know," it says, pinching at the muscles in its arms.

"Consume?"

"The creatures work on an energy input system. They ingest another's flesh in order to make their own function."

"How disgusting."

"I think it's neat. I wonder what sensation it causes?"

"I hope I never find out. We are supposed to observe, not go native."

"Some would say one has to experience to observe; data is hardly reliable otherwise. How do I look?"

The First Observer marshals its thoughts, processing the input from the human's eyes and trying to express it in the words it has to hand. It is impossible. "Like a human. What else do you want me to say? You are crude, unappealing and have some form of growth all over you."

"They call it hair. Have you explored your human's brain?"

"Briefly. It was depressing."

"How can you say that? So many thoughts and urges, so raw and energetic!"

"So basic. We will leave now."

"So soon? What have we learned?"

"Enough to know that there is nothing of interest here for us, it's all so…" it pounds at the earth with its borrowed hands until the small bones inside it snap "…pointlessly fragile. How have they have managed to exist this long?"

"They call this Asia," its colleague says, looking around.

"Who cares?"

"I do. I want to stay for a while, see how they function."

"No, we are leaving. It was only a point of… they don't even have the vocabulary… meticulousness that merited exploring thus far. Sitting in this mess of a construct I have learned all I need. This place is beneath us."

"I disagree!" its colleague insists, bringing a rock down on its fellow observer's head to open the fragile skull.

"I enjoyed that," it says afterwards to the rivulets of blood pushing their way through the sand. "It was interesting."

Now alone on the wide Asian plain, it wonders what to do next.

CHAPTER FOUR

Young men were supposed to have big dreams, but for Tom there had been only one ambition. Nothing beat playing a piano for a living. Tom would assure people of this, anybody that was still around at the magical time – say three in the morning – when the martini took over and Tom quit speaking for himself. He would stop playing, pour himself straight up on to a barstool and graze on olives and punjabi mix until his tongue felt like a tramp's sock during a downpour. "It's, like, pure," he would burble, pointing at invisibles in the air between him and his audience and fixing them with an earnest stare. The sort of look that says its owner knows... OK? He just fucking knows.

On the night in question, Tom still had some semblance of balance left, having arrived late for work and therefore being two rounds light on his normal consumption. Not that he was what you might call straight. He still had to expend a considerable effort windmilling his arms and breathing deeply so as not to smack his teeth on the bar as he'd done that time in Chicago when a combination of whisky sours and a pair of Quaaludes had sent him carpetwards with a hard-on and a smile but no real consciousness to speak of. When the TV above the bar showed silent news footage of distraught fans gathering at Graceland to pay tribute to their lost idol he was capable of figuring out what had happened. "The King is dead, baby," he slurred, raising a glass. He took a sip and then pushed the glass away. He needed to maintain a modicum of muscle-control tonight; it was Thursday and that meant Elise would be dropping by on her way home from her shift at the *Neon Melon*. Tom liked Elise, in fact he loved her almost as much as he did Jim Beam and Lord Buckley, which – for an emotional retard like Tom – was tantamount to obsession.

"Knock me your lobes, daddy-o," he said to Terry behind the bar, a man who ran out of the very little creativity he possessed thinking up names for happy-hour cocktails. "Frilly Maiden", "Velvet Sunrise", "Fruit Sunstorm"… after that he was spent.

"You talk like a dick, Tom," Terry commented, whipping a dank towel at the bar as if it had been misbehaving.

"And you have no jive."

"But plenty of liquor so I'm sure you'll bring yourself to forgive me."

"You may well be right. What time is it?"

"She'll be here soon enough."

Tom smiled. That Terry was one smug son of a bitch.

He took the brave step of slipping off the barstool and taking himself to a window booth, a journey so long and perilous for Tom by this stage of the evening that he felt entitled to call it a goddamn quest. He was an inebriated Frodo Baggins heading to the leatherette and formica landscape of Boothor... This idea gave him the giggles about halfway across the shiny carpet and he had to grab hold of a particularly rubbery rubber plant in order to steady himself.

"You cool?" Terry asked, only too aware of how difficult Tom was likely finding the journey.

Tom waved, signalling that all was fine, before letting go of the plant and risking a few more steps toward the window.

Outside, Ninth and Hennepin was taking a beating from the rain. Tom pressed his nose against the glass and imagined sailing paper yachts along the gutter, floating the hell out of there. A man has to dream. The neon of the Triangle Pool Hall buzzed like a trapped bluebottle, winking in and out as if tired. Fat Eugene, the owner, was sheltering under the smudged green awning, pushing cotton-candy balls of cigar smoke into the wet air to be smashed apart by the raindrops.

"When you gonna quit moonin' over her, for Christ's sake?"

"Just as soon as she sees sense and gives in, Terry."

"I've as much chance of getting a BJ from Barbara Streisand."

Tom, baffled at the best of times, was utterly confused by the notion of this. "Would you want to?"

Terry, still making a pretence of cleaning, nodded. "Who wouldn't?"

Tom guessed there was little to be said to this without causing offence so he went back to staring out of the window. Fat Eugene had returned to the seedy hop-musk of his pool hall and the street was now empty... No, there was some guy hanging around in the front doorway of Verbinski's Pawn Shop. He was wearing a fedora and raincoat, a regular Philip Marlowe, Tom thought.

"Perhaps he's on the trail of a red-hot dame," Tom muttered in his best Bogart impression, "surviving on rye and smarts."

"What you talking about now?" Terry called. "And wipe your goddamn chin – you're dribbling on the upholstery."

"Nothing, just watching some guy..." but "Marlowe" had gone and Tom's attention was elsewhere, watching Elise – a folded copy of the *Times* over her wild, electric-shock red hair – running down the street towards them. Tom yanked his brown suit into shape; it had a habit of looking as if it was trying to worm its way off him. He tried to work his hair into respectability but as usual it refused, sitting like whipped ice-cream on the top of his head.

"Oh, she's on her way, is she?" Terry said with a smile. "I'll get the grill warmed up."

Elise burst through the door in a shower of rain and cussing. "Jesus, but it's biblical out there," she roared, heading over to the bar. The sodden newspaper hung from her hand like shed lizard skin. She dripped on Terry's carpet but he sure as hell didn't care; maybe the damn thing would grow more luxuriant if she watered it enough.

"Grill's on, give me five and there'll be patty melt and fries to take the edge off the cold," he said, walking out back to kick the fat-fryer into life.

"Hey, Elise," Tom offered from his booth, hoping to hell he'd made it sound non-committal rather than the bark of a desperate man.

"Hi, Tom," Elise replied, "good night?"

"I've been shaking down the jazz and blues as surely as you've been shimmying those curves of yours. I dare say neither of us really got the appreciation we deserved."

"I dare say." Elise joined him in his booth, just as Tom had hoped, dragging a snail trail of rain across the leatherette from the damp ass of her coat.

"You want that whistle of yours wetting?" Tom asked, nodding an inebriated forehead towards the bar and the rows and rows of seductive possibilities it offered.

"I'll take a Martini, something long, cold and strong as hell – I'll leave the rest up to your creative imagination."

"I am a veritable Manet of the Martini, a Hopper of the Highball."

"Then refresh your thirsty nighthawk, Tom, she's had a damn long night as always."

Tom threw a wink in Elise's direction. Catching his reflection in the window, he thought it looked more like the facial twitch of a man who had just been shot. He really ought to keep the expressions to a minimum; he was long past the point of being able to pull them off.

Terry was whistling along to the hiss of sizzling hamburger and fries. It was the only tune he knew.

"Hey, Terry," Tom asked, "fix the lady a drink, would you? Something to wash down the melted Velveeta and cockroach thigh she has forthcoming."

"Hell with that, I keep a clean kitchen as well you know. Fix it yourself, but mind..." Terry brandished a spatula with conviction "...don't get carried away, I'll be watching you pour."

"Pour... *poor* me." Tom shuffled his way around the bar hatch and began to throw gin, vodka and vermouth at crushed ice and lemon zest. There was something about his coordination that improved when it came to going through such automatic functions as playing a piano or mixing a cocktail. They were the sort of moves that, unlike walking or trying to look cool, came naturally to him. He throttled the shaker, ice-cold condensation biting into his palms through the chilly chrome, and poured some over one lucky bastard of an olive.

"Now that's a whistle-wetter." Tom nodded his approval, pouring one for himself, just to be sociable.

Terry appeared from the kitchen with a hot sandwich and fries and carried them over to the booth before leaving Tom to it with a half-smile.

"Something to chill your teeth, my good lady." Tom placed the drink next to her plate and took a big sip from his own, just so it was easier to carry to his side of the table. She tried it and acknowledged her approval while gasping for air.

"If that doesn't kick away the pole-riding blues then nothing will. Thanks, Tom."

"No problem at all. So how were things this evening down at that most esteemed of all skin joints?"

"I shook and rolled, while the pasty-faced and well-heeled steadfastly refused to notice anything above my nipples. Same old same old…"

"The damn fools missed your eyes," slurred Tom, then immediately wished he hadn't. The problem with fancying a stripper was you felt a heel hitting on them. Just another purveyor of corny chat-up lines.

Tom worried too much. Elise gave him a genuine smile. "You're a sweetheart, Tom," she said.

"Hell, Elise, I don't know much but there's two things I can swear to: I know beautiful eyes when I see them, and I can mix a Martini." He took a big mouthful of his own, just to shut himself up.

"I shouldn't complain," said Elise, tucking into her patty melt, "a few years of tips and I can pack it all in for a job that allows for more than glitter and tassles. Having said that…" She dug into her coat pocket. "What do you make of this?" She handed him a small wooden box.

Tom lit a cigarette – as he was wont to do when thinking was required – and turned the box over in his hands. "Looks like the kind of thing you stash your dope in when you've got visitors."

"Trust you. Try to open it."

Tom did but, no matter how he ran his fingers over the box's edges, he couldn't find an opening. "Weird."

"Damn right." She tugged at a stray strand of melted cheese that ran from the corner of her mouth like tacky spider's web. "Some guy gave it to me as I was leaving. 'A sign of my immense appreciation', he said."

"Did you tell him you preferred foldable appreciation?"

"I was just glad to get the hell out of there."

"Was he Chinese?" Tom pointed at the writing on the box's surface.

"Nah, some old white guy, not the sort of clientele we normally attract. He had his pants done up for one thing. Dressed like out of some old movie... hat and coat, you know, 'The Shadow knows...', that kind of thing."

A bell of recognition rang in the back of Tom's head but Elise licked her lips and he lost his train of thought. "The Shadow knows..." he murmured, to stop anything more provocative spilling over his ver-mouth-soaked lips.

He went back to looking at the box, sure he must be blushing. "So what you going to do with it?"

"Damned if I know. Think it's worth anything?"

"Oh yeah, a box that doesn't open... There'll be a line around the block for the chance to own it."

"What I thought..."

Tom looked out the window, hoping the sight of rain would wash his numb brain.

"Marlowe's back," he mumbled, sucking down the final dregs of his Martini in case the answer to Elise's problem was hiding under the olive.

"Huh?"

"Nothing." Tom nodded towards the window. "Guy stood out in the rain, thinks he's a private detective or something."

"That's him," Elise said. "That's the guy…"

"He's coming over." Tom started to get to his feet. "Think he wants his box back?"

The man reached into his raincoat as he strode towards them, and pulled out a large handgun. With no hesitation he opened fire and the large plate-glass window cracked like river-ice in spring.

"Jesus!" Elise dropped to the bench. Tom, quicker than he would have ever given himself credit for, grabbed her arms and pulled her down to the floor next to him.

"What the *fuck*?" Terry shouted. He looked in a mood to argue until a second shot knocked the window through in a waterfall roar. That took all the fight out of him and he decided that crouching behind his bar was the only sane response to the situation.

Tom hugged Elise hard, burying her head in his chest, the hard corners of the box pressing between them.

Terry worked his way along the floor to a strongbox he kept stashed beneath the till. Swearing repeatedly, he yanked the strongbox on to his lap and fished in his pants pocket for his keys. "What's the goddamn point of having the thing if you end up dead trying to get the fucker open?" he whined. He rifled through the keys on his bunch. "Fucking thing, fucking thing…" He picked the smallest out and tried to force it into the strongbox lock. It wouldn't fit. He heard the sound of shoes grinding glass to powder on the sidewalk outside. Panicking further, he emitted a high-pitched whine and started punching the lid. He picked another key and tried it. It turned the lock and opened the box. He grabbed the .45, stood up and pointed it at the man climbing through the window. Then he noticed the live rounds rolling out of the spilled strongbox at his feet. "Dumb fuck…" he whispered before deciding to bluff the situation out. "Drop the gun!" he shouted, "or I'll drop *you*." That sounded so embarrassing he'd have turned the gun on himself were it loaded.

The man clambered over the booth table and on to the floor. Terry was surprised to see how old he was – in his late seventies at least.

"There's no need for anyone to shoot," the old man said, holding up his own gun. "I just want the box." He gestured to a small wooden box on the floor and Terry was baffled to see there was no sign of Tom or Elise. Maybe they'd got out somehow?

"Take it and leave, real slow…" Terry said.

The old man sank to his haunches, picked up the box, dropped it into his coat pocket and stood upright, keeping his gun levelled on Terry throughout. He looked at Terry's gun and smiled. "That ain't loaded," he said. To prove his conviction he turned his back on him and walked slowly out of the front door.

Terry dropped quickly, grabbed a couple of rounds off the floor and loaded them into the Colt. By the time he'd stood up again he was alone in his bar. No sign of the old man, Tom or Elise. "Well…" he scratched at his baffled face and stared at the Thursday night pouring in through his broken window "…fuck me sideways."

As far as Tom was concerned, he and Elise had fallen through the floor of Terry's bar. The impossibilities of that didn't occur to him; he was just glad to be away from mad bastards with guns. They tumbled through utter darkness for a couple of seconds before landing on what felt like a stack of rough pillows. Tom coughed as a cloud of dust erupted from under them. He pulled himself away from Elise, knowing he was going to be sick. His hands grabbed at rough hessian and he guessed they had landed on a pile of sacks, flour by the feel of the powder all over his face. He rolled off the sacks on to a cold floor and got to his feet just as he started to throw up. Blind to his surroundings, he hoped he wasn't upchucking all over his shoes.

"Elise?" he asked, once done. There was no reply. Spitting his mouth clean he retraced his steps up the pile of sacks, pulling his cigarette lighter out of his jacket pocket to give him some light. "Elise?" he asked again, feeling her limp arm and starting to worry. He brought the light to her face to see a panicked look in her eyes that at least meant she was conscious. Conscious but unable to move… it occurred to him that wasn't a good thing at all. "Elise? Can you hear me?" Her eyes flickered but that was all the response she could give. Tom started to panic. It didn't help that his head felt strange… airy and brittle. He realised it was because he was sober, not an experience he had had recently.

He needed to find some light. "Don't worry, Elise," he said, an empty promise and he knew it. He climbed back down, let the lighter go out and waited for his eyes to adjust. As the blue and yellow afterglow of the lighter flame faded from his eyes the darkness moved in. Turning around he saw a thin beam of light ahead and walked towards it. He stuck out his hands to stop himself bumping into anything. After a few seconds, his palms hit the far side of the room. Rubbing the surface he decided it was wood and therefore, as hoped, a door. Moving his hand down he groped for where he would expect a handle. His hand gripped metal, he turned it and the door swung open bringing the light from outside with it.

On the other side of the door was something completely unexpected: a large oldfashioned kitchen, filled with wood and tile, large dressers and stone work-surfaces. It was the sort of kitchen you saw in old movies, where fat cooks wore white hankies over their hair as they chopped up meat and vegetables. The sort of kitchen that really shouldn't be in the basement of a New York bar.

"Bad jive, daddy-o," Tom whispered, before deciding that there would be time enough to worry about where they were once he had seen to Elise. They had landed in the kitchen's larder, sacks of flour perfectly placed to offer a soft landing. Except… the ceiling above was intact, no sign at all of where they might have fallen in. He propped the door open with a clay bottle of oil and – trying not to look at where he had been sick – grabbed Elise and carried her out of the larder.

As soon as he'd lifted her on to his shoulder he realised this was the wrong thing to do. You weren't supposed to move someone who had been in an accident, just in case you made things worse. He paused, not knowing what to do next. He wasn't a man used to making executive decisions, definitely a "go with the flow" kind of guy. Well, there was little point in worrying about it now; he'd picked her up, the damage – if there even was any – was done and there was no going back from it. He lay her down as gently as he could on a large marble-topped preparation table. He brushed her hair from her face and gently unbuttoned her raincoat. He felt her arms and legs delicately. She seemed OK, nothing obviously twisted. Elise mumbled something… Tom, hyper, had his ears to her lips in seconds. "What was that, Elise, honey?"

"*Cnt muvve*," she repeated.

"I know that…" he replied, trying not to sound exasperated. "You'll be fine, it's probably just…" he had no idea what it might be "…shock or something."

That was lame and he knew it. "Just relax, every-thing's going to be fine." That was somewhat overconfident too, wasn't it? At that moment though, her hand twitched and grabbed his, which made him so stupidly happy he was willing to con-tinue thinking positive. Then it occurred to him that if they were beneath Terry's bar – *Except you know it ain't so, don't you, Tom? We ain't in Kansas no more and the sooner you admit the fact the better* – perhaps the gun-man was going to follow them down to finish the job? In a surge of panic he moved around the room hunting for the door so he could block it, get some kind of barricade going.

There was no door.

A large stove took up one wall, several thick chrome pipes leading off it and into the bricks be-hind. It made him think of a church organ. Thin wisps of smoke were escaping from its various hatches and seals, like a steam-trawler boiler ready to blow. There were rows of saucepans hanging from a rack on the roof, old and beaten like a war-damaged knight's armour. A heavy porcelain sink took pride of place on another wall but where, above it, you would have expected to see a window there was nothing but red brick. The wall was painted with dust and cobwebs, suggesting the kitchen hadn't been used for some time, though the fire in the wrought-iron grate said otherwise. Logs crackled and spat their disapproval as Tom moved around the preparation table, checking out every part of the room. A large hatch in the wall to the left of the fireplace was probably a dumb waiter, he decided; certainly it fitted the period. But no, other than the larder they had fallen into there was no door. He checked the larder, climbed up on to the sacks and shone the flame of his lighter on to the ceiling, it was completely intact. They could not have fallen through it.

But they had.

"Do not adjust your *goddamn* set," he mumbled to himself, talking nonsense as he did when in need of a morale boost. He went back to Elise and rubbed her arm gently, pleased when it began to twitch.

"Pins and needles," she said, "feeling coming back." Her speech was still slurred but clearer than it had been, another sign she was recovering. "Where the hell are we?"

"I just don't know," Tom replied. "It's freaky shit, I have to tell you. We, like, fell through the floor, yeah?"

"I've no idea what happened... that guy was shooting at us and then, I don't know, I blacked out or something."

"It felt to me like we were falling but..." he looked towards the larder and decided not to think any more about it.

"Are we still being shot at?'

"No."

"Then, for now, it's all good."

"Yeah... copacetic..."

Tom couldn't stand still, he was feeling too damned twitchy. He squeezed her hand and began to pace, sure at any moment that something hostile and terrible was bound to descend on them. "Just makes no sense..." he muttered, beginning to open the cupboards around them. "Completely whacked..." He opened a large cupboard to the left of the oven and stumbled backwards in surprise at the sight of the small man who stood inside.

"Hello," the man said, pulling a puffy white chef's hat from the pocket of the stained smock he was wearing. "Who's hungry then?"

CHAPTER FIVE

Pablo hit the stairs rolling and if it weren't for his boot getting caught between the uprights of the banister he would likely have continued for some time. He hung there upside down, hanging loose and fearing the worst. He couldn't move. Had the old man shot him? Or maybe he had landed badly? A year ago he had seen one of his father's crew fall from the mast of the ship. It was his own fault, he'd been playing the fool, making the others laugh. The man had lost his grip and plummeted to the deck, his spine snapping audibly as he bounced off the wooden planks. Nobody had laughed at that. The man had survived but lost all mobility from the neck down. He was now angry and fat, pushed around the harbour by his son when he wanted to sharpen his anger on the sight of the ships. Perhaps that was what had now happened? Was his spine broken?

Where the hell was he?

His limited vision offered what seemed an infinite run of half-carpeted steps. The wood was dark, the carpet thick and deep red. The wall to his right was mostly taken up with panelling, slats of the same dark wood as the steps jutting up into a sky of paint the thick cream of homemade custard. To his left, the solid balusters propped up a heavy handrail, their bulbous curves like pirouetting fat ladies.

His foot began to hurt, twisted and taking all his weight. Pablo was a little relieved by that as he supposed it meant his spine was intact, though his ankle might not be if he hung there much longer. His duffel bag was still on his shoulder, the weight of the rope pulling the strap into his flesh.

Slowly, feeling began to creep back into his face as it swelled with blood. His eyes began to lose focus, white stars pulsing in front of them. He grew light-headed, even as his cheeks and jowls threatened to burst from the pressure. He imagined himself growing purple, then black… a grape turning to rot as it hung on the vine. For a while it seemed to him that he could feel the flesh of his face blossoming and curling as the rich juice seeped out. Perhaps the blood to his head was bringing on delirium?

His fingers twitched, his right hand going into spasm as every nerve-ending in it tried to remember what it was for. His head continued to spin, his thoughts becoming more ill-defined with every moment. By rights he should be panicking, but his dreamy state of mind wouldn't let him. Perhaps if he just stayed here someone else would come along eventually and tell him what the hell had just happened.

• • •

"There must be other people here," Miles said as he and Penelope continued to walk along the interminable corridor.

"What makes you say that?" asked Penelope. "I fail to follow your logic."

"Well…" In truth, Miles was speaking from the perspective of hope rather than logic. "All the furniture and everything…"

"But no sign of actual habitation," Penelope pointed out, "there's all the peripheral things – the decoration of a house – but no clothes, no untidiness, no half-empty glasses of water by the bedside, half-read books, crumpled sheets, dirty ashtrays. The whole place is lifeless."

"I suppose you're right," Miles admitted, "but if we appeared here then surely others must have too? The two of us have no connection and yet we wake up in this…" he looked back at the absurdly infinite corridor behind him "…*impossible* house. The odds would suggest we're not alone."

"I don't have a lot of faith in odds."

Miles shrugged "I can't say I've had much success following them either. Shall we try another?" He pointed at a door off the corridor.

"Do we have any choice?"

"Not really."

They stepped into another bedroom. The carpet seemed to sigh miserably at the sensation of feet on it.

"See." Penelope waved her arm around the room. "Nobody's ever slept here. You can feel it – it's like a theatre set, all the right trimmings but none of the soul."

Miles was cautious of the window after his last experience but walked over to it anyway. Like before it was pitch-black beyond the glass. Penelope yanked open the doors of the wardrobe, still hoping that she might chance upon something more becoming to wear than a curtain. With a yelp she fell back as a large brown shape burst from the wardrobe and whipped upwards. The shape flattened as it hit the ceiling, expanding across the sickly cream paint and reaching towards the corners of the room. The air was filled with a crackling noise, like frying fat. In the low light it took a few seconds for Miles and Penelope to appreciate what they were looking at.

"Moths?" Penelope said, getting back to her feet.

"*Lots* of moths," agreed Miles.

They watched for a few seconds as the moths thrashed against the ceiling, circling around the room.

"Weird," Miles whispered, unable to take his eyes off them.

"Disgusting," Penelope replied. "Shall we leave?"

"Yeah…" Miles tore his eyes away from the ceiling and walked towards the open door. The moths immediately arced down toward him, making him dart back to the window and stand with his back against the glass. The moths returned to the ceiling.

"OK," Miles said, "now *that* freaks me out – the moths don't want me to move."

"Don't be ridiculous," Penelope replied, moving towards the door herself. "They're moths, they can't..."

Again, the moths cut down, a phalanx of them whipping at Penelope as she approached the door. She stepped back towards the wardrobe, watching in relief as they returned to a flat sea above their heads.

"Tell them that," said Miles.

Eventually, Pablo was able to move, turning his throbbing ankle to dislodge it from where it was wedged. The sole of his boot held fast against the wood of the balusters and he had to yank it free, the momentum sending him rolling backwards down the stairs. He stuck his arm out to stop himself from rolling too far and his hand slammed against the stairs and jarred his shoulder. Sore and nauseous from being upside down so long, he turned over so that he sat against the wall. He stayed still for a few minutes, just to let the blood settle from his head. He rolled his arm in its shoulder-socket and straightened his bag on his back. Ahead of him the stairs stretched on and on with no end in sight. He turned to look behind him but the view was no more hopeful, the steps reaching up into darkness with no sign of a destination. Slowly the dizziness and sickness faded and, deciding that walking down stairs was less work – and surely they must lead somewhere in the end? – he got to his feet and began to descend.

• • •

"This is ridiculous," said Penelope, "they're only moths, it's not as if they can harm us, is it?"

"I suppose not," Miles replied. "Shall we just make a run for it?"

"On three, we charge the door and just push our way through."

"OK… who's going to count?"

Penelope smiled. "Silly man, like it really matters."

"I'll do it then."

"If it makes you happier."

"OK… one… two…"

"Don't move!" A man stepped into the open doorway. "Or they'll cut you down where you stand!"

Pablo didn't own a watch, though he was sure that if he did it would tell him he had been descending these stairs for far too long. His thigh muscles were beginning to cramp and he decided to sit down and stretch them for a while before they gave out entirely. It didn't help that his bag was so damned heavy – though, even in his current bizarre circumstances, he feared his father enough never to consider leaving the equipment behind. Then it occurred to him what that equipment was: he was carrying fifty metres or so of rope. He got back to his feet and looked over the bannister. There was nothing to be seen. Still, his current plan was getting him nowhere; a change in direction was worth a try. He began to yank the rope out of his bag.

• • •

The man in the doorway was dressed in old-fashioned explorer's clothes: pale khaki jacket littered with pockets, long shorts, desert boots and a pith helmet. "My dears," he said, in a cultured voice richer than a port-soaked stilton, "if you value your lives as you surely must, I beg you heed me. The wildlife here is unpredictable and predominantly deadly. You dismiss it at your peril." At this he gave a jolly smile, his long bushy moustache rising like theatre drapes to reveal his shining teeth.

The moths, perhaps sensing they were being discussed, swirled even more dramatically around the ceiling, the noise of their wings building in volume.

"Am I still the only one here that realises we're dealing with moths?" Penelope asked. "Possibly the most inoffensive creature imaginable."

"My dear lady," the stranger replied, "maybe you would feel somewhat different toward our lepidopteran friends were you an old sheet. Any creature, when found in sufficient number, might be defined as threatening; in this terrible domicile you can be sure of it. Nothing in this building is to be taken lightly, my dear, nothing at all."

"You have a suggestion then?" asked Miles.

"Indeed I do," the man replied, reaching to one side of the door and pulling a long-barrelled rifle into view.

"Oh, dear lord," Penelope sighed, "the fool intends to shoot our way out."

"The 'fool' in question, my dear lady – if one can

really refer to a young woman wrapped in nothing
but soft furnishings as a 'lady' – is none other than
Roger Carruthers, world-famous explorer, big-game
hunter and expert in matters zoological." With the
rifle slung on his shoulder he reached down again,
this time picking up a storm lantern. "I can assure
you there is very little in this world that I have not
tracked, catalogued and shot. If I wished to pick
these chaps off one by one I would most certainly
have the aim – if not the munitions or time – to do
so. The moths, however, are not my target." He lit
the lantern and turned the wick up high so that the
flame blazed beyond the glass. He looked at Miles.
"Might I suggest, sir, that you have the good sense
to duck?" With that, he stepped inside the room,
pushing the door closed behind him. He levelled the
rifle at Miles and emptied both barrels.

Pablo tugged at the knot around the handrail. Accepting that it was strong enough, he tied a loop in
the loose end – so he would have a foot-hold – and
tossed the coil of rope over the banister, watching it
drop away into the darkness. His hope was not that
it might reach the ground (if it were only fifty metres
away he would be able see it) but rather that he
might gain a new perspective on things once off the
stairs. Perhaps there was something beneath them,
a wall or even balcony, that he might be able to
reach. If the worst came to the worst he would just
climb back up and carry on his journey; at least he
would have tried. Wrapping the rope loosely around

his arms and legs, he climbed over the banister rail and began to descend.

As Miles hit the floor he heard the glass of the window explode outwards. Covering his eyes slightly he peered towards the doorway, at a loss as to what the madman was planning. Carruthers shifted his aim and fired three more times, shooting the gas lamps in the wall.

"Oh, brilliant!" Penelope shouted, "now the lunatic wants to blows us all up!"

"Not with this calibre, my dear," Carruthers replied, holding up the storm lantern, now the only light in the room. "Just encouraging a modicum of darkness." He threw the lantern across the room. As its flame threw a flickering light across the undulating moths, Miles saw the insects surge after it, following the light through the broken window and into the darkness beyond. "And now," Carruthers continued, "I suggest you take the opportunity to join me back out here in the hallway where I will be only too happy to answer your many questions."

Pablo dropped lower and lower, feeding the rope cautiously through his fingers, not wanting to move too quickly. Eventually he came to the end, poked his foot through the loop and hung there. He had hoped that he would see something of use from below the stairs but there was nothing. He stayed still for a moment, in case his eyes needed to adjust to the darkness, gently swinging on the rope, turning in the air to check every direction. Above him he could see the side of the stairs, the dark wood banister. Underneath was as dark and featureless as everywhere else, as if the stairs only existed when viewed from above or to the side.

He was in no rush to climb back up the rope but didn't see that he had much choice; he could hardly hang here for ever. With a sigh he reached up and took hold of the rope, preparing to yank himself upwards. As he tensed his muscles a feeling suddenly struck him and he held himself utterly still. He couldn't say what it was that had changed but he knew that he was no longer alone. Something was in this darkness with him, and it was coming closer.

"Allow me to take this opportunity to introduce myself under more convivial circumstances," said Carruthers once they were safely back in the corridor. "Roger Carruthers, author, adventurer, after-dinner speaker and Chairman of the West Highbury Gourmands – 'If it walks, flies, swims or slithers we'll eat it!' I have no doubt I may be familiar to you from my many public appearances and articles?"

"Never heard of you." Penelope held out her hand. "Penelope Simons, American, débutante – well, more of an old hand if I'm honest – and most certainly a lady, however fashionably indisposed. I take it this is your house?"

"Nothing could be further from the truth, madam." Carruthers was clearly put out not to be recognised but covered it with grace, kissing the back of her hand and nodding courteously. "I am merely an explorer in these wild corridors and chambers. In fact I am of the opinion that nobody could be said to own the place; like the African wilds and those more inhospitable corners of your own nation it is a place that simply *is*. An environment to be endured, a place where one has no greater fight than that for survival. It is a fight I can thus far lay claim to winning. And your name, sir?" He turned to Miles.

"Miles Caulfield, antique dealer, failed gambler and possessor of what I begin to suspect is the most ludicrous mental breakdown imaginable."

"Aha!" Carruthers clapped his hands together. "You are not long upon our shores, I surmise?"

"We haven't been here that long if that's what you mean."

"I suspected not. I too believed this place a delusion on first arrival." He patted Miles on the shoulder. "It's quite real, old chap, and we must consider ourselves lucky for each new day we manage to avoid death. You are both welcome to return to my camp. Let us hope you are the measure of the journey, eh?"

Pablo began to climb, yanking himself up the rope with all the speed his aching arms could muster. He could still feel the presence – or presences, it was impossible to tell, so all-invasive was the feeling that he was not alone – but he reasoned that he would be in no position to defend himself while hanging in mid-air; his best hope was to reach the solid ground of the stairway and take whatever stand was needed there. The fear felt solid around him, a physical sense of something trying to pull him back down the rope. It took all his concentration to fight it and keep moving. He was not inclined to nerves, and the sensation was so alien that he couldn't help but feel it was an external force, buffeting him like wind or rain at sea. Closing his eyes he pictured his situation as just that, afloat on the Mediterranean during one of her cruel days, wrestling with the rope as the elements tried to grab him for their own.

He risked a peek upwards to see how far he was from the banister and as he did so something collided with him. He swung to one side, digging his hands and knees into the rope as he arced through the air. This time he had to look but, twisting his head, there was nothing to see but the dark. The force came again, a rock-solid weight that hit him so firmly in the back he had no doubt it must have left a bruise. Still he could see nothing. He tried to keep climbing but the swinging rope made it almost impossible. When the third blow came it was violent enough to leave him swinging by one hand, spiralling out of control, thrashing his legs in an attempt to steady himself. He grabbed hold of the rope again but it was a lost cause. The fourth blow tore it from his grip completely and he fell back into the darkness.

CHAPTER SIX

Alan seemed to spend his whole life being hot. Living in Kissimmee, Florida, one accepted the humidity of the state; running between islands of air-conditioning, fighting off the sweaty air with iced drinks and cold showers. Now, sitting in what appeared – but most certainly *couldn't be* – a jungle, he was perspiring again, the sweat running into his eyes, blurring his vision. He would give anything to be able to wipe them. Propped up against the thick bark of a palm tree, his body was not his own. An immovable, overweight lump that had no more responsiveness than most of his lecture students. He had known this would happen – knowing altogether more about the workings of the box than most – but it was still an effort not to panic about it. He tried to distract himself by identifying the plant species around him. Botany wasn't his subject but he had a mind for minutiae and he was faintly pleased with the fern and palm species that his memory kicked up.

• • •

Making his way off campus, Alan waded through air thick and hot enough to fry pork in. He loosened the collar of his shirt and yanked his tie down a couple of inches. What the hell, he was sure his students had seen worse. Although he was old-school enough to believe a teacher should always be dressed formally, he had no intention of dying over it. He sat on a stone bench, polished smooth by the buttocks of thousands of would-be bus passengers over the years, and watched Kissimmee broil, served alongside the fat yolk of a Florida sun.

He opened his leather satchel and hunted for the half-sandwich he knew he had left in there. Ham and mustard, sweating as much in its Saran wrap as he did in his cotton shirt and slacks. Nibbling a wilting corner, Alan thought about nothing very much and let the tiny amount of breeze chill his sweating brow. There was nothing quite like the emptiness that ended his days. After hours of questions if he was lucky – barefaced indifference if he was not – it was refreshing to sit in the open air and let the thoughts just fall out of his head.

The bus appeared and he pulled himself on board. He waved at a small group of his students through the window. They pretended not to have noticed him. He smiled. If being ignored was something that you couldn't bear, you would hardly become a teacher. He jerked in his seat, startled by the sight of a small, blond-haired boy running past him, swinging on one of the support poles and then running back towards him.

"Since when does Tarzan take a bus?" Alan joked.

The boy stared at him, as if angered by the fact Alan had chosen to speak. "What's Tarzan?"

Alan chuckled and the boy looked even more disgusted, then resumed running towards the back of the bus. Alan turned around, smiling at the mother, a thin, nervous-looking young woman who was clutching a baby in one arm and the straps of a gurgling toddler in the other.

"Tires you out, I imagine?" Alan asked.

She gave him a weary nod. "You better believe it. Got some of your own?"

"No, life never quite worked out that way, I teach... next best thing, I get to send them home at the end of the day."

She nodded as if he had said something incredibly wise and returned her attention to the baby as it coughed a spittle bubble on to her cheek. Alan left her to it, settling further into his seat and closing his eyes. He was nodding off within five minutes.

The young mother – having heard Alan request his stop to the driver – tugged cautiously at his shirt cuff to wake him as the bus drew close to his destination. For a few seconds he was disorientated, then he smiled his thanks, got to his feet and stepped out on to the sidewalk, where the hot air beat on him mercilessly. Sighing with the intensity of it, Alan made his slow way along the street, feeling as if he was trying to move through water. Rebecca's office was only a few minutes' walk but the two flights of stairs up from street-level were nearly enough to finish him. He really should take better care of himself, maybe enrol in a gym. He had hit fifty a few months ago and had suffered from frequent bouts of guilt ever since, staring at his belly in the bathroom mirror, running his hands over it and imagining it gone. If he stared at it long enough the depression soon kicked in and with the depression came the food, trying to poke the grey moods down with hunks of cinnamon pastry or barbecue as if they could be swallowed and shat away.

He entered Rebecca's office and, as usual, was greeted by the sight of himself in the mirrored walls of the reception. It was an unflattering reminder of a sweating man's middle age and guaranteed his self-esteem would be at subterranean levels by the time he made it through to the therapy couch.

"Hello, Alan," said Stacey, Rebecca's incessantly chirpy receptionist, around the straw of her iced frappuccino. "She won't be a minute, her 4.30's overrunning."

"No problem," Alan said with a smile, "I'm sure their need's greater than mine."

Stacey gave him the sort of smile you offered a small child when they'd said something amusingly precocious, and returned to sucking the hell out of her iced coffee.

Alan sat down on one of the leather sofas, half reached for a magazine and then stopped as he realised there was nothing he wanted to read. He found himself awkwardly balanced between sitting and standing as he scanned the covers, trying to find anything he could bear to be seen flicking through. Everything was a glossy testament to celebrity lifestyle, perfect people pretending perfect lives. He glanced at Stacey but she was engrossed in Facebook on her computer and clearly hadn't the least interest in what he got up to. He dropped back into the sofa and put his hands into his lap. Glancing at his reflection in the mirror he was struck with the unpleasant image of a fat man playing with himself and so shifted his hands to his sides where they looked even more awkward. Who the hell put mirrors in waiting rooms, anyway? What sort of act of cruelty was that? He shifted in the seat, watching his reflection and trying to find a pose that he could live with. He was still trying when Rebecca's door opened and a woman stepped out, pushing her nose into a crumpled tissue as if trying to hide it.

"We'll get to the bottom of it next week, Sandra," said Rebecca, following her client out. "We've made some wonderful progress, I'm sure you agree?"

If Sandra did agree she wasn't about to admit it, shuffling straight past Stacey and out the front door. Stacey gave a small shrug and returned to updating her online status, no doubt with some witty variation on "You don't have to be mad to work here…"

"Hello, Alan," said Rebecca, holding her hand out to him.

He had never felt so disadvantaged, the sofa having sucked him back into it just as he wanted to leap to his feet. She was wearing her usual outfit: a tight pencil skirt and light cream blouse, half austere, half enticing. He managed to get to his feet but she was forced to step back as his momentum sent him into her personal space.

"Sorry," he mumbled, taking her hand and then being horribly embarrassed by how clammy it must feel.

"What for?" Rebecca asked. He wished she could save the awkward questions until they were inside.

"Nothing," he said, hoping to dismiss it. "Hot, isn't it?"

"I'm sure it is," she half-agreed, though in that non-committal "that's your opinion and it's not my place to disagree" way that therapists did so well. "I'm lucky enough to have been in the air-con all day." Alan nearly started talking about the campus air-con – a devilish contraption of pipes and vents that spat staleness sporadically into the lecture halls – but stopped himself just in time, having realised it was the most boring subject known to man. Instead he nodded and tried to stop smiling. He couldn't. "Well," she said, "let's get settled."

She led him into her office and he took his seat in the patient's armchair, a soft entrapment of furnishing that seemed designed to limit movement. She sat opposite him, crossing her legs, and he tried not to stare at the inch of thigh she offered. Were all patients so attracted to their therapist? He found himself spending more time trying to perceive her bra through the cotton of her blouse, or imagining how the lining of that skirt might slide up and down her thighs as she shifted in her seat, than he did actually thinking about her questions.

It was with something approaching horror that he realised he was developing an erection.

"So, how've you been?" she asked.

"Fine, great really, nothing major." He tried to shift in his seat to cover his arousal.

"Dreams?"

"Oh, you know, the usual." The more he tried to will his erection away, the more the bastard stiffened.

"Talk me through them."

"Do I have to?"

"I think it would be helpful."

Alan crossed his legs, hoping it would help. "It really is the same old stuff, me before the accident, being... well, not being nice. I really would rather not go into it."

"And the box?"

"The box is just a hobby. You said hobbies were good."

"They are, but obsessions are bad."

"I wouldn't say I was obsessed," Alan leaned forward defensively and Rebecca raised an eyebrow. For a moment he thought she was looking at his trousers (the thought of which made the problem more profound), then he realised she was sceptical about the box. In which she was quite right, of course.

"You read about a 'magic box' in a junk conspiracy magazine" she said, "and then dedicate all your spare time to finding it. That's obsessional."

"It's curiosity."

"It's displacement."

This actually threw Alan, giving him enough change of focus for his erection to dwindle of its own accord. "Displacement?"

"You're missing twenty-odd years of your life – the memories of them anyway – but you don't want them back, you'd rather focus your attentions on a mythical object, something to distract you from the important business of recovering your lost memory."

"Nobody but you even thinks it's lost."

"It is rather unprecedented..."

"Yeah, well, I manage without it. The box is far more interesting."

"The mythical box."

"Aren't you a bit confrontational for a therapist?"

"It's my style."

Alan didn't know what to say. Everything about his "accident" (as it had been so carelessly labelled) bored him. It was baggage he had carried for thirty years; it had almost become comfortable, for Christ's sake. He only kept coming to these sessions because he liked seeing Rebecca.

"Why do you come to my sessions?" she asked, her timing making him think she was far better at reading his thoughts than he gave her credit for. "I know it's part of your agreement with the college but still, it's not just that, is it?"

"They like to know they're not employing a mad-man, for sure." She stared at him, refusing to fill the silence until he answered the question. "No, it's not just that. I don't like the gap, the mystery, the dreams, all of it. If I could make it go away I would. At the same time, though, I am used to it, like to think I get on fine despite it, and there's a big part of me that thinks I'd be better off just, well, forgetting about it. The box helps me do that."

"See, displacement."

Alan sighed; he couldn't argue it. "Strike one to you."

He gave up for the rest of the session, alternating between recounting his thoughts and dreams in mind-numbing detail and fantasising about what a woman like that would never dream of doing with a guy like him. He also thought about the box, that impossible box…

At the end of the session he dutifully booked another – and Rebecca must know what her bending over the desk to check her appointment book did to him, she *must* – and headed back out into the heat to wait for his bus.

By the time he climbed up the steps of his wooden porch, his clothes were sticking to him and there was no other thought in his head but the glass of iced tea he planned on drinking the minute he got through the door.

Inside, he threw his briefcase on to the table beside the phone, hit the flashing message button of his answering machine and headed to the kitchen to slake his thirst.

"Mr Arthur," came the first caller message, "just to let you know that the book you requested, *The*

Imagineer by Gregory Ashe, is back in stock. We shall hold it for you for up to three days."

The iced tea was perfectly cold and Alan drank it greedily, taking the first glassful in one go before re-filling.

"Mr. Alan," came the next message, the heavy Chinese accent getting his name wrong as usual, "your suit is ready for collect. See you soon, bye."

Alan smiled around his second glass of iced tea.

"Alan Arthur?" The third message was from an entirely unfamiliar caller. "I have the box."

Alan dropped the glass and it shattered on the tiles of the kitchen floor, peppering his shoes with minted tea and glass crystals.

"If you're willing to pay what it's worth – and mind me here, I fucking *know* what it's worth – then you'll meet me at Home Town, out on I-4, tonight, 11.30. Just keep walking around. I'll find you."

He felt his toes twitch within the soft leather coffin of his loafers: a small sign of life. In the distance the foliage ruffled as something made its way through the leaves. He hoped it wasn't a creature on the hunt for dinner. He might be able to blink at it really hard but that was about it as defending himself went. He would move again soon enough, but Alan had never been much good at waiting.

"Home Town" – as a student of history Alan had less patience than most with plastic nostalgia. The place was a cheap recreation of Fifties Americana,

boardwalks and Buddy Holly, milkshakes and
reproduction Wurlitzers churning out flimsy rock 'n'
roll while families trudged between shops and
lacklustre fairground rides. He had been there for ten
minutes and already he could happily trash the place
with a baseball bat.

This wasn't the first time someone had got in
touch with him claiming they had the box in their
possession. He made no secret about his search, had
been interviewed in a number of counter-culture
magazines and websites, and made himself easily
contactable... how could he hope to get his hands
on it otherwise? More often than not the interview
would culminate in an outrageous financial demand
and the presentation of a worthless trinket – likely
picked up on a package holiday or from a cheap im-
port furniture house. At this point Alan would
simply apologise for having wasted their time, explain that it wasn't the correct box and give them a
small payment as an appreciation of their good in-
tentions. Generous, yes, but having once lost his
patience with a young chancer in Long Island only
to find himself staring at the messy end of a packer's
knife, he kept calm and always deferred to the
would-be seller.

He did as he had been asked, strolling aimlessly
along the boardwalks and killing time until he was
approached. He visited a small magic store, taking a
few moments to admire a miniature treasure chest
that – as the owner demonstrated – was crafted so as
to make anything placed inside it vanish. He was

sufficiently impressed with its design and efficacy that he bought it. At least now he was guaranteed not to leave the resort empty-handed. He walked further up the parade and entered a coffee shop that threatened to suffocate under its own enforced sense of nostalgia. From the chrome fixtures to the black and white floor tiles, the red leatherette seating and the elderly black guy glowering under his white, peaked hat.

"Help you?" he growled.

"Black coffee, small." Alan didn't try and make small talk with the man; it was obvious that such niceties weren't on the menu. He took his coffee, paid and sat down at a window seat. He'd walked enough, damn them; he was sure the caller could live with meeting in a coffee shop. He'd buy the man a damned drink to sweeten the pill.

Alan's coffee had barely cooled before a man walked in and headed straight over. He was small, his clothes expensive but badly crumpled. He looked as if he had left his home weeks ago and never re-turned. His jacket looked slept in, his trousers so creased they seemed like a cotton mosaic built around the man's thin legs. He was carrying a small leather holdall but Alan suspected the heavy baggage was carried internally.

"I take it you're my mysterious caller?" Alan asked, not altogether seriously.

"Yeah, well, can't be too careful." The man was English, which was another slight surprise. You saw many over here on vacation but Alan couldn't imagine this guy was a fan of the Mouse House. "I like to keep the odds in my favour, y'know?"

"Gambling man."

The man stared at him and there was a look in his eyes that alarmed Alan. This was a man who liked hurting people. "No," he said, "that's my fucking point, innit? I know gamblers... taken 'em for every fucking penny... I'm not one of 'em."

Alan was suddenly put in mind of that young man in Long Island, a kid who had just been waiting for the first excuse to pull a knife. This guy was the same, he wanted to snap and start hitting people; he just needed an excuse. Alan must be careful not to give him one.

"So," he said, eager to get to business and then go their separate ways, "you think you have the box?"

Wrong phrasing. The Englishman slapped the table with the flat of his hand. "I don't fucking *think* anything, mate... I've got your box, don't you worry about that." He reached into his holdall, pulled out a bundled plastic carrier bag and tossed it carelessly on to the table between them. "Question is, have you got the price?"

"May I?" Alan gestured towards the uninspiring package in front of him.

"Help yourself. Just don't go getting any smart ideas. You ain't fast enough to outrun me."

Alan attempted a placating smile but was too scared to completely pull it off. There was no doubt in his mind that he was about to unwrap yet another in a long succession of counterfeit boxes; the only uncertainty was what the Englishman would do when he announced the fact. Was he going to have to pretend it was the genuine article and pay accordingly? It would be heartbreaking to hand over any great sum of money for a worthless...

The box fell into his hands and immediately his brain quietened... this was no trinket. This was the real thing. His fingers trembled just to hold it.

"No bollocks, eh?" The Englishman smiled. "Got a fucking bite to it, ain't it?"

"Where did you...?"

"A man did a runner owing me a lot of money. That was what he left behind. I want ten grand, what he owed me... point of principle."

"Fine." Alan didn't care about the money, never had.

"Sterling mind... you can keep your fucking dollars... cash too."

"Fine, no problem." Alan held the box up, trying to catch the light from one of the overhead spots. The Englishman flinched and sat back in his chair. He's scared of it, Alan thought, he knows what it's capable of and he's terrified. A vicious streak bubbled up in him. He had felt intimidated; now he knew he could throw some of that back.

"It's more than just a box, you know," Alan said.

"Yeah, whatever."

"But you already know that, don't you?" Alan pushed the box in the man's direction and smiled to see him flinch.

"Look, just pay up and I'll be off, yeah?"

"Don't be ridiculous, I obviously don't carry that sort of cash – in sterling no less – in my back pocket. You'll have to wait, or take a cheque."

"All right, cheque's fine… I'll trust you, OK?"

"Changed your tune." Alan smiled. "You've seen what this can do, haven't you?"

"Don't fuck with me, OK?" the Englishman replied, trying to claw back a little control. "Just be glad I'm happy to make this business quick."

Alan smiled, put the box down between them and pulled his chequebook out of his jacket pocket. "Maybe this debtor of yours even used the box?" he asked. "It has a reputation for stealing people away. There have been many of them over the years. You wouldn't believe the years I've spent researching it, tracking it from one owner to another."

"Happy fucking day then, innit?"

"You swear too much."

"And you talk shite… now give me my money and I'll leave you to it."

"Call it seventeen thousand in US dollars, I'm inclined to round up." Alan tore off the cheque and held it out to the man. "Oh," he said, pulling the cheque back, "one last question: how did you find me?"

The Englishman leaned forward and snatched the cheque from Alan's hand. "Piece of piss," he replied. "The fucking box told me."

He grabbed his bag and marched out of the building, leaving Alan with the object of a life's obsession sat in front of him.

● ● ●

Both of Alan's legs were filled with pins and needles, a sure sign that he was on the mend. A trail of sweat dripped from his nose into his lap but he couldn't feel enough to be discomfited by it. A sharp pain began to build in his left hand but he couldn't turn his head to find out why. As the feeling grew he managed to lift his hand slightly. There was something attached to it but he couldn't tell what. Still, if that was the limit of his injuries he could hardly complain, considering what they would have been had the box not performed as expected. He was lucky to be alive.

Alan drank his coffee slowly, staring at the box. What came next was daunting and he was in no great rush. He had confidence in his research – it was pretty much all he had, so he wasn't going to doubt it now. Still, if he was mistaken... No, no point in thinking that way. He had set aside the majority of his life in the name of this box. There was nothing to be gained by getting cold feet now.

He drained his cup, picked up the box and walked outside. The crowds were thinning out as the hour grew late, holiday-makers heading home to their motels and rented villas. Alan would not be going home. He walked past his car – ignoring it completely – and headed towards the Interstate. Even now, the road was busy, airport traffic and those kicked out from the parks making their way home, bellies sloshing with junk food and soda.

He held the box firmly in his hands and stepped out into the traffic, gritting his teeth in panic as the horns began to cut through the thick Florida night.

It was some time before he felt anything else.

His hand was still hurting and, slowly, he managed to lift it to his face so that he could find out why. A thorny vine was imbedded into his palm, small purple holes leaking blood in thin trails toward his wrist.

A movement ahead drew his attention. A girl, fourteen or fifteen, had stepped from out of the undergrowth and was staring at him. He tried to speak but his mouth was slack and unresponsive. He turned his hand towards her, intending to show that he meant her no harm but with the vine and blood it occurred to him the gesture was rather grotesque. She continued to stare, utterly expressionless, then walked over and crouched in front of him. Delicately she pried the thorns out of his hand and flung the vine to one side. Job done, she stood back up and began to walk back into the undergrowth.

"Wait…" Alan managed to say, "please… wait…"

She stopped and turned to look at him. After a few seconds, she came to a decision, sat down in the foliage and waited for him to come round.

They sat together for a while, lazy light tumbling down through the thick canopy of leaves above. Occasionally, Alan would mumble something, whisper reassurances or impatient apologies as, slowly, his legs and arms came back to him. The girl said nothing.

Slowly, Alan began to move, stretching his legs amongst the fallen leaves and moss.

"How long have you been here?" he asked, massaging his cramping legs. The girl didn't reply. "It must have been quite a shock," Alan continued, undaunted, "snatched from wherever you were and ending up..." he looked around him "...well... I must admit this wasn't quite what I had expected." He pushed against the tree and pulled himself upright. "I've been researching the box... you know about the box, well, of course... you must know... well, as I say, I've been researching it for years. Reports of people taken from their day-to-day lives and transported here into..." he looked around again "...well, most accounts agreed it was some sort of house, not quite like this at all." He took his first few hesitant steps. "Very few reports exist from people who have claimed to return so I suppose it's only natural that there may be more to it all than meets the eye... but they all talk about a large mansion, English, Victorian, but with, well, certain rather weird differences... endless corridors, impossibly large rooms, a building that has dismissed the more fundamental laws of physics."

Alan walked, somewhat unsteadily, over to the girl. "A disturbing place, certainly, a nightmare of a building but... full of possibilities." The girl looked at him but her face was expressionless. He had assumed it was shock but, as he looked into those solid yet empty eyes, he began to wonder if it wasn't something a little more permanent.

"I'm talking a lot," he said, "not like me, sorry." He removed his tie; maybe it would help if he looked less austere. "Nerves, I expect."

They looked at one another for a moment then she stood up and began to walk into the trees. "Quite right," Alan said with a smile, "a doer not a thinker… let's see what we can find, shall we?"

INTERLUDE

The troops are fragile. Months of famine and abuse from the neighbouring Chinese have made them as weak as they are bloodthirsty. If determination were a weapon they would be victorious, but the renegade observer knows it isn't enough. They'll need all the help they can get. He trots between the brothers-in-law, Li Jinzhong and Sun Wanrong, enjoying the feel of the horse beneath him, the domination of another animal still a hobby he favours over all others.

"Do you think they will fight well, my chieftains?" he asks.

"They will defend their honour," Jinzhong answers.

"You make them sound like virgins." The renegade smiles. He is by no means certain there are any virgins left in the Khitan tribes. He has seen to a good number of them himself. Women are like horses, he has found: good for riding.

"When it comes to battle they are," says Wanrong, "they can fight off wolves from their farms, maybe even deter the odd band of outlaws, but stand up to the Chinese? This will prove… *interesting*."

"Well," replies the renegade, "as always, I'll see what I can do."

Jinzhong chuckles. "Yingzhou will remember the day it was visited by the Bringer of Tricks!"

Indeed it will, thinks the renegade, trying to decide what he might do on the battlefield. Perhaps he will turn the ground to swamp so it sucks the Chinese away? Or maybe animate the trees to tear them apart? As soon the ideas are visualised he is bored by them. It is sad how quickly such theatrics pall.

Later, having infected the Chinese with a lethargy close to his own, he wades through their soporific army, hacking and slicing until there is no opposition left. Blood-soaked and apathetic, he sits down on a rock and considers where to go next. Six months of being the personal deity to the Khitans is no employment for one of his abilities.

He needs to think bigger.

CHAPTER SEVEN

"Who's hungry then?" the man repeated, stepping out of the cupboard. There was no more than five foot of him and a good portion of that was the hat: white and puffy, the sort of thing you only saw on cartoon chefs. The little man walked over to the stove and stroked its wrought-iron curves with tenderness. "A light meal, perhaps a stew... or something more refined?" He turned to Tom and smiled, his face pink from the heat of the stove, his little moustache furred up like a rat in a storm-drain.

"Look..." Tom finally managed to find his tongue. "My friend's not well, she... Well, we don't know what happened but she can't move and..."

"Oh, nonsense," the little man insisted, "she'll be right as rain in a few minutes. It always affects newcomers that way – it hammers the nervous system travelling here." He fixed Tom with a curious stare. "In fact I'm surprised you're not suffering from the same thing." He stepped closer to Tom and sniffed deeply. "Ah… alcohol! How interesting! It must make for a smoother journey."

"That's my creed, brother," Tom muttered. "So…" he took hold of Elise's hand "…she's going to be cool?"

"Absolutely," replied the little chef. "Which is why we must get to work quickly." He pulled a knife from a drawer and firmly inserted the tip into Tom's thigh. "It's such a bugger to prep them when they keep thrashing about, after all."

Tom fell to the floor with a shocked yell that took a frying pan to the brow to silence. Elise cried out too, but the little man slapped his hand on her mouth like a lid on a screeching kettle.

"Shush now," he said, leering over her. He smiled, showing off large yellow teeth, chipped from gnawing the edges of bones. "It's distracting." He tugged a long paisley handkerchief from his pocket and began forcing it into Elise's mouth with fingers that smelt of old meat and body cavities.

He whipped off his leather belt and wrapped it around her face, tightening it around her jaw to keep the handkerchief in place. "Feel free to chew on that while I cut and slice and peel." The butchery that lay ahead was exciting the man. He was getting breathless and needed to steady himself for a few seconds by holding on to the marble top of the preparation table. "Sorry," he whispered, "I'd hate you to think you were in the hands of anything less than a dedicated professional, it's just been so long." He straightened up and began tugging her blouse from the waist of her jeans, smacking and squeezing her exposed belly. "By all means, if you have any particular preference for a dish, a rump cut or braised thigh perhaps, then do let me know, otherwise I'll just follow my gut."

He ground his thumb into the meat of her hip and licked at the ragged fur of his moustache, tasting its salt as seasoning for his imagination. He picked up a large knife, pulled a grey stone from his pocket, spat on it and began to sharpen the blade. "I'm tempted to open an artery," he commented, "make some pudding. When pickings are as slim as they are in this kitchen you want to make sure you make the most of every opportunity. I apologise but I simply haven't the patience to force-feed you, though I'm sure I could make art from your liver if only my stomach wasn't so eager to be filled... some corn and a pipe... pump you up like a ballon until you were a masterwork of rupture and distention. Ah! My mouth waters at the very thought. But there is no need to dine on dreams, is there, my dear? When some of your most succulent portions can be searing within minutes." He leaned in as if to kiss her and licked her face with enthusiasm. "My belly aches for you sweet calf." He walked out of Elise's field of vision and she could hear the rattle of pans and bowls. She desperately fought to move her arms and legs but her hands flicked on dead wrists and her toes wriggled pointlessly in the toes of her sneakers.

The man returned with a large basin and propped her head up against the brim. "Just a pint or so," he said. "You can never keep it fresh and I wouldn't dream of wasting precious blood-sausage on flies."

Elise looked up at the ceiling and tried to prepare herself for the knife. It didn't come. Directly above her, a young man appeared, bursting from the ceiling like someone erupting from water. He fell directly on her would-be butcher, who crumpled beneath him with a high-pitched wail.

The young man was first to his feet, backing away as the screeching chef ran at him with his knife. Looking around, the boy grabbed the frying pan with which the chef had hit Tom. He swung it once to knock the blade from the man's hand and then again, bringing it down with a resounding clang on the man's forehead. The chef stared at him, a rather flatulent look on his face. A trickle of blood appeared at his hairline and crept down his forehead like the yolk from a perfectly boiled egg. The blood continued to run, flowing in a thin stream across his cheek and down towards his moustache. The little chef licked at it, smiled with approval and fell flat on his face.

The boy continued to back away, scared and confused. He looked at Elise, then up at the ceiling, unable to process what had just happened. Tom groaned, as consciousness forced its way rather rudely into his aching head. He sat up, pressing his hand to his bruised temple, before remembering the knife-wound in his thigh and giving another pained cry. The boy, still disorientated and afraid, raised the frying pan towards Tom.

Elise moaned against her gag, trying to sit up, trying to warn Tom, but there was no need.

"Stay cool, kid!" he said, holding his hands up in a gesture of surrender, "we're all cats here."

"English?" the boy asked, slightly lowering the frying pan.

"American," Tom replied, "but don't hold that against us. The name's Tom and that there is my good friend Elise. Didn't catch that son of a bitch's name," he gestured towards the prostrate chef, "but can't say I'll lose any sleep over the fact."

"I am Pablo," the boy replied, "Spanish but I speak good English – better than you, I think, for I know what a cat is and there is none here that I can see."

"So," Carruthers' voice rang out along the corridor as he marched back in the direction Miles and Penelope had come from, "you found yourselves washed up on this foul land, no memory of how you came to be here – except, I warrant, the suspicion that a box lies at the root of the mystery – and, after an interminable time of immobility, you began to explore your new home. Did you travel together or was your meeting the same stroke of good fortune that brought you into my company?"

"We came separately," Miles replied, quickly so that he might fit the words into the brief pause Carruthers took for breath.

"I suspected as much. Whatever carriage lies within that box, it seems only to afford a single berth. A further detail: at the moment in which you left our world, might your lives have been in peril?"

"Yes, I suppose so." Miles replied

"That adds some fuel to a thought of mine. I wondered why the box didn't open the minute I lay my hands on it. Obviously there was some extra factor that unlocked it. I had wondered if that might be mortal danger. I was being shot at at the time, you see…"

"I was being beaten up," Miles continued, "by a right vicious little bastard–"

"I say, old chap," Carruthers interjected, "ladies present."

"I had been stripped in preparation for being raped and murdered." Penelope said, "so I can assure you the word 'bastard' has long since lost its ability to bring a rouge to my cheeks."

Carruthers stopped dead in his tracks and turned toward Penelope with a sincere look of remorse. "Oh, my dear lady," he said, "I have been most terribly insensitive… I cannot hope that you would ever forgive me. My time here has robbed me of a good many of my social graces and I confess I gave no thought as to the possible reasons for your…" He gestured towards the curtain wrapped around her. "I just…"

"*Assumed*. Yes, I know, you're forgiven. And please don't start fussing, I'm made of sterner stuff than that. I am alive, relatively untouched and, correct me if I'm wrong, but we really do have more pressing concerns at the moment."

Carruthers bowed towards her, a smile of the utmost admiration on his face. "I am in awe of you, madam. Your bravery shames us all." He gestured for them to continue walking.

"So," Miles said, after a moment, "where are we?"

"I have been here for several months and yet I fear I am no closer to solving that particular mystery. It looks like a house, certainly, but that is merely the surface. These walls obey no natural laws I am aware of and the dangers here are limitless. I cannot explain, I cannot comprehend. But my eyes have seen countless impossibilities before: Alaskan nights afire with colour, lizards the size of hounds, leviathans in the ocean, fish flying through the air... and if there's one thing it has taught me it is that there is no such thing as the impossible, merely the unexperienced. Yes, our learning demands that we dismiss this place as utterly impossible, and yet we are here, so what is one constructively to do except get on with it?"

"I can see your point," Penelope conceded. "Like Alice I have found that my ability to believe the impossible expands by the minute."

"Exactly, my dear! One simply has to survive and hope! I have held on to a solitary mission since my arrival here and I will follow that mission until either I succeed or it kills me."

"And what is your mission exactly?" Miles asked.

"Why, what else, dear boy?" Carruthers laughed, throwing his hands into the air. "I intend to find my way home!"

"I'd settle for a way out of this corridor," Miles replied, with a smile brought on by the man's good humour.

"Aha!" Carruthers pointed towards one of the doors. "That I can do." He grinned widely. "Though naturally it is *extremely* dangerous."

"Naturally," Penelope sighed.

"You're lucky," said Elise as she finished binding the wound in Tom's leg, "there doesn't appear to be any serious damage."

"Yeah, cool," said Tom, "'lucky'… just the word I was thinking of."

"I know a man on my father's boat who lost his foot," Pablo said.

"Careless of him," Tom muttered.

"He get it caught in engine piston, it badly twisted, like mincing meat. He bind his shin with belt and cut off foot. Still worked the rest of the trip."

"OK!" Tom shouted. "I get the message, I am a baby for complaining about the little bit of stabbing my leg has received. From now on I shall shut up, sit back and enjoy the pain."

Elise kissed him on the forehead. "Nobody's saying you're a baby."

"Sure feels like it."

"Well, they're not."

"Promise?"

"Promise, now stop going on about it, you big baby."

"Ha ha."

"I am thinking," said Pablo, changing the subject, "that this man who shot you is the same who I see."

"I think you're right," said Elise, "though it doesn't help make sense of it."

They had swapped stories while Elise had come around and looked to Tom's wounds. Not that there was that much to tell, all three being as much in the dark as each other about the hows and whys of it all.

"Well," said Tom as he got slowly to his feet, "at least we know that wherever *here* is, there's more to it than just a groovy old kitchen and a kinky cannibal."

"I guess," Elise agreed, "though it doesn't help us figure a way out."

Pablo grabbed a poker from beside the stove, climbed on to the preparation table and tapped at the ceiling, now resolutely solid. "It is not a way back through here," he said, jumping back down.

"Even if it was I can't see we'd be much better off," said Elise. "From the way you described it I'd say we were safer here."

"I think I know how to get out," Tom replied, "though I can't say the idea appeals much." He limped over to the hatch in the far wall and opened it.

"A dumb waiter?" Elise asked.

"I know someone like this," Pablo added, "he is too stupid to keep his job, he make wrong the people's orders."

"'Dumb' as in silent, El Toro," Tom explained. "It's how the food was sent to the dining room upstairs in these oldfashioned kitchens: you put the stuff in here, yank on the rope and winch it up to the next floor."

"I not like the sound of being lifted like soup through the walls."

"You and me both, Jack."

"My name is Pablo."

"He talks weird, Pablo," Elise explained. "You'll get used to him. Will it take our weight?"

"The rope looks strong enough…" Tom pounded the base "…and the box sure is. As for the pulleys… well, there really is only one way to find out, ain't there?"

"Jesus," Elise sighed, "this can't be a good idea."

"Maybe not, baby, but it's the only one on the menu."

"I am less heavy," said Pablo, "I try it first."

"The Spanish bull takes one for the team. Like your style, Pablo. Hop on board the gravy train."

"He means 'get in'," Elise explained.

Pablo climbed into the wooden box. It was large enough for him to sit in if he pulled his knees up high and clutched his duffel bag tight to his chest. "Make gravy train leave station, cat," he said to Tom with a nervous smile.

Tom laughed. "You've got the jive, Spanish bull, hold on tight." He began to pull on the rope, grunting with the effort as Pablo rose out of sight.

"A couple of years ago," Carruthers said while ushering Miles and Penelope into a bedroom almost identical to all the others, "I traversed the Great Victoria desert, that arid wasteland in Australia, filled with little but lizards and the most bizarrely painted fellows I have ever had the fortune to meet. In fact, had I completed the journey a week earlier it might not have been named after our Queen at all, but that damned Giles beat me to it. Still... who wants 450 miles of sand named after them, eh?"

"I have a Martini in my name," Penelope admitted, "which is probably just as dry."

"And eminently more practical."

"Anyway..." Miles butted in, "your point was?"

Penelope smiled. "Don't mind him, he's just sore that nobody's ever named anything after him."

"The desert was an unreliable place," Carruthers continued, "you could never guarantee the solidity of the ground beneath your feet. When the sandstorms descended, navigation became impossible and the landscape would be utterly changed once the light returned. It was ever shifting, ever fluid. This house has certain similarities." He gestured for them to join him at the window. "Out there," he said, pointing into the darkness, "is nothing the human eye can discern and the house is filled with such spaces. Great swathes of absence that demarcate the barrier between one location and the next. As far as I have managed to comprehend it is impossible to travel far in this building without crossing these spaces."

"And how, precisely, are we supposed to do that?" asked Miles.

"Oh, you'll see, my dear boy. But first I must warn you of the wraiths that police the barriers."

"I think I may have met one earlier."

"Aha!" Carruthers patted Miles on the arm. "And lived to tell the tale, eh? You will know then that the wraiths are invisible phantoms that prey on the mind as much as the body. They fix you with terror, until – transfixed like one of our moth friends in a killing jar – the wraith strikes!"

"Erm… yes, wonderfully dramatic… strikes *how* exactly?"

"Oh…" Carruthers waved his hands in he air as if such details were not in the least important "…they can pulverise a man down to his very atoms, render him little but red mist and screams. But we're too clever to let it get to that, aren't we, my dears?"

"I'm glad you seem to think so," Miles muttered.

"Look at this way, dear boy," Carruthers said with a wink, "I'm still in the land of the living, eh? You just mark me well as I teach you the knack of it."

"We're all ears," Miles replied.

CHAPTER EIGHT

Sophie decides the fellowship building is neither warm nor cold. It is No Temperature. It is also not too dark or too bright. The sun is shining today but a filter on the glass roof takes away the glare. She decides that the roof is made in the same way as her sunglasses and she holds them above her head to compare the two. The lenses in her glasses are darker. The roof does not look dark at all and yet somehow it does the same thing. Sophie decides this is very interesting and forgets to listen to the officer's words as he drones on about "a life well lived" and "a woman cherished in the memory of those she has left behind". Sophie finds the officer hard to listen to. His voice is a monotone. He sounds like a buzzing fridge. He is not interesting. The glass is interesting. Besides, mothers die every day. It happens to lots of people. It is very common. It is very boring.

Sophie looks at her father. He is not bored, she thinks (or maybe he is – she has heard people talk about being "bored to tears", perhaps this is what has happened to her father). He is crying a lot. Watching his eyes squeeze out all that water (it is like sweat but it is not sweat) makes Sophie forget about the glass and think about tears instead. It is very strange, all that water coming out of someone's eyes. Sophie wonders what it is for. It seems to her that it serves no purpose. She cannot understand things like this. Her father looks at her and tries to smile. Perhaps he is not so sad after all. So why is he crying? All of this contradiction has stopped being interesting; now it is just confusing, and that makes her angry. She stares at the wall, humming quietly. This is how she becomes empty, how she becomes calm. The wall is what most people would call white but it is not white, there is a grey in it and a pearlescent sheen that makes it look as if it comes from the ocean. She studies it until she knows it, humming, humming, humming. Then she is calm.

Outside, her grandparents lead her and her father to their car. Her grandmother kisses her on the cheek. She doesn't like that as her cheek felt perfect and now it is wet and won't sit right. Her grandfather doesn't kiss her, in fact he hardly looks at her. This is because he finds it hard to understand her. She can relate to this and therefore understands her grandfather very well. She likes her grandfather because she understands him. She feels they are quite alike.

They are not going home; they are going to stay at her grandparent's house. This angers Sophie but she can tell that there will be no changing it so she doesn't shout or scream. She just sits quietly on the back seat, holding her head against the window so that the vi-brations of the motor make her head shake and her teeth tickle. It feels as if she is cleaning her brain.

When they arrive at the house she remembers that she does not know it. Her grandparents used to live in one place and now they live in another. This is not something that Sophie understands – why would you change where you live? Perhaps it is straighter, perhaps it is easier to draw. Sophie has drawn her house many times but there are so many rooms and they are all different sizes so it is difficult to get it right. What she needs is a piece of paper as big as the house, then she could trace it and get everything just right. She doesn't think it is possible to buy such paper.

Inside the house she realises she has not remem-bered to listen to her grandparents. They have been asking her questions but she didn't hear them. She doesn't try and answer them now, it is too late. She just smiles – often this is the only answer people want anyway – and begins to get to know the house. She goes into each room, walking around the out-side, running her hand against the wall. This is a good way to understand a room. You get to know its shape and what it feels like on the edges (which are the only bits of a room that are real anyway, every-thing else is just air).

The house is quite big and this takes her a while as she has to do it three times. Three times is a good number, it is the amount of times it takes to really know something.

Once she has finished she goes back outside. Outside is not the problem for her that some people assume it is. People think she will find the outside uncomfortable because there are no walls. This is a silly mistake. Here are the reasons:

1. *Outside there are not supposed to be any walls.*
2. *Without walls you cannot build a perfect box.*
3. *Outside will, therefore, always be random, always be untidy.*
4. *Outside is doing exactly what it is supposed to do, therefore she understands it and likes it.*

It is things that don't work as they should that make her uncomfortable.

There are trees outside, planted in rows. Sophie walks along the rows, counting the trees. This is a good thing and she is happy to do it for hours. In the end she stops because it is getting too dark and it is hard to count.

She goes back inside and eats her tea. She has spaghetti. She always has spaghetti because that is what she likes. If that is what you like then why would you eat anything else? Afterwards she eats half a tin of cold rice pudding. She knows it was half a tin because her grandmother lets her measure it. This puts her in a good mood and she goes to bed happy and smiles as she counts the way into sleep.

In the morning she wakes up and there is a moment where things are difficult. She likes her mother to make her toast – medium, brown, plain, no butter or jam or marmalade or Marmite or honey or any-thing, *plain*. Her mother knows how crisp toast should be, she likes it cooked on toaster setting number four, that is the best setting. When she goes downstairs she remembers that her mother is dead and dead people cannot make toast – though they are cooked like toast. Her friend at school, Anya, has told her so: "They'll toast your mother," Anya said, "toast her until she's dust." Sophie thinks this must mean that they are using a setting that is higher than four. Her grandmother promises that her toaster – which looks very different from the toaster Sophie is used to, it is white not silver – also has a setting for number four and that they can make the toast together so that Sophie knows everything is fine. It is fine and Sophie takes her toast outside to count the trees again.

After a while she doesn't want to count the trees any more, she wants to know new things. She walks through the forest only stopping every now and then to brush the pine needles off her boots (boots should not have pine needles). Soon she hears the sound of the sea. She has forgotten her grandparents now live near the sea. Lots of people like to live by the sea, it makes them happy. Sophie does not mind the sea but it does scare her a little bit. She can swim, but to swim in the sea is not to control the sea, it is to try and stop the sea controlling you and that is not the same thing at all. So the sea makes her a little bit scared. She walks toward the sound of waves anyway. There may be other things that are interesting to know, so it is worth being a little bit scared.

The forest opens out and Sophie has to sit down for a while to close her eyes. There is too much sky and she has forgotten how big it can be. After a few minutes' humming and emptying herself she opens her eyes knowing that the sky is there and that she cannot fall into it. The sky is not scary any more; it is just there as usual. The ground falls at a slight gradient towards the coast and she continues to follow the sound of the waves.

Once she reaches the edge of the cliff she takes the time to look and understand. There is a lot of sea, but that is all right, she has been expecting a lot of sea. The cliff is very tall but that is all right too, tall cliffs were only bad if you walked off them; if you didn't walk off them they couldn't hurt at all. She walks along the cliff back towards the house. Maybe she can even walk in a square (out of the house straight ahead into trees, turn right towards sea, turn right, walk along cliff, turn right, walk back to house). That would make her very happy: squares are good and always turning in the same direction is good. There is a lot around her that is not ground. There is a lot of air and a lot of water and a lot of space. It is like a very large room. She is enjoying it.

Then she sees the box.

The box is lying in the grass on the edge of the cliff and it should not be there. Not only is it the sort of box that should be inside a house, there is something wrong with the way the box is. It is like standing next to an electricity pylon. The box buzzes.

Sophie sits down for a moment so that she can decide what to do. The box makes her uncomfortable
and she would like to run away from it. But if she
does that then it will still be there. She is not quite
sure if it will still be upsetting even when she cannot
see it, as she will still know it and sometimes that is
just as bad. But the only way to make it right is to
pick the box up and take it back to the house. Then
the box will be inside a house. That is good. But,
deep down, she knows that the box will still be
wrong. That is not good.

She has an idea. She can throw the box in the sea.
The box is not supposed to be in the sea and that is
not good but the sea will break the box down – turn
it into broken bits of wood. You do get broken bits
of wood in the sea, she has seen them on beaches.
She still has to be brave enough to pick the box up
and that is not good. But it is the only way. She emp-
ties herself again, becomes calm. Then she stands up,
walks over to the box and picks it up.

*Theboxbiteshertheboxbiteshertheboxbitesherthe-
boxbiteshertheboxbitesher!!*

She is so scared when she feels the pain in her
hand that she slips on the edge of the cliff. She falls,
and that is not good. The box is still in her hand because she has forgotten to let go of it now that
something more interesting has happened. She is
falling through the air. Sophie is not supposed to be
in the air. Sophie vanishes.

This is good.

• • •

Instead of crashing into the sea below she finds herself lying on her back in the middle of a jungle. Her feelings about this are complex. She would not have wanted to die. She has not. This is therefore good. However, people do not vanish from the space halfway between a clifftop and the sea to reappear in the middle of a jungle. This is Not Something People Do. Never, never, never. But she has just done it. This is not good. The conflict between these two states is hard to reconcile and it takes precisely twelve minutes of counting and humming to achieve contentment (twelve is four multiplied by three, the sides of a box by the times it takes to know something, a good, solid, dependable number). After she has done this she sits up and prepares to understand the jungle.

She thinks of counting the trees she sees, but the planting is too random, and the fat rubbery leaves or long palm spikes far too unusual. They are best not counted. Let them just be. The ground is made of thick compost. She has seen compost in bags. Her father once tried to grow tomatoes in a bag of compost that he slit down the middle. Sophie did not like this and eventually he got rid of it. Plants grew in the ground, not in bags. Tomatoes came from the supermarket in nice shrinkwrapped punnets, their skin perfectly clean, perfectly shiny. She liked to stroke them with her thumb. She did not eat them because they were not spaghetti but she liked to touch them. They were not misshapen and dirty from the compost or rain. This is not how tomatoes were. She does not like the compost on the floor because of this. But the compost is there and nothing can be done about it so she must try not to think about it. The rest of the vegetation is OK. It is thick and it has taken away most of the sky (like in the forest). This is OK, as long as she remembers that there will come a point when she leaves the jungle and there will be a lot of sky. She does not mind the creepers, does not mind the noise of the parrots above her head, does not mind the shuffle of undergrowth either side of her as other creatures move through the leaves. All of these things are normal in a jungle and so they are fine.

Then she finds something that is not normal in a jungle: she finds a man sitting against a tree. He turns his hands towards her and they are very wrong indeed: they are bleeding and there is a branch stuck in one of them. This is something that Sophie can put right. She walks over and carefully removes the branch. The man is silent as she does this, which is good as she needs to concentrate on not being too scared by the fact that he is there. Once she has removed the thorns she decides the simplest thing is to walk away, then she can stop worrying about the fact that the man is sat there.

"Wait…" he says as she leaves, "please… wait…"

She stops walking and thinks about things. It is wrong that he is there but then it is wrong that she is there. Perhaps now both of them are in the jungle it is no longer wrong, it is no longer a strange "one thing. It has happened twice. Twice means it might happen three times and four times and five times and six times… When something happens this many times it is not wrong any more. So maybe it is better to stay with the man as that will prove that her being there is not wrong. Also it will prove that he is not wrong either. This will be good. She turns and looks at him again. He seems the sort of man you would expect to see in a library, quite old – father old, not grandfather old – and with smart clothes. Perhaps a professor. Perhaps a doctor. Perhaps a teacher. Perhaps a social worker. Perhaps.

She sits down. She will do as he says and wait.

He doesn't move. Sophie thinks he is probably emptying himself though she cannot hear the sound of his hums. After a few minutes he begins to move his arms and legs. He begins to talk to her but she has forgotten to listen because she is thinking about how all toasters must have setting number four on them so why bother with the rest? Why put settings on things that you do not want to use? Isn't this a waste of time? Isn't this trying to confuse people?

The man gets to his feet and walks over to her. "A disturbing place, certainly, a nightmare of a building but… full of possibilities." These are the words he says but she has no idea what they mean as they carry on from other words, words she has not heard. She thinks about answering him with a smile but they do not sound like smiling words so she just stares at him and hopes he will not ask questions she cannot answer.

"I'm talking a lot," he says, and this is a fact so she is happy. "Nerves, I expect."

Sophie gets to her feet and walks into the trees. She means him to follow her and he does. He says something more but she does not hear it. She is sure it will not matter. Then she remembers he knows facts and so she decides she will make a special effort to listen so she can learn more facts. Facts are good.

There is a lot of jungle and this makes walking through it difficult. Sometimes the plants tug at her clothes and hair and this makes walking through it difficult (and reminds her of her grandmother, always hugging, kissing, brushing). The Man Called Alan keeps talking about facts and this makes walking through it difficult. She remembers to listen to some of his facts. This is what they are:

1. *Alan knows about the box.*
2. *Alan has spent a long time looking for the box.*
3. *Alan has spent a long time reading about people who have owned the box.*
4. *Most of those people have vanished.*
5. *Some people came back (but very very few).*
6. *Those people who came back said the box took them to a house. Two or three people saying that makes it right so Sophie agrees that the other people who vanished probably went to a house too. But they did not come back.*
7. *They are not in a house, they are in a jungle. This is strange (and might be Wrong).*
8. *Alan sweats a lot but this is probably because he is Fat.*

9. *There is something else in the jungle, following*
   them (but this does not upset her as much as it
   seems to upset Alan; this is a jungle, of course
   there are other animals).

There is one other fact she discovers and this is a
big fact and is so Wrong that she has to sit down and
empty herself after she has learned it.

"Oh, my God," Alan says, "that's unbelievable."
Ahead of them the jungle appears to disappear. Between the leaves and branches there is nothing but
darkness. This is not the fact. Though it is a fact.

Alan walks forward and touches the darkness.
"Unbelievable…"

This is the fact:

The jungle is surrounded by a wall of glass.

CHAPTER NINE

"It's all about finding the entrance," Carruthers explained, "which, when your door is a black rectangle on a black background, can sometimes be rather hard."

"One can imagine," said Penelope.

"Which is why I have come up with this!" Carruthers opened the wardrobe and pulled out a bundle of rope and planks. He began to uncurl the contraption. "The Carruthers Reality Bridge!"

"It's a swing, " said Miles, "the sort of thing children play on."

"Ah, but this is no toy, dear boy!" He pointed out of the window. "You will note that I have constructed a pole that juts out from yonder balcony. The traveller hooks the ends of the rope to aforementioned pole so that, when lowered into the darkness on this wooden platform…"

"Or 'swing seat'," Miles interrupted.

Carruthers gave him a defensive look. "Mock all you will but I have made this journey countless times and know of no other way to leap from one portion of this domicile to another."

"Countless times?" Penelope asked.

"Countless, my dear!"

"Countless?"

Carruthers laughed and threw his hands in the air. "Very well, you devilish woman, four times, happy now?"

"As long as we all know where we stand."

"Or rather sit," Miles said. "So, we go swinging next to the outside of the building… what then?"

"Firstly," replied Carruthers, "you must prepare yourself for the fact that once you are suspended from the balcony there will be no outside of the building. From that perspective you will no longer be able to see the house; you will see nothing except yourself and the box of Carruthers Reality Pocket Locators I will give you."

"Produced by none other than the Bryant & May match company, I notice," Miles said.

"Yes indeed, pure London craftsmanship. You light the C.R.P.L. or 'match' if you insist and drop it earthwards while swinging gently on the Reality Bridge. When you are directly above the point of egress you will note that the match disappears from view more swiftly than at other points on your trajectory. Once satisfied that you have pinpointed the position of the exit along your arc, you dismount and traverse at your leisure."

"You jump off?" Penelope asked.

"Precisely, my dear, nothing could be simpler, eh?"

"And what about these 'wraiths' you mentioned?" asked Miles.

"Oh, well, naturally they will be attacking you with gay abandon throughout the whole process."

"How absolutely lovely," Penelope sighed. "So, what's to stop them pulverising us while we do all this?"

"Nothing but good fortune and speed, my dear. We must move swiftly enough that they do not have the chance."

"Oh, that's all right then," Miles said, "as long as we have a really good plan."

"I did warn you it was dangerous. In fact I seem to remember going on about it rather."

"In fairness he did," Penelope said to Miles.

"He did indeed," Miles replied, "it's the whole 'absolute bloody madness' thing I don't remember being discussed." Miles sighed. "Balls to it, let's just do it, shall we?"

"That's the spirit!" Carruthers replied. "Might I suggest you go first? It would be most ungallant of me not to bring up the rear and one can hardly ask a lady to take the first step 'unto the breach', can one, eh?"

"No, one can't." Miles was finding it very difficult not to run around the room screaming the most obnoxious swearwords. He assumed it was nerves.

"Splendid." Carruthers gathered the rope swing. "You stay in here for now, m'dear," he said to Penelope, "it doesn't take three of us and there's no point in exposing yourself to unnecessary risk." He turned to Miles. "Ready?" Miles nodded, counted to three under his breath, then grabbed the handle of the French windows and stepped outside.

He was struck again by how dead the air felt, as if they were still standing in a room, just one so infinitely large its boundaries couldn't be perceived.

"Don't dither, m'boy!" Carruthers scolded, pushing Miles to the edge of the balcony. "Remember time is of the essence!" He hooked the ends of the rope on to the pole and tossed the seat over the balustrade. He pressed the matches into Miles' hand. "Don't light more than you have to. I have several boxes but nonetheless there's no point in wasting them. Now lower yourself over the edge, quickly as you can!"

Miles swung his leg over the balustrade, took hold of one side of the swing and began to slide down the rope. Already the fear he had experienced before was building in his chest.

"It's coming!" Carruthers shouted. "Can you feel it? A tightness in the chest, a shortness of breath? The damn thing is terror personified! Concentrate on the job in hand. Focus on the darkness, not what's in it."

Miles reached the end of the swing and pulled himself on to the wooden seat. He was so scared he was close to hyperventilating so he took a moment to close his eyes and focus on becoming calm.

"Don't just sit there, lad," Carruthers called down, "nobody's going to give you a push!"

"Fucker," Miles whispered, sliding the match box open with his thumb and starting to swing.

"That's it!" Carruthers said, "bit higher, cover as much space as you can."

Miles was swinging several feet to either side of the balcony and he noticed Carruthers popping in and out of vision as he did so. It was just as the man said, beyond the balcony there was nothing. The window hung there in the darkness; move in a steep enough angle either side and it vanished altogether.

"That'll do!" Carruthers shouted, "now... only drop a match on the backswing, that way you can follow it as it falls. Drop your first at the farthest point and then each successive one a second or so further back on the arc, you get me?"

"Yes!" Miles replied, adding, "of course I bloody get you" under his breath. He lit a match and nearly spilled the whole lot. He managed to grip the box in his fist at the last moment but missed the furthest point of his swing so he waited, sailing backwards before the momentum held him still for a fraction of a second and he moved forward again. At the farthest point he dropped the match, watching it as he once again swung backwards. The tiny orange light dropped into the darkness, twinkling smaller and smaller until he was no longer able to see it. He lit another and dropped it a second or so into his return swing, about two feet away from the first. Again, it sparkled for longer than he could keep track of.

"Quickly now!" Carruthers shouted, "the wraith... can you feel it?"

Miles could, he knew instinctively that the creature was heading towards him, zooming in on his tiny swinging form as it sailed through this absence in search of intruders. He dropped another match: nothing. Next time would be four seconds into his backswing, almost directly down from the balcony. Something moved past him in the darkness, setting him spinning on the swing. He pushed the ropes apart as they threatened to entwine with one another, gritting his teeth as he waited for the creature to return. While holding the ropes to try and swing straight he couldn't light a match, couldn't do anything but wait for the wraith to strike. It hit him again, setting him spinning in the opposite direction.

"Keep moving!" Carruthers shouted, "it's your only hope!"

The swing was spiralling, despite Miles' best efforts to keep it on a straight arc. The wraith came again and this time Miles could hear the slight displacement of air as it hit him head on, knocking him backwards off the swing. He managed to instinctively throw his legs wide, hooking the rope with his feet to stop himself falling. The matches were still in his hand and he tried to grab another one, his head swimming from being upside down. The matches spilled from the box as he fumbled it, spraying out in a trail behind him. He gave a yell, frustrated and terrified at the sight of them falling away. Then he noticed a gap in the line of matches, a point of blank space. Either side of that point he could still see the matches as they fell but – for a span of maybe four feet – there was nothing. He had found the hole he needed. He followed it with his eyes as the swing pulled him away, desperately trying to fix the point so that he would know when to jump. The wraith flew past him again, this time narrowly missing him but coming close enough to clip the tip of his nose. He would have one chance at this, he'd never be able to keep track of the hole unless he jumped… *now!*

Penelope stepped out of the way as Carruthers yanked himself through the French window and back into the bedroom.

"Miles?" she asked, rather nervously.

Carruthers smiled. "Tell me, my dear, might you be willing to place your utter trust in me?"

Miles landed on a pair of mattresses stacked in the corner of a colossal library. Still panicking, he rolled on to the floor – knocking away the handful of matches that had preceded him as he did so – stood up and backed away, keeping his eye on the ceiling.

"Well, bugger me…" he muttered, "'the daring young man on the flying trapeze'."

The ceiling erupted in a splash of paintwork and Penelope appeared, landing on the mattresses as the ceiling re-formed behind her.

"Well, that was an experience," she said, tugging her curtain around her and shuffling to the floor just in time to avoid Carruthers, who dropped down behind her.

"Aha!" he laughed, "I must say it's much easier when there's three of you."

"Speak for yourself," Miles said. "It was bloody terrifying!"

"But you so expertly led the way for the rest of us," said Carruthers "You're much easier to follow than a lit match."

"He threw me off the damned balcony!" Penelope cried.

"Proving my excellent aim in the process," Carruthers added, climbing off the mattresses and gesturing around the library. "Pray welcome to my most literary camp!"

The library was ludicrously large. The walls were filled with books accessed from a huge brass and iron scaffold, with gantries every ten feet or so. Five stand-alone stacks – loaded with volumes on both sides – stretched away into the distance.

"There must be billions of books here," Miles said, "more than you would have ever thought written."

"They are very special books," Carruthers explained, taking him by the shoulder and leading him among the stacks. "This library specialises in biography." He turned and beckoned Penelope to follow them. "Come on, my dear, it's a fair walk yet, I'm afraid."

"Why don't you camp close to the mattresses?" Penelope asked.

"Miss Simons, there are many mattresses here. In my time here I have plotted twenty points of access into this room alone. In fact I am of the opinion that this library is central to the whole house, a hub if you will to its disparate chambers and corridors."

They came to a junction in the stacks and he turned left, cutting into the next row. He pointed in the opposite direction. "Half an hour's walk that way would see you in the gargantuan landscape of the 'S's and the route to the kitchens but we are heading to the rows set aside for 'C'."

"'C' for 'camp'?" asked Miles.

"Ah, no, 'C' for 'Carruthers'."

"At least you'll never forget where you left your bed," Penelope joked

"There's a little more to it than that," said Carruthers, grabbing a book at random from the shelf next to them. The cover was plain, with the title in a heavy sans-serif font.

"'Madeleine Fauston'," read Miles. "Never heard of her."

"No reason why you should. Like most of the people here Miss Fauston will have lived a perfectly normal life, far away from the gossip columns and society parties. Her story, one imagines, will not be unlike many other volumes here: childhood with all its hope and promise, then the dissatisfaction and impatience of adolescence followed by the begrudging acceptance of maturity. Finally the disappointment of one's twilight years."

"You make life sound so joyful," said Miles, flicking through the book.

"Well, there are always exceptions," Carruthers replied. "One could hardly class the three of us as having conventional biographies; simply being here has scotched that. Still this library contains all of it, every single human being who has ever lived or will ever live, their stories condensed into one of these slender volumes. It is the ultimate social history of the world."

"And predictably you wanted to stick close to your own particular part of it?" asked Penelope.

"Well, naturally, my dear, there is very little to be constructively achieved in my current situation by reading someone else's history."

"But…" Miles was in shock at the scale of it. "How is it possible? I mean, how many books would you need to chronicle everyone?"

Carruthers gestured around them. "Why, this many, obviously."

Miles flicked to the end of Madeleine's book.

"Let me guess," said Penelope, "she dies."

"Don't spoil it for me," Miles replied with a smile.

"I wonder what it's for?" asked Penelope as they carried on walking.

"Indeed, my dear," said Carruthers, "that is rather the question, isn't it? This room provides an indubitable link with the world we have left behind. This house knows all our stories. I wonder what it might wish to do with them?"

"How far did you say the 'S' section was?" Penelope asked.

"A considerable trek, I am afraid to say. However, Miss Simons, there is more to this phenomenon than you yet know, as I shall illustrate once we reach camp. The answers one might expect to find in a book of one's life are not so easily found."

"You mean I can't read my book and find out the future?"

"Indeed not. But, please, allow me my theatrical whims and let us say no more about it until I can demonstrate with my own ghost-written memoir."

"If this room contains all of human history," said Miles, a new thought occurring to him, "then the house exists outside of time."

"Oh, indeed, surely that was already clear? I could tell from your vestments that you hail from an era alien to my own. What year was it when you left your natural world?"

"2009."

"Aha! Nigh on a century away from my own slice of the human clock!"

"It hadn't occurred to me," Penelope said, looking at Miles in a new light. "I was so distracted by everything else."

"And the outfit you were wearing at our first encounter was positively timeless," joked Miles. "What year are you from?"

"1933, a positive antique by your standards."

"I've always been rather at home with antiques."

"Charmer."

"It's true!" Miles laughed. "It was my business. That's how I got my hands on the box – it was part of my stock."

"For me it was a trek to a Himalayan temple," Carruthers said, "a journey of such arduous length I could scarcely conceive it would be the initial step in a far lengthier journey. A journey beyond imagining!"

"Well," said Penelope, "without wanting to rain on your parade, we've all made the same journey."

"Aye, you have a singular point," Carruthers sighed, "and neither are we three the only ones to have travelled this path."

"I meant to ask about that," said Miles. "How many other people are here?"

"Oh, do not be misled – as far as I can tell they are few and far between. I have met a handful of other individuals. In all cases the appointments were brief and not altogether pleasant. There is a terrifying young lady whose path I once crossed. Her mind was not the measure of her experience; she is quite, quite mad. I have heard her more often than seen her, howling great insanities in the night when the gas lamps grow dim."

"There's a nighttime?" asked Penelope.

"Oh, most certainly, the lighting is beholden to its own temporal whims. The entire house becomes black as pitch for several hours a day. It is during those hours that it is at its most deadly. You would scarcely countenance the beasts I have heard awaken at twilight."

"Oh, I think I could hazard a guess," replied Miles, thinking of the hostile taxidermy he had witnessed when first arriving. "Who else?"

"Hmm? Oh, there are two that weigh particularly heavy, though I am at a loss to say whether they are more or less fortunate than our shrieking banshee. I came across them in one of the dark spaces. A pair of young men, little more than boys... frightened out of their wits, running with no purpose in our direction through the darkness. The first, a blonde-haired lad with a Scandinavian look to his features, was obliterated swiftly by one of the wraiths. It descended upon him like the very hammer of God. One minute he was running, the next he compressed upon himself in a terrifying spectacle of splintered bone and distended muscle... Oh, my dear." He touched Penelope lightly on the shoulder. "You must forgive me, this is not a discussion for a lady's ears."

"My dear Carruthers," Penelope replied, "as I hoped I had made clear earlier, I have no desire to be treated with kid gloves. I have already experienced more than I would care to but have no doubt there will be worse to come. Let us hear the facts of it and to hell with misplaced sensitivity."

Carruthers nodded. "You are right, of course, but there is no need to dwell on detail. Suffice it to say the young lad must have perished instantly, for there was no recognisable body for him to inhabit after the creature had struck. As for his companion, he was not so lucky. The wraith dragged him high and low, swinging him in its imperceptible jaw like a terrier with a rat. I hazard to guess he took some time to die. It is to my certain shame that I did not loiter to find out."

"I don't blame you," said Miles.

"A kind sentiment but I feel sure the young lad may not have shared it. I should have, at the very least, attempted to aid him. As it was I was struck so fearfully by the sight of it that I ran – without the slightest glance over my shoulder – returning here to a coward's sanctuary."

"Surely you must know there was little you could do?" asked Penelope.

"Perhaps, but there is no nobility in logic. I left a man to die and that is that. But let us talk no more about it!" he shouted, returning to his jubilant self, "for we are arrived at my little home from home."

Turning around the corner of the stacks they were faced with a selection of tents that brought to mind a sheik's desert camp. They were constructed from bed-linen and curtains held aloft by a cat's cradle of ropes strung between the stacks. There was a large central area littered with cushions, a small camping stove and a pile of books. Behind that was another section that they guessed from the sheeted mattress that poked out of one corner to be a sleeping area. Behind another sheet, bunched and slung to one side like a curtain, was a stack of canned foods, Carruther's makeshift larder.

"You have been industrious!" said Penelope.

"Even in the most adverse circumstances there is no excuse for a gentleman not bringing order and civility to his environs. I even had the foresight – or, more honestly, *hope* – to construct guest quarters!" He pointed to beyond his own bed where a long strip of eiderdowns concealed further mattresses.

"I don't suppose," asked Penelope, "that amongst your home comforts you might possess something so welcome as a change of clothes?"

Carruthers smiled. "My dear lady, while I cannot offer anything approaching *Parisenne* fashion I am certain that I might be able to improve on your current sartorial misfortunes. The house is filled with supplies and I confess to having hoarded considerably. Avail yourself of whatsoever you desire from the third tent on the left while Miles and I transfer our attentions to dinner."

"I can't believe you've managed to gather so much stuff," said Miles as hacked his way into a tin of beef.

Carruthers lit the small gas stove and set the flame low. "The supply of provisions seems limitless. The kitchen is more modest in size than the library but its larder has the most peculiar habit of replenishing itself. Though I must warn you it's all rather tasteless, like an idea of food rather than the real thing. I suppose that is not surprising considering its unconventional and supernatural provenance. It fills the belly but there is little pleasure in it."

"That describes most meals I cook anyway so I'm not sure I'll notice. I don't suppose you might have found any cigarettes on your travels?"

"There is a case of cigars that I will gladly share after we have dined. Again, the tobacco satisfies not one jot but there is something wonderfully civilised about smoking after one's meal."

"Or before it?" Miles asked hopefully.

"Patience, my dear chap, it will take but a few moments to warm this unappetising fare."

"Fair enough," Miles replied, scraping the beef into a saucepan, wanting a cigarette more than ever.

"How do I look, gentlemen?" Penelope asked, stepping from Carruthers' wardrobe tent. She was wearing a gentleman's evening shirt and trousers a good two sizes too large for her. A decorative sash cinched around her midriff attempted to hide the voluminous folds.

"A vision, my dear!" Carruthers announced gallantly.

"It's an improvement, certainly," Miles added, stirring some peas into the beef to make a lazy stew.

"You damn me with your faint praise," she replied before holding up her feet, which were bound in pillowcases. "The footwear leaves a lot to be desired but there simply wasn't a thing that would fit."

"We are hardly trekking the Asias, my good lady," Carruthers reassured her. "Footwear is not the necessity it was on my previous expeditions. Now, while our supper warms, allow me to show you my biography." He strolled over to the pile of books and selected a large volume which he offered to Penelope.

"It's certainly better presented than the saga of Madeleine Fauston," she commented, opening it up and flicking through the pages.

"Perhaps," Carruthers replied, "but nowhere near as definitive. Peruse the last page and tell us what it says."

Penelope flicked to the back and began to read: "*'Carruthers lit the small gas stove and set the flame low. "The supply of provisions seems limitless. The kitchen is more modest in size than the library but its larder has the most peculiar habit of replenishing itself. Though I must warn you it's all rather tasteless, like an idea of food rather than the real thing. I suppose that is not surprising considering its unconventional and supernatural provenance. It fills the belly but there is little pleasure in it.'"*

"That's what you were saying just before Penelope came out," said Miles.

"Indeed. My story continues to write itself."

Penelope gave a startled shout and dropped the book.

"What is it?" Miles asked, dashing over.

"Oh, don't fuss," Penelope hissed, angry at herself for her display of panic. She picked the book back up. "It surprised me, that's all."

"My dear, if it makes you feel any better I threw the thing several feet when I first saw its trick." Carruthers stepped over to her side. "Show Miles," he said. Penelope turned the book away from her and opened the pages in Miles' direction.

"Bloody hell..." Miles whispered, staring at the words that were flowing across the page. "It writes while you're watching!" Even as he said it he saw his own speech replicated between gothic quotation marks and unfold across the yellowing paper.

"And in that it is unlike any other book here," said Carruthers, "though I'll warrant that at least two other volumes are behaving in a similar manner as we speak. Do you not think, Mr. Caulfield?"

"Caulfield..." Miles dashed towards the stacks, running his eyes along the spines.

"Calder... Callett... Callisto..." He began to run along the shelf, stopping every few seconds to trace his progress. "Cattleman... Catyda..."

"You may need to climb my boy, but mind your footing."

Miles stopped at "Caulder" and began to back-track, scaling the stack to his right.

"Careful!" Penelope shouted as he began to rise by several rows.

"It's all right," Miles called back, "the shelves are deep, it's like climbing a ladder. Caulfield! Dear God, there's so many of them..." He continued to climb, twenty or so shelves above the ground now. He passed the Stephens, the Roberts and the Olivers until he found the Ms. "There are far too many people called Michael Caulfield!" he shouted. "For that matter there's a fair few called Miles, something you wouldn't have guessed when I was at school." He steadied himself on his elbows and began to pull out a book at a time until he found a narrative he recognised. "Got it!" He clamped the book in his teeth and began to descend.

Back on the ground he suddenly felt selfconscious, flicking through the pages and seeing so many pitiful moments from his recent history. He began to regret fetching the book and could only hope that Penelope wouldn't try and read it. The fact that this concerned him pulled him up short. Now was hardly the time to be trying to impress the ladies, was it? There were far more important matters at stake than getting his leg over. Mind you, she was incredibly attractive and, try as he might, he couldn't stop picturing her naked. He shook the thought away.

"It's just the same!" he said, glancing at the last page and turning it around so the other two could see.

"Oh, my dear chap," Carruthers blustered, reaching for the book.

"No you don't!" Penelope knocked his hand away and began to read aloud: "*'There were far more important matters at stake than getting his leg over. Mind you, she was incredibly attractive and, try as he might, he couldn't stop picturing her naked'*?"

Miles threw the book away in embarrassed shock. "I don't know what it's talking about," he said, growing deeply red in the face.

"I bet." Penelope glowered at him.

"Dinner's ready!" Carruthers shouted, clapping his hands together and turning Penelope away from Miles and towards the stove.

"I think I've gone off the idea," Miles muttered.

They ate in silence, and, when done, Penelope was quick to excuse herself. She retired to the bed Carruthers had allocated her – though it was clear this was out of embarrassment rather than actual tiredness. Miles was relieved, whatever the reason. Carruthers brought out the cigars and suggested they walk while they smoked. Miles jumped at the idea.

"That was so bloody embarrassing," he said once his cigar was lit.

"Yes, it was rather," agreed Carruthers, moving a match-flame around the end of his cigar to ensure it lit evenly, "though, in hindsight…" he puffed a majestic ball of blue-grey smoke above his head like an angry thought-balloon "…damned funny as well!" He gave a booming chuckle and put his arm around Miles' shoulder.

"Glad you think so." Miles muttered.

"Oh *tish*, all will be fine by the morning. As you said, there are far more important matters at stake and Penelope is a splendid sort, she'll let you off the hook quick enough, mark my words."

"Or stab me to death in my sleep." Miles inhaled deeply on his cigar. "I see what you mean about the cigars, by the way. We may as well be smoking a pair of carrots."

"Aye, but if you close your eyes and imagine, you can just about recreate the taste."

"I'll take your word for it. So, what comes next?"

"Well, as I mentioned earlier, I am not a man who settles for imprisonment. I have festered here, truth be told, hopeful of finding more like myself."

"And now you have."

"Indeed, and while I might have dreamed of greater numbers, to delay further is just prevarication. We must set forth, my friend. Come the morning we shall strike this mockery of a camp and venture out into the unknown areas of the house. If one can enter one must be able to leave."

"Possibly."

"Definitely! We must not think in negative terms.

We must believe our real homes lie in wait for us, beyond this mockery of a dwelling. In truth, Miles, what else is there to do? I have spent my whole life wishing to be anywhere but home, exploring the farthest reaches of our planet in search of new experience and knowledge. Well, no more... I wish for my hearth and will not be denied it. Will you join me?"

Miles puffed listlessly on his cigar, trying to find some pleasure in it. "Of course I will," he replied, "if only so that I can find something worth smoking!"

Carruthers laughed and patted Miles on the back. "That's the spirit. They won't put us down easily, eh? Now, the lights are beginning to fade." Miles looked around them and saw that it was so, the pools of light from the gas lamps slowly receding as their flames drew in. "The nights are not safe, even here," Carruthers continued. " We would do well to be tucked up long before the last of the illumination is stolen away."

INTERLUDE

He holds the heart up and turns it over in his hands. It looks like nothing more than lunch and yet the humans cannot function without it. He gives it a curious lick but it has insufficient taste to merit the considerable chewing it would take to consume it.

"What are you doing?" demands Jinzhong from the open flap of the renegade's tent.

"I took one of the serving maids apart to see how she worked. In hindsight, I shouldn't have bothered. I am left with little but tidying up and the need to fetch my own drink."

"My people are not toys for your amusement!" Jinzhong shouts, his hand hovering too close to the handle of his sword for his own good.

"*Everything* is for my amusement," the renegade answers, "at least that had been my hope. It's all a bit boring these days. Time I moved on."

He gets to his feet, drops the heart into the bowl of the dead woman's ribcage and licks his fingers clean.

"You would do well to remember who is your chieftain," says Jinzhong, pulling his sword free and pointing it at the renegade.

"You see, there we go," the renegade sighs. "Whenever I start to think I have some interest in your species you demonstrate your complete lack of intelligence. You know my capabilities – rely on them in fact – and yet it somehow occurs to you that I can be intimidated by a small length of sharpened metal." The renegade agitates the atoms in Jinzhong's sword until it is far too hot to hold, then takes the Khitan leader's face in his wet, red hands. "You are not my chieftain, Jinzhong," he says, "you are simply my ally and that is a position constantly open to negotiation." He digs his fingertips into Jinzhong's skin, infecting it with an amusing selection of plague bacteria. Instantly Jinzhong's body fizzes with disease, pustules rising and popping on his skin like the surface of a hot mud pool.

The renegade steps out of the tent and stares at his adopted world. He needs a change of scenery: nothing a few hundred years and a shift of continents won't fix.

CHAPTER TEN

Inside the house – in fact at its very centre – there lies a small room. Unlike many parts of the house, there is nothing particularly terrifying or surreal about this room. It is realistically sized and comfortably decorated, from its compact bookshelves to its hard but attractively furnished bed. The room has a small en-suite bathroom, and this is, again, perfectly safe and respectable in both plumbing and fittings. No sea creatures roam the bathtub, mustard gas will not billow from the taps, the toilet does not bite. It is simply a bathroom and is intended to be used for all the purposes asked of such a thing.

The room's resident has never used the bathroom, has never seen the need. Despite this, he appears as normal as his accommodation. He is a small man, balding, prone to cleaning the thick lenses of his spectacles on his woollen tanktop when deep in thought. He appears overweight, despite the fact that he never eats. One of those mole-like gentle-

men that one imagines having done nothing of con-
versational value in a bank for many years. You
would guess he might be called Brian, or Lionel, or
Gordon. Actually, if he has a name it has been forgotten, by him as well as everyone else. He has no
need of a name; there is nobody else in this room to
call him by it. There has never been anyone else;
this room – in fact this entire house – was intended
for him and for him alone.

One thing that makes this room slightly abnormal
is that there is no window. The only light is from a
candle that sits, never-ending, in a cone of its own
dripped wax on a table in the middle of the room.
Sometimes he lights it. Like the bathroom he doesn't
need it but he likes the flame. He sets a match to it
and watches the shadows dance on the walls. The
patterns can be quite diverting.

When he wants contact outside his four walls it is
the house he talks to. He is not supposed to be able
to do this – his captors intended utter isolation for
him – but over the years he has picked up many
skills they would be uncomfortable with. The house
is particularly talkative at night; it is then that the
building really lets itself go. Under cover of darkness
it stretches its bricks and mortar, flexes its ancient
wood and begins to play.

He smiles often in the darkness, sensing the cruelty that has crept into the building's psyche. It is a
cruelty he can relate to. He closes his eyes and tunes
in to the structure, feeling the invasive footsteps of
those brought here as they fight to avoid the house's

attentions. Sometimes he can even taste their thoughts, their fears and confusion.

If nothing else it passes the time.

Pablo rose up through the wall. The creaking of the rope echoed in the small box as it worked its way around the pulleys above his head. He was not comfortable in enclosed spaces. He was used to wide skies and a strong breeze; this groaning coffin made his palms sweat and his breathing shallow. Eventually the box juddered to a halt, an external mechanism clicking into place in the narrow passage.

"It has stop!" he shouted.

"I noticed," came Tom's distant voice, "can you get out?"

Pablo extended his arm, his fingers tapping on a wooden hatch. He gave it a push and the doorway clicked open on to a large dining room lit by rows of gothic candelabra.

"Yes," he replied, "it is dinner room." He climbed out.

"Close the hatch!" Tom shouted and Pablo did so, hearing the box begin to descend immediately. He looked around the room. It was gloomy and not somewhere he would ever want to eat a meal. Mounted animal heads lined the walls, forced to watch their fellow creatures consumed at the central table. There was a lion, a tiger, a bear, several deer, their savage-looking horns casting shadows in the candlelight like the branches of winter trees. Pablo had never understood people who hunted. His father fished to fill his belly and his wallet, not simply to boast. There was nothing difficult in taking another animal's life.

Behind him the dumb waiter was making a return journey so he walked back over to the hatchway to wait. When the box clicked into place he opened the hatch and took Elise's hand to help her climb out.

"OK?" shouted Tom.

"Is fine!" Pablo replied, closing the hatch so that Tom could bring the dumb waiter back down. After a few moments the sound of the winch stopped and Tom shouted up again.

"There must be a way to pull me up from where you are. Can you see it?"

Pablo looked around and spotted a looped cord in the corner. "I think so."

"OK." There was a roar of pain.

"Are you all right?" Elise shouted.

"Just enjoying my leg wound. I'm all aboard."

Pablo began to pull on the cord and the dumb waiter rose.

"You want me to help?" Elise asked.

"It is easy," Pablo replied, "I am used to this kind of thing." Just as the dumb waiter was a few feet short of the hatch there was an almighty screech and Pablo was yanked off his feet as the pulley system was torn from its casing. Pablo shot towards the roof. Flipping over, he managed to wedge his boots against the ceiling, stopping the dumb waiter's descent. Elise grabbed him under his arms but she couldn't pull the weight of both him and Tom combined.

"What's happening?" Tom shouted.

"Too heavy!" Elise shouted.

"Bullshit, baby!" Tom shouted, "I've eaten nothing but bar olives for six months, how the hell can it not take my weight?"

"We do it!" Pablo hissed between his teeth, "climb on me, let rope take both weights."

"Jesus…" Elise grabbed a chair from the dining table to give her some extra height. She reached up so that she could wrap herself around Pablo's midriff and then kicked the chair away. The two of them dropped towards the floor, Pablo grunting as Elise landed on him.

"Stay still," he mumbled from beneath her. "You ballast."

"Not something I've been called before," she said, "and believe me, it's not often I can say that in my line of work."

Pablo began to slowly pull the rope, feeding it hand over hand. The dumb waiter rose the final foot or so and locked into position. The hatch burst open and Tom tumbled out, not wanting to trust his life to the small box a moment longer.

"Second floor," he moaned, holding his wounded leg, "haberdashery and heartache."

Pablo let go of the rope.

"You can get off me now," he told Elise.

"Oh, sure." She rolled off him and got to her feet. "Sorry."

"Is no problem for me, most fun I have in long time."

Using the back of one of the dining chairs, Tom pulled himself to his feet. "Way to go, El Toro, you strong like bull."

"And you fat like pig." Pablo smiled.

"Grab his legs, honey," Tom said to Elise, "and help me shove the little bastard back down to the kitchen."

Elise ignored him, walking over to a pair of drawn curtains at the far end of the room.

"Let's see where we are shall we?" she said, pulling them apart.

"Is nothing." Pablo said, looking over her shoulder, "just night."

"Like a Sunday night in New Jersey," Tom added. "Weird… can't see the ground."

"Or the stars," said Elise, "or *anything*."

"Yeah, well, let's keep moving." Tom limped around the table, towards a pair of double doors. He pulled them but they stayed resolutely shut. "You have got to be kidding me," he sighed.

"Try push," said Pablo, coming up behind Tom and shoving hard at the wood. The doors swung open and both he and Tom tumbled forward. Running flush with the doorway was a large wooden slide, bright blue and yellow. Tom and Pablo careered down it, coming to earth in a pit of white ping-pong balls.

"This house is so uncool," Tom said.

They were in a large playroom, every available space taken over by toys and games. One part of the floor was painted as if for Snakes and Ladders, another offered a climbing frame. There were rocking horses, lined up as if for their own Grand National; a merry-go-round painted with stars; a trampoline surrounded by fat beanbags. Everywhere you looked there were teddy bears, wooden soldiers, puppets dangling from their strings.

"Shall I just leave the two of you to play for a while?" Elise asked from the doorway.

"Hell no, come and join us, I'll give you first go on the rocking horse."

Not seeing much alternative, Elise dropped to her haunches and slid down after them.

"Why you have playroom right next to dining room?" Pablo asked. "It make no sense."

"I don't know if you've noticed, El Toro, but not much here does." Tom climbed out of the ball pit and looked around for the door. "Well," he said pointing towards an arched passage on the far side of the room, "I don't know about you but I'm not in the mood for playtime, let's keep moving."

Pablo and Elise climbed out after him and the three of them clambered their way over stuffed toys towards the exit.

"Is creepy," said Pablo. "I not like things that try so hard to be cheerful."

"There speaks someone with a bad childhood," Tom laughed.

"No… is just very… not real," Pablo replied. "It make me nervous."

He walked on to the floorboards painted with the Snakes and Ladders board and was immediately sent

shooting up into the air as the two dimensional ladder beneath his feet erupted into three dimensions.
"I tell you!" he shouted, grabbing on to the rungs to
stop himself falling. "I tell you but you not listen!"

"Keep back!" Tom said to Elise, tugging her arm
before she set foot on the playing board. The whole
thing was now a cube, the ceiling parting to accommodate it. The squares had become transparent
boxes with ladders poking through the various levels. The snakes blossomed too, writhing between
their demarcated sections.

"What do we do?" Elise asked, trying, and failing,
to see a way around the game.

Tom pointed towards an alcove in the wall that
was now spotlit from above. In the alcove were three
wooden dice, the size of a man's head. "I think we're
expected to play."

"Play how?" Pablo shouted before he found himself being pulled back down the ladder he was on
and yanked along the confined passage to the starting square. He tried to climb out but was unable to
move. "I stuck" he said, "give me number box,
thing."

"'I speaks good English,' he says," Tom muttered,
walking over to the alcove and lifting out the three
dice. "There is no way this can end well, kids, you
do know that, don't you?" He fumbled one of the
dice and it fell to the floor, rolling along until it
stopped on a six. "I don't know though," said Tom,
"my luck's clearly on fire right now." Suddenly he
flew forward, the dropped dice following on behind

him as an invisible force pulled him into the game. He shot past Pablo and stopped six boxes in on the lowest level. "When will I learn to keep my goddamned mouth shut?" he shouted, the dice winding him slightly as it collided with his stomach.

Elise walked towards the other two dice, jumping out of the way as one of them flew past her and straight into Pablo's hands. "Looks to me like we're not being given a choice," she said, picking up the remaining dice and walking towards the start of the game.

"Lady first!" said Pablo with a smile.

"Thanks a bunch." She squatted down and gave the dice a gentle roll. "Four," she said, flinching in anticipation. She was pulled inside the board, landing two boxes short of Tom.

"Hey, honey," he said, rubbing at his sore leg, "how's it hanging?"

"OK." Pablo rolled. "Only two!" He waited to be pulled along but nothing happened so he shuffled forward.

"Why the hell are we playing fair?" Tom said. "I'm damn sure this place won't. Screw the dice, let's just get ourselves out." He made to shuffle forward but, as one, all the snakes turned to face him, their flat tongues tasting the air, their glistening black eyes staring soullessly. The closest one to him hissed, tilting its head on one side and opening its mouth to expose fangs wet with venom.

"Careful, Tom," said Elise, "something tells me the rules are strictly enforced."

"Yeah… stay cool, snake eyes…" Tom sat back in his alloted box holding out his hands in surrender.

"Roll the dice," said Elise, "quickly."

"OK, OK." Tom rolled the dice down the passage in front of him. "Give me a five, baby," he muttered, eyeing the foot of ladder that the score would see him reach. It was a four. "OK, cool, four, I can groove with four." Cautiously, he walked forward on his hands and knees. "Just the four, OK? I'm sticking to the rules, man, let's be chilled with the whole fang thing…" He reached his box and sat down. The snakes turned back in the direction they were facing.

"That could have been nasty," said Elise.

"The game ain't over yet," Tom replied. "What do you think's going to happen when one of us lands on a snake square?"

"I do not like snakes," said Pablo.

"Can't say I'm too fond myself," muttered Elise, "especially when they're the size of subway trains." She rolled her dice "Five." She crawled along to one box behind Tom.

Pablo rolled six, ending up one behind Elise.

"One or a five, one or a five." Tom rolled a five and shuffled along to the fifteenth box where a ladder took him up to thirty-four. "Bite me," he muttered, sticking his middle finger up at a snake that coiled a couple of levels above him.

"Don't encourage them," Elise whispered, rolling a two and also climbing up a ladder, albeit only to box twenty-eight, a row beneath Tom.

"Hey," said Pablo, rolling his dice, "you two are leaving me behind." He also got a five, taking him to box fourteen.

"What can I say, El Toro?" Tom rolled a six. "It's all in the wrist. Oh…" The six placed him in box forty but he had to go straight past a snake's jaws to do so. "Shit…" he muttered, pressing his back against the wall of the cube, keeping as far away from the snake as possible. Its head followed him as he slid through box thirty-nine. He froze, transfixed by his own reflection in its expressionless eyes. It stretched its jaws wide, great pink and blue folds of tissue hanging down around its thick fangs. "Oh Jesus…" Tom said, "this is not cool."

"Keep moving," shouted Elise. "Don't antagonise it."

"I ain't antagonising the thing," Tom replied, "I'm experiencing an honest-to-God moment of ass-quaking terror." Slowly, he continued to move past, pulling himself into box forty. Desperate to be as far away from the serpent as possible, he began to inch into forty-one and – at terrible speed – the snake's head darted forward, snatching his foot in its mouth.

"Hey!" Pablo shouted, running into the next box and the next, "hey, snake thing!" The snake let go of Tom and looked down at Pablo, the rest of the snakes following suit as he threw his dice at the serpent closest to him and continued to run. "Get out of way, Tom!" Pablo shouted, "and you, Elise! I take one for team."

"Don't be stupid, you whacked-out Spaniard!" Tom shouted. "They'll kill you!"

"We not get out of game alive, I think," Pablo replied. "Better one than all. Now run!"

The snakes slithered free from their positions and began to descend. Elise was forced back against the wall as one pushed its way past her.

Pablo turned on his heels and began to run back towards the first square. Hoping that the invisible forces that had pulled them in didn't reappear, he dived for the entrance, sailing through and landing on a soft bed of teddy bears.

"No way are we leaving him," Tom said, limping towards the ladder and dropping down it, just behind the last of the snakes that were chasing Pablo out into the play room. "Get to the finish line!" he shouted back at Elise, "maybe there's some way of flattening the cube."

Elise hesitated, not wanting to turn her back on Tom and Pablo. Finally – her commonsense admitting that Tom's idea was for the best – she worked her way forward.

Pablo ran towards the merry-go-round, grabbing on to it and spinning out of the way of a snake's jaw as it shot towards him. Jumping off he bounced on the trampoline and launched himself across the room to the climbing frame. He wriggled inside it, judging correctly that the gaps between the bars were small enough to keep the snakes out. They curled around the frame, hissing and bashing their heads at the bars.

Tom stepped out of the cube. With a sigh he re-alised that Pablo was now safer than he was. He gritted his teeth against the pain in his leg and ran for the slide just as one of the snakes caught sight of the movement and turned towards him. "I got the cold-blood blues!" he shouted, skirting the ball pit and running up the slide, "with its dead-eye shimmy and the shine of its tongue, that lowdown bastard got me on the run, if I end up feeling its pointy teeth, don't send help, send a goddamn wreath!" He ran around the dining table as the snake's head appeared in the doorway. "I've got rhythm, fork-tongue!" he shouted, grabbing one of the candelabra from the table and shoving the flaming candles in the snake's eye as it darted towards him. "Skiddley bee-bop, *pow*!" The snake reared up, bashed its head against the wall and impaled itself on the antlers of a particularly dead stag. "Double whammy!" Tom laughed.

The snake thrashed, driving the antlers deeper into its head until they found their mark, whereupon it stiffened and crashed to the floor.

"Strike one!" Tom ran to the doorway but rather annoyingly found he couldn't get through it due to the huge dead serpent in the way. "Typical…" He peered over the top of its back "How are things in España?" he shouted.

"They are OK," Pablo shouted back. "They cannot bite me, this is good thing."

Suddenly all of the snakes lifted their heads as if having heard something. As one, they turned away from the climbing frame and returned to the game cube.

"What's bugged them?" Tom wondered.

Once inside, the cube glowed briefly and then collapsed leaving a rather startled Elise on the far side of the now two-dimensional game board.

"OK…" she said, "what did I do?"

"I'm not sure you did anything," Tom replied. "Something sure as hell spooked them though."

Slowly the lights in the walls began to fade.

"Er… Tom?" Elise said, "maybe you should come back in here now, OK?"

"I'd love to, honey, but I got myself one of those reptilian blockage issues, y'know?"

"It get darker," said Pablo.

"No shit, señor," Elise replied, "but that ain't what's really freaking me."

"What gives you the freak?"

"I'm not convinced I like the idea of hanging around to see what gives a giant snake the wimwams…"

The light continued to fade.

"Tom!" Elise shouted, "we've got to get out of here, you need to squeeze past."

"Easy for you to say," Tom replied, looking at the snake. "You'd better be dead, fork-tongue." He put his hands on its dry back, preparing to pull himself on top of it when a thought occurred to him. He dashed over to the table, blew out a few of the candles and, trying not to scald himself on the hot wax, shoved them in his jacket pocket.

"Come on, Tom!" Elise shouted,

"I'm coming, I'm coming…" He pulled himself on to the snake, grimacing at the feel of its muscle beneath his hands as he pulled himself along. He had to press his face into it, forcing his chin against its scales so that he could squeeze his head under the door jamb. "Oh God..." he mumbled, trying not to panic. The snake twitched. "Oh, screw you," he said, "the motherfucker's still alive!"

"Be quick then," suggested Pablo, looking around nervously as the lights continued to dim.

"The toys," said Elise, "wouldn't you know it? It's the fucking toys!"

One by one the stuffed animals were beginning to move, stretching their soft furry limbs.

"Screw that," said Tom with a laugh, "we've just faced off giant snakes – you think teddy bears scare me? I'll organise a picnic, that'll get them off our backs." Beneath him the snake twitched again and he wriggled faster. Once his feet were clear, he rolled off and slid into the ball pit. The snake's tail flicked slightly as Tom clambered out and headed over to Pablo and Elise. The stuffed animals were getting to their feet; a large purple bear roared at Pablo, exposing ridiculously large teeth.

"OK," said Pablo, "we go now."

The snake thrashed in the doorway, pulling itself back into the room. It veered widely, out of control, the antlers in its skull having damaged its brain.

"Yeah, go now," said Tom, backing towards the far side of the room, "good plan."

The snake threw itself towards them, landing off to one side where countless toys jumped on it and began to bite and chew.

Skirting the games board, Tom, Elise and Pablo ducked through the archway just as the lights gave out altogether.

CHAPTER ELEVEN

"Oh my God," said Alan, "that's unbelievable." He stuck his hand between the branches of the palm tree and stroked the glass beyond it. "*Unbelievable*," he repeated. "We're inside some kind of structure… a greenhouse perhaps."

Behind him Sophie gave a loud moan and sat down on the floor, closing her eyes and humming. He ran over to her and put his arm around her shoulders. "It's OK, honey," he said, "don't panic."

It hadn't taken him long to realise that Sophie's manner wasn't down to shock but a symptom of something deeper. Knowing that didn't help him figure out how to deal with it, mind you, but he figured a bit of gentle support could do no harm. She wriggled out from under his arm, humming even louder, so he stepped back to give her some space. She immediately became quieter so he guessed he'd done the right thing.

A few feet away the undergrowth started to rustle. They had been surrounded by noises as they'd walked, movement in the bushes around them and in the trees above their heads. He'd tried to dismiss it as nothing to worry about, not wanting to scare Sophie, though in truth he was terrified. If a hungry animal had their scent he didn't fancy their chances much: a fat guy and a special-needs kid wouldn't make the hardest dinner to catch.

There was a high squeal and the bushes parted to reveal a fat boar, its tusks a chipped nicotine yellow, the hair on its back matted by mud into a spiky Mohican. It stared at them for a moment then squealed again and charged. A man burst out of the trees and dropped on the boar with a yell. Brandishing a wooden stake, he stabbed aimlessly at the creature, his own frenzied shouts matching the animal's panicked screams. Alan instinctively turned away in disgust, though the noise turned his stomach just as badly as the glimpse of spurting blood had done. As an afterthought he dropped down in front of Sophie to block her view, though she didn't appear aware of what was happening, still humming in her own private world. The noise stopped, the animal finally dead. Alan turned to face the savage-looking hunter, hopeful that he wouldn't prove a danger now that he had something for his fire. The man didn't appear threatening, in fact he seemed confused, staring at the dead beast as if it was something he'd stumbled upon rather than created. Suddenly he jumped to his feet and pulled himself together.

"Hey," he said, tugging a spectacle-case from the pocket of what – now Alan looked closer – appeared to be a pair of badly torn pinstripe suit-trousers, "sorry about that." He pulled a monogrammed handkerchief from another pocket and wiped the boar blood from his hands and cheeks. He opened the spectacle-case and placed a pair of thick-lensed glasses on his nose. "Couldn't afford to damage these puppies, blind as the proverbial without them. I'm somewhat of a blunt instrument when it comes to hunting, though – keep clouting the bugger till it lies still."

Alan stared at the man, taking in all the bizarre details: those pinstriped trousers, the headband that was surely once a red silk tie, the tatty brogues, toes open to the elements, sock-suspenders yanking on holed and dirty argyles.

"Oh, forgive me," the man continued, "lost all my social graces. Toby Whitstable, 1984, London, housebound three years." He stuck out his hand and Alan – on reflex – shook it.

"Alan Arthur," he replied. "Not sure I follow the rest."

"Ah! Newcomer, eh?" Whitstable chuckled with a snort not unlike the boar he had just slaughtered. "Just the way of things in our tribe. Name, year in the real world when you were taken, where you were taken from and how long you've been here. Sort of name, rank and serial number."

"Oh, 2010, Kissimmee – that's in Florida, in case you didn't know – and..." he checked his watch "... about an hour."

"I say! A real spring chicken! Fab I bumped into you, and who do we have here?" he looked over

Alan's shoulder at Sophie, who had stopped humming and was now staring at them.

"I don't know her name, she's…"

"Sophie," she said, "three is good."

She stood up and walked over to them, silent again.

"Oh," said Whitstable, "yeah, three's super isn't it?" Not quite sure what else to say, he grinned inanely for a moment and then regained his stride. "So, you two had better follow me, I guess. It's not safe out here on your own, especially not with nighttime on its way…"

"Night?" Alan looked up at the canopy above them.

"Oh yes," Whitstable replied, "not long now and only a fool or a spring chicken would wander around out here then." He walked over to the dead boar and lifted it on to his shoulders with surprising ease. "Get piggy here on the go and there'll be grub all round, eh?"

Seeing little choice in the matter Alan nodded and turned to Sophie. "That all right by you, Sophie?" She nodded.

"Brill! Follow me then." Whitstable strode off into the vegetation, Alan and Sophie a little way behind.

Alan tried not to stare at the dead boar as they walked. Its fat purple tongue swung from the corner of its mouth as Whitstable marched. He dearly hoped he wasn't going to be expected to eat some of it.

"You say you've been here three years?" he asked, moving next to Whitstable so he wasn't staring at the boar.

"Amazing, eh? I worked in the City, financials, now look at me! Gone native!"

"You came here through the box?"

"That's right, bought it off a stall in Portobello Road, thought it would be a stellar gift for Monica – that's my wife... well, *was* my wife... you know. Next thing I know, here I am, utterly bemused, no idea what's going on."

"It's quite an experience."

"Absolutely! I'm lying arse-up in a giant fern, thinking I've gone doolally. Lucky for me I was found by a couple of the boys and they were able to show me the ropes. Bit like I found you."

Alan looked over his shoulder at Sophie. "You OK, honey?" he asked. She didn't respond, didn't even seem to hear him.

"Bit on the slow side," said Whitstable. "Knew someone at school like it, always laughing but none of us could see why. Not much to laugh about licking windows all day."

"I don't know what her condition is," Alan replied coldly.

"Oh, hey... no offence. I get a bit confused with some of the changes since I left, everyone tells me I'm tactless."

"It's fine."

They didn't talk for a while. Whitstable whistled "Club Tropicana" rather loudly to break the silence.

Alan noticed that the light was beginning to fade, the shadows deepening between the trees.

"How much further?" he said. "It's getting pretty dark."

"We're there," Whitstable replied, tugging a large bush to one side to reveal a hole in the ground shored up with wooden props and a tarpaulin.

"Underground?"

"Absolutely," said Whitstable, "keeps us out of sight of the beasties."

Alan looked at Sophie, who was staring past them at the cave mouth. "You OK, Sophie?" he asked. "Not scared of the dark, are you, hon?"

She didn't reply, just kept staring.

"Do… not… worry…" Whitstable said, as if trying to communicate with an unruly dog, "no… scary… in… dark."

"She can understand, for Christ's sake," Alan hissed, "you don't have to talk to her like she's an idiot."

"Just trying to help," Whitstable replied, offended. "I could have left you out there, you know?"

"I know," said Alan, "you're a saint, just let me talk to her, OK?"

"Whatever, make it quick. I'm not staying out here any longer than I need to, not once the light's gone."

Alan nodded and went over to Sophie. "Hey, honey," he said, "I know you don't like the look of it, can't say I fancy it much myself, but we can't stay out here, it's too dangerous." She didn't look at him. "Sophie? Sophie honey?" She turned to look at him, a confused look on her face as if she hadn't heard a word he'd said. She stared for a few seconds then smiled and walked past him into the tunnel.

"After you then," Whitstable muttered, turning to follow her.

Alan shook his head, exasperated. He followed them inside.

The tunnel was narrow but not as long as he had imagined. Once past the opening, they turned a sharp corner, light streaming in from ahead.

"Well hidden, eh?" said Whitstable.

The tunnel opened out into a huge chamber. A network of thick ropes criss-crossed the beamed roof with lit torches hanging from it. In the centre of the roof a vent hole sucked smoke up from a roaring bonfire into which people as wretched-looking as Whitstable were poking wrapped parcels for cooking. There were around thirty people in all, though it was difficult to be sure as the various shadowy piles in the dirt might be sleeping natives or stacks of clothing. Some people worked at knocked-up tables, fashioning tools or weapons, some were simply sitting around, staring into space and thinking their own thoughts. It had the air of a refugee camp. Everyone was thin, dirty and rough.

"Home is the hunter!" Whitstable called. Several people looked towards him with undisguised enthusiasm at the boar he carried.

"Toby!" An emaciated woman came running over, rubbing her hands at the sight of the fresh meat. "We were getting worried, it must be nearly night by now."

"I've not been caught out yet, Lauren. Toby Whitstable is a man that keeps his promises!"

"And you've brought company, I see?"

Alan introduced himself and Sophie, who had walked past them towards the fire. She stared at the flames, muttering under her breath.

"They've just arrived, poor things," said Whitstable "Least we could do was offer them a warm welcome, I thought."

"Of course," said another woman, much older than the first, "they are welcome to a meal and a bed." She turned to Alan. "Stefania D'Amaro, Milan, 1973, housebound four years."

"Alan Arthur, Kissimmee, 2010, housebound just this afternoon. I can't speak for Sophie, she keeps herself to herself, but we're touched by your hospitality."

"It's all we have. Come and join me closer to the fire."

They walked over to a table where she had been working. A dress, half-stitched, was draped over the back of her makeshift chair. She gestured to Alan to pull up a stool as she continued absentmindedly to fix the hem of the dress.

"You speak excellent English," said Alan, settling on to his seat.

"My husband was an American like yourself," she explained, "and I could never get him to learn Italian."

"You've built yourselves an impressive camp."

"It's wretched, but then our resources are limited."

"You've got heat and light, that's the main thing."

"The fire never goes out, nor the torches… don't ask me how, it's quite impossible but we've given up trying to understand it."

"As long as it keeps working, why should you?"

Stefania shrugged. She had little interest in discussing herself, it was him she wanted to talk about. "So tell me – it's traditional – how did you come to find yourself here?"

Alan related his story, the years he had searched for the box, the reports he had read from those who had been stolen away by it and yet found escape. This, in particular, was of great interest to Stefania.

"We had no idea there might be a way out," she admitted.

"I have to say a jungle was never mentioned," said Alan. "The reports were of a house – this wasn't at all what I expected."

"Perhaps the box can take you to many places?"

"Perhaps… but the glass surrounding the jungle, maybe there's something beyond that?"

Stefania waved the idea away. "We avoid the barrier. A few people have tried to break through but they learned to regret it. There are… monsters beyond the glass, in the darkness… they drag you away, never to be seen again."

"A dangerous place."

"And yet it is one you actively sought to find? I must admit I find that strange."

Alan nodded. "I can see that. It's difficult to explain…"

"Well, please try!" Stefania laughed.

Alan smiled and wondered where to start. "When I was a young man something happened to me, an accident... I was found wandering along the roadside with no memory of how I'd got there, who I was... anything at all, in fact."

"Amnesia."

"Yes, though I had one hell of a time trying to convince the authorities of that. It doesn't tend to happen, you see, outside movies anyway. People just don't forget great chunks of their life, not for long anyway. I was in a clinic for a while, lots of specialists... came to nothing."

"Very strange, though it doesn't explain the death-wish you seem to have developed."

"It's a fascination with lost people, I guess. I read about the box in a magazine. One of those grocery-store conspiracy tabloids, Bigfoot, crop circles, UFOs, you know the kind of thing... There was just something about the box story though, it grabbed the imagination. It was about a man, a Victorian explorer, named Roger Carruthers..."

"That's got to be a made-up name!"

"No, he definitely existed. He didn't put his name to anything ground-breaking but he was a compulsive essayist. Up until his last expedition at least; that was the subject of the article. History reports that Carruthers died in Tibet. He was one of the first Englishmen to visit the country after Francis Younghusband did his bit for the Empire by storming in there and forcing the acceptance of British occupation under gunpoint."

"The English have never been refined in their politics."

"Nobody building an Empire ever is. According to the report filed by the British Museum, Carruthers was simply there on an exploratory mission. This article reproduced a letter, allegedly from one of his colleagues on the expedition, stating that Carruthers had been searching for a specific artifact."

"Let me guess, a box?"

"Got it in one. The letter went on to claim that Carruthers found the box but, when he attempted to claim it in the name of the King, the Tibetan soldiers opened fire on his party. It was during this firefight that Carruthers vanished. So... a good story but as crazy-sounding as the rest of the stuff in the magazine."

"Though now we can guess that it's probably true."

"Oh every word, I have no doubt. Having been intrigued by it I tried to see if I could find any more evidence. I'm a history professor," he said as if it was an embarrassing admission, "so I have access to a lot of research material..."

"A man who has no history of his own becoming an expert in the subject... Freud would have a field day with you."

Alan smiled, "I'm an open book. Anyway, the box, however, was everywhere. Missing people reports, auction lists, even a dossier claiming Hitler's interest during the Second World War."

"None of which explains why you wanted to find the box and then use it."

"How else could I solve the mystery? To prove it utterly I had to use it. It's more than I can bear sometimes to have one mystery in my life I really couldn't tolerate two."

"How like a man. Is it so unbearable to have mysteries?"

Alan couldn't answer that.

The boar was butchered and roasted, chunks of it stirred into a large stew of roots and tubers harvested from the jungle. Alan couldn't in good conscience refuse the meal, despite the way that boar's swinging tongue sprang to mind with every chewy mouthful. Sophie had no such compunction; she simply sat down and stared at the flames, disinclined to interact with the group. Alan was almost envious of her at times, as he was introduced to one broken person after another, Helene (Lyons, 1964, housebound two years) sobbing over her children, lost to her for ever; Gregor (Massachusetts, 1992, housebound one year) and the wife he left at the altar, jilted not by a loss of affection but geographical circumstance; Pedro (Barcelona, 1936, housebound three years) and the family that may never have survived the war... One by one they came to the new man, eager to tell their stories to a pair of fresh ears.

"They are all so lost," said Stefania once they had been left in peace. "We are inextricable from our surroundings – pulling us from them is like uprooting a flower, we cannot thrive."

"And you?"

"Oh, I go hungry and my bones ache but I left nothing behind of any consequence. It's easier for me. I view my situation as one to be endured as simply as possible. I am stuck here but while some dream of going home, I simply live by the best and most comfortable means available."

"Is that why they all look up to you?"

Stefania smiled. "People are drawn to the fearless. They think we know better than they do."

"And what do *you* think?"

"I think that I am willing to do what is best for the community and that will always mean they need me. I make decisions others do not want to make. I take responsibility and I live with the consequences." She looked at Sophie. "She was lost before she ever came here, I think."

"She's all right, just a bit different. She helped me when I needed it and that's all the proof I need of someone's worth."

"Worth? Yes, that is the question isn't it? What are people worth?"

"I don't tend to think in such terms." The conversation was becoming uncomfortable; a strange mood had settled over Stefania, and Alan was becoming uncertain what he should say. "It was just a figure of speech."

"But it is the key to survival. Worth – and nature's assessment of it – is what keeps a species strong."

"Perhaps, in a general sense…"

"No!" Stefania sat forward in her chair. "In a very real sense. Look at Toby…" Still high on his success

as a hunter, Whitstable was telling all who would listen how he had stalked the boar through the
undergrowth. "Yesterday he was a joke," Stefania
continued, "stuck behind his ridiculous glasses, and
his silly accent, his talk of financial indices and the
money he made in 'the City'. What use was he? He
was nothing but an extra mouth, one portion less for
everyone else, a drain, a waste."

"Well, he proved himself today, didn't he?"

"Oh, yes, when he had to, when his future was
at stake."

Alan was starting to grow concerned at the direction this conversation was taking. "His future?"

"I told him we needed to eat. Either he brought us
something for our pot or he went in it himself."

Alan's mouth grew dry. "But you didn't mean it–"

"Of course I did. Like I said, I make the decisions
others are not willing to make."

"But you wouldn't have actually…"

"Lionel Tailor, New York, 1948, two years, I
dashed his brains out myself while the others held
him down. He was the first. Stephanie Kray, London,
1989, six months… Dear fat Stephanie was not cut
out for the wild life. We ate well for three days. As
for sweet, pregnant Louise–"

Alan jumped to his feet, knocking over his stool.
Stefania stared at him calmly. "Sit down, you foolish
man, scared of mysteries and big decisions. If you try
and run you will fill our stomachs tomorrow. As it is
I have a better suggestion: tomorrow you hunt. If
you find us meat, if you contribute to our society,

then all will be well and we can put this conversation behind us."

"And if not you'll eat me?"

Stefania laughed. "Dear Lord, no. Though I grant there's a few dinners on you, we'll eat the retard. It's about all she's good for."

Alan lunged to attack but he felt hands on his shoulders before he had got within a foot of her.

"See?" said Stefania, "fear for your safety makes you willing to harm another. Would you kill me if you thought it might let you or the girl survive?" She smiled. "I think you would. We are no different."

Sophie sits and watches the flames. She does not like it here in the cave so this is the best place to be. While watching the flames she can forget that she does not like it here and then nobody will get cross. She does not want Alan to get cross. She likes Alan. He knows facts. Facts are good. The people here are not like Alan. The people here are Wrong. They wear Wrong Clothes. They eat Wrong Food (and they ask her to eat it too but she will not, it is not spaghetti and she knows better). Some of the people here look at her in a way she does not like. They look at her in a way that you do not look at other people. Not the look that people use when they do not understand her. Not the look people use when they are scared of her. Not the look people use when she is making them feel uncomfortable by being with them (she thinks this is because people think she is Wrong, and, like her, they do not like Wrong Things). These people look at her in a way she does not quite understand. They look at her in the same way her father looked at a whisky bottle after her mother died. But this does not make sense. Sophie is not a bottle of whisky. Sophie has heard that sometimes people can be drunk but she does not think it is true as she has never seen it. People are too thick to drink, they're just not squishy enough. Sophie hopes she will not find out she is wrong when these people drink her later.

For a minute Sophie thinks the people are going to try and drink Alan. Then she thinks that maybe they just want to help him empty himself, help him become quiet. He is very angry about something, he is shouting a lot. They're not helping when they grab him. Alan is like Sophie, he doesn't like people touching him like that, it makes him shout even more. Sometimes he shouts about her but this makes her worry that he is angry with her so she turns away and looks at the flames for a while. She doesn't want to think that Alan could get so angry with her. When she looks back the strange people have stopped touching him. They have tied him up and sat him far away from the fire. He seems calm now. This is good. She wonders whether she should go and see him but the old woman is talking to her and now she is worried as she hasn't heard what the woman was saying. The old woman looks very serious so Sophie nods. Old people like it when you agree with them, it is the main thing that makes them feel the world is right.

"You have no idea, do you?" the old woman says. Sophie shakes her head. The old woman smiles. Sophie knows how to please old people, it is easy.

Sophie walks over to see Alan. Now he is calm she likes him better.

"Hello, Alan," she says, thinking this will help make him even happier. Grownups like it when you speak to them. Usually Sophie is too busy thinking about other things to remember this. But she remembers it now.

"Sophie, honey," he says, "listen to me, this is really important, we're in trouble and you need to…" but Sophie forgets to listen because she is wondering why Alan keeps calling her honey. Honey is something her mother used to have on toast. Sophie does not have honey on toast. Sophie likes her toast medium, brown, plain — no butter or jam or marmalade or Marmite or honey or anything, *plain*. But her mother eats honey. This is because everyone likes things different. Sophie doesn't like that but she accepts it. But why does Alan call her honey? It is very strange. Sophie realises she has been forgetting to listen because Alan looks very very very sad. It's all right though. Sophie knows how to make grownups feel better when she hasn't been listening. Sophie smiles.

Alan gave up trying to fight against the ropes; he wasn't strong enough and all he was succeeding in doing was cutting deep grooves into his wrists. One by one the people in the cave were falling asleep.

Alan tried not to hate them all, tried to convince himself that they were just people driven to inexcusable actions by their experiences. He didn't manage; he wished them the very worst. He looked around the chamber, trying to think of a way out of the situation. He was still thinking when, exhausted, he fell asleep.

Whitstable woke him. "I've said I'll help you," said the financier, throwing a sturdy club at Alan's feet.

"Keep an eye on me, you mean?"

"That too."

"Let me guess – if you let me get away she'll have you on the menu tonight as well."

"She wouldn't do that to me," Whitstable scoffed, "I've proven myself…"

"…of worth, yes, I know. Well, not in my eyes. Untie me and let's have this done."

Whitstable gave him a cautious glance and began to work the ropes loose. "Don't even think of trying to fight," he said, holding up his sharpened stake. "I'm not afraid to stick you with this."

"I don't doubt it," Alan replied, standing up and stretching his aching legs. "Can I warm myself?" he asked, nodding towards the bonfire. "My circulation's not what it once was and being tied up all night hasn't done me any favours."

"Help yourself," said Whitstable.

Alan picked up the club and made to walk over to the fire but his legs buckled, pins and needles working through them like a colony of ants.

"This is stupid," said Whitstable, grabbing hold of Alan and keeping him on his feet, "there's no way you're going to be able to hunt."

"I know," Alan admitted, "that's the problem. It's not a fair fight, is it?"

"Life isn't fair," said Whitstable, "it's kill or be killed, survival of the fittest."

"It shouldn't be," Alan replied. "I wish it wasn't." He looked over at Sophie, who was still watching the fire. "Sophie?" he said, "three is good, isn't it?"

She turned to look at him, her attention grabbed by his words. "Three is good." She walked over to them. "Three is the times it takes to really know something."

Alan nodded. "Look over there," he said to her, pointing towards the door, "this is something not worth knowing."

Sophie turned to look and, reassured she wouldn't have to watch, Alan grabbed hold of Whitstable's shoulder and pushed him into the fire.

Whitstable's screams echoed around the cave as Alan shoved his club into the flames until it caught. "Everyone keep back!" he shouted, thrusting the flaming club above his head as the panicked savages began to circle him. Alan grabbed at Sophie. "Three is good," he whispered in her ear, "remember that. I know you don't like me holding you but I need to right now, it's important." He hummed in her ear and she relaxed slightly.

Whitstable rolled clear of the fire, still screeching, and ran into the gathered crowd. Someone threw a

blanket over him and pushed him down into the
dirt.

"What are you doing?" asked Stefania, calmly
waving a few braver souls back as they inched towards Alan. "Let him have his moment," she said,
"it won't last long."

"I'm acting as loathsomely as the rest of you," Alan
replied, "in order to save Sophie's life. I'm also proving a point."

"Which is?"

"Worth is not just measured in strength, it's measured in intelligence."

"Oh, so you're cleverer than us? Is that it?"

"I must be," Alan replied, "because only a bunch
of absolute idiots would suspend a network of flaming torches above their heads."

His flaming club finally burned through the rope
above him and the strands either side swung down,
whipping the torches through the air. The fires found
their mark, igniting people as well as the piles of rags
and bed coverings that littered the floor. The cave
erupted in panic, people running to put out the fires
and save their friends. Alan ignored the lot of them,
waving the lighted club around him as he ran for the
exit.

He hummed in Sophie's ear, relieved to hear her
hum back, drooping on his shoulder as she vanished
inside herself. He ran back in the direction they had
travelled the day before, thankful that they had left
a clear enough trail to follow. The sound of pursuit
wasn't long in coming, the shouts of the savages and

the snapping of branches. His breath drew painfully short in his chest. He wasn't fit enough for this sort of thing, he carried far too much flab. His shoulder throbbed with Sophie's weight, the muscles in his legs quivering with every step. He just hoped he had enough adrenalin to keep him going. Behind him the natives were calling to one another, no doubt trying to get ahead so they could cut him off. He was sure they weren't overly worried about losing him. As far as they were concerned he was running towards a dead end.

He made it to the clearing where they had met Whitstable the day before, marked by the boar's blood still staining the ground. He sat Sophie down and walked up to the vast transparent barrier. "'There are monsters in the darkness...'" he quoted to himself as he raised his club towards the glass. Well, maybe that was so, but there were monsters here too. He brought the club down on the glass, a stabbing pain erupting in his shoulder as the wood reverberated against the glass. He brought it down again, as hard as he could, while the sounds of people beating their way towards them grew louder and louder. This time the glass cracked. Once more would do it, would have to do it.

There was a terrible scream from behind him and he turned to see Whitstable, still smouldering, running towards them, his glasses bent around his shining, burned face. Behind him were a crowd of natives, the rage in their faces transforming them into the animals they truly were. No time... Alan hit the glass again and it shattered, the cracks shooting up through the large panes, a rain of crystal shards pouring down on him. Covering his face he grabbed Sophie and stepped through the hole he had made into the darkness.

CHAPTER TWELVE

Carruthers was woken by the sound of movement outside his tent. It was the tiniest noise, a slight rustling, but an explorer learns to keep his wits about him. Many years ago, Carrutthers had been trekking in India when he woke one morning to find a Bengal Tiger in his tent. Coming face to face with a man-eater who has designs on your legs is no way to start a day. Since then his subconscious had learned to wake him at the slightest possibility of danger.

He reached for his lantern and revolver before slowly creeping outside. Someone was walking through the stacks towards them; he could hear the soft slap of their feet, the shifting of their clothes. Carruthers' senses were ludicrously attuned – he was damned if he would get caught napping twice in his career. Turning his back on the noise he lit the lantern, fixing the metal coverings in place so that no light would escape until he wished. Treading silently, he positioned himself in the centre of the aisle between the stacks, waiting for the intruder to step a little closer. With one fluid movement he un-hinged the flap on the lantern – bathing himself and the intruder in a beam of light – and trained his re-volver on the centre of the illumination. Recognising Penelope he whipped the gun-barrel away.

"My dear!" Carruthers cried, "I might have shot you!"

"Well, I'm ever so glad you didn't," she replied.

"What on earth possessed you to go wandering?" asked Carruthers. "I had hoped I'd made it clear how perilous this place is during the hours of darkness."

"I couldn't sleep so I thought I'd find a book to read," said Penelope with a smile.

"You jest, my lady, but I can assure you I don't ex-aggerate the danger. There is no book worth the risk."

"No doubt you are right," Penelope said, "I just… " She shrugged with embarrassment. "There was someone's biography I wanted to read. I told you what happened to me before I came here, the things my fiancé threatened to do."

"I would have thought that was the last thing you would want to re-experience."

"Oh, I didn't want to re-experience it, I wanted to understand it. I thought I knew Chester, knew him really well. Turns out I didn't have the first idea."

Carruthers nodded and put his arm around her shoulder to lead her back towards the camp. "I do empathise, of course. You saw, no doubt, the small stack of volumes I have collected? In some cases I simply wished to know how a few select friends had fared since my departure but the book I sought out first – in fact the very moment I came to realise what these volumes represented – was the life story of Lady Vanessa D'Lacey."

"A sweetheart?"

"Oh, very much so, since a young age. We were to be married, in fact."

"What went wrong?" she asked.

"Exactly what I wanted to know. This was before I started travelling and I was nothing if not an attentive beau. Still, a handful of days before the wedding she called it all off and vanished to Vienna. I was utterly at a loss to comprehend it. Had I done or said something to upset her? Had there been someone else to whom she pledged her affections? I was, I am ashamed to confess, in a terrible state."

"Nothing to be ashamed of."

"You are kind. I decided the only thing for it was to change my circumstances, I had always been interested in other cultures and there was nothing in England to bind me, so I became an obsessive traveller, hoping, I now appreciate, that if I walked far enough I might be able to escape the blue funk that had gripped me. Of course, time is a great medicine and the pain lessened over the years. Still, I would be lying were I not to admit the conundrum clung to me. Why had she done it? When faced with this room I had the opportunity to find out, to read her side of the story and finally understand what I had done to drive her away."

"What was it?"

They were back at the camp now and Carruthers hung the lamp from one of the ropes. "It was quite simple: she didn't love me. There was no more to it than that. Such an obvious answer really and I shouldn't have needed the book to tell me. Your situation's no different: this fellow did the most unutterable things to you for no more reason than that he was a terrible man. It is no great mystery."

"You're right, I know, I just can't quite dismiss the notion that maybe…"

"It was something to do with you." Carruthers nodded. "Of course. But we must let others take responsibility for their actions. You had the misfortune of crossing this monster's path and I wish it were not so. However, the fates are terrible ladies and they do not always act as one might wish."

Penelope gave Carruthers a kiss on the cheek. "You're a good man," she said, "and I hope Miss D'Lacey realised what she had lost."

"Bless you." Even in the low light, Penelope could tell that Carruthers' cheeks had reddened slightly. He lifted the lantern, meaning to extinguish it, but a pool of light fell on the shelves behind him and he gave a cry of disgust. The shelf was filled with fat worms, writhing over the books. The size of a man's forearm, they recoiled at the light, their circular mouths flaring to show glistening bristles that may have been needle-thin teeth.

"Cool your boots, kids," said Tom as the three of them stumbled around in the darkness, "I'm actually prepared for this." Elise and Pablo listened as Tom rummaged in his pockets. There was the click of his lighter and then they were bathed in orange light as he held up a lighted candle. "Who's your daddy?"

"He would not have liked you, Tom," said Pablo, smiling in the candlelight, "he was an angry man."

"Just what he world needs more of. Here," he handed the candle to Pablo, "I've enough for everyone, just mind the wax." He pulled out another, lit it and gave it to Elise, finally taking another for himself.

"May I suggest we keep moving?" said Elise, "I don't like the idea of those toys following us in the dark."

"I'll beat the stuffing out of them," said Tom, "have no fear." Nonetheless he started to move down the corridor. As he held up the candle to get a sense of their surroundings, the flame showed rows of oil portraits on both sides. "Handsome dudes," he muttered, grimacing at the dour jowls and effete ringlets of a particularly satanic-looking figure.

"They built them beautiful in the old days," replied Elise.

The corridor ended in a pair of panelled wooden doors.

"Maybe keep us safe if hairy things follow?" asked Pablo.

"You have a point, El Toro," Tom replied, "though, knowing our luck, there's probably a goddamned rollercoaster rigged up on the other side."

He reached for one of the wrought-iron knockers, tapping it cautiously before grabbing it and pulling the door open. A musty smell crept out into the corridor.

"Am I the only one who's already thinking, 'Out of the frying pan and into the fire'?" said Elise.

"You think that bad you should visit my house," said Pablo, "fishermen make houses smelly."

"Sounds lovely," Elise replied. "Come on then, it's not like we can go back the way we came, is it?"

"The lady speaks the truth," said Tom, swinging the door wide open. They stepped inside, holding out their candles.

"Well, bless me father!" said Tom, shining his candle against a stained-glass window, "looks like we've found religious sanctuary, kids."

Pablo looked up at a large crucifix fixed on the far wall. The blood on the pasty forehead of the plaster Jesus was black in the low light. "I don't like churches," he said, "I spend too many hours in them."

"Well, kid," Tom replied, swinging the door shut and bolting it, "looks like you're going to spend a few more in one. If you like we could sing some hymns, cheer you up some?"

"Songs about dead people, I do not see where is fun."

"I thought all Spanish were Catholic?" said Elise.

"I thought all American wear cowboy hats, is very disappointing."

Tom laughed. "The rest of us all look like Presley."

"I do not know him, but he must be funny looking."

"You don't know Presley? Jesus… what have you been doing with your ears?"

They settled down on one of the pews, thankful for the opportunity to do nothing but sit.

"My ears?" Pablo was confused. "I do not understand half of what you say."

"Feeling's mutual, kid."

"I speak good English!" Pablo insisted, his pride hurt.

"You speak it better than Tom," Elise interjected. "Don't let him get to you, he's just spoiling for a Martini."

Tom made to argue then realised she wouldn't believe him if he did. They'd been busy enough for the thirst to be all but quelled. Still, it bubbled away, a background constant like the hum of a power line. This was probably the longest he'd been sober for about fifteen years and he couldn't say he was enjoying the experience much.

"What is Martini?" asked Pablo.

"Liquid sunshine," Tom grumbled, "can we get off the subject?" He rooted in his jacket for cigarettes. He offered the pack to Pablo and Elise, both only too happy to take one. Using their candles they lit them and sat silently, as if the act of smoking took every ounce of concentration in the human body.

"Feels strange smoking cigarette without having to watch for my father," said Pablo. "He think cigarettes kill you."

"He might well be right," admitted Tom, "but I don't think it's the major concern to your health right now."

"We will not die here I think," said Pablo.

"I admire your confidence," said Elise.

Pablo shrugged. "It is just a thing I think."

"Well keep thinking it, El Toro, I like your style."

"Shush!" hissed Elise, "I thought I heard something."

All three stood up, moving their candles around to throw as much light into the darkness as they could. A thin shadow of Christ reached for the ceiling behind Pablo as he lifted his candle in front of him. "I cannot hear anything," he whispered.

"Wish we had more light," said Elise, moving between the pews to stand in the middle of the chapel. "Wherever we stand you can never see all of it."

"There is nothing here," said Pablo, "I am sure of it. Think of smell, there's no way anyone has been in here for years."

"That's logical, kid," said Tom, "but I think, what with the giant snakes and killer teddies, we can safely say logic is not always on the setlist."

There was a ruffling of feathers.

"Trapped pigeon maybe?" said Elise, testing the safety of one of the pews with her hand before stepping on to it, holding her candle up towards the ceiling.

The light fell on the chubby face of a toddler, wedged between the rafters. Two wide-spanning wings sprouted from his back, the feathers off-white like aging paper. "Not a pigeon," she whispered. The cherub looked at her with milk-white pupil-less eyes, its head moving with the jerkiness of a bird.

"Careful," Tom whispered, creeping slowly towards her.

"It's all right," Elise said, "I think it's just curious."

The cherub opened its mouth to exhale a piercing note like a damp finger rubbed along the rim of a glass. Letting go of the rafters it swooped towards Elise, knocking the candle from her hand and plunging both of them into darkness.

"I need to put you down, honey." Alan lowered Sophie from his shoulder, keeping hold of her hand. "But we have to keep running, OK?"

The darkness was impenetrable with no distinction between the ground and their surroundings. With the exception of the light streaming through the hole behind them, the jungle was invisible from this side of the glass. Alan hoped that the natives were too scared to follow them. Stefania had certainly viewed whatever lay this side of the barrier as a no-man's land not to be entered. Stretching out an arm he was relieved to feel the cold sensation of glass to his left, so the barrier *was* still there. Perhaps somewhere along its surface there would be a door. Only one way to find out...

"We've lost them," Whitstable wailed as the rest of the tribe caught up with him. He couldn't stop moving; his seared skin was beginning to blister. He stared into the darkness beyond the broken glass and howled in a mixture of pain and frustration.

"*You've* lost them," Stefania said, coming alongside him. "It was your job to keep him under control, remember?"

"That's hardly fair!" Whitstable shouted, "I didn't see you helping much."

Stefania slapped him across the face making him squeal in pain. "Stand up to your responsibilities," she said, "or we'll finish the job of roasting you ourselves."

"But you can't expect me to go in there…"

"It's entirely up to you – either you fetch the girl or take her place."

Whitstable yelled in frustration, staring into the darkness beyond the glass. "Damned if I do…" he muttered, and stepped through the hole.

Miles was startled awake as Carruthers and Penelope climbed inside his tent. "Don't tell me it's morning already," he groaned.

"I'm afraid not, old chap," said Carruthers, "more a case of safety in numbers – we seem to be suffering from an infestation."

"Of what?"

"Bookworms," answered Penelope, "and before you laugh, they're the size of small dogs so they may have a taste for more than antique paper."

"Oh, lovely," Miles replied, sitting up on his bedroll. "Well, at least with this really thick bedsheet in the way they can't get at us, eh?"

"Yes, Miles," Carruthers replied drily, "I'm quite aware of our limited fortifications. Let us hope that we're of no interest to them, shall we? Certainly they have never invaded this section of the library before. I would say that any creature whose diet consists primarily of vegetable matter is unlikely to start feasting on humans."

"If you're that confident then what are you both doing in my tent?"

"My considered zoological opinion is one thing – and it has been sought by the greatest establishments in the Empire – but I would prefer not to stake my life on it."

"Surely, even if they're as big as you say we could easily defend ourselves against them? One stout kick and it's a long old crawl back for a rematch, isn't it?"

"Come here," said Carruthers, closing all the shutters bar one on his lantern so as to focus the beam.

Miles shuffled over next to Carruthers at the mouth of the tent.

"Look," Carruthers said, pulling back the sheet and pointing the light out into the library. The shelves and floor were covered, hundreds of the worms writhing over one another. Now they were silent the sound of the worms' grazing was audible, like the crackling of a badly tuned radio.

"Oh," said Miles, "perhaps we should stay here then."

"Yes," said Penelope, smiling, "perhaps we should."

"It won't be long until first light," said Carruthers, "and one would hope they'll retreat before then."

"Would that be your zoological opinion we're staking our lives on?" Miles asked.

"Yes, though I'd rather you didn't dwell on the fact."

"Elise!" Tom ran towards her, bashing into one of the pews and stumbling to the floor.

"I'm all right," she called, "it's scuttled off. The little fucker bit me though!"

Tom crawled towards her voice, holding out the candle. "Let me see," he said, as he found her.

"I don't think it's bad." She held her hand up to the light, Tom angling the candle so he could examine the small wound in the ball of her thumb.

"Let's hope angels don't carry rabies," he said, "we're a hell of a way from getting you a shot."

"We are having big problem," said Pablo, still standing by the altar.

"Tell that to someone who isn't bleeding!" Elise replied.

"No, listen."

Above them there came the sound of beating wings, first one, then another, then another, swooping above them in the shadows of the roof.

"Cool," said Tom, "I was hoping there'd be lots of them."

Pablo ran down the middle of the chapel to the door. "We need to not be in here now," he said, "I think we're better back the way we came."

"Wait!" Tom shouted, before Pablo had opened the door. "Let's think about this a second. We know there's no way out that way, it's just back to the playroom and those toys."

"Or we stay here with angels that bite."

"I didn't say the options were good."

There came a scratching from the other side of the door, growing louder and louder as more claws added their efforts.

"OK," said Pablo, "now is no go there either."

"Maybe there's another way out?" Elise suggested, taking another lighted candle from Tom.

"Doesn't hurt to look," he agreed.

They began to make their way around the walls, the cherubs still swooping above them from one side of the room to the other.

"There is no door!" Pablo shouted. "It make no sense, how you go from dining room to playhouse to church and not go anywhere else?"

"Maybe we missed something in the corridor?" Elise suggested. "It was pretty dark."

"Or maybe this is a house that just loves to fuck with expectations," Tom replied. "There's no point in angling for this shit to make sense, it hasn't so far." A cherub swooped down from the eaves with the same piercing song as before, snapping at Tom's candle with its puckered mouth. "Oh, fuck you!" he shouted in exasperation, shoving the candle at it. The cherub's mouth stretched like rubber, chisel-like teeth dotted around its pink gums. It swallowed the candle whole and flew back up to the roof.

"How long until it's light?" asked Miles. "You know… roughly."

Carruthers sighed in exasperation. "I have told you, time is inexact here, the night usually lasts for five or six hours."

"Did you tell me that?" Miles asked, genuinely confused.

"Once or twice but it's no matter."

"Sorry."

"Honestly, no matter."

"I'm trying to sleep!" whined Penelope, rolling over on the mattress.

"Don't get all agitated then," said Miles with a smile, "otherwise you'll never drop off." Penelope scowled at him but said nothing.

"I used to be able to sleep through anything," said Carruthers. "I remember once, during a trip across Australia, trapped in swampland but crippled with exhaustion, I tied myself to a tree, sleeping the sleep of the just for a full five hours before cutting myself loose and continuing on my way."

"Got any rope?" Penelope murmured.

"Is there anywhere you haven't been?" Miles asked, "places you always planned on visiting but never managed?"

"Oh, many, my boy. I have long been fascinated by tales of the Arctic, to conquer the Northwest Passage… now there would be a thing. Knowing my luck that swine Amundsen will have survived his attempt in my absence. Takes more than ice to knock the Norse, the chilly beggars are used to it. Always thought that was cheating somewhat. Now, Franklin there was an explorer!"

"Didn't he kill off his whole expedition?"

"Nonsense! The man was a hero!"

"A hero that trapped two ships and their crew in ice through bloody-mindedness and poor leadership."

"Mind your tongue, sir! You happen to be defaming a hero of mine."

"I read they ate one another in the end."

"I'll eat you two if you don't shut up!" Penelope shouted. "Dear Lord, it's like being trapped with a pair of little boys."

They sat in silence for a few moments, Miles and Carruthers intentionally avoiding each other's eyes.

"Or was it a big Eskimo monster?" said Miles in the end. "I'm sure I read about it…"

"Eskimo monsters! The man's delirious!"

"Oh yes, because being besieged by bookworms isn't weird at all."

Carruthers was about to argue but saw the pointlessness of it. "Yes, well, 'there are more things in heaven and earth' and all that."

"Indeed."

They said nothing for a while. The only noise was the grazing of the worms and the occasional irritated grunt from Penelope as she tried to get comfortable.

"So," said Miles in the end, "how long until it gets light?"

"Oh, for goodness sake!" Penelope sat bolt upright. "It's utterly pointless."

Carruthers gave Miles a conspiratorial smile. "It's difficult to tell, it varies from night to night."

"We know!" sighed Penelope, "you've told him often enough, it's about five hours!"

"I say, my dear," replied Carruthers, "how on earth did you know that?"

"You've said it about four times now," Penelope replied.

"I'm sure I hadn't mentioned it."

"Of course you have, Miles keeps asking you."

"Does he?" Carruthers looked baffled at Miles. "Can't say I remember anything about it, do you, old chap?"

"I wouldn't have asked if I did," Miles replied defensively. "Who's Miles anyway?"

Penelope stared at them in exasperation. "This is not in the least bit amusing."

"I'm not trying to be amusing" Miles turned to face Penelope. "Are you feeling all right?"

"Nothing an hour's sleep wouldn't fix. It's not me that claims not to know his own name."

"Don't be silly," Miles scoffed, "of course I know what my name is."

"It's Carruthers, isn't it?" Carruthers said. "That certainly rings a bell."

"You're not joking, are you?" asked Penelope. "Neither of you actually remember."

"Remember what?" asked Miles. A look of confusion crossed his face. "I don't feel very good," he said, pressing his hands to his temple, "my head's pounding…"

"Something's very wrong here." Penelope got off the mattress and sat face to face with Miles. "What's your name?"

Miles' face crumpled. "I don't know!"

The cherubs continued to strafe the room. At first it seemed it was the candles that were attracting them. Certainly the flames were their initial target – they snapped at them with their elastic mouths or their pudgy little fingers. Then one yanked at Elise's hair, wrenching out a handful and flying back into the darkness with it, that high note sounding all the more triumphant.

"Perhaps it wish to build a nest?" Pablo suggested.

"Well, it can screw itself," Elise moaned, rubbing at her sore head.

Another cherub dropped from the air, grabbing Pablo's face and sinking its teeth into his cheek. "*Cosa de mierda!*" Pablo swore, wrenching it free and flinging it to the floor. He tried to stamp on it, holding his hand to his bleeding cheek, but it was too swift for him, taking to the air with a red smile.

"You OK?" Elise said, grabbing hold of Pablo and trying to see his wound.

"Later," Pablo said, "now is not time for nurse."

"The little bastards are playing," said Tom, ducking as another cherub dive-bombed his head. "I swear the fuckers are enjoying this." He moved towards the altar, keeping down in case one of them tried for another strike. He grabbed a large brass candlestick off the altar and held it in one hand like a club.

"I will take one of those, I think," said Pablo.

"Me too," added Elise.

"There's only two," Tom said, throwing the spare to Pablo.

"Sexist pig," Elise muttered.

"It is all right," Pablo said, "I will protect you."

Elise stared at him. "You have no idea how close I am to taking that thing off you and braining you with it."

A cherub flew down at them. Pablo swung the candlestick but missed.

Tom fared better; swinging the candlestick upwards he caught the cherub in the belly, flipping it in the air. Not satisfied, Tom brought the candlestick straight back down again, clubbing the cherub hard on the back of the head. It dropped to the floor only to be snatched by a couple of its fellows an instant later and carried up into the roof. Within seconds there were lots of tearing noises and the air was filled with feathers and whistling as the cherubs fed on their fallen comrade.

"Smooth," Tom muttered with a scowl. "Cannibal cherubs."

The taste of the meat incited the rest of the flock as the whistling noise increased and they began swooping *en masse*.

Suddenly a couple of gunshots rang out over Tom's shoulder, and two cherubs all but exploded in mid-air as they were hit.

Tom fell over in shock, holding his hand to his ringing left ear.

"You need to be quick," said the man who had appeared from behind the altar, "they'll be almost uncontrollable now."

"Where the hell did you come from?" Elise shouted.

"There's a passageway that comes out under the altar," he answered, "but might I suggest we discuss it while we're using it rather than standing here like sitting ducks?"

Whitstable was crying as he ran, every footstep agony. "Fucking kill you!" he screamed. "Fucking kill *both* of you!"

Alan stopped running for a moment, looking around. "Did you hear something?" he asked Sophie but she was utterly lost, humming loudly, her eyes vacant. "I definitely heard something," Alan said, searching the darkness for sign of company.

Whitstable appeared out of nowhere, only feet away, screaming and stabbing the air with his sharpened stake. "*Fucking kill you!*" he roared, the words mangled into little more than noise. Suddenly he was knocked to one side as something invisible collided with him. Alan stepped closer to Sophie, searching for what it was that had struck. Now that he had stopped running, he could feel a half-presence, a suspicion of something in the dark. A force collided with his already throbbing shoulder, knocking him off his feet and making him cry out in pain.

Sophie stopped humming, reaching out in front of her.

"No," she said. "That is wrong. Stop it."

Alan got to his feet with a groan. He wasn't going to be able to stand for much longer, he was taking too much of a battering. Unfortunately Whitstable still had more fight in him and was crawling on all fours trying to find his weapon, mumbling obscenities. Deciding to do without it, he charged at Alan and Sophie, happy to tear them apart with his hands. The invisible force struck him again, sending him several feet backwards in the air. With a scream he hit the glass barrier, which shattered to reveal a wood-panelled corridor. Alan took Sophie's hand and pulled her through.

"The books," Carruthers mumbled, holding his head in his hands, "it must be the books."

"What about the books?" Penelope asked, trying not to panic.

"Eating," said Carruthers, "eating history. Oh, my Lord, but it hurts."

"Eating history?" Penelope asked, "what on earth do you mean, eating…" The penny dropped. Both Carruthers and Miles had left their biographies outside where the worms could graze on them, chewing great chunks of their written lives from the pages. The damage to the books was affecting their subjects. She grabbed Carruthers' lantern and stepped outside the tent. The worms were everywhere, rolling over Carruthers' camp, nibbling at the sheets and ropes, the wood of the shelves, the books... She bit her lip and ran into the middle of them, kicking at them with her bare feet, grimacing at the feel of their pale, slick skins. Some had grown bloated by their feast, rolling aimlessly as they tried to move on distended bellies.

She saw Carruthers' biography first; it had several wet holes in its cover, and its pages were soggy from saliva. She picked it up, kicking out at a particularly grotesque worm lying next to it. The worm's outer skin burst, too stretched to take even the lightest blow. Groaning in disgust she tried to wipe the ichor from her toes as she hopped away from the camp towards where Miles had thrown his volume. There were books everywhere, in various stages of ruin, from the odd serrated bite-mark to a scatological pulp of confetti and leather. Flipping each book over she hunted for the one with Miles' name on it. She tried not to notice how the worms were becoming aware of her, turning their fluted snouts towards her as if scenting her binding. She found it, but nearly dropped it again as one of the worms latched its mouth on to her heel. She kicked back, flinging it loose. The worms were wriggling towards her, dropping from the shelves all along the stack and inching their way in her direction, intrigued by the appearance of a new volume. She backed against the shelves, preparing to make a run for it, stamping every single one of them in her path if need be. Then the lamps in the walls began to softly glow as dawn crept into the library. The worms froze, twitching their snouts in the faint light. Then they began to move, wriggling away into the depths of the stacks to burrow and sleep.

Penelope dropped to the floor and rested her back against the shelves.

"It's safe," she shouted, "they're leaving."

A few moments later the sheet parted at the mouth of the tent and Miles shuffled out, shortly followed by Carruthers.

"The pain's fading," he said, rubbing at his temples, "and I think some things are coming back."

"What's your name?" Penelope asked.

"Miles," he said with a smile, "though it still feels strange, as if it's not quite a part of me."

"It was the most blessed thing," Carruthers added, "I could feel great chunks of me breaking away. People I knew, places I'd been. The important things – the essence of who we are – are not isolated incidents, they are something we carry with us at all times. Let us hope they are a little harder to destroy in a couple of mouthfuls."

"There are great chunks of my life they were welcome to," said Miles. "Can't say I would have missed them. One thing, though, who's he?" He pointed to a prone figure, lying quite still behind one of the tents. "I'm sure you'll laugh but I can't remember him for the life of me."

INTERLUDE

The renegade has fallen deeply in love with Constantinople. The city has such scope for excess. Where else can one drink a few beers and watch 60,000 people slaughtered?

The Byzantines have finally lost all patience with the Latin Europeans, and are routing them out with the sort of vigour only a deranged mob can achieve. He has lent a hand, naturally, stoked the flames a little. Now he is happy to sit back, enjoy the feel of the sun on his face and the screams in his ears. A small group of people gathers a few feet away and he wonders what new piece of street theatre is to be offered. They separate with a cheer, setting a dog to run through the streets, the head of Cardinal John – representative to the Pope here in the city – tied to its tail. It bounces behind the animal, its mouth popping open as if the holy man wishes to take a bite out of the hound's rump.

The renegade laughs along with the crowd. You can't beat a little light comedy to break up an afternoon's massacre; it's tiring work casting the bodies into the sea and everyone needs their spirits lifting. He drinks his beer and watches the reef of dead bodies building off shore.

CHAPTER THIRTEEN

Sophie doesn't like any of this. In fact Sophie hates it. Everywhere Sophie looks there is something that makes her head shout. Her thoughts are like her father's car alarm, they go on and on and on and on. She wishes she could turn it off but she doesn't have the key. She has tried to empty herself but Alan will not let her. Alan needs her to stay still. Alan needs her to run. Alan needs her. Alan does need her. Alan does not look good. He is old – though more father old than grandfather old – and old people often do not look good. This is because they are nearly dead. Sophie hopes Alan does not die just yet, she would not like to be here without him, it is too Wrong. It is a place that needs company.

She had hoped for three but one of the three was not a good man. Now he is lying on the carpet and that serves him right. He can just stay there. He is pink and he shouts and he says the word that means "I have just hit my hammer with a thumb" or "You are not a very good driver" or "You shouldn't have left that toy on the stairs as now I've fallen over it". She knows this because her father has used the word too and she has figured out what it means. She looks at Alan. He is bent over and finding it hard to breathe. Perhaps, like her, he is finding this very wrong and it is making him sick. They have just stepped out of a mirror and that is wrong. Mirrors are for practicing your "I Understand" smile. They are not for walking through. Also, you do not break them. If you do then father will say that word again and he will say it Very Loudly.

Sophie decides she must be strong for Alan. She takes hold of his hand (she does not like holding hands but he does it a lot so he must like it so she does it to make him feel better). "Come with me, Alan," she tells him, "we will find a quiet place."

She leads him down the corridor. They should not be in a corridor. They should be in a jungle. She tries not to think about that as she has to be strong for Alan. She opens the first door they come to and walks him inside. She closes the door. The walls of this room have a lot of tiles. This means it must be a kitchen or it must be a bathroom. The tiles are blue so this is probably a bathroom. It is very big for a bathroom. Though it has a lot of water so that is good. There are towels in very tall stacks. There are benches on which to sit. This is not a bathroom, she understands. This is a swimming pool. That is why it has the sea in it. You can swim in the sea, it's allowed.

She locks the door. Which is confusing as bath-rooms have locks but swimming pools do not have locks. She knows bathrooms have locks as sometimes she locks herself in them to stop other people being with her. This lock will stop the pink man from being with her. This is good. But Alan can stay. She likes Alan.

Alan sits down on one of the benches. Then he lies down. Something in his shoulder makes him yell. Sophie yells too even though there is nothing wrong with her shoulder. Sometimes she cannot help copying people when they do things she doesn't understand. Sometimes it helps her understand. Alan looks worried because she has yelled like him. She shows him her "I Understand" smile. He still looks worried but his eyes close and his face stops being worried and starts being about pain. Alan does not understand and it hurts him. He needs to go quiet for a while so she leaves him to do so.

She goes to look at the sea. It is the sea. She wasn't sure because she knows you don't have a sea in a house. It fills the world as far as she can see. It makes waves that push the long fluffy rugs up and down that lie at the edge of it. The rugs do not float out. The rugs stay. This is also wrong.

Sophie has an idea. Everything here is wrong. If everything is always wrong then perhaps it is right for here. This feels like a fact. This is good. She does not feel so bad now she knows that wrong can be right as long as it is always wrong.

She sits down on a dry part of the rug and watches the sea go in and out. She wonders if it would be good to swim. Sometimes she likes to swim. The water feels good. It holds her and bounces her like it is pleased with her. Sometimes she does not like to swim. The water feels bad. It pushes and shoves her like it is angry with her. Sophie wonders what mood the sea is in today.

Sophie thinks about the sea she nearly fell in when she found the box. That did not look like a happy sea. Its waves were bigger than this sea. This sea looks like it might be happy. She will try it.

She goes to get a towel and looks at Alan. She thinks Alan is now sleeping. This is not unusual. Sometimes when she is very upset she falls asleep too. Sleep is easy, nothing happens there.

She gets a towel. It is very big and very white and very nice. She holds it to her face and hopes the sea will be as happy as this towel.

She walks back to the edge of the water. She takes off some of her clothes. You do not take off all your clothes when you swim as it is Not Allowed. You keep your pants and bra on. It is a rule. And a fact. Sophie thinks all rules are facts. Unless you break them but Sophie would never do that. Sophie makes her clothes neat. Clothes are nice when they are neat. Socks next to each other, facing the same way, tidy feet waiting to walk.

Sophie steps into the water. It is not cold. This is good. If the water had been cold Sophie would not have gone in, cold water is angry water. Sophie goes a little further. The water is as far as Sophie's knees and it has not been angry. She thinks that if the water was going to be angry it would have done it by now. The water is happy with her so she gets in completely and starts to swim. Swimming is easy as long as you remember you can do it. Sometimes it is easy to forget. Especially when the sea is angry. When it throws a big wave that hits your face and steals your air. Then you can forget and you start sinking. Thinking about this, Sophie nearly forgets how to swim but she stands up in the water and remembers again. She wonders if any fish live in this sea. There should be fish. The sea is where fish live. She cannot see any fish and the water is clear. The water is clear like those pictures of the sea you see that ask you to go on holiday. The water is as clear as it is in the swimming pool. Underneath the water are tiles like in a swimming pool. This is wrong. This is good. Sophie is so glad she now knows that wrong can be right, it makes things much easier.

Sophie swims some more. Sophie wonders if France lives on the other side of the sea. It does where she lives but this is probably not the same sea. She looks back at Alan. He is still sleeping on the bench. Sophie decides she will look for France while she waits for him to wake up.

The throbbing in Alan's shoulder woke him up. He hoped he hadn't dislocated it. He'd seen people in movies pop a dislocated shoulder back into place but he didn't fancy trying it. He sat up and looked around. They had swapped one impossible room for another, jungles in the greenhouse and oceans in the bathroom. Where was Sophie? He looked around but couldn't see her anywhere. Then he spotted the clothes and looked out across the water. Dear Lord... please don't say she had...?

He pulled off his shoes, shirt and trousers and limped into the water. What had he been thinking? Leaving her on her own like that, it was obvious she couldn't fend for herself...

He swam as fast as he could, shouting her name above the gentle sound of the surf. He noticed the ground beneath the water was tiled; not the sea at all then, just a pool big enough to form waves. He dived beneath the surface, dreading catching sight of her sunken body. Surely she wouldn't have swum so far out? Though he had to admit it was easy going. He took a taste of the water; there was no salt, yet it seemed to carry him forward. It felt as if this was water you could never drown in, water to embrace you, to relax you, water that made you feel a part of it.

"Sophie!" he shouted again, catching sight of a shape bobbing nearby. "Sophie?" He swam towards it, overcome with relief when he drew close enough to tell it was her, flat on her back in the rippling water. "You had me worried, honey," he said as he drew up next to her.

"Not honey," she said, "plain, no butter or jam or marmalade or Marmite or honey or anything, *plain*."

"Er... OK. We should swim back now though, OK?"

"No. The sea is happy. Lie back and see."

Alan made to argue but stopped himself. What the

hell was the harm, hadn't they earned a moment's peace?

He flipped on to his back and tried to relax. He always struggled to float, too damn tense… Not in this water, in this water he could float just fine. Slowly he let himself go. He was no longer floating on the water, he was the water, rising up and down with the tide. He imagined himself dissolving, breaking up, fizzing, losing the cohesion that weighed him down with every moment. Not just the time in the house, all of it: the hot Florida sun, the students, the sweat, the ignorance, the apathy, the therapy sessions.

All of it.

Gone.

Nothing but the water.

"This is wonderful," he whispered.

"Shush," said Sophie, "they are coming."

And they came. Great shoals of fish, swirling around them, their little mouths puckering against his body, tickling, stroking, kissing.

Alan had never known a peace like it.

CHAPTER FOURTEEN

"He looks like someone from my era," said Penelope as they carried the stranger to a mattress. "It's all right," she shouted, leaning over him, "you'll be able to move soon!"

"My dearest Miss Simons, I am quite sure deafness wasn't part of the transference process," said Carruthers.

"Oh, yes, sorry..."

The man was incredibly old, his skin a mess of soft wrinkles and liver spots. Miles picked up a fedora hat from where it had fallen from the stranger's head. He dropped it on to his own at a rakish angle. "The name's...erm..."

"Caulfield," said Penelope, rolling her eyes.

"Sorry, still a bit shaky on that one. *Ahem*... the name's Caulfield... Miles Caulfield. What's a good-looking dame like you doing in this joint?"

"Socialising with mad limeys," she replied, "and that has to be the worst American accent I've ever heard."

"Fair enough," Miles replied, taking the hat off and placing it next to the man. "Think we should take his coat off too?"

"We don't have to strip the poor man," she replied, straightening the tails of his gaberdine across his legs, "just keep an eye on him while he comes around… Oh…" She held up a large handgun. "It was in his pocket." She looked down at the old man. "I wasn't checking your pockets, it slipped out when I was straightening your coat, sorry!"

"If you wouldn't mind, my dear?" Carruthers held his hand out for the gun. "A little more advanced than a revolver in my day," he said, taking it off her. He pulled the barrel pin and emptied the cartridges into his palm. "Though the principle is much the same." He handed the gun back to Penelope. "Return the man's property to his pocket with my apologies for making it redundant."

"Wise move," said Miles, "he could be a raging nutter for all we know."

"I haven't the faintest notion what one of those is," admitted Carruthers, "but on the assumption that it's the sort of cove one would dislike to see running around with a weapon then we're in agreement."

"Exactly one of those sorts of coves, yes," Miles replied.

"He can hear you, remember?" said Penelope. "As you just kindly reminded me, there's nothing wrong with his ears."

"I'm sure no reasonable gentlemen would be-grudge us a degree of caution," Carruthers assured her. "I will, of course, return the gentleman's prop-erty to him once we are utterly reassured that it is safe to do so. Now, rather than crowd the poor chap might I suggest that we get on with our preparations and allow him to come around in his own good time."

Penelope nodded. "You're quite right, of course." She noticed a book on the floor. "In all things it would seem," she said, holding it up. "Chester's bi-ography, now with great chunks of it missing. It seems I was never meant to know."

Carruthers smiled. "Abandon it, my dear. The past is too weighty a burden to carry with us for ever."

Penelope tossed it to the floor and returned to the piles of spare clothing Carruthers had gathered (after all, she couldn't travel without a small selection of outfits – a lady had to have some principles).

Miles walked over to Carruthers. "Do you think he'll want to come with us?" he whispered, gestur-ing towards the old man.

"Who can say?" Carruthers replied. "He doesn't look sprightly enough to get far. Not that we can re-ally leave him here…"

"I don't see why not, it's not like you plan on re-turning to the camp."

"That is neither here nor there. As last night proved, he is no safer here than anywhere in this godforsaken building. If we leave him our con-sciences must accept the consequences."

"You never know, he may be stronger than he looks."

"In that case he will be more of a benefit travelling alongside us than not. Anyway, it's all immaterial, it must be his choice."

"I suppose." Miles noticed the old man's fingers beginning to twitch. "Won't be long before we can ask him."

"How many bags are we taking?" Penelope shouted. "Just so I know how many shirts to take."

"Dear God," Carruthers muttered under his breath, "perhaps it's Penelope we should leave behind?"

Miles smiled. "One bag each, I'd say." He looked at Carruthers. "Agreed, o seasoned explorer?"

"Agreed." Carruthers nodded. "And maybe you might like to bear in mind some of the essentials we'll have to split between us before you fill yours?"

"How is a shirt not essential?" Penelope asked. "It's not as if I'm suggesting cocktail gowns, is it? What could be more essential than a shirt?"

"Food?" asked Miles.

"Ah." Penelope looked at the pile of shirts draped over her arm. "There is that. Maybe only five or six then, you'd say?"

"Or less?" Carruthers suggested.

"How many less?"

"Five or six less?" Miles replied.

Penelope scowled at him. "Very funny."

"You really won't be able to carry more than one change of clothes, my dear," Carruthers explained.

"A lack of crisp, laundered cotton will not kill us, whereas a lack of tinned beef may."

"What a wretched and beastly excuse."

"But true."

The old man exhaled a rasp of breath, one arm twisting and turning spastically as he tried to lift it.

"It's all right," Penelope said, dashing over and taking hold of his hand, "just relax, let it come." The man's face was twisted in either pain or terror, she couldn't tell which. "I don't think I was this bad," she said.

"I was," said Miles, "but then I did have the added stress of animated taxidermy trying to kill me."

"I say," Carruthers said, all ears, "you didn't tell me about that."

"Well, didn't want to bore you, savaged by a tiger-skin rug, we've all been there."

"This house…" Carruthers shook his head in disbelief.

Penelope brushed his thin fringe from the old man's eyes. "Don't get too close," Miles said, passing her on his way to their supply of tinned foods.

Men! she thought, so suspicious, seeing danger in everyone. They didn't possess the intuition women had in such things, too busy trying to look bigger and stronger than everyone else. There was no danger in this man, Penelope simply knew it. She could tell from his watery, powder-blue eyes and his full lips. They were lips that were born to smile, not scowl.

He mumbled something but she couldn't hear. "What was that?" she asked.

"Who is it?" he whispered.

"Penelope Simons, honey, of the Massachusetts Simons. Over there you have Roger Carruthers, the renowned explorer, and Miles Caulfield the... well... Miles Caulfield."

"Penelope?" he repeated.

"Yes, dear, and I'm sure we're all going to be the best of friends so don't you worry about that."

"Friends..."

"That's right, real friends. And don't worry about what's happening to you now, it really doesn't last long – a few more minutes and you'll be back on your feet again. It's what always seems to happen when you arrive here in the house. Oh, not that you know anything about that, of course... the box, do you remember the box?"

"Yes."

"Well, somehow it brings you here, please don't ask me how as I couldn't even begin to tell you, it really is the most disturbing thing one can imagine... *anyway*, 'here' is a house, well, sort of a house, it's not really a normal house because sometimes the corridors just go on and on and on, and you wouldn't believe the size of this library – and the books all tell the life stories of real people, I mean, can you believe it? Your whole life written down as a biography... unless you're here, of course, in which case the book just sort of keeps writing itself. We think this is probably because we're out of time here... as in 'outside' of time, of course, not out of time as in 'run out of time' because hopefully that's not the case, or maybe it is? I hope not, obviously, but then you wouldn't believe the creatures here, we've just been infested with bookworms the size of babies, one of them bit me – do you want to see? Course you don't, why would you want to see that? You just want to get back on your feet again, don't you? We're going to try and find a way out of here and you're only too welcome to join us, more the merrier! As I said, Carruthers is a famous explorer so that's got to be good – if anyone stands a chance of getting us out of here it's him, don't you think? Of course, you couldn't really say, could you? You haven't even met him. Maybe you could say you've heard of him though as he really is terribly sweet and I just know it would mean the world to him. Not that I know him that well myself, or Miles, but sometimes you just have to trust, don't you? When you're in trouble – and we are certainly in trouble – then you need to band together and rely on each other. That's what I think anyway. Oh dear God, I'm talking and talking, I've started wittering, haven't I? I'm so sorry, it must be the nerves, it's just all started flooding out. Maybe it's because you've got kind eyes?"

"Or maybe just that I can't interrupt?" the old man said with a half-smile. "I can feel my legs."

"Oh, that's wonderful!" Penelope wanted to climb into one of the bigger books and slam it closed on her silly waffling face. "Do you think you can sit up yet?"

"I can certainly try," he said. With a groan and a lot of help from Penelope he managed to get himself upright.

"Back in the land of the living, eh?" asked Carruthers as he stepped over.

"On my way, I think," the old man replied.

"Splendid, Roger Carruthers, explorer, adventurer, diarist..."

"I've heard of you, of course," the old man replied, not acknowledging Penelope's smile as he did so, "though I must admit I haven't read your work. My apologies."

"Oh, don't be silly, dear chap," Carruthers replied, quite beside himself with glee, "never enough hours in the day, eh? Why, if you could only see the books piled in my study that have waited years for my attentions."

"Miles Caulfield," said Miles, having also joined them. He extended his hand and the old man made a valiant effort to return the gesture, Penelope supporting his elbow in the end so he could at least brush Miles' hand with his own.

"Pleased to meet you."

"And you are?" hinted Carruthers.

"Oh... Gregory Ashe, forgive me, it's just..."

"Disorientating," Penelope said, "we quite understand, don't we?" She looked at Miles and Carruthers.

"Naturally, you must have a lot of questions."

Ashe smiled. "I think Miss Simons here must have answered any it were possible to have!"

"I did go on rather," Penelope admitted.

"Well, I'm sure she can continue in the same vein," Carruthers continued. "You must forgive us but Miles and I need to continue preparations for our journey. As Penelope may have mentioned we are planning to find a way out of this most unnatural imprisonment and you are only too welcome to join us in our efforts."

"Thank you," Ashe replied.

"Not at all." Carruthers gave a half bow and tugged on Miles' sleeve to ensure he followed him.

"Seems all right, I suppose," Miles muttered as they walked away.

"Really?" Carruthers said, leading Miles into the next row of stacks, "I found him deeply unconvincing personally. A man wakes up in the middle of an impossibly large library surrounded by strangers. Do you expect me to believe he simply accepts he has been transported through a box to a magic house? And 'My dear fellow, don't worry, we're all your very best friends, why don't you join us on our mission to find a way home?'"

"Perhaps he's just trusting?"

"Trusting? He'd have to be mentally subnormal, if you will forgive the vernacular."

"So why did you invite him to join us then?"

"All the better to keep an eye on the fellow."

Carruthers was walking at a hell of a pace and Miles was struggling to keep up. "Expedition started already?" he asked, sarcastically.

"Just a little research," Carruthers replied, running

his fingers along the bookshelves as he searched for the right section.

"Ah…" said Miles, "thought you'd read up on him, eh?"

"Aha!" Carruthers climbed three rows off the ground and began yanking books from the shelf, scanning the last page and then piling them at the far end.

"But how can you tell which one is him?" Miles asked. "It's not as if we know anything about him, is it?"

"We know enough," Carruthers replied. "If he's in this house then his book will be in a state of flux, updating itself as the new experiences happen." He was speeding through the books, scanning them and slapping them to one side. He grabbed a stack of them and dropped them down to Miles. "Would you mind? I'd rather he wasn't left alone with Miss Simons any longer than absolutely necessary."

"Oh! I hadn't thought of that. You really think he might be dangerous?"

"Penelope's a strong woman and I have no doubt she can look after herself, especially now that he's not armed." He gestured to Miles to start checking the books. "I just think it's best to apply a little caution."

"He certainly looks as if a strong wind would knock him for six."

"Indeed… no, none of these." Carruthers climbed up another shelf and started checking more of the books. "Whatever the truth behind our Mister 'Ashe' we cannot afford to delay our departure for any longer than absolutely necessary. We want to get as far as we can before the next nightfall – it is perilous enough without that to contend with."

"Do you have any idea where we're going?"

"Some, I have explored a good deal of this place in my time here – well, I assume it's a good deal, who knows how big the house really is?" He waved the thought away. "No point thinking like that, won't get us anywhere. I've explored extensively and certainly know a lot of routes we should avoid. If I am right in that this library is a central hub for our prison then one of the crossing places accessed from here should set us on our way. By avoiding all the routes I know lead nowhere we have a solid start."

"You'll forgive me if I say that doesn't sound dreadfully hopeful."

Carruthers shrugged. "It's not very hopeful at all, but we'll never find a way home by any other means. Any luck?"

"Hmm? Oh… the books, no, they all seem normal." Miles smiled. "How quickly we adapt our attitudes – there's nothing remotely normal about any of them."

"Man is the great evolutionary animal," Carruthers said, working his way through the last few volumes, "we can adapt to anything." He slammed the final book shut. "None of them. Can't say I'm surprised but at least we now know one thing about our new addition."

"Really? Seems to me we're utterly in the dark."

"We know for a fact he's a liar, and for now that will have to be enough."

"Just wait until I confront him!"

"Let's see what he's about first, shall we? I'd rather have him with us than behind us. We shall keep him close and, as long as we retain our wits, we shall learn his secrets soon enough."

On their return, Ashe was pacing up and down to shake out a few twitches and kinks in his legs.

"Feeling better?" asked Miles.

"Much," Ashe replied, "and relieved that I had you guys to keep an eye on me. I would have hated to be here on my own."

"We can certainly show you the ropes," Carruthers said, "keep you on the straight and narrow."

"Sounds like I'll need it if everything Penelope says is true."

"It's true," she assured him.

"How can it be possible, do you think?" Ashe asked, looking at Carruthers.

"I am at a loss to say," he replied, "and until we unearth its secrets the best we can do is accept that it *is* and keep on our toes. We should continue further discussion as we travel. As Miss Simons may have explained, the nights here are treacherous and it would certainly be in our favour to get some miles beneath our feet before dark."

"Nighttime, inside a house!" Ashe exclaimed. "It's crazy!"

"I'll remind you of those words come dusk, my friend. Now, I have rucksacks for us all. We should fill them with as much food and water as we can carry and little else. We need to travel quickly and safely, that is best done by travelling lightly."

"That means only one shirt apparently," Penelope said to Ashe.

"Well," he replied, "I have nothing but the clothes I stand in and I guess I'm happy to keep it that way as long as nobody minds the smell."

"If something smells suspect about you, sir, I have yet to notice!" said Carruthers, laughing.

They were ready within ten minutes, Carruthers organizing them as he distributed the essential supplies. They bulked their packs out with a light selection of spare clothing. Carruthers presented a map that he had sketched over his time in the house. It looked more like a family tree, the library at the centre surrounded by linked boxes filled with scribbled descriptions of what the rooms contained.

"'Jungle Hothouse', 'Play Room (beware of snakes)', 'Bathroom (need dinghy)'." Miles scratched his head. "My, but I'm looking forward to exploring further."

"If it's any consolation they're all places we won't be going," explained Carruthers.

"Erm... nope," Miles replied, "no consolation at all."

"Which way do we head first?" asked Penelope.

"We need to aim for the eastern wing of the library," Carruthers said, leading them off between the stacks. "All four corners of the room contain access to other parts of the house and I have tried to be methodical in my exploration thus far. I am convinced that the route to freedom does not lie in any of the other three corners."

"Why?" Ashe asked.

"Because I've been through each and every discernable access point in them and am still not at liberty." Carruthers smiled. "My being here is your proof of their inefficacy."

"Good enough!" Ashe replied with a grin. He tipped his hat back on his head, looking at the books around them. "Never imagined there could be so many books in the world," he said.

"Was Miss Simons good enough to explain what they contain?" Carruthers asked.

"Indeed she was, unbelievable…"

"Were you not tempted to seek out your own volume?"

"I'm not the kind of guy that sneaks a peek at the last chapter of a mystery, I believe life should be a surprise."

"An admirable attitude," Carruthers agreed, "I have no doubt this house will help you maintain it."

After a couple of hours walking with the view not substantially altered, Miles began to grow concerned. "This reminds me of a certain corridor you and I enjoyed for what seemed like a couple of years," he said to Penelope.

"Don't worry," Carruthers assured him, "the library isn't infinite, just incredibly large. We shall reach the end in another few hours."

"A library where you should bring your car if you wish to browse," Miles muttered.

"Car?" asked Carruthers.

"Automobile… horseless carriage, whatever you used to call them."

"Oh… don't tell me those silly things took off."

"They were moderately successful, yes," Miles replied with a grin.

The horizon soon began to alter, the far wall coming into view.

"So how do you find the exit?" Penelope asked once they had reached the end of the room.

"I used to throw books around until one of them vanished. Now that we know the books and their subjects are linked, that seems somewhat unethical. I'd hate to be responsible for someone in the real world having a breakdown because I was hurling his biography around. I thought these would be just as successful." He removed his pack and pulled out a bag of golf balls. "I liberated them from a golf bag in one of the bedrooms, thinking the odd round or two might while away an evening."

"How did that work out?" asked Penelope.

"Terrible, I couldn't aim if my life depended on it. Besides, thrashing a ball around a library really isn't all that entertaining."

Carruthers dipped his hand into the bag and began tossing the balls into the air, like a farmer sowing fat seeds. The balls ricocheted off the walls forcing them to duck.

"It's not a very exact science," Carruthers said apologetically. "I know there's an entrance about six foot up the wall directly facing the stack but I've used that one and have no great desire to expose you all to the terrors of the broom cupboard."

"Tell me you're joking," said Miles

"I cannot recommend getting into a fight with an army of mops, dear boy, they can be quite vicious."

"He's joking," Miles muttered, "I refuse to believe he isn't joking."

"There's one!" Ashe shouted, "the ball just vanished."

"Where?" Carruthers asked. "I wasn't throwing–"

"It was your last ball," he replied, moving towards the wall and dropping to his hands and knees, "it bounced off the bookshelves and rolled towards the wainscoting. It vanished here." He stuck out his hand and it vanished up to the wrist, moving through the wooden panelling as if it were water.

"Excellent!" Carruthers walked over to join him. "This is a completely unknown exit, most promising."

"Did she warn you about the wraiths?" Miles asked Ashe.

"No, can't say she mentioned anything like that," he replied.

"Every passageway between the areas of the house is protected by a barrier of darkness. The wraiths roam that darkness. They're invisible but you soon spot them once they start smashing you to a pulp."

"Nice. I look forward to making their acquaintance. How do you know how to get beyond the barrier to the other side?"

"You don't."

"Maybe I should have stayed back at the camp after all."

"It's not as bad as all that," Carruthers assured him.

"Really?" asked Penelope incredulously.

"Well," Carruthers looked awkward, "not quite that bad anyway. This time we're not swinging in midair trying to find the entrance below us."

"You have a cunning method then?" Penelope asked.

"It's stood me in good stead on my many trips thus far." Carruthers removed the lantern from the side of his pack, lit it and then strapped his pack back in place. "We use a focused beam from the lantern, noting where the length of it is cut short."

"Of course we do," Miles replied, "in fact that's exactly what I was going to suggest. After you then, 'lad of the lamp'."

"Too kind." Carruthers dropped down in front of the wall and, pushing the lantern in front of him, wriggled through the exit.

"We need to follow quickly," Miles said to Ashe as Penelope vanished from sight.

"After you, son, by all means," Ashe replied with a wide smile.

"Wouldn't dream of it," said Miles, "I'll take the rear."

"Whatever you say." Ashe dropped to the floor and crawled through the wall.

"Yeah," Miles muttered, following on, "you keep that up and we'll all get on just fine."

On the other side, Carruthers was on his feet and sweeping the lantern beam through the darkness, Penelope stood at his shoulder.

Ashe got to his feet and looked around. "Not much to see," he commented, straightening his hat from where it had slipped during his crawl.

"You may look back on this as your favourite part of the journey," Miles replied, shuffling his pack so that it sat straight.

"There!" Carruthers shouted pointing to their left. He swayed the lantern beam to prove it, the light truncating measurably as it fell on the area he was pointing at.

"Get on with it then," said Penelope giving him a shove, "I can feel those things coming." They ran through.

Miles nudged Ashe to follow them, but the old man made a show of being in no rush whatsoever. "Just taking in the sights, son," he said with a wink.

"If you don't get a bloody move on they'll be the last sights you see!" Miles pushed him through the exit, striding after and coming to a startled halt on the other side. "You have *got* to be shitting me," he whispered as he took in what lay ahead.

He turned around. Behind him was a wood-panelled wall, an embroidered recliner, a stand-alone ashtray and a small bookcase containing a selection of Dickens and Brontë. Perfectly normal. He turned back again… ahead was a snow-covered mountain, its peak vanishing into white cloud. A few feet from where they stood snow lay on the floorboards, thickening the further you entered the room. "Welcome to bloody Narnia, Miles," he whispered. "Hope you remembered to pack the Turkish Delight."

CHAPTER FIFTEEN

The stranger led the way, with Elise, Pablo and, finally, Tom following. One of the cherubs nipped at his hair as he vanished beneath the flagstone floor and into the darkness of a winding staircase.

"Close the hatch!" the stranger shouted, "or we'll have the damned things in here with us."

Tom did as he was told, yanking a rusted chain that pulled a slab into place above his head. "Cool," he muttered. "Confined space, plenty of darkness, lovin' it."

The stairs wound tightly against wet brick, a constant, metallic percussion of dripping water beating time for them as they descended. A warm glow of firelight began to pour itself up the staircase as they drew close to their destination: a large chamber of sooty brick lit by flickering sconces.

"Nice, medieval chic," Elise commented.

"It's gloomy as hell," the stranger agreed, "but lacking in anything trying to kill you, for now at least." He was young, American and well-dressed in a pinstripe suit with wide lapels and shoulders you could launch a seaplane from. He stuck his hand out for shaking. "My friends call me Chester."

"A man that saves my life is the best friend in the world, Chester," Tom replied, shaking Chester's hand. "Tom."

"Goes the same for me," said Elise, giving him a peck on the cheek to go with the handshake, "and my name's Elise."

"I am surrounded by America," said Pablo with a smile, "and still no cowboy hat! I am Pablo, thank you for shooting flying babies."

"No problem at all," Chester replied with a smile, "I was on my way to the kitchen to stock up on food – can't say I expected company."

"Ah…" Tom shifted awkwardly, "we may have broken the dumb waiter if that was your ride."

"It is because he is so fat," explained Pablo, pointing at the stick-thin Tom without a hint of sarcasm.

"Well, that might complicate things in future," Chester admitted,. "I guess we'll just have to hope there's another way in there."

"How long have you been here?" asked Elise. "You're obviously an old hand at all this."

"A couple of months," Chester replied. "I've been staying on the move, spending a lot of time in the cellars. Grim it may be but at least you can move around easily. There's elevators and passageways everywhere that lead up to the house."

"Great, we love the house" said Tom, "especially the killer snakes and the cannibal in the kitchen… hey, you bump into him?"

"Little feller? Moustache? Yeah… I met him."
Chester held up the gun. "I dissuaded him from feeling too hungry around me."

"We found a frying pan did the same trick," Tom
admitted, "though the bastard stuck me a good one
in the leg."

"Noticed you were limping. Lucky escape, huh?"

"Not as lucky as these two without bleeding thighs
and shooting pains whenever they walk."

"He's a baby about it," said Elise with a wink.

"Always making with the moanings," Pablo added,
"like a kind of girl."

"Still," said Chester, grinning at Tom, "with such
good friends it can't have been too bad?"

"Walk in the park, feel free to shoot them at any
time."

Chester smiled, a thick veneer of charm that
would hide anything. "Shall we get moving?" he
suggested "I have, well… guess you could call it a
camp, about an hour away, we could gather up my
stuff and travel on together."

"Sounds like a plan," said Elise. "Please tell me you
know there's a way out of here…"

"Oh, I'm sure there must be. If you can get in, you
can get out, right?"

"If you say so," Elise replied. "We haven't seen
much of the place but it all seems designed to make
your stay permanent."

"This place is like one of those old commercial
warehouses," said Tom, as they made their way
through several brick arches and countless open

areas. "You know, those dockland dives you see in old movies? The kind of place you expect smugglers to be working from until The Shadow turns up and shoots 'em all."

"'Who knows what evil lurks in the hearts of men?'" Chester quipped. "The cellars stretch on like you wouldn't believe. You could build a whole city down here if it wasn't for the wildlife."

"Please tell me he didn't just say 'wildlife'?" Elise sighed, looking around nervously as they crossed the damp concrete of another chamber before entering a winding tunnel to the next section.

"It minds its own business for the most part," said Chester reassuringly, "but you're never far from something unpleasant." He stopped walking and held his hand up for silence. "Listen."

They stood still, the flickering fire from the sconces the only noise they could hear. Then – as either their ears became more sensitive or the creatures around them grew braver – they began to discern other sounds. The faint chattering of insects; the breathy sigh of something fat pulling itself along a wet concrete floor; a rustling of chitinous body parts and the patter of numerous pin-thin legs. Chester reached for one of the torches in the wall, sliding it carefully from its bracket and flinging it towards the darkness at the far end of the chamber. Lit briefly, a group of what appeared to be mammoth woodlice scurried across the brick wall, their white carapaces glittering as they retreated from the light.

"Oh great," said Pablo, "is bugs."

"Bugs, rats, worms, some kind of weird crab things…" Chester shrugged. "They're all down here with us."

"Well, hey," said Tom, "if we can't get back to the kitchen there's always worm steaks."

"I wouldn't like to try and catch one," Chester admitted. "Even with the gun, the things get riled when you move close – defending themselves, I guess. Some of the caterpillars have mouthes on them perfect for chewing a man's hand off."

They carried on walking, the sound of running water growing louder as they passed through yet another tunnel.

"There some kind of river down here?" Elise asked.

"There's a whole network of them," Chester said, "sewerage canals, I guess, though they don't smell too bad. We'll be travelling on them in a minute."

"You have a boat?" Pablo asked.

"A little motorboat, yeah. I found it moored up when I first got down here, wouldn't be without it." No sooner had Chester spoken than they entered another section, the rushing canal mere feet away. The boat was tethered up, bobbing impatiently on the water.

"All aboard," Chester said, untying the rope and beckoning the others to climb in. The boat rocked as Tom clambered in, trying not to put all his weight on his wounded leg. Elise steadied him before he fell overboard. "Thanks," he muttered. "A swim in this is about all I need to polish the day off."

"You are not used to water," said Pablo, hopping in and sitting down at the front.

"I'm used to it just fine, even drunk a glass or two in my time."

"Now that I find hard to believe," Elise joked as Chester climbed aboard, flung the rope on to the deck and turned on the ignition.

"It doesn't go that fast," he said, "but it sure beats walking."

The boat chugged along the canal, dipping into a low tunnel that threw the throaty sound of the engine back at them. "We should pick up my stuff and then get straight on," suggested Chester. "Maybe find some food from somewhere. There's a jungle in the greenhouse, there must be something there worth eating."

"Jungle in the greenhouse," Elise repeated, "cannibals in the kitchen, snakes and ladders in the nursery, God save us from the men's room."

The boat re-emerged into open space, moving through a cavernous chamber with a single sack marked "almonds" in the centre of it.

"Nut stocks getting low," Tom commented as they dipped back into a tunnel.

The geography of the cellars was as skewed as everywhere else; the canal twisted in a manner that should have seen it bending back on itself and yet somehow it never crossed its own path. They passed through chambers of varying sizes, most empty, some home to scurrying insects, some containing boxes or sacks. One was set out like a bathroom:

steel bath and stand-alone shower, toilet, bidet and sink, all unplumbed and wrapped in cobwebs.

"You find anything of use down here?" Tom asked.

"Sometimes," Chester replied, "but mostly it's just junk. I found a big crate of torches, for example, but no batteries to go in them. More cutlery than an army would know what to do with… a whole bunch of pink shirts about six sizes too big for me… weird stuff, no rhyme or reason to it."

"That's this place all over, isn't it?" said Elise.

"Oh no, the house has a purpose, I'm quite sure of that," Chester replied. "I refuse to believe there's not some underlying reason for every room or corridor. This isn't a natural occurrence, it's been built… though God knows how, the physics is screwy as hell… still, someone or something has made this place. Why? Got to be a reason."

"Everywhere's designed to screw with you," said Tom, "like the Snakes and Ladders, it was a game… not a very groovy one but there to test the poor mooks who stumbled on to it."

"Test or kill?" asked Chester. "I'd say they were more defences than games. Everything's out to kill you."

"Is true," Pablo agreed, "is not good but is true."

"You know how many people I've met here before you three?" Chester asked.

"Including Chef Boyardee?" Tom replied, " I don't know… if we're here there must be plenty more."

"Four people and I know for a fact that two of those are dead because I saw it happen – never trust the broom cupboards in this place. Still, as you say, there must be one hell of a lot of people who end up here – we did, right? So where are they all? Dead, that's where. I reckon most folk are toes up within a few hours of arriving here."

"But why bring people here just to kill them?" Elise asked. "Maybe I'm just not enough of a psycho but that doesn't make sense to me."

"I don't know," said Chester, "I guess it could just be sport, something to amuse whoever built the place. Either that or it's just a bad design."

"Meaning?"

"Meaning the box is designed to bring someone in particular here – someone specific – but it can't pick or choose so it just keeps grabbing until it has what it needs. Kind of like fishing for tuna with a net the size of Cleveland: you'll get your tuna but you'll get a hell of a lot of other stuff as well."

"The scattershot method," said Elise.

"Exactly. It's just a theory, of course, but it's logical, and however illogical this place may seem there's a point underneath it all somewhere. And if there's a point there's ultimately logic…"

"You're kind of an analytical feller, ain't you?" said Tom with a grin.

"I've thought about it a lot," Chester admitted. "I like to know what I'm dealing with in life. Besides, if all of this is being done for a reason there must be something to gain, and I'm a man that never gets tired of gain." He smiled unselfconsciously as the boat vanished into a tunnel. The roof was particularly low, only just allowing clearance for the boat and its passengers. The sides scuffed against the wall as they pushed their way through the darkness. After a moment, the sound of wood against brick increased as the tunnel narrowed even further. Tom, the tallest, had to duck as the roof began to knock his head.

"Wrong turn, you think?" he said, stooping so that he didn't graze his scalp.

"It's like this sometimes," Chester admitted, "the house gets all turned around and the routes change. We'll just have to work our way back." He cut the accelerator and applied reverse power, and after a few seconds the boat began to scuff the sides again.

"Now how is that possible?" asked Elise. "You telling me the tunnel has narrowed since we've been through it?"

"I told you, this sort of thing happens," said Chester. "The house likes to shuffle itself around. It rights itself in the end."

"I hope so as we very stuck!" said Pablo.

Chester killed the engine and the boat bobbed in the small middle section where, for now, it continued to fit. "Let's just hope this bit doesn't shrink," he said.

"Oh, yeah," said Tom, still hunched, "because it's bound to be the one tiny section that stays wide enough for us to move in... this from Mr. Logic."

As they were speaking the boat began to bounce off the edges. "It get less wide here too!" Pablo shouted.

"What if it gets too narrow to fit us, let alone the boat?" Elise said. "We need to get out of here, swim back to the last open section."

"I'm not abandoning the boat," Chester insisted.

"Don't be stupid," she replied, "either it'll get crushed in here or it won't. There's nothing you're going to be able do about it one way or the other. There's sure as hell no point sitting around to watch it happen."

"I am not stupid!" Chester shouted, his charm giving way to a childish anger now that he was losing control of the situation.

"Keep it chilly, Chester," said Tom, "the lady's got a point."

Chester controlled himself. "You're right," he admitted, "sorry I snapped."

"Don't worry about it," Elise answered, "but I'm serious that we need to move." She reached out her hands. "The tunnel's about the same size as the boat now and shrinking all the time."

"Oh, I hope this not smell," said Pablo, clambering off the stern of the boat and dropping into the water. "It fine," he said, splashing around, "bit cool but fine."

Tom rolled in afterwards, hitting the water with a shocked roar. "'Bit cool', he says! It's colder than a well-digger's ass."

Elise came next and finally Chester. They began to swim back the way they had come, the creaking of the compressed boat behind them filling the tunnel.

"Maybe it'll be OK," said Elise, "and we can swim back to it?" There was a loud cracking noise as the wood and fibreglass split and the boat began to fold in on itself.

"It not all right," said Pablo, swimming faster.

The further they went, the narrower the tunnel became. Tom's fingertips began brushing the walls on either side, forcing him to change stroke.

"We're not going to get clear," said Elise. All four of them were performing a thrashing doggy paddle; the tunnel was no wider than the breadth of their shoulders.

"Keep moving!" Tom shouted, turning on his side as the tunnel narrowed further.

It became harder and harder to move. All four of them were sideways on, squeezed tightly by the brick. Suddenly, the wall stopped moving. They floated there in relieved silence for a few seconds.

"How lucky are we, eh?" said Tom. "An inch more and I'd be popped all over this damn place."

"Another one of Chester's dead unfortunates."

"Shush," Pablo hissed, "there is something in here with us."

"Oh, fuck off..." Tom whined, "this is not even funny any more."

They listened and, true enough, there was the sound of something moving through the water from the direction they had come.

"Well, at least there's one thing we know about whatever it is," said Elise.

"Which is?" Chester asked.

"Given the size of the tunnel it ain't huge."

They continued pulling themselves towards the entrance. Over the sound of their own splashing they could hear whatever it was that pursued them: it sounded like a wet sound of applause, a rippled clapping.

"Is it in the water?" Elise asked. "Sounds like it's moving across the brick rather than swimming."

"Who knows?" Tom replied. "Let's get out of here before we have to find out!"

To their right the mouth of the tunnel became clear, the flickering of torchlight showing they were only a few metres away. Performing a weird, crab-like dance, they thrashed faster and faster. Pablo, still in the lead, pulled himself clear of the tunnel, turning around to help Tom then Elise.

"It's right on top of me!" Chester was shouting as both Tom and Pablo grabbed hold of him and yanked him out. He wasn't wrong: the creature that had pursued them had hold of Chester's other arm, and was emerging into the light. Its wide gelatinous face was pulled back on either side by the bricks, like a plastic surgeon's hands eager to cinch the deal. There was something of both amphibian and human ancestry to it. Its skin was off-white, like a glass of milk on sixty cigarettes a day. The eyes were much bigger than any eyes have a right to be, rolling around in sockets that held them as fast as holes in mud grip a stray foot. The mouth wasn't smiling, however unnaturally wide it stretched, and the teeth looked no more solid than gristle or single grains from a sieved rice pudding. Apart from these characteristics the rest of the physiognomy was recognisably human: a man that had been left in the water too long, perhaps, wrinkled and bloated all at the same time. Tom put it best when he said, "What the fuck is that!"

"I can tell you what it isn't," said Elise from behind him. "Lonely."

They turned around. The creatures were everywhere, climbing, swimming, running… all heading towards them.

INTERLUDE

"Well, I can't see that Scotland's worth the fuss, if I'm honest," says the renegade, washing the words down with some particularly foul wine. He holds the liquid in his mouth for a moment, analysing its composition and seeing what could be done to improve it. Deciding that there are limits to even his abilities he swallows the drink and vows to avoid it in future. "It's cold and filled with men that shriek as much as their women. Unless you think it possible to cut the damn thing off and push it out into the ocean I would suggest your attention is better spent elsewhere."

"If only that were possible, my friend," the young Edward replies, scratching at the thin beard he wears to add authority to a youthful face, "but a King needs to remind people of his strength. Wars are fought on principle as much as for acquisition."

"My liege!" A messenger runs into the hall, remembering to bow deeply before delivering his news. "We have reports of French ships off the south coast."

Edward sighs. "Not the French again…"

"Need I remind you of Philip's statement when he reclaimed Aquitaine, your majesty?" asks the renegade with a smile. "I think it's time you reminded the phlegmy bastards who their sovereign is."

"I suppose there's nothing like a good war to keep the spirits high," admits Edward.

"Indeed," replies the renegade, "and something tells me this one could run and run…"

CHAPTER SIXTEEN

It grew colder the further they walked, the untrodden snow punctuated by misplaced household furniture. An easy chair sagged under an extra cushion, an icy antimacassar glittering on its back. A standard lamp offered a pool of light within which fauns might loiter. A dessert trolley rested – rather disconcertingly – in the centre of a swirl of concentric circles that its coasters had made in the snow. There were no footsteps to be seen so one could only assume it had danced around under its own steam.

"Bet you're in your element, aren't you?" Miles said, grimacing at Carruthers as he trudged through the snow. "Probably start dancing with joy if there's a snowstorm later."

Carruthers marched with conviction, each stride twice the length of Miles'. The latter had to canter in order to keep up.

"I am at home on the ice, yes," Carruthers admitted, "though I worry for Miss Simons' feet, naturally."

They had paused at the doorway so that they might wrap themselves in as many layers of spare clothing as they could and improvise some more suitable footwear for Penelope. On each foot she was now wearing four pairs of socks and three pillowcases, so that her legs looked like a turkey's, white-capped for display on the carvery table.

"They're probably warmer than mine," Miles moaned. "Trainers aren't suited for snow."

"They are very silly shoes," Carruthers agreed. "I can't understand why you wear them – they're quite impractical and, if you'll forgive me saying so, look rather foolish."

"All the rage where I come from, pal," said Miles, "an era in which, 'if you'll forgive me saying so,' you would have looked a right tit."

"A bird? Save me from the future, it's like a foreign country."

"'They do things differently there.'"

"Clearly so."

"It's a quote."

"Probably from one of your silly future books… 'they do things differently in the future'… hardly Shakespeare, is it?"

"The quote's actually… oh, never mind, it's hardly important." He looked up at the mountain ahead. "How tall do you think that is?"

"Compared to the peaks of Tibet it's a mere foothill."

"Oh yes, we'll be up it in half an hour."

"We'll be fine."

"Including Ashe, it would seem," said Miles. "He's pretty spry for an old guy."

Ashe was walking alongside Penelope a few feet behind them. It was clear that he was slowing his pace for her sake rather than the other way around.

"We'll see how he manages with the altitude," said Carruthers, "that's the real challenge on a trek like this."

"Foothill my arse."

"They are very crude in the future too, I have noticed, always talking about their rumps."

"Don't come the puritan with me, the Victorians were a filthy bunch."

"I can assure you I am entirely pure. My body is slave to my mind, not the reverse as seems the case with you."

"Oh, my body's slaved to my mind too, it's the things the mind makes it want to do that are the problem."

"Most amusing."

"Mind you, in this temperature it doesn't want to do a thing. Be like trying to knock a nail in with an overcooked broad bean."

"Dear Lord, save me from this man's corrupting influence…"

The ground began to rise as they approached the mountain, their calf and thigh muscles aching and their pace slowing.

"Not exactly what I expected," Ashe commented, his hands shoved deep in his pockets as he tried to keep them warm.

"I've thought that at every step so far in this house," Penelope replied. "What next? Volcanoes in the coal scuttle?"

Ashe chuckled. "An ocean in the bathroom?"

"Exactly, filled with tropical fish."

"I like sailing. I'd prefer it to a trek like this."

"You don't appear to be struggling much."

"I try and keep fit."

"Obviously, you make me look like a sloven."

"I have the benefit of shoes, it makes quite a difference."

"Actually my feet are incredibly comfortable, warm and padded – they're the only part of me that's enjoying themselves."

"Perhaps I should try the same method," Ashe muttered, "I think my toes are snapping off one by one."

It took them an hour or so to reach the base of the mountain. Carruthers clambered up into the rocks, surveying the trail that lay ahead.

"Aha," he shouted, brushing at a ridge in the snow to reveal a thick wooden banister, "I think I've found the way up." He squatted down, continuing to sweep away the snow. What had looked like undulations in the rock were in fact stairs.

"Well," said Ashe, "that should make things easier."

"You wouldn't think that if you'd ever walked to street level from the platform of Covent Garden tube," replied Miles.

"I have!" Ashe replied. "Never use an elevator when stairs will do."

"The man's mad," Miles muttered, "absolutely insane."

"Or simply fitter than you," Penelope said with a smug smile.

"Yes," Miles said, "thank you for noticing that."

They began to climb the stairs, Carruthers leading the way. To begin with, the climb seemed easy enough. The snow blurred the definition between the stairs but the banister was a useful guide and they found their rhythm. After a while their legs began to ache, and the effort to keep lifting them slowed their pace to a crawl.

"My legs are going numb," said Penelope, "they keep wobbling."

"Your muscles are cramping," Carruthers replied. "We'll stop and rest in a minute, just a few more steps."

They climbed in silence, each of them too breathless to talk. Miles had to grab the banister tightly for fear of toppling. His legs jerked beneath him. The tops of his thighs pulsed with muscle pain, the only sensation in limbs that otherwise felt no part of him. "No good," he huffed, "have to stop." He sat down on one of the steps, his head dropping between his shaking legs as he tried to slow his breathing. The others followed suit, only too happy to rest.

"We have barely even begun," said Carruthers after a few moments, "though, believe me, I wish I could say otherwise."

"Any worthwhile journey is hard," commented Ashe.

"That's all right then," said Miles, "I'll think of that while enjoying my coronary."

"We will take it slowly," said Carruthers. "Tackle a short section, rest, then tackle another."

"How long do you think it's going to take?" asked Penelope.

"I wouldn't like to say, my dear."

"Days," said Ashe, "at least two, more likely three."

"I'm not sure I can bear the thought of sitting on a mountain for three days," said Miles. "How about we pop back through to the library and see if we can't find a door that's less crippling?"

"No," said Ashe, "this is the right way."

"How would you know?" scoffed Miles "With all due respect, mate, you've only just got here, so maybe you're not quite the expert, eh?"

"Don't be horrible, Miles!" Penelope snapped.

"It's all right," Ashe said to her, "he's right. But I feel this is the right way."

"Perhaps you might feel your way towards giving me a piggyback then?" Miles replied.

"Miles!" Penelope turned to him. "Why are you being so beastly to Gregory? It's hardly his fault, is it?"

Miles looked at Carruthers, who had sat in silence throughout. He gave no sign of having heard the conversation. Sighing, Miles held up his hands. "Sorry," he said, "I'm just tired and pissed off, I don't mean to take it out on anyone."

"I should think not," scolded Penelope.

"Please," said Ashe, "it's fine. You've been through a lot, I quite understand. Maybe we should just go back…?"

"No," said Carruthers, finally snapping his eyes away from the distant wall of the room. "We'll go on." He got to his feet and continued to climb. They hiked for several hours, breaking the steps up into small batches and taking regular breaks.

"We need to find somewhere to shelter," Ashe suggested after a while. "Get our strength back."

"We weren't prepared for this," Penelope added. "Walking through the house… that's one thing. This…"

"Ashe is right," said Carruthers, "we need shelter."

"Yeah… not a lot of that about," Miles said, rubbing at his aching chest.

"Let's go on a little further," Ashe suggested. "When we get around the next bend we might see somewhere."

"Or we might not," said Miles.

"No harm in trying," Carruthers said, "a few more minutes won't kill us."

"Speak for yourself," Penelope replied.

They got back to their feet and followed the stairs a short distance. They worked their way around a fold in the mountain, entering a shallow groove in the landscape. There was a forceful wind blowing by now, stirring the dry powder of the snow into eddies that danced around their feet as they pulled themselves further on. The recess allowed them a small amount of cover but Carruthers knew it wouldn't be enough to protect them while they camped. They had their bedrolls and a few sheets that he had intended to rig up as a tent but in these conditions they needed greater protection if they wanted to survive the night.

"There!" shouted Ashe, pointing to a circle of darkness in the cliff face ahead.

Carruthers smiled and forged on with renewed energy. "A cave!" he shouted, above the increasing wind, "a perfect place to rest for the night."

Within a few minutes they were out of the wind. Carruthers lit a lantern and walked ahead to see how far the cave extended. "Come in!" he shouted, beckoning the rest of them away from the daylight. "You might be pleasantly surprised!"

The narrow tunnel opened into a furnished cavern. An embroidered *chaise-longue* rested its curved feet against the tufts of a bearskin rug. Two sofas proffered their fat cushions to the weary travellers and a large wrought-iron grate sat – prepared to be lit – at the end closest to the exit. "All the home comforts!" Carruthers announced. "There's even a gramophone!" He wound the machine up, then dropped the heavy brass-mounted needle on to a crackling Ennio Morricone record. A narrow passage extended deeper into the mountain and Carruthers went exploring.

"Am I the only one who finds this somewhat disconcerting?" Miles asked.

"You said yourself: there's no accounting for logic in this place," said Ashe, dropping on to the *chaise-longue* with a relaxed sigh. "Don't look a gift horse in the mouth."

"Well," said Penelope, "there's no doubt we wouldn't last the night out there, so I don't see we have much choice."

"Quite right, my dear," said Carruthers, returning to the cave. "The passage extends a few feet beyond here but then is blocked. There's no danger of someone sneaking up on us from that direction." He looked baffled at the strange whistling noises and Sixties kitsch coming from the gramophone. "People listen to this, do they?" he asked Miles.

"Not many," Miles admitted, "but I rather like it – he wrote a lot of good stuff for Spaghetti Westerns."

"Only you know what you're talking about, darling," said Penelope, lying back on one of the sofas, her feet propped up on the arm.

"*The Good, the Bad and the Ugly, Django, Il Grande Silenzio*," listed Ashe, miming a gun with his fingers at Miles. "Corbucci was good but Leone was king."

"Yes!" enthused Miles, "*Once Upon a Time in the West*! That opening... The flies, the harmonica... Bronson when he was still cool."

"Bronson was always cool."

"Without wanting to interrupt your social club, gentlemen," said Penelope, "might we have the fire lit?"

"Oh," said Miles, embarrassed by his enthusiasm, "yes, of course."

Ashe chuckled and closed his eyes as if to doze.

"Here," said Carruthers, throwing Miles the matches. "Is there enough wood, do you think?"

"Erm, should be," Miles said, before catching Carruthers' eye and realising the man wanted a private word, "though I suppose there's no harm in checking outside… in case there's any more close to hand."

"Allow me," said Ashe, opening his eyes and swinging his legs off the *chaise-longue*.

"Wouldn't hear of it," said Carruthers. "You looked about to drop off. Rest a moment. Miles and I are perfectly capable."

Miles stepped back from the crackling fire, dropping the match into the grate. "Absolutely, I could do with stretching my legs!" he joked.

"Warm up for a minute first," said Penelope. "Stop being so butch."

"More a case of seeing what can be found before night falls, my dear," Carruthers replied. "The darkness cannot be far off."

"Oh, hooray," Penelope replied sarcastically, "the nights are *such* fun here."

"Indeed," Carruthers replied, "all the more reason to ensure we have plenty of light and warmth." He and Miles walked back down the short tunnel and into the open air.

"Worried?" Miles asked.

"Always," Carruthers replied, gesturing to Miles to walk a little further, "but not about our accommodation."

"I don't know," said Miles, shivering against the wind, "all seems a bit convenient to me."

"Oh, it is," Carruthers agreed, "and, more to the point, Ashe knew exactly where to find it."

"What, all that 'this is definitely the right way' and 'let's have a peek around the corner' stuff?"

"Precisely. Our Mr Ashe knows precisely where we're going, don't you think?"

"I had wondered. Bit weird as he's supposedly new here."

"Yes, well, I think we can dismiss that as a notion, he knows far too much." Carruthers began scraping at the snow beneath his feet, looking for vegetation.

"So why are we just going along with it?" Miles asked, following Carruthers' lead and unearthing a tiny root with far more enthusiasm than it deserved.

"That should keep us warm for a second or so," Carruthers remarked, flinging the root away. "I see no reason not to follow his directions for now. He clearly has a destination in mind and it may be one that benefits us all."

"Or it may be a trap."

"Rather a laboured one, surely? Besides, I'm inclined to believe that he had just appeared in the library when we found him."

"He could have snuck in while we were distracted."

"And then lain down amongst the worms to wait for us to wake up? I doubt it – besides, wouldn't Penelope have spotted him?"

"She was rather distracted."

"True. I don't know, you may be right... but my gut tells me that that at least was genuine. And if it was..."

"The only way he could know so much about the place is if he's been here before."

"Precisely: been here, left and then returned. Wouldn't that be interesting?"

"But if that were the case why doesn't he just tell us?"

"Oh, he's playing some devilish game or another, no doubt about that." Carruthers unearthed a wizened bush and began to kick at its root bole to try and loosen it from the ice. "We just have to decide whether it's worth playing along, using his knowledge and keeping on our toes for the moment he turns."

"Sounds like a bloody big risk to me."

"What isn't here? We know nothing, he knows a great deal… I'm fairly certain I haven't the emotional wherewithal to torture the information out of him – what about you?"

"If he keeps chatting Penelope up I might find the odd punch to the testicles in me." Miles wrenched a slender branch from the snow.

"I hardly think he presents a threat on that score," Carruthers replied with a smile. "The man's postively monosyllabic. Nor am I convinced that now is the time for romantic inclinations."

"Oh," blustered Miles, "I wasn't thinking… that is, I haven't…"

"Do be quiet, old chap, it's obvious you like her."

"Well, yes, obviously she's very nice but… look, can we get back to the subject in hand?"

Carruthers nodded. "Those red cheeks of yours should keep you warm out here."

"It's the wind, that's all… oh, shut up." Miles smiled, he couldn't fight his corner and knew it. "OK, so we carry on for now."

"Good, and given that he knew about this place and seems only too happy in it I'm inclined to think it's safe. A logical assumption?"

"I suppose so. Though I'm sleeping with one eye open just in case."

"Then I look forward to seeing how exhausted you are in the morning!" Carruthers looked up. "The sky is beginning to bruise, old chap, what say we take our meagre stock of firewood inside and see about some dinner?"

They returned to the cave, dumping their pathetic supply of sticks next to a fire that crackled its contempt.

"Well," said Penelope, "as long as we're all agreed that was worth it."

"The ice was just too thick," said Miles. "It was like trying to grab things off a shop shelf from the wrong side of the window."

"I'm sure the fire will last," said Ashe. "It's been burning solidly for a while but you wouldn't know it to look at the wood."

"As long as it makes its presence felt on our victuals as surely as it does on our bones," said Carruthers, "might I suggest we prepare some food?"

"And what choice delights await us this evening?" asked Penelope. "Did we pack a rack of lamb? I forget. Or perhaps a little beef filet?"

"Beans with little sausages in!" Miles announced rifling through the tins, "I bloody love those!"

They heated a tin each, Carruthers insisting that they needed to fill their bellies if they hoped to climb a respectable distance the next day. After their meal was done, Penelope put the gramophone to use again, shimmying to the sounds of Sixties jazz. The music was incongruous but certainly didn't care, guitars and flutes bouncing off the cave walls without the least concern. Ashe closed his eyes, appearing to sleep despite the music. Following his example, Carruthers begged exhaustion and bedded down shortly after. Within a few minutes his snoring was competing with Ashe's.

"Well," sighed Penelope, turning off the music, "they sure know how to kill a party."

"Oh yes, the canapés, the conversation, the constant threat of bears sneaking in and biting our faces off."

"Well, you're a morbid chap this evening," Penelope said with a smile.

"Not at all, actually," Miles admitted, rooting around in his pack for the box of cigars Carruthers had demanded he leave behind due to their being "utterly inessential". "I did all my wishing for death before coming here. I'm now determined to live an obscenely long life…" he held up his cigar "…and I'm sure this will help. Want to come and stand in the doorway and watch me smoke it?"

"Watch you? I'll join you… It's obviously the only entertainment on offer this evening."

They walked to the mouth of the cave, the temperature dropping the minute they passed the warm curtain of air offered by the fire. Miles lit their cigars with a match, peering over his shoulder to make sure that Carruthers was asleep. Penelope thought he appeared quite the naughty schoolboy and told him so. For a few minutes they stood and silently smoked. Miles hadn't the first idea what to say now it actually came down to it. Penelope was shivering and Miles was torn between suggesting they abandon their cigars, offering her his jacket or even… imagine… putting his arm around her. He was just deciding that the latter was so damn terrifying he would be happier jumping off the cliff, when she gave him a big hug. "Some gentleman you are – I'm freezing to death here, the least you could do is put your arm around me or something."

"Right," said Miles, trying not to do any of that screaming-with-joy business, "sorry."

"No problem," Penelope replied, "as long as you do a good job of it now."

Miles felt absurdly happy, puffing on his cigar and rubbing his hand up and down Penelope's back. He smoked *very* slowly.

CHAPTER SEVENTEEN

Alan was no stranger to loss; in fact one might say his life had been built on it. People lost all manner of things, from loved ones to jobs, limbs to marbles. But few had lost as much as he: great chunks of history, vanished so completely he couldn't even feel the hole. Still, he had known no greater agony than when they pulled him from the ocean. The thick water droplets pouring from his hair and skin felt like the best of him falling away. What was left, this construction of meat and bone, this shitting and wheezing absurdity... what sort of burden was this? He had been grace; he had been the ebb and flow across infinite distance; he had been the tide; he had been the chill breeze across the surface, the ripple and splash; he had been the ocean. Now he was flesh, solid, barely able to move due to the sheer, suffocating weight of himself. He had cried as the hands held him up, carrying him into the dark where the air felt brittle as glass next to the skin, not like the soft blanket of the water, the perfect, folding embrace of the waves. As they left him there, closing the door and abandoning him to the darkness, he could imagine himself swollen to the size of a moon: a fat rock trapped in the pointlessness of space. He would have welcomed death, if only he could have lifted his leaden arms to find a weapon with which to achieve it. Even if he could have done so, how sharp a blade must be needed to hack through this skin? And what would he find beneath? Dust? Grit? Ball-bearings? He closed his eyes and solidified until sleep took him to dreams of water.

He woke several times, often delirious. At one point his screaming brought company: those same terrible hands that had torn him from the water now returned, this time forcing him down on to the bed, its thin mattress a poor imitation of the water's soft support. One hand clapped across his wide mouth, attempting to silence him, its fingers tasting of tar and sweat, fat and odious, solid things. He thought about biting the fingers but couldn't bear the thought of them bleeding in his mouth, filling him with even more of that leaden juice. They were strong, these hands, but his traitorous body made their work light; he could barely move as it was.

At one point he awoke, certain that there had been something in the room with him. Something invisible, like that force in the darkness between the jungle and the house. This reminded him of Whitstable and for one moment he imagined he could smell him: a sweet pork roast, sharpening his wooden stake and planning where to strike. Then he wondered if this presence might be young Sophie, who must be suffering as much as he. The shame he felt at having forgotten her entirely, so consumed with his own selfish loss, shook the delirium clear for a moment and he called for her. There was no answer and the mental funk returned as he slipped back into unconsciousness, listening to the sound around him: a creaking and straining like a man hanging from the gibbet.

"Are you awake?" a voice asked and Alan was surprised to find that he was, his head clear, his body once more his own. A lamp revealed the room to him, a small cabin, dark wood and bare of decoration. He sat up in the bed, a thick woollen sheet falling from him and releasing a fug of his own night sweats. The room still creaked but he knew the sound for what it was: the stretching of a boat on the water as its planks and beams ground against one another, buffeted by the swell.

"I'm on a ship," he said.

"Indeed you are," the voice replied. The speaker yanked open a rough curtain to let in the white light of the outside world. He was a man close to Alan's age, though he wore the years more visibly in the salt of his beard and the creases of his skin. His hair was long, pulled back into a ponytail that hung in thick, greasy lengths down his back. His clothes weren't the rags of the jungle natives – he wore a thick white shirt and black trousers – but they showed the same signs of hard weather and long wear as their owner, patches marking old wounds in the fabric. The man snuffed the lantern and sat on the end of Alan's bed. "The good ship *Intrepid*, in fact," he said, "a schooner held together by spit and imagination." He smiled "Nonetheless you are as safe as one ever can be and our honoured guest."

"Thank you," Alan replied, "though you'll forgive me if I'm a little cautious: the last people that offered me hospitality wanted to eat me."

The man laughed. "No fear of that. As much as the crew tires of hard tack, you don't look the most appetising of cattle. Besides, most gentlemen would consider it an unbreakable rule never to eat something they could also have a conversation with."

"These people didn't share your manners."

"Well, what can I say? His Majesty's navy has a scurrilous reputation but it has yet to descend to cannibalism."

"And which Majesty might that be?"

"Edward, though I confess I have been released of my fealty to him for some years."

"Where is my friend?"

"The girl? She is in her own cabin – we run with few hands and have spare beds aplenty. We will go and see her. Once reassured, you and I can share our stories. I've left you some clothes. I trust they will be suitable. There is also some soap and water should you wish to scrub away the fever. I'll wait outside." He walked out, pulling the door closed behind him.

Alan got out of bed, stretched – his aching muscles now much improved, though by the water or his period in bed he would never know – and rifled through the clothes the captain had left. A denim shirt, some black combat trousers and a sturdy-looking pair of army boots. Functional, hard-wearing stuff. He couldn't help but hold the underwear up to the light to check it was clean. A small table held a bowl, jug of water and bar of soap. He filled the bowl and worked up a lather in his hands, scrubbing at his skin as if the memory of the last few days could be removed by anything as simple as washing. He made a mess of rinsing himself, splashing the table and the floorboards as he tried to remove the suds from his armpits and groin. He was used to the modern convenience of a shower cubicle and the bowl was empty by the time he had finished, its contents spread liberally around the room. He dried himself on a rough towel, his skin stinging from his indelicate attentions. Once dressed he sat down on the bed to pull on his socks and boots; both fit fine. All done, he stepped out into the corridor.

"Better?" the captain asked.

"Much. The boots fit perfectly."

"I held them up to your feet while you were sleeping."

Alan nodded. "Sophie?"

The captain smiled and gestured towards the cabin door at the end of the short corridor. "I believe she's still sleeping so you may wish to be quiet."

Alan opened the door gently and peered around it into the room – still suspicious and half expecting someone to leap on him with a carving knife or basting brush at any moment.

"Here." The captain offered him a lantern.

"Thank you."

Alan entered the room, holding the lantern out in front of him and tiptoeing over to the bed. Sophie was, as promised, fast asleep. Wanting assurance that she was all right, Alan settled on the edge of her mattress, placed the lantern on her bedside table and brushed the hair away from her face. She mumbled something and rolled over. He held his hand to her forehead: no sign of fever. If she had been as delirious as he had been – and he had to assume she had – then it had passed in both of them. He was tempted to wake her, to thoroughly reassure himself that she was all right, but it seemed cruel. She was content for now and contentment had come in short supply thus far. Let her have as much of it as she could.

He went back out into the corridor. The captain was smiling at him. "Thank goodness that's over, now we can get on with being friendly! The name's Hawkins. It's a pleasure to have you on board. May I invite you to take a stroll on deck?"

"Alan Arthur, and you certainly may."

They walked along the corridor to where a wooden staircase led them up to the deck. Alan squinted as he stepped out into the light.

"Too long below deck," Hawkins said. "Not a problem from which I suffer. As I said, we are short-crewed. There were more but sadly..."

"Sadly?" Alan's suspicion returning.

"It's no life," Hawkins admitted, "working all hours with little hope of seeing a friendly shore. They gave themselves to the water. You have seen the opiate effects of the ocean here: it lulls you to its breast and smothers you until you are lost." He noticed the quizzical look on Alan's face, "Oh yes, friend, had we left you or the girl in the water for much longer I fear we would never have been able to fish you out. The body breaks down, dispersing into the water like sugar in a cup of tea. The waves we ride on, even now, are thick with the essence of those it's stolen. You will see the result come nightfall. But let us save the darkness till later."

Alan looked out over the waves, remembering how he had felt when borne upon their weight. "It was beautiful," he said.

"Aye," Hawkins nodded, "death sometimes is. Come, let me introduce you to the rest of the crew." He led Alan across the gently swaying deck towards the front of the ship where a boy of no more than thirteen was swinging from the rigging as if the ship were a school playground. "This gentle idiot is Ryan, our cabin boy."

"Avast ye!" the boy cried, gurning wildly, "hoist ye mizzuns and up the forebrace!"

"He has no idea what he's talking about," Hawkins explained with a smile, "but he thinks it sounds good."

"Damn your eyes, cap'n!" Ryan replied, giggling. He tucked his legs through the rigging and hung upside down, extending his hand to Arthur to shake.

"Well met, me hearty!" said Alan with a smile, shaking the boy's hand.

"See!" said Ryan in a Cockney accent, "'E's a land-lubber and even 'e knows 'ow to give it a bit of the old skull and crossbones!"

"And I dare say – no offence, Alan – that he knows as much about sailing as you do."

"No offence taken," Alan replied, "You're quite right, I've never so much as set foot on a sailing ship before."

Hawkins ruffled Ryan's hair and led Alan to the fore of the ship where a tiny man was sitting on a kit box fixing the holes in a large net. He was resting his feet on the base of a harpoon gun. When the man turned around Alan was startled to see he was wearing two eyepatches. "This is Jonah," Hawkins explained, "blind as a bat but with a nose for the sea like no other. Excuse the patches, he thinks it's funny."

"Who said that?" Jonah cried before cackling at his own joke and showing Alan the solitary tooth he possessed in his upper gum.

"Alan Arthur," said Alan, sticking out his hand to shake before suddenly realising how stupid a gesture it was. Jonah surprised him by crooking his head slightly to one side and then grabbing hold of the extended hand with his own and giving it a forceful pump.

"Well met," Jonah said. "You still stink of the ocean, Alan. You're lucky to be in one piece."

"So I hear."

"Well, let's hope your luck rubs off, eh? We'll take all we can get on this vessel."

Hawkins began to work his way around to starboard, Alan following.

"If you look up there," Hawkins said, pointing to the crow's nest atop the foremast, "you'll see Barnabas. He's a miserable bastard, always convinced that each new day will be our last, so I keep him out of everyone's way as much as possible. Any sights of interest, Barnabas?" he shouted.

"Nay, Captain," came the reply, "but I dare say there'll be something horrible along any minute. Who's that? The bloke we fished out of the water?"

"It is!" Alan shouted back. "Good to meet you."

"You won't be saying that for long," Barnabas replied. "I give you a day before you're begging us to throw you back in."

"See what I mean?" Hawkins said quietly, "absolute bloody misery. I'll throw him overboard one of these days." He cut across the deck towards the cockpit where a the ship's wheel was being manhandled by a woman almost as broad as she was tall. Her hair was so curly and proud from her head that she looked as if she was permanently facing into a storm.

"And, finally," said Hawkins, "this is Maggie, the Queen of the Wheel, my Commander and, for that matter, wife."

"In which relationship I think you'll find I outrank him," she said, giving Arthur a wink.

"I am led to believe this is usually the case," Alan replied. "Alan Arthur. Good to meet you."

"And you. I hope Hawkins is looking after you?"

"He is." He looked at the captain. "Even your wife calls you by your last name?"

"You haven't heard my first name."

His wife laughed. "Do you want to tell him or shall I?"

Hawkins shrugged. "You'll likely get more pleasure out of it, dear."

Maggie leaned over to Arthur. "His full name is Admiral Benbow Hawkins. That's not the rank, you understand, he never made it past captain. That's 'Admiral Benbow' as in–"

"The pub from *Treasure Island*."

Maggie howled with laughter. "You've got it!"

"My father was a fan of the novel," Hawkins explained.

"Could have been worse," Alan said with a grin. "Could have been 'Moby Dick'."

"That's just what I calls him when we're being romantic," joked Maggie with a lascivious wink.

Hawkins sighed. "As you might imagine, the long evenings fly by. Might I suggest – as long as my beloved has everything under control – we head below deck? I have no doubt you'll have a lot of questions and I'm only too happy to answer them if I can."

"Please do," Maggie said to Alan, "he only gets under my feet when he's up here."

"Mutinous creature," said Hawkins, giving her a peck on the cheek.

• • •

Below deck, Hawkins led Alan into the captain's quarters. They were larger than the bare cabin he had woken up in but not as lavish as he might have imagined.

"I know," Hawkins said, offering Alan a chair at the central table. "Not exactly plush, is it? We make do."

"I'm still at a loss as to how the ship's even here."

"It came with us. Look, the story is long, let me pour us a drink and tell it from the beginning. I have some brandy – I put a couple of bottles to one side when we first arrived here, intending to crack them open if a suitable occasion came along. This is as close as I've got so let's throw caution to the wind."

"I was about to say it's a little early," Alan said, "but if your clock's right then I overslept more than I realised."

Hawkins glanced at the clock, which gave the time as just past six. "We have less time before nightfall than I might have liked but I shall tell my story briefly. You were asleep for four days, so don't be surprised if you're somewhat disorientated."

"Four days?"

"The water's effects cling to a man, Alan. You really were remarkably lucky we chanced along when we did."

"Chanced along… no, OK, too many questions. I'll take that drink and let's hear your story."

Hawkins nodded and pulled a bottle and two glasses from the sideboard. He placed the glasses on the table and poured them both a measure. "Right," he said, raising his glass towards Alan, "your health."

He took a sip and leaned back in his chair, organising his thoughts.

"As you will have guessed from my name, my parents always hoped I would have a future on the ocean. I joined the Navy when I was a lad and did moderately well, sailed the world, rose through the ranks as far as captain and then found myself under Jellicoe at the Battle of Jutland."

"The First World War?"

"I know of no other. I won't bore you with interminable war stories, have no fear. I have no urge to discuss the battle; it put me off service for good. The blast of the heavy guns, the dead bobbing in the water like driftwood, great fleets of them... When the *Queen Mary* went up, the fire and smoke... I simply lost my taste for it." Hawkins gave Alan a nervous glance. "A coward's response, I know."

"Hardly. Nobody should have a taste for war."

"I served out the conflict but when the Kaiser fled so did I, taking decommission and a civilian life. This boat was my retirement. I couldn't altogether abandon the ocean. I hired a crew and sailed as a private charter, ferrying those who could afford my services, asking few questions – the hallmark of the trade – and maintaining a peaceful existence. Then, in 1921, I accepted a commission from a man claiming to be an archaeologist. He was an elderly countryman of yours who wished to transport certain 'archaeological items' from India to the States. He was a shady character. Nonetheless, I needed the fee he was offering and so accepted the job.

"We took the cargo on board – a single packing crate, no more than six foot square – and set sail. Our employer chose to spend his time between the hold and his cabin, examining the various artifacts. I can't say we cared for his company so he wasn't missed. As we skirted past Malaysia towards the South Pacific we encountered bad weather: a string of storms that threatened to sink us, each more vicious than the last. The gentleman was altogether disparaging about my abilities – as if it were within my power to control the weather – and one night grew so abusive that I must confess we almost came to blows. Were it not for his extreme age – he was eighty if he was a day and built as thin as if his bones were matches – I suspect I might have lost control and given him a beating. I am not by nature a violent man but Mr Ashe – that was his name, or at least the one he gave when signing my services, Gregory Ashe – challenged my limits. In the end I returned half of his money and declared my intention to put him aground at Indonesia. He could make further arrangements from there. Me and my crew would have no further dealings with him. After an initially violent response he seemed to accept I was immovable and retired to his cabin. I should have known that would not be the end of the matter. Maggie always accuses me of being too soft and I confess she is invariably right.

"That night, Ashe crept into my cabin with a handgun to further bolster his argument. He threatened to shoot Maggie were I not to accede to his demands." Hawkins took a large mouthful of his drink then topped up his glass. "I am reaching an uncomfortable point in my story, Alan, but I hope that you might understand: when a man's wife is threatened he acts in a manner that is wholly without restraint."

"I understand," Alan assured him. "This Ashe was clearly a dangerous man. Whatever you did to defend the life of your wife and crew can hardly be deemed unreasonable."

"Perhaps you will no longer think that when I tell you what I did." Hawkins took another sip of brandy. "I made an initial show of agreement, just so that I could get close to him, but the minute an opportunity presented itself I took advantage, striking him a resounding blow to the head and disarming him."

"I would have thought that was exceptionally restrained."

"My real crime came afterwards. I was incensed! How dare this man threaten to kill the woman I love in return for ferrying him and his trinkets? It was all I could do not to shoot him, right then and there. It was Maggie who calmed me, pointing out that everyone was perfectly safe and that no harm had been done. She was right, of course, but I couldn't bear the thought of him on board my ship a moment longer.

"By now the storms looked as if they would blow themselves out. In the distance the lights of the Malaysian port of Kupang were just visible. I wonder, are you familiar at all with the story of William Bligh?"

"*Mutiny on the Bounty*? Only vaguely…"

"After the mutiny Bligh was set adrift in an open boat with those few crewmen still loyal to him. They didn't expect him to make shore; it was all but a death sentence. However, Bligh was one hell of a sailor and managed to navigate as far as Kupang, where he landed safely."

"I think I begin to see where this story is heading."

"I imagine you do. The *Intrepid* had two lifeboats and I set Ashe adrift in one of them. He had a solid chance of reaching safety: land was visible and, as long as the storms didn't return to full strength, he had an even chance of success."

"I still think you acted reasonably. The man was a risk to you and your crew, and you had to put their safety first."

"Perhaps. Though if I'm honest I simply wanted Ashe to suffer. I was hot for revenge. I wanted him *scared*. And he was… though not for his own life, damn him, but rather for his precious artifacts! He began screaming like a lunatic, insisting that he would follow us every step of our journey, hunt us down and cut our throats while we slept unless we gave him his belongings."

"So what did you do?"

"I gave them to him, one by one, over the side of the boat, figurines and busts, tapestries and paintings… all of them were hurled into the waves. Maggie endeavoured to calm me down but I was wild and would have none of it. To make matters worse the sky had begun to darken, as if the clouds were as angry as I. The storms were returning and, as the rain began to fell, there am I, captain of my boat, ignoring all issues of safety, pelting this bastard with antiques. In truth he seemed no more concerned about the storm than I was, still screaming his threats.

"The ship began to rock. We needed to take measures but I was focused on only one thing. Then I came upon the last item in his cabin, the most precious of all, it would seem."

"A Chinese box?"

Hawkins nodded. "You are familiar with it. I grabbed the thing, meaning to hurl it off the side with the rest. That was when the storm really broke, thunder, lightning, the very worst God can hurl at us. As the rain lashed the deck and the boat rocked, I lost my footing, falling back down the hatch, the box slipping from my grasp.

"The next thing I know, the storm has stopped and we are surrounded by silence. I had lost consciousness in the fall, fetching my head a sound blow on the stairs. I could only assume I had managed to sleep through the whole thing. On climbing up to the deck, imagine my surprise: not only was it daylight but we had lost all sight of land. Still, I could only assume the storm had blown us off course. It took the reports of the crew to clarify otherwise…"

"You had been transported here."

"Indeed. All of us, crew and boat, the whole affair, scooped from the edge of the Indian Ocean and dropped here. Needless to say, of Ashe there was no sign." Hawkins drained his brandy and glanced at the window. "Our story must continue later. The night is coming and you will soon see that that is something into which we do not sail lightly. May I suggest you check on your young friend and then join me on deck? I would appreciate your help in the hell that will soon be on us."

Sophie was still sleeping. Alan wondered if it was due to her longer exposure to the water; after all, she must have been floating there some time before he had arrived. He checked her window was closed – whatever terrors were due tonight, he wanted to ensure she was locked away from them – and headed back up to the deck.

Hawkins was pacing up and down. The quiet, self-reflective man now quite absent to be replaced by Hawkins the Sailor, the efficient man of the ocean.

"What do you need me to do?" Alan asked.

"For now, nothing. We've got the lockdown to a fine art. Later, though, you can add to the defences."

"Defences against what?"

"The water, naturally – it is our major enemy here, you will see…" He began moving towards the fore of the ship. "Jonah! Come on, we need to be anchored, now!"

Alan looked above him. The white roof was darkening as if the illumination were within the very paint on its surface. The water was becoming restless beneath the boat, the gentle rolling of the day replaced by an irritated choppiness. A storm was on its way; there was a charge to the air that was unmistakeable.

"How on earth can you have a weather system inside a house?" he wondered to himself.

"Same way you can sail a boat in it," said Barnabas, walking past. "The whole place is mad and will likely kill us any minute."

Clouds were beginning to form. Alan looked over the prow, watching the waves lengthen in the gloom. The water took on a strange quality in the half-light, moving as if independent of the wind on the surface. Waves contradicted each other, moving in opposing directions. They came to a peak only to hold themselves for a moment before crashing back down with an aggressive slap. Alan thought about what Hawkins had said: the water itself was the enemy...

As he watched, the sea began to undulate towards the boat. Peaks extended to form the shape of human hands, hundreds of them waving to one another in the stormy air. One by one they approached the boat and began to clap on the hull, the slow drumming building in volume as each watery hand joined its fellows.

"Quickly, man!" Hawkins shouted to Jonah, "they're upon us!"

Jonah manned the harpoon guns, turning them – rather disconcertingly – towards the aft of the ship rather than facing out towards the water.

"What's he doing?" Alan asked, having to shout loudly over the drumming noise.

"Anchoring us," Hawkins replied as Jonah cranked a lever that lifted the harpoons towards the sky rather than the deck. "When the water is unreliable we must look above for stability."

With a cry, Jonah fired the harpoons skyward, where they sailed through the building clouds whipping their ropes behind them. They found their mark, embedding themselves in the plaster of the roof with a double thud. The ship creaked to a halt, the ropes pulling taut. Alan grabbed hold of the rail to stop himself losing his balance. "Now what?" he asked.

"Now we fight!" Hawkins replied, throwing him a plank of driftwood. "They break up if you hit them hard enough."

"What do?" – but the answer was already climbing aboard: men moulded from the water around them, their transparent muscles glistening in the torches that Maggie was lighting all over the deck. Alan watched as Ryan ran at one of the invaders holding a plank of his own. The boy swung the plank and the creature exploded in a splash across the deck. He swung at another but the blow was too light: the man's shape distorted but ultimately held its form. Barnabas leapt in, giving the creature a stout blow to the shoulder-blades that saw it dissipate like an upturned bucket.

"Spread out!" Hawkins shouted, "cover all sides!"

Alan saw one of the creatures clambering aboard a few feet to his left and struck at its head. It opened its mouth in a silent roar a moment before the head dispersed in a shower of vapour.

"Aim for the body!" Maggie shouted as she ran past him, a skillet in her hands. "The head's not enough."

She was proved correct as the man's features re-formed, the extra water flooding up from its shoulders. Alan waited until it was half over the rail before hitting it again where its watery ribs might lie, closing his eyes as it exploded in a shower over him. Another had made the deck to his right and he turned to attack it, unaware of yet one more creeping over the rail behind him. He stuck the plank in the man's solar plexus and whipped it outwards, the torso gushing forth, its raised arms pouring to the floor as it disintegrated. He felt himself grabbed from behind, the grip surprisingly strong as it lifted him from the deck, one watery hand pushing into his mouth to drown him. Suddenly the creature dissipated, hit from behind by Barnabas.

"Told you," he moaned, slouching off with his oar to attack elsewhere, "we'll all be dead in a minute."

Picking himself up off the deck, Alan wiped his wet hair away from his face and struck another man clambering over the rail. Above them, the storm continued to roar, forks of lightning slicing their way through the deluge and throwing light on the sea's surface, where more and more of the men could be seen to form, rising up and wading towards them through the foam.

"How many are there?" Alan shouted.

"Sometimes there are whole legions, sometimes only a handful," Hawkins replied, moving to stand back to back with Alan and grunting as he dispatched another. "The attack never lasts long, no more than five minutes, but each night, when it comes, one cannot help but wonder if that will be the night their numbers overwhelm us."

A pair of them appeared from behind the rigging, the reflection of lightning adding a whiteness to their grinning teeth. Alan struck at one, Maggie the other, plank meeting skillet with a celebratory clang in the resulting shower of water.

"No end to the fun on board this ship, eh?" she said with a laugh before spotting more invaders behind her and dashing off to deal with them.

Alan was quick to tire, the pain in his shoulder returning. He wondered how long the attack had lasted. Surely it must end soon? Out of the corner of his eye he could see Jonah, whipping an oar around him, like a character from a martial arts film. The blind man had hit upon a surefire method to compensate for his lack of sight, keeping his weapon on the move at all times, turning constantly so that he couldn't help but hit something if it came anywhere near him. Ryan still seemed to be enjoying himself, whooping and jeering as he ran to and fro, dropping to the deck and sliding towards his targets. It was amazing, thought Alan, how the crew had adapted to their circumstances. They remained undaunted by the odds of their survival and met the challenge head on. He was glad to have found himself on board, proud to fight alongside them. He just hoped he survived the experience…

Barnabas slipped on the deck, dropping his oar as two of the attackers bore down on him. Alan came up behind them and dispatched them with a roar that was half triumph, half pain, his shoulder protesting terribly by now. "There," Alan said, spitting out a mouthful of the dispersed creatures, "you won't be dying just yet."

"Only a matter of bloody time," Barnabas moaned, climbing to his feet and picking up his oar.

The attack ceased. There was one final explosion of thunder and then all the watery men poured away leaving the crew tired and soaked but alive for one more night.

"Thanks for your help, Alan," said Hawkins, "good to have another pair of hands. We should be safe now. Let's leave the storm to blow out while we warm ourselves and eat."

"Bet it's stew again," Barnabas said, slouching off towards the hatch.

Hawkins rolled his eyes, miming clubbing the man down with his plank to the amusement of the others. "Come on," he said, "let's go and eat some bloody stew."

They gathered below deck in the mess. It was a room that took its name to heart, with discarded clothes, papers and even the odd bread roll hiding under the table. Hawkins had given Alan a change of clothes and he had checked on Sophie again but she was still fast asleep, the sound of the storm and fighting having disturbed her not one jot.

"Don't worry," Maggie said as she stirred the predicted stew, "she'll be all right but it takes it out of you. We found young Ryan there floating in the water three or four months ago now, it took him a week to come round."

Alan looked over at the cabin boy, who was laughing and pulling mocking faces at Barnabas. "Certainly hasn't harmed him in the long run," he commented. "So Ryan wasn't part of your original crew?"

"No, he was driftwood, just like yourself."

"Are you not tempted to leave the ocean?"

"We prefer to stay aboard ship. It's our home and we know the risks here. From what we can tell the house has a never-ending set of surprises."

"'Better the devil you know.'"

"Exactly, though I worry sometimes that we'll never find a way home if we stick to the water. We've sailed so much of it and found nothing."

"Is there any other land out here?"

"Not that we've seen."

Hawkins came in, his hair hanging loose to dry around his shoulders. "Stew, is it?" he said with a smile, sitting down at the table. "Your favourite, Barnabas."

Barnabas growled, picking at the wood of the table with the blade of his knife.

The stew was served into bowls and they all sat down to eat. It was bland but filled a hole and Alan could at least be grateful that it contained no boar. Once they were done Hawkins asked him to tell his own story, which he did, describing his life in Florida and what had driven him to hunt for the box. He told them about meeting Sophie and trekking through the jungle, the escape from the cannibals and the darkness between the walls. He found himself enjoying it; certainly it was an adventurous tale and nobody could claim to be bored. His life had always been quiet and predictable, split between his research, his therapy and his students. While he couldn't say he relished the danger, he had to admit that – having survived what the house had thrown at him – he was the better for it. Of course he might change his mind once he saw what terrors tomorrow brought.

"It would seem," said Hawkins, "that our fishing you from the water was just the latest in a string of narrow escapes."

"No doubt about it," Alan replied. "I just hope my luck holds out."

"It won't," Barnabas muttered before crying out as Ryan punched him on the arm.

"Well, the question now is whether you're willing to join us for a while," Hawkins continued. "I don't make a habit of keeping people on board against their will so if you want me to sail for shore and put you aground just say the word."

Alan thought about it for a second. It was true that the *Intrepid* could be nothing more than a holding pattern; they certainly hadn't found a way home yet. Then again, he liked their company and there was no reason to assume he would have better luck continuing his wanderings through the house. "I'll stay," he decided, "as long as you're happy to have me."

"Only too happy," Hawkins said with a smile, "I need all the able hands I can get."

"I want to get home," Alan said, "and if what I've read is true – and it must be – there is a way. Are we agreed that that is the ultimate goal of this trip?"

"Damn right we're agreed," Jonas said, "I for one can't wait to set my eyes on home again!"

Everyone at the table groaned.

"I confess I had grown accustomed to the thought that we would live out the rest of our lives here," Hawkins admitted. "However brief they may be. From what you've said though, it would seem there is a chance we could return home. Let us hope we find it."

Alan couldn't sleep, which was hardly surprising. After a few hours of staring at the wooden ceiling he decided to stretch his legs, maybe get himself a glass of water. He shuffled quietly out of his cabin and made his way towards the mess. As he was pouring himself some water, he heard a creaking sound on the stairs that led up to the deck. Wondering what someone else was doing creeping around – the fact that he was doing exactly the same never occurring to him – he walked out into the corridor just in time to see Barnabas stepping on to the deck. The storm had abated now and Alan could see no danger in following.

He crept up the stairs, keeping his feet to the edges so they might not creak. He peered over the hatch opening to see if Barnabas was in sight: he was, walking towards the fore of the ship. Alan stepped on to the deck and was about to call out to him when something changed his mind. Perhaps it was still suspicion, or the oppressive stillness that had settled on the ship after the storm, or maybe he just didn't want to risk waking the rest of the crew. He couldn't have said. Nonetheless, he followed Barnabas silently, walking delicately on the still wet deck, fearful of slipping.

Once Barnabas had reached the front of the ship he leaned on the railing for a moment as if weighed down by something terrible. Alan assumed he probably was; certainly he wasn't a man filled with the joy of existence. Then Barnabas pulled himself up on to the railing, swung his leg over the side and prepared to throw himself overboard. Alan dashed forward and grabbed hold of the man's arm as he fell.

"Oh, for God's sake," Barnabas said, hanging over the waves, "wouldn't you just guess that might happen?"

Alan pulled on the man's arm, trying to haul him back up on deck. Barnabas didn't fight; in fact, after a second or so, he reached for the railing, pulled himself back on board and sat down with a sigh. "Why couldn't you just keep your nose out of it?" he said. "None of your bloody business, is it?"

"What were you thinking?" Alan asked. "You would have got yourself killed."

"Not much chance of that, what with all the busy-bodies around," Barnabas moaned and then, much to Alan's surprise, he started to cry, his body slumping like that of a dejected child as he began to sob. Alan felt suddenly awkward, dropped down next to him and tentatively put his arm around his shoulders.

"It's all right," he mumbed, not knowing what to say.

"How do you reckon that then, eh?" Barnabas replied. "I've been here for months, stuck here in this ungodly place just waiting for something to kill me. I can't be doing with it. We all know we're never going to get home so why put up with it? This is no damn life."

"You don't know you won't get home," Alan said, "weren't you listening earlier? There is a way, there must be or I could never have heard about it."

"Oh Christ, that almost makes it worse," Barnabas whined, rubbing at his snotty nose with the back of his hand. "There's nothing more terrible than a tiny bit of hope, is there? At least if you know something's impossible you can get on with it, but imagine spending the next six months here actually hoping that something might happen every day. And then having to face the fact that it didn't... I just don't think I can take that. Better the water, it feels good and then you're nothing, the problem's gone."

"There is a way," said Alan, "and it can be found. I can't say how long it might take, who knows? But I do know it's there and, knowing that, how could you give up now? I could understand if you'd just been told there was no way home. Hell, I'd dive off there with you if I thought that. But once you actually know you could escape...? Imagine if we found a way home tomorrow and here's you, missed it by twenty-four hours just because you can't bear a little hope."

"Miss it by a day?" Barnabas replied, sniffing loudly. "Aye, that'd be about right, that. Just my bloody luck."

"There you go then," said Alan. "Let's get back to a miserable but bloody-minded Barnabas, shall we? No more of this threatening to jump off."

"Oh, I ain't going nowhere now. I'd be too bloody embarrassed. Don't you dare tell the others either!"

"Wouldn't dream of it," Alan agreed.

Barnabas got to his feet and, with a gentle nod, slouched back off to his quarters. Alan watched him go, then turned to look out across the prow. There was nothing discernible ahead of them; with no moon or stars to light their way the boat might as well be floating in mid-air, the gentle rocking the only clue that the water was even there.

"Thank you for that," Hawkins said from behind him.

Alan spun around. "You nearly gave me a heart attack!"

"Sorry."

"It's all right, just didn't hear you coming. But then my ears are obviously not as highly trained as yours."

"Nobody walks around on this ship after lights-out without me hearing them. It was better Barnabas heard that from you, though, so, again, thank you."

"No problem. I just wish he had a little more hope in him. Easy for me to say, I suppose, I've only just got here."

"It's not just that. Barnabas isn't stupid, he knows there's a fly in the ointment that nobody's acknowledging. Come into the light." They walked over to one of the lamps and Hawkins pulled a small leather case from his pocket and handed it to Alan. "Take a look."

Alan flipped the case open to find a compass, its point slowly revolving. "Ah…" he said, "I hadn't thought of that."

"Wherever this house is it's not beholden to the normal laws of the earth. That includes a magnetic field." Hawkins nodded towards the sky. "There's no help up there either, of course, as easy as it is to forget that it's a roof. No stars to guide us, nothing."

"So how do you navigate?"

"We don't. We sail aimlessly until we fall across something. When we come within sight of shore we land and stock up. It's never been planned. For all I know we've just been turning around in circles – small circles at that."

"So what's the solution?"

Hawkins shrugged. "Your suggestion of 'hope' is pretty much all we have."

Alan nodded. "Then I guess it'll just have to do."

CHAPTER EIGHTEEN

Nobody ever got warm or fat off the dream of bacon, but that didn't stop Miles trying as he stared at the roof of the cave, summoning up the energy for another day's climb.

"I can't climb mountains today," he whispered, "my mum's given me a note."

"Well, I'll give you a kick if you're not upright in two minutes," said Penelope, stepping over him and going to stand by the fire. "Still going strong," she said, "unlike the rest of us."

"Speak for yourself," Ashe announced while stretching.

Watching, Miles could imagine every sharp little vertebra snapping into place. "Dear God, don't tell me he's a morning person... I can't bear morning people."

"I'm an 'all-day-long' person," Ashe replied, straightfaced.

"Breakfast!" Carruthers exclaimed, pulling out a carton of crackers and some dried meat.

"That's not breakfast," Miles complained, "that's a selection of items that would make a brick seem succulent."

"And will fill our stomach for hours."

"Concrete would do it for years, doesn't mean it's a good idea."

Carruthers handed Miles some of the crackers and meat. "Drink lots of water with it."

"I could take it with a bottle of vodka and it wouldn't be any more palatable."

Carruthers handed food to Penelope and Ashe. The latter immediately started chewing on it.

Once they had eaten they wrapped themselves up and headed out into the snow. The winds had hidden the staircase from view but the route was obvious enough. Carruthers led the way, adopting the same plan as the day before: marching for a few minutes then taking a brief breather before continuing.

As they curved around the mountain the view of the walls began to vanish behind thin veils of cloud. The cream paint of the roof blended with the air. The ceiling rose was still visible, its knotted vine motif like a two-dimensional sun, empty of warmth, the cornicing a lofty horizon line on all sides. The higher they climbed the colder it got, the air burning their lungs as they breathed it in. The wind grew so chilling it filled their cheeks with the sensation of paper cuts. By the time they had been climbing a few hours their skin was too sore to touch.

"I'm just not built for exploring," Miles moaned. "In future I will only deal with ice that is thoroughly drowned in gin."

"If we get to a bar I'll buy you one," Penelope said. "In fact I'll join you."

"Shush," whispered Carruthers, waving his hand at them.

"Yes, Dad," Miles muttered.

"We're not alone," Carruthers said, turning on the spot and scrutinising the mountainside.

"We've been followed for the last couple of miles or so," Ashe said.

"You didn't think that worth mentioning?" asked Penelope.

"Didn't want to panic anybody. There's a good chance they won't attack unless there's enough of them."

"*What* won't attack?" asked Miles.

"Wolves," Carruthers replied, pointing above them to where a white shape darted out of sight.

"Oh, yes, obviously... a pack of those house wolves, isn't it? Like earwigs but *toothier*." Miles kept spinning around trying to catch sight of them.

"Keep moving," said Ashe.

Carruthers carried on, marching faster up the steps. "We can't outrun them," he said.

"No," Ashe replied, "but we can hope they leave us be. If there's only a couple of them we should be fine – no animal takes on a bunch of humans unless the odds are thoroughly in its favour."

"Is that true?" asked Miles.

"Yes," Carruthers replied, before adding "usually," with a somewhat non-committal shrug. "Ashe is quite correct in that our only choice is to keep moving."

"Perhaps they're just waiting for us to tire ourselves out," Penelope suggested.

"I'm there already," Miles admitted. "They may as well just get on with it. It would be a nice change of pace just to lie down in the snow and have a good bleed."

"Of course, one of us does have a weapon," said Ashe "Now might be the time to use it."

"I think not," said Carruthers, "let's wait until there's a very real threat, shall we?"

"What will it take to convince you of that?" asked Miles, "fatalities?" He kept looking around him as they walked, hoping to catch a glimpse of the animals. He saw nothing, but then someone like Miles would only notice a creature as stealthy as a wolf when it was chewing their throat.

"If we start shooting now we bring attention to ourselves..."

"As opposed to subtly strolling around smelling of tired cutlet," Miles muttered.

"If they attack," Carruthers continued, "we defend ourselves. If they continue to just observe we leave them alone and conserve our bullets."

"*My* bullets," said Ashe. "Not that I mind contributing them to the cause."

They continued to walk. Every now and then a slight flicker on the periphery of Carruthers' vision let him know they still had company but the animals came no closer, happy to escort them up the mountain.

After an hour or so, Carruthers stopped for lunch. "We've got to keep our strength up," he said, "whatever the company. Besides, I think if they were going to strike they would have done so by now." He broke out more dried biscuits and meat.

"This may put them off," said Miles. "We should leave some behind just to break their stomachs."

They ate quickly, none of them inclined to loiter over an uninspiring meal in such daunting company. Within ten minutes they were walking again, trudging up the snow-covered steps, the peak of the mountain drawing closer at a speed normally reserved for indolent bricks.

"You think we stand a chance of making it to the summit by nightfall?" Miles asked, knowing the answer but hoping he was wrong.

"I think we'll be doing well if we manage it by tomorrow night," Carruthers replied. "It's a long way and – with the best will in the world – we're hardly travelling at speed."

The snow to their left suddenly exploded outwards, sending a curtain of ice down on their heads. Carruthers, backing away in surprise, nearly toppled over the banister but managed to retain his balance. A six-foot-tall polar bear, its fur patchy and stained a sickly yellow, reared up out of the snow. It roared, the stench of its mouldy breath strong enough to feel solid as it hit them. It was the odour of rot and wet carpets, of houses left to ruin. When it moved it was with a stiffness that suggested it might be wounded in some way, a creaking reluctance to its limbs as if it had been frozen and only half thawed out.

"It's stuffed!" Miles shouted, knowing only too well the nature of taxidermy within this house.

"So are we unless we defend ourselves," Carruthers replied. Ashe levelled his handgun at the beast and emptied three rounds into it. The bear's head exploded like a ruptured cushion, its snout flowering into a mess of wire and kapok. It fell forward a couple of feet from them, a sour scent of age pouring from its open body cavity.

"Spare bullets," Ashe commented. "Didn't think I'd mention them. Trust goes both ways." He reloaded, flipped the safety catch on the gun and dropped it back into his pocket. "I think I'll hold on to them too if it's all right. I'm not quite relaxed enough to hand over my only means of defence."

Carruthers glanced at Miles and gave a gentle shake of his head. Now was not the time for making a stand. Ashe had a point and as long as he was looking out for his own skin he would be protecting theirs as well. "Well," he said, advancing on the empty bear carcass, "I for one am most grateful for your quick reflexes and sound aim. I would not have enjoyed being on the receiving end of one of these paws."

They resumed their climb, the dose of adrenalin giving them more of a boost than lunch. They took the next fifty or so steps at speed before the throbbing in their legs started to slow them down again.

"You know what this place needs?" Miles said as they sank down for another brief rest, "a ski lift. Or even an escalator."

"I've been thinking," said Penelope, "what guarantee have we got that we're even doing anything worthwhile by climbing this? For all we know we'll get to the top and then end up having to climb all the way back down again."

"Not me," said Miles, "I'd insist that Ashe shot me at that point. I'm close to asking him now."

"I may even agree to do it," said Ashe.

"Nice… he's going to shoot me."

"Just after a little peace and quiet."

"He shoots me to make me shut up!"

"Would anything else do it?"

"I'll shoot the pair of you in a minute," said Penelope. "It's like going on a trip with my young nephews."

Carruthers had been keeping an eye on the mountainside, doing his best to ignore the squabbling between Ashe and Miles. "The wolves are still following," he said. "I can't see them, they're too quick for that, but after a few years of this you get to know when something's got you in its sights."

"Like the bear?" Ashe asked.

"All right," Carruthers admitted, "I'll admit that one crept up on me."

"It crept up on all of us," Penelope added, happy to come to his defence. "And luckily no harm was done."

"To us at least," added Miles, "Ashe here made sure the bear couldn't say the same."

"You complaining?" Ashe asked.

"Not at all, I'd have kicked his hollow corpse off the mountain if I thought it a worthwhile way of expending energy. If anything else tries to eat us you have my heartfelt permission to blow its face off."

"Consider it done."

"When you've quite finished trading metaphorical gunfire," Carruthers interrupted, "I suggest we get moving. There's no doubt that we will be forced to spend another night on this godforsaken mountain and I, for one, am not looking forward to doing so in the elements."

"Do you think we might find somewhere else to shelter?" Penelope asked.

"It would seem logical," said Ashe. "Why build one if you're not going to build others?"

"We can but hope," Carruthers replied.

They continued their climb, always aware that they were being observed as they did so. The thin clouds fell down around them, scarves of chilling vapour that left their skin wet as they passed through them. Visibility dropped, and the whole mountain was shrouded in a white haze.

"Now I get really nervous," Carruthers admitted. "I couldn't see the wolves before but at least we knew we would have a few moments' grace should they attack. If they come for us now then the first we'll know about it is when we smell their breath on our cheeks."

"Cheery thought," Miles replied. "Revolver at the ready, Ashe."

"It never leaves my hand," came the reply.

While tired there was no doubt that they were getting more used to their environment. The altitude and exertion took their toll but they made better progress than they had the day before. They took the same frequent breaks but lingered over them less, always eager to resume their journey in the hope of finding its conclusion. Even the absurdity of it began to wane; as with everything in the house, you could only be in awe for so long. Yes, they were climbing a mountain in a drawing room… but its location made it no less a geographical inconvenience and thinking about it didn't get you up the damned thing. That said, they still took a few moments to appreciate the bizarre sight that met them in one of the frequent grooves in the landscape: a pyramid of sofas that had solidified into a natural feature, paisley upholstery sparkling beneath its sheen of ice crystals.

"I don't know much about art," said Miles, "but DFS have a corking sale on this year."

"Do you have any idea how little the rest of us understand you?" asked Penelope with a smile.

Miles chuckled. "I'm used to it, at least I entertain myself."

"Great to be so easily pleased," Ashe commented, pushing past them and continuing up the stairs.

Miles bent over to Penelope. "He's always buttering me up, do you think he fancies me?"

Penelope snorted with laughter, giggling all the more at the baffled looks Ashe sent her way.

They walked on and, as the afternoon passed, they once more became eager to find somewhere to spend the night. Carruthers was confident, despite what he had said to Ashe earlier. He knew that if the man believed they would find shelter then they likely would. He was uncomfortable with the man knowing much more than he let on, but he had to admit it set the mind at rest in some areas. Not only were they travelling with a worthwhile destination – otherwise why was he walking alongside them? – but there was little risk of a night of exposure ahead. He'd played that hand squarely when the subject had arisen. Hopefully it wouldn't be much further…

They found the shelter half an hour before nightfall. A narrow tunnel leading to yet another furnished cave. There was a selection of sofas, a laid fire in the grate, even a small stove on which to heat their meagre supplies. Miles spent some considerable time circling the stove, looking for pipes or chimneys but finding none. For that matter he couldn't even find the fire… "I give up," he said in the end, "it's physically impossible but as long as it cooks our equally impossible food I for one will not be giving a toss."

"What's on the musical menu, I wonder?" Penelope said, discovering a gramophone no less aged than the one they had used the night before. She held the disc up to the light. "Roger Whittaker?"

Miles took it from her hands and threw it out of the cave. "My turn for a timely rescue," he said. "That could have been just as lethal as the bear."

"Might I suggest," said Carruthers, "that we organise a rota to keep watch this evening? There is still the matter of a pack of wolves to be aware of. Catching us all asleep may be just the opportunity they were waiting for."

"I've gone off the idea of sleeping a wink," admitted Miles.

"Then you can have first watch," said Ashe. "I don't intend to lose all my sleep over it."

"That's agreed then," said Carruthers with a smile. "You won't mind giving Miles the gun, of course? Hardly fair to expect him to stand guard without it."

This clearly hadn't occurred to Ashe though he was quick to cover it. "Fair point," he admitted.

"Excellent. We can break it down into shifts of two hours each. I'll go second with you seeing us through until dawn, Gregory."

"And how does that work, exactly?" Penelope enquired. "There's four of us, in case you'd forgotten."

"I'm sure all the gentlemen will agree that we're only too happy to take the burden."

Miles put his hand up. Carruthers gave him no more than a brief glance. "Except for Miles, naturally, but then he loves sleep almost as much as he does the sound of his own voice."

"Oi!" said Miles, though it was clear Carruthers was pulling his leg.

"I will do my shift," Penelope insisted, folding her arms. "Just because I'm a woman doesn't mean I am any less capable, or do you think the mere sight of

an overambitious fur muff will send me into hyster-
ical panic?"

"I wasn't meaning to suggest…"

"Perhaps I will get distracted by thoughts of pretty
dresses and ponies? Or maybe I'll be too busy fixing
my makeup to notice as a naughty wolfikins starts
chewing on Miles' legs?"

Carruthers sighed. "Four shifts of an hour and a
half each, Miles first, then Penelope, then me and finally you, Gregory, that all right?"

"Fine," said Miles, "though I can't swear I won't
be too busy thinking of fast cars and breasts to concentrate."

Carruthers threw his hands up in the air. "That's
it, mock a man for coming from a civilised age!"

"One day she'll even be allowed to vote, you
know," said Miles, "but for now… why haven't you
made us our dinner, woman?"

Penelope punched him on the arm. "Get working
on the stove, boy, I'm hungry."

"Yes, mistress." Miles tugged a nonexistent fore-
lock. "Sorry, mistress, coming right up, mistress.
You can help, Carruthers, old chap, by way of
penance."

They moved over to the stove, where Carruthers
hoisted up his knapsack and dug out some tins of
soup. "I say," he whispered, being careful they
wouldn't be overheard, "do women really end up
getting the vote in your day?"

Miles chuckled. "Damn right they do, and why
shouldn't they?"

"No reason," Carruthers blustered. "I can see it might be something of an oversight in my era."

"Now, as to whether they actually get anyone worth voting for... well, that's another story. But the emancipation of women is one of the biggest steps forward of the twentieth century. In fact they rule the world by 2010 and all men have to wear dresses."

"No!"

"And thongs... really pinchy ones that cut their way through your crack like a wire through cheese."

Carruthers was baffled. "Again, I have no idea what you're talking about, though I suspect I am, as usual, being made a fool of."

Miles smiled. "I'm pulling your leg, yes, but nobody could ever make you a fool."

They dished up the food and it wasn't long before Carruthers, Penelope and Ashe took to their beds. Miles went to the cave entrance to smoke his sneaky cigar, Ashe's gun held tightly in his right hand. He practised aiming it, imagining himself a grizzled gunslinger or no-nonsense cop. Then he wondered why men never grew out of being utterly childish when it came to handling weaponry. Then he imagined being a cowboy for a bit more.

His shift passed without incident, nothing but the wind stirring at the mouth of the cave. Though he nearly shot Penelope when she came to relieve him, so uptight was he due to the recurring mental image of wolves charging towards him.

"Get yourself to bed," she said, once she had taken the gun from him. He started to speak but she interrupted him. "If you even try to tell me how the gun works I'll use it on you."

"Actually, Annie Bloody Oakley, I was going to say I would have another cigar before bed if you didn't mind the company."

"Oh… sorry."

"No worries." Miles lit a cigar with a smile, not in the least bit wanting it but happy to have an excuse to hang around a bit longer.

"So," he said clumsily, "you got a boyfriend back in New York?"

"That would be Chester, the man who gave me the box and tried to rape me."

"Oh… right… yes, of course." Miles considered shoving the cigar in his eye or perhaps head-butting the side of the cave until he just stopped *being*. In the end he did the only thing a man can in that situation. He tried to talk his way out of it. "I hadn't realised he was, you know, an actual boyfriend, just some passing nutter, you know…"

"We were engaged to be married."

"Narrow escape there then." Oh. Dear. God. Miles really wished he could stop his mouth moving. "I mean, you could have ended up marrying him and then… well… you know, that would have been… well… not worse, of course but–"

"Do I make you nervous, Miles?"

Miles stopped blathering. "Erm… a little bit. Sorry."

"It's all right." Penelope smiled and kissed him on the cheek. "It's funny. Now finish your cigar and go to sleep before you say something *really* embarrassing."

"Right, yes... good plan." Miles flung the cigar away, smiled in such an over-the-top way it made his face hurt, and skipped his way to bed.

The next thing he knew was the sound of a gunshot and Carruthers yelling: "They're coming!" Utterly disorientated, Miles leaped to his feet, nearly falling over as his still half-asleep brain tried to take control of his legs. The gun fired again and Carruthers was rolling back into the cave, a wolf bearing down on him. The gun skidded across the floor, and Ashe grabbed it even as another of the beasts leaped at him. He couldn't get the gun up in time but toppled to the floor, the wolf tearing at his coat with its fangs.

Using his discarded socks as a glove, Miles grabbed a log from the fire. He thrust the flames at the wolf that was wrestling with Carruthers. The animal howled in pain and fled from the cave, the stench of burned hair following it like a second tail. Miles looked for Penelope, who was hurling the heavy gramophone at another of the animals, its stout wooden corner impacting against its skull with a crunch. Meanwhile Ashe had turned the gun on the wolf that was still tearing chunks from his coat. He put a bullet under its chin and out through the top of its head. He took a second shot at a wolf just entering the cave, then a third at one directly behind it.

This was enough for the pack's sense of self-preservation to kick in. The animals fled back into the cold, the lingering smell of a singed pelt all they left behind. The whole attack had lasted no more than a few seconds.

"They came so quickly," said Carruthers. "Forgive me – I tried to hold them off but my aim... the shot was more powerful than I imagined."

"The recoil sends your arm up unless you're used to it," Ashe said. "Should have warned you, they make guns more potent in my time."

"You OK?" Miles asked Penelope.

"I'm fine," she said, "no damage at all... I..." Her eyes had fallen on the cover of a book that had spilled from Ashe's coat during the attack. "That's your book from the library," she said to Miles, "and Carruthers' and..." She stared at Ashe. "What are you doing with that?" The name on the third cover chilled her more than the pack of wolves had done.

Ashe looked down at the book, opened his mouth and then closed it again, unable to think of an excuse.

"What is it?" Miles asked.

"He's got Chester's book!" Penelope replied.

"*My* book actually," Ashe corrected her. "I might not have been telling the whole truth when I said my name was Ashe – first name that came to me, read a bunch of his books."

"Chester?" Carruthers asked, staring at the cover. "It doesn't say Chester."

"Chester was his nickname," explained Penelope, "after the president. His real name's–"

"Alan Arthur," Ashe interjected. "Wish I could say it was a pleasure to meet you."

INTERLUDE

"Did you think we wouldn't find you?"

The renegade looks up from his coffee, trying to place the two gentlemen standing by his table. They are of a particularly bland type, the only thing of note being their varying heights, one tall and thin, the other short and fat. They can only have been paired by someone with a sense of humour. After a moment's reflection, it is their complete lack of distinction that gives the renegade a moment's concern. He has always adopted the most nondescript of faces to hide behind, something soft and curved to hide all his sharp edges, and there is no guarantee that these people have not done the same. "Do I know you?" he asks, making a point of sipping his drink slowly, glancing casually at them over the rim of his cup.

"We know you, that is enough."

"I somehow doubt that, gentlemen." He smiles and reaches for his pack of cigarettes. He has taken the habit up recently and is enjoying consuming as many as possible in a day. He pulls out a cigarette, puts it in his mouth and digs in his coat pocket for a lighter. There is no need: the tip obligingly ignites itself, or at least appears to.

"Still enjoying the native life?" the tall man asks, smiling at his little trick. He reaches over and plucks the cigarette from between the renegade's lips. He sucks on it, drawing the entire tube of tobacco into his mouth in one inhalation. Letting the smoke emerge from his nostrils he drops the filter on the ground. "Fascinating, I'm sure. How clever to have mastered inhaling smoke. What are they going to do next? Ingest liquids? You're wallowing so far down the evolutionary ladder it's an effort to even communicate with you."

The renegade is trying to put a name to the terrible sickness he is feeling; it's a new sensation and he doesn't like it. It makes his stomach churn, the hair follicles on his skin tighten, his muscles tense. It is terribly uncomfortable. He has an idea it might be fear. Deciding to act on it rather than simply endure it, he shoves the table away and runs down the street, managing a few steps before the ground beneath him loses its solidity and he is left to thrash around in a grey taffy of road surface.

"What is the name of this place?" asks the tall man as the couple draw alongside him.

"Stalingrad," the renegade answers breathlessly, "and if you think it's boring now then hang around twenty-four hours, we're about to have a bit of fun."

"We are aware of what you consider fun. How many are to die this time?"

"About two million."

The tall man stretches his inherited bones. "I find it astonishing they can be so active in these meat sacks of theirs." He cricks his neck, grimacing in discomfort. "But then they do have a great deal of encouragement, do they not?"

"A little cheering from the sidelines, nothing too vulgar."

"It's all vulgar, you ridiculous specimen."

"Each to his own."

The tall man pokes at the renegade with his foot, pushing him back down into the sticky mess of tar. "Your philosophy is utterly contaminated... you are an embarrassment, a disgrace."

"To you, perhaps, but here I am a God. These things are relative."

"A God? I can't even pretend to know what one is... no matter, we know what you are: you're a renegade and as such will not be tolerated."

The small man drops to his haunches and opens his mouth. There is a cracking noise as his jaw dislocates, his lips parting until his whole face is nothing but mouth. With workmanlike patience, he eats the renegade whole.

CHAPTER NINETEEN

Sophie wakes to the sound of an explosion. It shakes her in the dark and she is scared. Explosions are Never Right. They are loud and dangerous. They break things. They can never be anything but Bad. She told her mother and father this when they tried to take her to see fireworks. Fireworks were just colourful explosions. Fireworks were bad. She screamed and screamed and screamed until they stopped. They never took her again.

This was not a firework, it did not sound the same. Still it made her scream until Alan came and told her it was all right. She does not know how Alan can think explosions are all right but she knows Alan is a man of facts so she has no choice but to believe him.

He opens the curtains so Sophie can see what she already knows: she is not in the water, she is in a room. The room is small and dark and made of wood. She thinks the room must be a shed. She knows sheds. She has been in sheds before.

"The noise was Jonah freeing the anchor," Alan is saying, though the words mean nothing to her and she worries that she has forgotten how words work. "He climbs up the ropes and sets a small charge on the roof to blow the harpoons loose, hell of a sight." Sophie is really worried now, Alan is making no sense at all. Maybe he's gone mad?

"Sorry," he says, "you probably have no idea what I'm talking about, do you?" Sophie shakes her head, glad that Alan is once more a man of facts.

Alan tells her that they are now not in the water, they are on a ship. Sophie thinks about this. It would explain why the shed is moving up and down and creaking. She thought it was just angry with her for screaming but maybe this is how it is supposed to be. Ships go on water and they were on water so maybe they are now on water in a ship. This doesn't sound too wrong so maybe it is right.

Alan tells her about everything he has seen while she was asleep. She is thinking about sheds for a lot of it so she misses most of what he says. She picks up some things. The names of some people which don't mean anything as names are no good without faces. He says something about people made from water but she must have missed the important part of that as men are Not Made From Water so it doesn't make sense. In fact, she decides, most of what he says doesn't make sense so she gives up listening and thinks about clothes. She left her clothes in a very neat pile on the bench. She is hoping Alan has brought those clothes with them. She cannot

walk around in her bra and panties, that is a rule. It's
all right in the water or going between the dry land
and the water (as long as it's not far) or when going
to bed or when going between bed and the water.
Probably. She's never done it. She doesn't think it's
all right on a ship. So has Alan brought her clothes?
She gets out of bed to look for them but can't find
them. This makes her very sad. She left them so
neatly. What if something comes along and makes a
mess of them while she's gone? What if they move
her socks, her perfect, walking, empty feet? She sits
on the bed and starts to empty herself, her humming
sounding very loud in the small shed. She wonders
if Alan will worry about this. She thinks that he
sometimes needs to empty himself so maybe he will
understand. She opens her eyes once she feels better
and Alan is still there. This is good. He is holding up
some clothes for her and she wonders if he has read
her mind. They are not her clothes. They are big
clothes for a man but he says they will be all right
and he speaks facts so they will be. He leaves her to
put them on and she does so. They are too big but
they are funny. Floppy shirt and trousers that she has
to turn up so she can walk. She will wear them until
she can get her proper clothes back.

She joins Alan and they leave what isn't a shed
but a room. They walk up to the deck of the ship. It
is very strange there. It is like outside but it is not
outside. It is just a very big inside. This is like the
jungle that was not a jungle but a very big inside.
She has seen this before so it is not so Wrong. The

water still looks like it is very happy with her, though
Alan says it is dangerous and she must be Very Careful. She already knows you have to be Very Careful
with water but Alan seems to think it is Important
so she adds it to her list.

Very Careful now includes:

1. *Fire (or things that make fire).*
2. *Broken Glass.*
3. *Roads.*
4. *Tall Places (she has learned this to be true
   because cliffs are Tall Places and she has now
   fallen off one).*
5. *Water.*
6. *Strange Men (but all men are strange except for
   Alan and her father, so this confuses her a bit).*
7. *Knives.*
8. *The iron (do not touch it!)*
9. *Some Animals (ones that bite or sting).*
10. *This Sea Especially.*

Alan introduces her to all the Strange Men on the
ship and, because she has remembered they are on
the Very Careful list, she is on her guard. They do
not seem too strange though. Except for the blind
man, the grumpy man, and the young man that giggles all the time. She changes her mind: they are
very strange. She likes the woman. The woman is
Very Strange Indeed but nobody said anything about
being careful with strange women so she likes her.
She has good hair. She helps her with her clothes

and does not touch more than Sophie likes. She is good. The captain is good too. Though he has far too much hair. Maybe she will tell him this when she knows him better. People don't like it when you tell them things about how silly they look unless you know them a lot.

She watches the strange men make the boat work. It is nice. It is soft and soft things are good. It is good being on the water but not in the water as you get to have the softness without the wetness. She sits down and watches them for a long time. They talk about going home. Sophie would like to go home though she hasn't got to understand everything here yet so maybe she should do that first. She will see.

Alan seems happy but Sophie knows that Alan is one of those people that can pretend to be happy when they're not so she is not sure if it's true. She watches him as the strange men teach him how to make the boat work. He seems to want to help make the boat work A Lot so maybe he is happy. Maybe he likes pulling and climbing and lifting. Her father used to like pulling and climbing and lifting. He had a place he would do it in. The place was called Jim. Which is a wrong name for a place but her father liked it so she tried not to think about it.

After a while she gets bored watching the men make the ship work so she goes down inside the ship and gets to know all the little rooms that are like sheds but not sheds. She goes into each of them, walking around the edges in the way that lets you understand a room properly. This is difficult in some of the rooms as they are very untidy and it is hard to walk. She decides she will be nice to the strange men and put their things in good piles. They will like her for this and maybe they won't be strange any more. In the bigger of the bedrooms she finds a bottle of brown drink that makes her think of her father. It smells like his face when he kisses goodnight. She holds it to her face. Yes, it is nearly the same. But not quite the same.

Once the piles have been made it is much easier to understand the rooms and she goes all around them again. Three times. Three is a good number.

This has taken a long time but there was nothing else she was supposed to do and the strange men will be pleased. That is good. She goes back to look at the men and the water. They have not changed. The men are still pulling and climbing or lifting. The sea is still doing what seas do. This is good. But she does not know what her place is so she is restless. You cannot walk far on a boat and soon she has understood the ship three times. There is nothing more to understand.

She spends an hour hanging over the side, counting the different coloured tiles she can spy beneath the waves. She then realises this is making her very sick so she has to stop. She does not like being sick. It is messy. It is uncontrolled. It is food going the wrong way. It is bad.

She sits down on the deck and tries to make her belly stop feeling bad. This is not easy as she has let it feel Very Bad Indeed. She really won't be able to bear it if she is sick. She breathes slowly and deeply, counting to three over and over again in her mind. This is doing all the things possible to stop the bad things happening. It is enough. She is not sick.

In a way this has been good, it has passed some time and made her forget she is bored. Now she must think of something else to do.

She decides to go below again and make the kitchen work. The kitchen has so many things in the wrong place. This is good, it gives her a really big problem to solve. She will make it a good room again. She clears everything from the floor. There is food and knifes and packaging and a book and a sock and a teacup and some hair. She thinks the hair is from where someone has cut their beard sitting at the table. She does not know why anyone would do this. She does not know why anyone would have a beard. She does not know where to put all these things so she walks back up to the deck and throws them over the side of the boat. This is not good but she closes her eyes and pretends it didn't just happen. At least the floor now has nothing more on it than should be on it: tables and chairs are supposed to be left on floors, this is not mess, this is normal. She begins to tidy the other parts of the kitchen. In the cupboards she finds bowls and plates and things. She arranges these according to size until they look nice. They never look nice. It is hard to make a bowl look nice. She tries arranging them according to colour but that goes wrong straightaway so she puts things back to how they were and stares at them until she likes them. She moves on to the cutlery, making sure that there are forks then knives then spoons (this is the order in which you use them unless you have soup but soup has its own type of spoon, not like these, so it's still all right). She makes the forks and spoons sit inside each other so they are one stack of each. She cannot do this for the knives but she can make sure that all the blades are pointing the same way. This makes them look better. They are not all the same type of fork, knife and spoon so it will never be perfect but it will Just Have to Do. She is not always good at Just Have to Do (however much her mother tried to teach her how it worked) but she does her best. She realises that this means that her trying to make Just Have to Do work is a good example of Just Have to Do. Life is funny like that. She understands it a bit better for the realisation. Sometimes nearly is the best you can get. Yes. This is an important thing. Just Have to Do. A wise thing.

She has forgotten about tidying the kitchen but that's OK as she has lots of time. So, she has done crockery and cutlery, now she must do food. There is not much food but what there is is easy to make right. She looks for spaghetti as she is very hungry. There is none so she will have to stay hungry. She separates what there is into bags, packets and tins and makes neat rows of each. Some of the flour has escaped. Flour always escapes. It is like a mug of hot drink in that it always leaves a mark where it has been. Flour is horrid, horrid, horrid. She is tempted to throw the flour in the sea too but then it will make pastry and you cannot sail a boat on pastry so the strange men will be cross. She tries to make sure the packet will not leak, puts it down and then does not look at it again so that she cannot see whether it has leaked. The flour is fine. The flour will Just Have to Do.

She finds a cloth. This is a good thing, cloths make things clean. Though first she has to make the cloth clean. She does this by soaking it in some water and some salt. She has heard that salt is a clean thing. It doesn't feel clean but they use it to store things in so it must be. And when you cut yourself even though salt stings it heals and that's why it stings. So salt is good. She uses the cloth to make everything else clean. It takes a long time but once it is done it is good.

All of this has taken a long time and when she goes back up to the deck it is starting to get dark. The strange men are all running around as something very important is going to happen. Alan tells her again that when it gets dark the sea turns into men and the men attack the ship. This is silly and she doesn't want to see it. Water and men are very different. She hopes Alan hasn't become too strange by being with the other strange men. She decides the easiest thing is to stay below deck and ignore all the noise and the shouting. If she does this then she does not have to understand about men made from water as she hasn't seen them and things are only completely real once they have been seen. The noise lasts for twelve minutes, she counts them, this gives her something to do that isn't worrying. Twelve is also a good number. This is good.

Everyone comes down and they go in the kitchen and make it messy again. This makes her a bit angry but the nice woman says she has done a good job so that is good. She supposes she can always make the kitchen right again tomorrow.

She is tired and the conversation between the crew isn't something she needs to understand so she goes to bed to sleep.

It has not been a Really Good Day but at least nobody has tried to hurt her so it was better than some of the Really Bad Days she's had lately.

Alan didn't sleep well. But then he rarely did. His dreams were of the sort that left you too agitated for sleep. From typical anxiety dreams – answering a phone that he cannot find, typing on a typewriter whose alphabet is unknown by anything but itself – to mini-dramas that centred around the early life he couldn't remember. Rebecca, his therapist, was all too quick to dismiss this as his subconscious trying to fill the gap in his memory. Perhaps so, but he wished it would do it with a little less cruelty. He imagines himself as a young man, savouring the discomfort of others. A dream in which he rapes a young woman is particularly intolerable (and regular enough to partly explain his lack of interest in relationships). Then there are his dreams of the box. In his nightmares the box has always been a part of his life, though clearly this is not the case: this is a prime example of "retrospective editing" – only a therapist could come up with a phrase so unwieldy – in that the things that are important to him are now inveigling their way into his fantasies of the past. He doesn't much care what they are; he doesn't like them and would gladly consign them to the same fate as his history.

He awoke with the shocked conviction that he had just shot someone – how ludicrous, he's never even handled a gun, let alone fired one, yet he seemed to recall the recoil of the revolver, the spray of precious blood from an exit wound. The blood was as red as the woman's hair, both flying free in the air around her shocked face. Rebecca insists that this is his mind's inclination to fear the unknown. With less respect than he suspects he should owe, Alan always thinks – but never says – that Rebecca is full of shit. She likes the sound of her own voice more than she does his, and for a listener this is never a good sign. One day he'll cancel his meetings with her, one day…

He sat up in bed, not even tempted to try and drop off again just yet. Let a few minutes pass in the darkness. It's time for his brain to occupy itself with fresh thoughts, to dismiss the image of the gunshot wound in a woman's head, unfurled like a Valentine rose. Let him, instead, think about the here and now. About how he and Sophie might find their way home.

"Hmm… tell me about Sophie." Rebecca was

seated in the corner of his room. Not really, of course, that would be lunacy rather than imagination – but he had pictured her strongly in his mind and now she was here. As always she was asking questions.

"Nothing to tell," he whispered, feeling foolish to have given the fantasy weight by speaking to it.

"This constant fear that you're not a good man," she said, "this conviction that – despite the opinion of your peers – you are in some way an unpleasant individual, unworthy of respect, friendship or love. You wouldn't be trying to assuage it, would you? The kindly father to a special-needs child... you couldn't get more worthy could you?"

He ignored her this time. He wouldn't validate that opinion with an answer, however close it might be to the truth.

"Who couldn't respect such a man?" she continued. "What a good, kind, wholesome man. What a *worthy* man."

He stared at her, if only to make her vanish. Fantasies never bear up to scrutiny, not in the waking hours.

Now he had the room to himself he got out of bed and walked over to the window. He'd forgotten that there was nothing to be seen, no light to illuminate the water they sailed on. He rested his head on the sill, desperately tired and yet determined to stay awake long enough to wipe his brain clean of the dream that woke him. What to do? That was still the only pertinent question. He had surprised himself by enjoying the day spent playing a sailor, everything driven by simple reasons and purpose. There was much to be said for it. Now he was worried that it wasn't getting them anywhere, it was just a way of filling his time. They needed to find a way home but, adrift on this unreliable water, how exactly were they supposed to go about it? They couldn't navigate, all they could do was fight against the whims of the water and hope they stumbled upon something. How long might that take? Years?

Something had just occurred to him in his thoughts. He was brushing against a realisation of importance but was unable to pin it down. A phrase suddenly occurred to him and with that, all hope of sleep was lost…

"The water *knows*." Alan paced the deck, shaking with the weight of this thought.

Hawkins watched him, trying but failing to share in Alan's excitement. "The water knows what?"

"The water knows the exit!" It was all Alan could do not to shout it. "The sea is sentient, right? It has a consciousness? A sense of its own self?"

Hawkins nodded. "It seems so, yes."

"Then it knows everything about its environment! What sails on it, swims in it, what shores it touches."

Hawkins began to follow. "It is aware of everything around it, yes, I see that… if it can feel us it must feel everything."

"Precisely! So, on the understanding that there is a route through the water, the sea knows it."

"How does this help us?"

"I was in the water for a few hours and it was a part of me, I shared my thoughts with it, nearly became part of it. In a subconscious sense I communicated with it."

"Enough to know the way?"

"No, because I didn't ask the question."

"You're losing me…"

"I need to become part of the water again…" Alan held up his hand, aware that Hawkins was about to protest. "Not for long, just enough to try and ask the question."

"To ask where the exit is?"

"Yes!"

"Have you any idea how mad that sounds?"

"Of course I do! But I also know that we're unlikely to get anywhere just drifting around. This is a part of the house that we can talk to, however dangerous it may be. How can we not try it?"

Hawkins fell silent. He moved to the bow of the ship and looked out at the wall of the bathroom they had anchored themselves alongside. The checkered pattern of its black and white tiles was like a vertical chessboard, stretching as far as the eye could see. "There may be no exit," he said.

"No, there may not, but there's no harm in hoping, is there? And with the whole crew on hand to fish me out should things go wrong…"

"I don't like it."

"You think I do? But having thought about it I need to try it. What if it works? There's a possibility, and there's so few of those here that I can't ignore one, however much I might wish to." Alan put his hands on Hawkins' shoulders. "Don't worry," he said. "We'll be as careful as possible."

Hawkins nodded. Every sailor knows that sometimes careful just isn't enough.

They lowered him into the water in a net, the better to fish him back out again at the first sign of trouble. He poked his wrists and ankles through the mesh, coiled the rope around him and did his best to relax as he touched the sea's surface. A few years ago he had broken his arm, slipping on the ice outside the faculty building and earning a swan-neck fracture – and no few laughs from the gathered students. Later, at the hospital, he had laid back in the operating theatre, a cannula inserted into the back of his hand, and immersed himself in the sensation of the anaesthetic. The hot surge crept up his arm, riding the vein to the heart, knocking him out by the time he had felt it reach the top of his bicep. This was like that, a thick, liquid sleep that folded itself over him and rendered him as limp as a corpse. He closed his eyes, took a breath and dipped his head back into the water, offering himself to it.

He did his best to push away physical sensations. He remembered how it had felt to be part of the water, dissolving into it, evaporating until every ebb and flow was a muscular twitch, a sensation he was part of rather than just subject to. The water was happy to receive him, buzzing effervescently over his scalp, stroking and massaging him.

"This, of course, is a perfect example of a death wish." He opened his eyes to the voice, not in the least surprised to see Rebecca sitting cross-legged on her office chair on the sea bed. The water splayed her long hair around her head like a cartoon electric shock, and her blouse rippled with the investigation of fish as they explored cotton coral, tasting this new part of their landscape. "If you could only die in this brave attempt to save them all, what a glorious martyr, what a hero…" She spoke in air bubbles, the words popping out like marbles from between her lips.

"I'm beginning to think I pay you too much," Alan replied. "All you ever do is patronise me."

"But I'm the closest you come to a real relationship," she said, uncrossing her legs to let a small eel escape from the dark cave offered by her pencil skirt, "and you find me far too attractive to let me go."

"There is that," Alan admitted, "though I would never admit it to your face."

"Which just goes to show how unproductive our professional relationship is. What are you searching for?"

"Escape."

"Aren't we all?"

"Are you my subconscious or are you part of the sea?"

"Soon there'll be no difference."

"Are you here to help me or distract me?"

"I always want to help you."

"So how do we leave here?"

"I can't tell you, that's not how therapy works – you have to find your own answers."

"Some help you are."

"Let go of all of it, your fears, your perceptions, your flesh…" She arched her head back in the water, a small crab scuttling across her cheek and tapping her eye with its claw. "Go with the flow."

"I didn't hold with that in the Sixties, let alone now."

"The Sixties? I was under the impression you didn't remember them."

"I don't, I was being glib."

"And yet, when you dream of your life before it's not the Sixties you remember, is it? It's much earlier…"

"They're just dreams."

"You would love to believe that."

"It's what you've always said."

"Ah… but here I know better. How can you have memories of a time before you were born, Alan? How can that be possible?"

"It isn't. I'm just fantasising, imagining… That's not me I see when I close my eyes, it's the man I'm afraid of being."

"And you do right to be afraid, don't you? He's a terrible man, isn't he, Alan? A cruel and selfish man."

"It's not me."

"Of course it is. He's the man you were born to be

before you locked him away in a box, in a house, and refused to let him back out."

"It's not me."

"You said you wanted escape, so... escape!"

"It's not me." Alan could say no more; he refused to go along with the this line of conversation. She reached down beside her in the chair and pulled out an old leatherbound book. She held it up so he could see his name on the front cover. "Your notes?" he asked.

"Not mine, I don't keep such a full account as this." She opened the book and showed him the torn first section. "Though I'm afraid it hasn't been well preserved, as you can see: whole years are chewed away. Is it any wonder you can't remember? It doesn't become really legible until you find yourself waking up alongside a country road in 1976. Before that it's just fragments, the odd word here and there, the odd image... not that there's anything wrong with a bit of mystery. Who wants to know everything in life? Where would be the fun in that?"

"This is getting me nowhere." He closed his eyes, tried to push her from his thoughts.

"And that's the problem: you're offered the route to escape and you don't take it, you run back into your heavy, repressed cage to rot."

He ignored her, trying to reclaim the feeling he had experienced when last here. He tried to imagine what it felt like to have a boat floating inside you, a foreign object, a splinter you wanted to expel. After a few moments he felt the intrusion in his solar plexus, shifting and rolling as he tried to dislodge it with his tides. He held fast to that feeling, imagining his splayed fingers were part of the water, part of this house. He stroked the cool tiles that surrounded them. He tickled the bathroom shore with his toes, reached out and touched the wooden bench, pushed his big toe into the pile of Sophie's clothes. He moved his hands, running them along the wall on his right, sending them through the open expanse of water on the left. He felt fish dart between them and grabbed hold of that sensation, that feeling of the things invading his being. He stretched his hand, tapped the wall behind his head – oh, so many miles away – and the wall on his left, further still. He tried to differentiate between it all, the swimming of fish, the bobbing of the boat, the feel of the walls. He acknowledged those sensations and then blanked them out, seeing what was left. Something was buzzing in his ear, like a persistent wasp at a summer picnic, dancing just inside his awareness. That buzzing, that tingle of the other lying just on the edge of awareness, that was the door, and he now realised he had been hunting in the wrong direction. He reached for it, felt the coil of metal chain between his fingers, the soft edge of rubber. He reached for it and yanked it free.

"Alan! Can you hear me?" The crew pulled him out of the water with such vigour it was like being born; yanked from somewhere warm and safe and brought out into the bright, white cold of the real world.

"How long?" Alan gasped, spitting some water

from his mouth and trying not to imagine it as a finger or toe of their nighttime attackers.

"A minute," Hawkins said. "I wouldn't risk any longer."

"Felt so long…" Alan suddenly remembered what he had done. "We need to take shelter!" he shouted, "and hope the anchors hold."

The boat was beginning to rock violently, the sea whipping up a storm around them.

"What did you do?" Hawkins asked, helping him out of the net.

Alan smiled. "What else do you want to do when you want to get out of the bath? I pulled the plug out!"

CHAPTER TWENTY

The creature had a firm hold on Chester. As Tom and Pablo tried to tug him free, its arm stretched like the limb of a gooey children's toy, distending and becoming translucent in the torchlight. The skin, bone and muscle spread out to little more than a flat sheet. Chester had begun to panic, mindless of the weapon in his hand as the creature unhinged its wide mouth and took both the gun and his forearm into its throat.

"Shoot it!" Elise shouted, cutting through Chester's blank panic. He did so, and the bullet punched a gelatinous hole between the creature's shoulders. More in confusion than in pain, it let go of him, spitting out his arm and reaching behind itself to explore the wound with rubbery digits.

The creatures surrounded them, rolling their pipe-tongues around thin lips, wanting to suck on a warm morsel or two. They reached out glutinous hands and fingers, tugging at the humans' clothes and hair, trying to grab the piece of meat they wished to lay claim to.

A noise began to build from the tunnel: the rush of water being forced along the narrow passage. It grew louder and louder. The creatures glanced around, distracted from the hunger in their bellies. A curtain of warm, foul-smelling air pushed before the wave like the early warning of a tube train. When the water emerged, it did so with enough force to send all of them flying backwards. They were thrown on to solid ground as the water fanned out to fill the space. Tom fought for breath as he was sent spinning across the flagstones, and desperately tried to keep hold of Elise.

"Keep moving!" Pablo shouted. He was the first to his feet. Chester scuffled behind him, his leather soles slipping on the wet stone as they ran across the chamber and towards a far tunnel. Tom and Elise followed, hoping that the size of the chamber would buy them enough time to get clear. There seemed no end to the flood as it bounced off the ceiling, dislodging the rubbery creatures that still clung to the brickwork. Like the spout of a giant pressure hose, it was relentless as it forced itself through the narrow opening. The water had a life of its own, whipping into shapes as it sought to grab and absorb every living thing within reach. This was no ordinary water, this was water haunted by the many travellers absorbed into its waves. Human figures formed on the crest of the flood, shimmering surfers riding into the darkness of the drainage pipes.

Tom, Elise, Pablo and Chester ran through a tunnel that led off from the main chamber. The water gurgled around their feet, nipping at their toes as they tried to keep some distance ahead.

"It just keeps coming!" Chester shouted, "we need to gain higher ground."

"You're the cat who knows the tunnels," Tom replied. "Give us a dose of your wisdom – how do we get up a level?"

Chester was still too close to panic for clear thought, spinning around in the tunnel as he tried to remember the closest routes leading up to the house. "I know!" he shouted, like an enthused child who's just come up with a new game for the day. "There's a–"

The water exploded around him, elevating him several feet off the ground inside its translucent fist. The end of his sentence burst from his mouth in a series of air bubbles as he thrashed to pull himself free. Pablo jumped up, shoving his hands through the surface of the water, and grabbed hold of Chester's ankle. Elise did the same with the other leg. They dangled from his feet, tugging him down with all their weight. Tom grabbed hold of Elise's waist and pulled. That was all the extra weight that was needed and Chester dropped, the bubble bursting and showering them with water as they fell to the ground.

Chester lost all control, thrashing around, trying to rub the water from his face and hair. "Fucking thing, fucking thing," he repeated, panic rioting through him.

"It's all right!" Elise shouted, grabbing hold of him, forcing him to stand still and look her in the eyes.

"No harm done, we're still here, let's keep it that way, OK?"

"Saved my life," Chester muttered. "If you three hadn't have been here I would be dead, no question..."

"It's all cool, Chester," said Tom, patting him on the shoulder.

"Is like ice cream," Pablo agreed "but we need keep running before it melt!"

"Taught the cat everything he knows," said Tom with a grin. "Where were you about to suggest we ran to before being so rudely interrupted?"

Chester snapped out of it. "An elevator!" he shouted, "It's small but we should fit!" He ran through the tunnel, the others keeping pace behind him, all the time aware that the water was deepening. "I've never used it," Chester shouted over his shoulder, "but anywhere's better than here." He ran up a short ramp that led to the cabin of an oldfashioned cage elevator, just big enough to accommodate them.

"Press the button! Press the button!" Chester shouted, squeezed into the far corner of the cabin. Pablo stabbed the button that would begin their ascent and then gripped the mesh sides so that he could secure the gate behind him. The elevator groaned under the weight, climbing jerkily as it struggled under the load.

"There's too many of us!" Chester shouted, watching the water surge below them.

"We'll be fine," said Elise as the elevator continued to climb. "It's slow but it's managing."

"Fucking thing will probably snap halfway up!" Chester shouted, spraying Tom's cheek with spittle as he grew more and more red-faced. "No way is it going to make it."

"Chill out, Chester baby," Tom replied, "we're on our way, everything's copacetic."

"I am not dying in this stupid fucking elevator!" Chester screamed, grabbing hold of the bars of the cabin behind him, hoisting up his legs and kicking out.

"What the fuck?" Tom was winded by the sole of Chester's left shoe, while his right shoved hard enough against Elise to make her fall backwards with a cry. It was Pablo – only just managing to hang in there as it was – who took the brunt of the pressure, forced back against the gate, the metal cutting into his fingers as he grabbed the sides in order to steady himself.

"You will kill all of us, stupid America!" he shouted, giving a terrified yelp as the catch on the gate snapped behind him and the elevator stopped. The gate swung back, leaving him holding on to the sides of the cabin, his toes pedalling at the floor's edge, trying to get a grip. Chester kept kicking, forcing the other three back towards the opening of the elevator. "Please!" Pablo shouted. The metal was cutting into his hands enough to make them bleed.

"Mother fucker!" Tom wheezed, still partially winded but trying to grab Chester to keep him still. The elevator cabin shook violently as the young man kept kicking. It just couldn't take it. No longer able to hold on, his hands sliced raw by the bars, Pablo toppled backwards, flipping in the air and hitting the edge of the ramp before slipping beneath the water's surface.

There was silence in the elevator cabin, the three of them hanging above the rising water, Tom and Elise not quite able to believe what had just happened.

"What have you done?" Elise whispered, turning on Chester. "You stupid fuck… you killed him!" Tom stared at the water below, hoping perhaps to see Pablo reappear. He did not.

"What are you going to do?" Chester asked, his voice again like that of a child, a naughty young boy who has been caught in a terrible act.

"I don't know about Tom," Elise replied through clenched teeth, "but I have *every fucking intention of throwing you out there after him!*" She roared at him, hand raised to smack him as hard as she could across the face. Chester pulled the gun from his pocket and shot her squarely in the forehead. Tom screamed as blood splashed across his cheek, hot as a passionate kiss. He grabbed Elise as she fell backwards, her eyes rolling in her head, like a doll shaken by a child. Chester pointed the gun at Tom and pulled the trigger, but the hammer clicked down on to an empty chamber. And again. And again. He was out of ammunition. So he shoved them, the weight of Elise pushing Tom back out of the elevator, the look on Tom's face one of utter disbelief as to how everything could have gone to shit so quickly. They fell, Elise wrapped in Tom's arms. Chester didn't watch them fall; he didn't care. He simply – calmly – pulled the metal gate closed and forced the catch into its socket so it didn't trip the motor again. The elevator jerked back into life.

"They saved my life, they saved my life, they saved my life," Chester repeated, over and over, as he rode the elevator to its destination. "They saved my life, they saved my life, they saved my life."

The elevator clicked into place and Chester yanked the gate open. The bent metal refused to fold back properly, but he made just enough space to squeeze past and clambered into the carpet-lined corridor of the house. "They saved my life, they saved my life, they saved my life."

The gas lamps in the corridor were dimming with the night. Chester stumbled into darkness as he followed the curve of the corridor, running his hand along the dado rail for guidance. The paintings and sculptures that lined the walls began to flicker in the twilight of the lamps. In a mediaeval hunting scene, the painted torches the huntsmen carried began to move with real light and warmth. The huntsmen gathered at the edge of the frame to watch Chester stumble past. "They saved my life, they saved my life, they saved my life."

A bust of Medusa writhed, lit by a lantern hanging in a portrait above her. The mouths of the asps nipped at Chester as he passed. "They saved my life, they saved my life, they saved my life."

A stabbing sensation in his head forced a cry of pain from him and his legs crumpled. "They saved

my life, they saved my life, they saved my life." The
pain returned, savage and unbearable, as if something were being rammed directly between his eyes
(like a bullet perhaps? "They saved my life, they
saved my life, they saved my life"). He tried to crawl,
a string of spittle dangling from his mouth like a silver necklace, glittering in the light of the artistic fires
that burned around him. Several busts of Roman
Caesars watched with lofty disdain as he crawled
past, batting not a marble eyelid at the screams of
agony he issued, the pain returning time and again
as – unknown to him – a book of his life met the
eager mouths of hungry worms in the house library.
Mouthful by mouthful they ate away his past, the
pain as debilitating as if it were his meat they fed on,
not just his history.

He passed out, lying face down on the corridor
carpet. Around him the pictures cavorted: the mediaeval hunstsmen left their dense forest to dally in
the bushes of the water nymphs that hung close by;
a Tudor gentleman took a bite of Venetian red from
the neck of his wife; his neighbour, a miller by
trade, showed his disgust by squatting beneath the
silently revolving blades of his mill and defecating
a curl of raw umber; Whistler's Mother gazed las-
civiously at Rembrandt's Bathesheba at Her Bath,
parting her ridiculously long legs to frig beneath her
Puritan's skirt as the voluptuous Queen was
sponged and cleansed by her servants; Picasso's Boy
with a Pipe sucked on his opium as Matisse's
Bathers turned on the little turtle between them,

wrenching off its legs like drumsticks and chewing on its scaled flesh.

Chester was blind to it all, his brain having shut down in response to its injury. When morning came and the artworks returned to the two-dimensional safety of their own frames, Chester lay utterly still, his eyes open but empty. The hours passed. The corridor was silent but for the faint hiss of the gas lamps. Around mid-morning a young woman awoke in one of the rooms off the corridor, snatched from her Greek island to reappear in this most terrible house. Her visit was not a lengthy one, for she was plucked from an open window by the talons of a massive house-martin with chicks to feed. Her screams reached the corridor but Chester was unable to hear them. Lunchtime came and went. Chester's breath became laboured with the dust from the carpet, wheezing as the afternoon rolled on. By the time night came again he sounded like a leaking foot-pump. The noise was enough to bring the workers from Breugel's Corn Harvest down to investigate, poking at him with their hayforks and kicking at his exposed teeth.

The morning lamps shone on a bruised and bleeding face, the paintings having vented their frustration throughout the night. After nearly forty hours of unconsciousness, Chester came to life, spasming on the carpet, his limbs refusing to work after long hours of dysfunction. The pain had gone from his head and in that it was not alone: pretty much everything had gone from Chester's head. He finally got to his feet and stumbled towards the end of the corridor, his fingers tracing the solid door in front of him. He was a vacuum, empty of everything but motor movement, but, as the door fizzed beneath his fingers, he knew that there was something incredibly powerful on the other side. Something that waited for him. He tried to speak, tried to remember the words for things. After a few slurred noises, his mouth and tongue remembered the sound of a question.

"Who am I?" he whispered, as a surge of dizziness forced him to the floor.

"Open this door," said a gentle voice from inside the room, "and I'll tell you."

CHAPTER TWENTY-ONE

Alan was put in mind of a fairground ride as the *Intrepid* tugged on the ropes that held it fast to the bathroom roof. "I hope they hold," he said, staring up at the holes in the plaster where the harpoons were embedded.

"They won't," said Barnabas as he stumbled past, "we'll die an agonising death any minute, just you watch."

"Hold fast!" Hawkins shouted, clipping Ryan around the ear as the boy ran past giggling. "Stand still, damn you! The less we do to put strain on the ropes the better."

Below them, the water continued to swirl, coursing its way towards the distant plughole and beyond.

"Do you think we could ride the current?" Alan asked.

"For a certain distance perhaps," answered Hawkins, "but I wouldn't fancy our chances once we were on top of the sinkhole, would you?"

"Our best bet is to wait for the water to drain," Maggie suggested, "then drop down and make the rest of the journey on foot."

"You're no fun," moaned Ryan. "The first chance of a laugh we've had in months and you want to sit it out."

"We should lighten our load, Cap'n," Jonah suggested.

"Aye," Hawkins agreed. "We need to do everything we can to ensure that the ropes hold until the water level drops." He untied the remaining lifeboat and let it fall to the water below, where it shot off like an speedboat. "Maggie, start packing a few essentials. Ryan, give her a hand." He turned to Alan. "You go and get Sophie, she must be fair panicking by now." Alan dashed off, leaving Hawkins barking further orders at Jonah and Barnabas to ditch what they could above deck. The captain was in his element now, the adrenalin flowing and a crew to protect.

It was hard to walk, because the ship was swinging from side to side and knocking him against the walls as he ran down the stairs shouting for Sophie. She was sitting in her room, utterly calm. "The sea is angry," she said casually.

"Indeed it is," he agreed, "but not with us. We need to be careful though – we're going to get off the ship now and walk the rest of the way. I think I might have found us a way home."

"That is good," she said, standing up and walking out of the room as if there was nothing alarming about any of it. Alan couldn't help but smile.

The water level continued to drop, and Hawkins directed everyone to the rear of the ship. "Once the water is low enough we're going to tip up," he warned. "The front will rise towards the roof as the whole lot sinks backwards. If you haven't got a steady grip at that point you'll be going overboard."

They lashed themselves to the stern, using the railing to hold them as the prow of the boat rose vertical. On their backs they strapped the knapsacks that Maggie had prepared, hoping they would survive long enough to use their contents.

"And to think I put some faith into you!" Barnabas shouted at Alan. "Should have know you'd kill us all soon enough."

"Shut up!" said Hawkins. "We were going nowhere fast. Alan was right, we need to get off the *Intrepid* and take our chances."

"I'll remind you of that when we're lying crushed to a pulp beneath her."

The ship continued to tilt, the crew pressed back against the inside of the railing. The ropes creaked as the full weight was brought to bear on them, and showers of plaster dropped like hailstones.

"We need to be ready," said Hawkins, "as soon as the water drops to about ten feet we jump. It should still be enough to cushion our fall and hopefully the drag will pull us under the boat and clear before it crashes on top of us."

"'Should'?" Jonah asked with a chuckle. "I like the sound of 'should'!"

"Hopefully the sea has better things on its mind than trying to absorb us," Hawkins continued. "If not, we shouldn't be in it long enough to cause any damage. Just keep your mouths shut and your wits sharp." He looked down between his legs, judging the depth. "OK," he said, "on my command, one… two…"

"Geronimo!" shouted Jonah, throwing himself off and into the water.

"Blind bastard never could count," mumbled Barnabas.

"Now!" cried Hawkins.

Alan took Sophie's hand as the crew jumped into the rushing sea. He hit the water badly, winding himself, but kept a tight hold of Sophie's hand as the surge pulled them underneath the *Intrepid*. The shadow of the boat hung above them for a few seconds before the current dashed them away. After a short while, they began to slow down, the level dropping enough to let their weight counteract the swell. Alan grabbed a mouthful of air, holding up Sophie so that she could do the same. Eventually, they came to a stop, drenched and breathless. The *Intrepid* was a good distance behind them, hanging vertical from the ropes.

"Wahey!" Ryan shouted, skidding past them in the shallow water, "how good was that? I mean seriously. Again! Again!"

"That was not good," said Sophie, getting to her feet and looking down at her drenched clothes. "He is a Very Strange man."

Alan couldn't help it – he lay on the tiles and roared with laughter.

Sophie stared down at him, a frown on her face. "And sometimes you are a Very Strange man too," she said disapprovingly, which only made Alan laugh more.

"Well," said Maggie, wringing the water out of her long hair, "not the most comfortable way to disembark but as we're all here to tell the tale it'll have to do."

"Is this Portsmouth?" Jonah asked with a chuckle, getting unsteadily to his feet and readjusting his eye-patches.

"No," Barnabas replied, "so for once things could be worse."

"What about the ship?" asked Ryan.

In the distance, the harpoons gave up trying to bear their load and the *Intrepid* toppled forwards, crashing to earth in a shower of splintered wood.

"She's been better," Hawkins said, "like us all."

Alan finally got his laughter under control, only too aware how Hawkins must be feeling to see his beloved ship destroyed. "I'm sorry," he said.

"Don't worry," Hawkins replied, brushing water from his face and hoping it would cover the tears, "she was on borrowed time the minute we came here. She sailed well."

The crew followed the rivulets that trickled toward the distant plughole. The tiles were littered with dead fish gasping their last in the new environment.

They stopped to observe one sorrowful beast, a large squid, its single eye rolling in confusion as its arms thrashed for the familiar.

"If I had a gun I'd shoot it," commented Hawkins as the creature coughed a mouthful of liquid from its beak.

Night fell and they were forced to camp. They unwrapped the plastic-bound bedrolls from their knapsacks and maintained a watch rota, unwilling to risk sleeping in the open without a little security.

"The only threat at night was the water," said Maggie, using a hunk of bread to mop up some of the soup they had brought with them. "Alan seems to have knocked that problem on the head for us."

"Aye," Ryan agreed, "all in all it'll be a boring old night, I reckon."

"I can live with boring," Hawkins said, "in fact I can think of nothing I'd like more."

Once it was completely dark, they took to their beds, a circle of lanterns affording a few feet of light coverage so that they could see if anything drew near. Alan took the first shift alongside Hawkins, a pairing that made him uncomfortable. During their trek he had lost all sense of joy or relief, becoming guiltier by the moment at the chaos his actions had caused. He had meant to find a path through this small world but had, instead, destroyed it. He could just about live with the fish – though not if he brought to mind the thrashing squid – but the sight of the *Intrepid* crew as they walked along, bereft of

the vessel that had been their home for so long…
that weighed heavily.

"So," said Hawkins, breaking the silence that had
sunk around them, "we find the plughole and then
what? You think we can escape through it?"

"Yes," Alan admitted, "When I was in the water I
could sense there was something beyond there, a
way through. It's hard to put into words, it was an
impression – a vivid one – but nothing more solid."

"It'll do."

There was another pause, then Hawkins smiled.
"Stop worrying about the ship."

"That obvious, am I?"

"She was mine and I loved her but we were fools not
to abandon her long ago. We were never going to be
able to sail home. She was as much a prison as the rest
of this place and though it saddens me to see her lost
it's for the best. Next time you plan on doing something
that threatens our lives so dramatically though, perhaps
a little more warning might be in order?"

Alan nodded. "I'll see what I can do."

The silence that followed was more comfortable,
each of them thinking his own thoughts as the
lantern flickered. Their shift passed and Alan was
grateful for a sleep from which he could remember
no dreams.

Morning, and they rose to stiff backs and damp
bedrolls, only too happy to be on the move again if
only to stretch the muscles that had cramped during
the night's sleep.

Soon the plughole was in sight, a massive dark oval on the horizon that widened as they drew closer.

"Hope there's no spiders in it!" joked Ryan, sticking his tongue out and menacing Barnabas.

"You watch I don't just throw you in, lad," the grumpy sailor warned. "If anything could cheer me up it's that."

Another half an hour saw them at the edge, the hole stretching out before them like the mouth of a volcano.

"Now what?" someone asked.

Hawkins squatted down, looking over the edge at the six-spoked wheel lying across the opening. "We could maybe tie a rope to the inner fitting," he suggested, "though we have no idea how deep it goes..." His voice faded away.

"What?" asked Ryan, "don't tell me there really is a spider?"

"No..." Hawkins voice had grown dreamy, as if his mind were elsewhere, "it's..." It seemed a struggle for him to get his words out. "There's something..." He flew back from the hole as a great force burst upwards in a spray of drain water.

"I knew it!" shouted Barnabas, "here we go..."

Everyone ignored him, spreading out and spinning around to see if they could spot whatever it was that had flown out of the plughole. Alan, for one, suspected he knew exactly what it was. "I've seen something like this before," he shouted, "in the gap between the jungle and the house..." The wraith sailed down, sending up a v-shape of water as it skimmed the ground aiming directly for Alan and Sophie. Alan grabbed Sophie's hand, dashing to one side in the hope they could avoid it. The wraith curved in the air, knocking them towards the plughole. Alan tried to get to his feet but the creature was upon them again, pushing them force- fully towards the hole. There was no grip on the wet tiles, and there was nothing he could do to stop them tumbling into the darkness and vanishing from sight.

INTERLUDE

"There's no point in resisting," the taller man says as his dumpy colleague vomits the renegade on to the floor. "You may be potent amongst these apes but you're just another glitch to us." The renegade looks around the room, assuming initially that they have returned him to his hotel: the simple bed, the table and chair, the open door of the en-suite bathroom, they are all familiar. There is something amiss though; he can sense it rather than see it, an oppressiveness that hugs everything, a sense of isolation.

"You are not in their reality any more," the tall man explains, "we have made you one of your very own. I'm sure you will enjoy it just as much."

The renegade gets to his feet and, despite the orders of his captors, makes for the door. He is only a couple of feet away when the heat sears his skin, forcing him back over the table and into a pained huddle on the floor.

"Do listen," says the tall man, "there is no escape that way."

"Where are we?" the renegade asks, looking at his pink, burned fingers.

"In a little pocket reality we've built for you, a prison in fact, where you might be afforded the time to think over your actions."

"A prison?"

"Built from the subconscious of these animals you're so taken with. You exist as a notion, a concept, outside their reality but permanently linked to it. I confess their imaginations make an impressive power source. I begin to see why they might have been diverting... briefly, at least."

And with that his captors vanish.

CHAPTER TWENTY-TWO

"So," said Miles, trying to get his head around things, "this is the bastard that attacked you?"

Ashe's face fell, "I didn't…" He looked at Penelope. "Did I?"

"You know you did." The look in Penelope's eyes was colder than the wind outside.

"I don't know *anything* about you," Ashe insisted. "Look at the book," he said, kicking it towards them. "You know what the worms do…"

Carruthers picked it up and opened it. "The first section's all but eaten," he said. "You can't read a thing until you get to–"

"Me walking along a roadside with no knowledge of who I am." Ashe said. "Whenever we met – and you have to understand that it's news to me we ever did – it must have been before then."

"Oh," said Miles, "that's OK then, I suppose it doesn't count if you don't remember it."

"I'm not saying that…" Ashe ground his teeth in exasperation. "Look… a man is the sum of his memories." He stared pleadingly at Penelope. "I'm not the person you knew. You have to accept that."

"I don't have to accept a damned thing from you," she spat, "not then and not now. What about Dolores? Should I accept that you let your driver rape her? Should I accept that because you don't remember having done it? Well? Stripping me naked in the back of your car, beating me, threatening me... I should just accept all that, should I? And the box... if it wasn't for you then I wouldn't even be here in the first place!"

"I had the box?"

"Of course you had the box!" Penelope was screaming at the top of her voice by now, "it was because you wanted to open it that you did what you did!"

Ashe just stared at her, every dream, suspicion and uncertainty falling into place. He dropped the gun, fell back into one of the chairs and began to cry.

Carruthers grabbed the gun from the floor and held it loosely trained on Ashe.

"How dare you!" Penelope shouted, "how dare you be the one to cry! What have you got to cry about?"

Ashe sniffed, wiping at his face. "Because I hoped I was a good man," he said, "and that was all I ever cared about."

"Good?" Penelope scoffed, "you were the very worst!"

"Fucking *kill* you." Whitstable opened eyes gummed shut by drying blood, the lids peeling apart like

parched lips to reveal the ceiling of the corridor.
"Fucking *kill* you," he repeated. It was his mantra of
the moment, his motivational chant. In the real
world, his team had gathered at the start of each day,
a few minutes before the markets opened, and
chanted the team motto: "Buy cheap, sell dear!"
They would shout this over and over again like an
unruly football crowd or an army marching into battle. That and the couple of lines of coke he shoved
up his nose in his executive washroom – his snowy
breakfast – had been the fuel that got him through
the day. Now his motivation was even simpler.
"Fucking kill *you!*"

He rolled over to be greeted by the sight of his pink
and weeping face, multiplied in the broken shards of
the mirror that littered the carpet. He selected a
larger piece and held it up, taking in his cracked and
bent spectacles, the blisters and a smile that would
have terrified him had he seen it being worn by anyone else.

"Fucking *kill* you!"

"We need him, my dear," whispered Carruthers,
"which is not to lessen what he did to you, not even
for a moment, but he knows where we're going and
that is invaluable."

"How can he possibly know?" Penelope asked.

"Because I've been here before," Ashe interjected,
"in fact I'm here right now… twice over in fact."

Miles groaned. "What's he talking about? I don't
trust a word this arsehole says…"

"I have been to this house three times, once as a young man, then in my middle age and now one last time. All three visits take place in the same relative period for the house, so all three of me are here right now."

"How lucky," Miles said "As if one of him wasn't enough."

"Why come here so many times?" Carruthers asked.

"The first..." Ashe shrugged "...I don't know. Whatever my experience, I was left with no memories but a subconscious memory of the box. It drove me to hunt it out, thinking it would answer a lot of my problems."

"And why are you here now?" asked Penelope.

"Because I have to stop what's going to happen to Sophie."

Alan and Sophie fell for only a short time, the darkness around them thickening until they were hardly moving. Just when it seemed they would draw to a complete halt they were shoved forward, erupting in a spray of oceanic blue and titanium white from a portrait of an eighteenth-century sailing vessel.

"You OK?" Alan asked Sophie as they lay on the carpet of a house corridor. She didn't appear to be listening, just staring at the picture they'd fallen out of. "Sophie?" He tugged at her sleeve until she turned and focused slowly on him. "You OK?" he asked again. She considered her answer for a moment. To Sophie this was far from a simple question.

In the end she nodded, though Alan suspected that was as much because it was the easiest answer as anything else.

He looked along the corridor and realised they were not alone: a man lay slumped against the door at the far end, a man he took a moment to recognise. He pulled himself to his feet and drew closer, moving cautiously as if approaching a dangerous animal, which, in a way, he was. Alan dropped to his haunches and reached out to touch Chester's cheek.

"You," said Sophie, who had walked up behind him, "but not so Very Old."

Chester stirred, opening lazy eyelids. He tried to focus on Alan's face. "Do we know one another?" he asked.

"No," Alan replied. Chester's eyes drooped closed, his lips twitching as if about to say something but robbed of the strength to do so. Alan sighed. "And that's always been my problem."

"This house," Ashe explained, "you don't even begin to understand what it's for. It's a prison, and the creature it was built to contain... we *can't* let it out."

"Oh, can't we?" Miles replied, before realising that he was just scoffing automatically now, and that Ashe might actually have a point. "Erm... What sort of creature are we talking about exactly?"

"I can't even begin to say," Ashe admitted, "it looks human but..."

"Why are we even listening to him?" Penelope interrupted. "Do I have to remind you both who this is?"

"Of course not, my dear," said Carruthers reassuringly, "but you must accept that he knows more about all of this than we do. I'm not suggesting we offer him our trust but our attention costs us nothing, and we may learn something of value."

"I wish I could reassure you that I mean no harm," Ashe said, "but even if I knew how, we certainly don't have time." He glanced towards the mouth of the cave. "In fact we only have a few hours. Soon the door will open and after that… well, who knows how we can deal with him?"

"All right," Penelope said in exasperation, "talk and we'll listen, but no promises."

An arm erupted from the flood water, desperately trying to find something to hold on to. Wet fingers grabbed a rough edge in the brick, dug in their nails and pulled. Tom emerged behind them, his wild hair plastered across his face as he spat out water. He dragged himself on to the narrow ledge in the tunnel wall, his lungs desperately pumping air. For a moment he lay there, trying, and failing, not to think about Elise and the look on her face as she had fallen back against him with a bullet in her head. He thought of Pablo too but only briefly – sorry, El Toro, there was just no room for anyone else, hadn't been for years.

The flood was settling, having run its course. He sat forward, and a stomachful of water shot from between his lips. He wiped his mouth with the sleeve of his jacket, feeling wretched – not only from the death of Elise but also the contaminated water. He would move in a minute, just as soon as his head cleared. He passed out.

"What makes it even more complicated," said Ashe, "is that I remember all of it. What happens when he leaves the room, what he does to Sophie... I was there as a younger man – and will be there again, in this body, in a couple of hours' time. I know how it all works out... but I have to change it."

"Who is this Sophie?" asked Penelope. "Not some new woman, I hope? Knowing how you like to treat them..."

"She's a child," Ashe spat, angry at Penelope for the first time, "and she means a lot to me. We met here, she looked after me. I like to think I looked after her. Up until I let the prisoner touch her, of course... not that I could have stopped him, not then. Now that I know how everything works out I just need to make sure we get there first, stop the door from being opened. If he's never let out then everything will be fine, not just Sophie, everything... You have to understand: the power this creature has... if it gets out then none of us will survive it, here or back in the real world."

"Oh, nothing too worrying then," joked Miles.

"I mean every word of it," said Ashe. "Don't forget I've seen it. I know what it can do."

"Forgive my, perhaps, archaic comprehension of these things," said Carruthers. "Bar the romance of HG Wells I have no understanding of the workings of time travel – but if it has already happened then how might we stop it?"

"It's about perspective," offered Miles, "Ashe – I mean, Chester… Or Alan…"

"Stick to Ashe," Ashe suggested, "it makes it easier."

"Thank you," said Miles, somewhat dismissively; he was still far from sure he trusted a word the man said. "Ashe has witnessed these events from a dual perspective: he was there as a younger man and therefore has a memory of how things played out then. He also knows that he will be there as an old man – because he saw himself – though no idea of the events leading up to it from that point of view. So it all comes down to whether his foreknowledge will be enough for him to change how things occur this time."

"And, therefore, how they will have always occurred," Ashe chipped in.

"It's a paradox," added Miles.

"It's a nonsense" was Penelope's opinion.

"But can we afford to take the risk?" asked Carruthers. "I still can't claim to fully comprehend this but if, as Ashe insists, the stakes are so high then how can we not play the game out?"

"Because we don't trust him an inch?" suggested Penelope.

"I'm sorry," said Carruthers, "but that's not enough, people can change and if he has, and if what he says is true…"

"A lot of 'if's, you notice," said Miles.

"Indeed," agreed Carruthers, "but not enough to counter the final one: if he's right and we don't follow his lead then our obstinacy will cost the lives of countless others."

"We have to do it," said Penelope, "even though it makes me sick to spend a moment longer in his company."

Carruthers looked at Miles. "This is not a decision to be made lightly. Miles, are you with us?"

Miles sighed. "Of course, we do it." He looked at Ashe. "Though if you hurt Penelope in any way I'll bloody kill you, all right?"

Ashe smiled. "All right."

"So," said Carruthers, "with that agreed..." He held up the revolver and began loading it with the bullets he had confiscated earlier. "May I suggest you lead the way? You can explain more as we walk."

Elise came to Tom while he slept. She rose up in front of him, a line of brown liquid trickling from the hole in her forehead. A column of water reached up to the roof for her to grip and swing on, shaking the wares that had kept her rent paid when she was alive but were now just meat to swell and bloat and rot.

"No touching," she whispered, a dribble of water cascading over her blue lip, "no extras."

"Not who you were," Tom muttered, "not to me."

She moved slowly, to music only the dead can hear, swinging her hips to the trumpet of a graveyard Quincy Jones or Miles Davis, splashing Tom with spray from her body as she gyrated.

"Loved you," said Tom, "not for this… for Thursday nights, for your eyes."

He passed out again.

Ashe led them to the rear of the cave, running his hands over what appeared to be a solid stone wall. "In this place," he said as his hands disappeared into the stone, "nothing is what it looks like." He walked through the wall as if it weren't there, the others following behind him. "When we met, I told my younger self how to find the creature's cell," Ashe explained, "which means I can remember it now."

"Another paradox," said Miles, "in case anyone was wanting to keep count."

"As always, darling," said Penelope, "you make sense only to yourself." She squeezed his hand to reassure him she meant it kindly.

They were in a narrow tunnel, Ashe marching ahead with his lantern held aloft. Soon he had no need of it, as a faint luminescence in the walls brightened the further they walked. The tunnel began to change shape, becoming more regular, the walls, floor and ceiling flattening. A little further and a faint *fleur de lys* pattern could be seen in the walls, as if there was wallpaper just beneath the surface of the stone.

"It's becoming another corridor," Penelope observed, as they came upon a series of alcoves filled with decorative busts, "part of the house again."

"We never left, of course," said Carruthers, "however much our recent climb may have made us think so."

"The house is constantly changing," explained Ashe. "Though it looks like an old building it's nothing of the sort. It's more like a living being than bricks and mortar."

"But where is it?" Miles asked.

"That I don't know," Ashe said. "Outside the reality we're used to but still linked... in fact fuelled by it."

"Fuelled by it?" asked Carruthers.

"The library," Ashe answered, "though don't ask me to explain in too much detail. I only know the vagaries. The house needs human minds to perpetuate it. It is their imagination – nightmares, mostly, you'd assume, from being in the damn place – that gives it form and substance."

"Freaky," said Miles.

"And beyond my ability to comprehend, I confess," said Carruthers. "How can the human mind perpetuate something so solid?"

"The beings that built it are capable of bending reality," said Ashe. "To them it's all just clay, to play with as they like."

"And the guy they imprisoned?" asked Miles.

"Is one of them, yes."

"A creature that can create matter purely from thought, with the power to control or destroy us all on a whim?" asked Carruthers.

"That's about the size of it," admitted Ashe.

"I don't know about the three of you," said Carruthers, "but where I come from the only person we credit with those abilities is called God."

• • •

Tom was alone, Elise having danced away the hours while he slept. Night had fallen and with it the creatures of the tunnels had roamed, the insects and worms exploring his unconscious body and finding the seawater that still invaded his clothes not to their taste. They knew what the water was capable of, had seen the bodies emerging from it in the areas where it was not too diluted. They did not risk angering it here. Tom had woken for an hour or so the next day, still feverish and incapable of much beyond tears and prayers. When finally he lost consciousness again it was a blessing, both for him and for anything that roamed these cellars with sensitive hearing, his screams having carried some distance.

On the next day he woke again, still dazed and weak but with the fever broken and his thoughts once more his own. The nighttime creatures were gone, leaving little sign of their roaming (a few bite-marks in the tails of his jacket from one of the braver cockroaches, all beneath his notice). He shifted on his ledge, his arms and legs numb from the lack of movement. He stretched them, rubbing his thighs and calves to get a little life back into them. Once he felt he could move without falling flat on his face he inched off the ledge and lowered himself down into the water. It went up to his waist but was shallow enough to walk in. He began to make his way back along the tunnel.

Whitstable was enjoying himself. He had run along the corridors for some while, exploring the rooms (hoping to find something… anything… to stab with either his sharpened stake or his new toy, the piece of mirror). He found nobody, but amused himself with some wanton destruction anyway, tearing up wallpaper, engraving his name in the soft wood of an occasional table, taking a relaxing shit in a large vase of pampas grass. Sometimes he thought someone was talking to him, suggesting directions, fuelling the anger he felt towards the man and his kid. For a while he had assumed it to be Stefania; certainly he was used to her issuing commands and goading him. It didn't take long for him to recognise his mistake. For a start the voice, if he listened really intently, was male. Secondly, Stefania would never have taken care of him as this man did. When the lamps in the walls grew dim the voice had suggested where Whitsable could hide, directing him to the shadows beneath a large four-poster bed where he lay and listened to the booming feet of whatever roamed this wing of the house at night. It had been safe and comfortable and he had enjoyed his best night of sleep for months. He gave the voice thanks when he awoke, offering a bloody sacrifice of his ear lobe, sliced off by the mirror and left on the pillow like a mint in a five-star hotel. It made sense to him and he was sure that the gift would be appreciated as he continued through the corridors.

Proof – not that he had the self-doubt to need any – came a few hours later when he stumbled upon a young man, newly arrived in the house, paralysed and terrified, in an en-suite bathtub. Whitstable was overjoyed at the glories on offer, painting his thanks on the walls of the bathroom once he had finished rearranging the young man's organs to his pleasure. His new master was a fine master indeed and for Whitstable it was a joy to serve.

"I've just thought," said Miles. "If you've been and come back you must know the way out of here."

The passage had lost its stone trappings, reverting to a corridor not unlike the one in which Miles and Penelope had first explored the house. It seemed to them – and Carruthers endorsed it, having seen altogether more of the building – that this maze of corridors was the default appearance of the house. A network of seemingly innocuous walkways that led the unwary to a sticky end. Ashe had a baffling simple navigational method, turning right whenever the choice presented itself. It was as if they were constantly winding inwards to the heart of the building.

"The exit I used will be no use to us if we succeed," Ashe said. "The prisoner made it himself, with Sophie's help."

"Oh great," Miles replied, "and you didn't think to mention it?"

"I don't want to tell you any more than I have to," admitted Ashe. "You've got to understand that my telling you what I know could alter how you react, and that wouldn't be good."

"Why not?" asked Penelope, convinced her suspicions were about to be borne out. "Sounds like an excuse to me."

"I'm using what I know of the future to think of a way to change it. If you three don't do exactly what I remember you doing then that's no use."

"Well, I don't like it," moaned Miles, "you're asking for one hell of a lot of trust."

"Yes," admitted Ashe, "I am. But we're nearly there so you won't have to worry about it for long."

They turned the corner and Ashe rebounded against a barrier directly in front of them. "Something there," he muttered, holding his nose as it trickled blood.

Carruthers walked forward, holding out his hands. "Feels like glass," he said, running his palms against what appeared to be no more than thin air.

"Didn't see this coming then?" said Miles, knocking against it with his knuckles.

Suddenly the corridor in front of them rushed forward as if they were flying along it at speed.

"What now?" moaned Penelope, steadying herself against the wall as the sight of the corridor flying past robbed her of her balance. The house darkened. Turning to look over their shoulders, they saw the carpet and walls shift to re-form into a village square at night. There was a pond, a thatched pub, a winding road leading away into the darkness.

"No!" shouted Ashe, "the paintings! There were paintings lining the wall. We're there! Look!" He pointed beyond the glass and, as the corridor in front of them solidified, they saw the end of the corridor. There was a large door with a young man – whom Penelope recognised all too easily – slumped against it. In front of him was an older man and a girl. The man was reaching out to the handle of the door, unable to hear the shouts of his older counterpart, trapped as he was behind the glass of a rural watercolour hanging on the corridor wall.

"Quick!" came a voice Alan didn't recognise, distracting him from the sight of his younger self. "Let me out!" The voice was coming from behind the door Chester was leaning against. A man's voice, panicked, as if his very life was in the balance.

In this place, thought Alan, it most probably was. He reached for the handle.

"No," said Sophie "it is not good."

"Someone's in trouble, sweetheart," said Alan. "We can't ignore them."

He opened the door.

CHAPTER TWENTY-THREE

The prisoner sat down at his table and stroked the wood. For a moment he felt what it was to bend in the breeze, a skirt of leaves flapping around him. He felt worms and grubs burrow in his limbs before the whine of buzz-saws cut them away. Heady with the scent of sap, he rubbed his palms together to fashion six flat pieces of wood. He slotted them together, forming a box. *The* box.

He pinched the base of his brass candlestick, making molten metal that he fashioned into hinges. Holding the box open, he breathed inside, a wisp of his essence curling into the compartment. He closed the lid, trapping the tiny piece of him.

He placed the completed box on the table. As an afterthought, he picked it back up and burned a series of characters into the wood. This was something of a joke, the ancient and indecipherable Khitan script spelling "Bringer of Tricks". The first name he had been given, a signature on this work of art.

"Quick!" he shouted, aware that Alan had joined his younger self outside the door of his prison. "Let me out!"

He picked up the box and walked towards the door, sighing as, for the first time in centuries, the wood swung open. He felt a surge of renewed energy enter him alongside the air from the corridor outside. He breathed it deep.

The prisoner stepped into the corridor. "Thank you!" he said, smiling at Alan, "you have no idea how relieved I am that you came along."

"No problem," Alan replied, "have you just arrived here?"

"Oh no," the prisoner replied, "I've been here some time."

He sat cross-legged on the carpet and beckoned Sophie closer. She didn't move, Alan placing a protective hand on her shoulder. "I mean no harm," the prisoner said, offering a smile that dripped gentility. "But Sophie can get us all home if only she can be taught how." He looked at her. "You'd like to go home, wouldn't you, Sophie?" he asked. "To a place that is Right, to a place you can understand, to a place that makes sense?" She gave a slight nod. "Then sit with me," the prisoner replied, "and I will show you how you can understand everything."

"How do you know her name?" Alan interrupted, holding Sophie's shoulder more tightly.

"Oh, Alan," said the prisoner with a smile, "there's not much I don't know. Now shush, you're interrupting…" The prisoner slipped into Alan's mind, switching off a few brain functions. Alan stumbled back against the wall of the corridor and slowly dropped to the carpet.

The prisoner looked back at Sophie, reaching out to her with his mind, stroking her, reassuring her, silencing her confusion with a soft hum that only she could hear. One…two…

"Three," she said, sitting down in front of him.

"That's the way," he said, "that is good. Close your eyes for me, Sophie, and let us talk to a mutual acquaintance."

Sophie does not know what to think. Perhaps she should be Very Careful of this thing that has come out of the room. Certainly it is Very Strange. It is not a man and she is surprised Alan is not able to see this. It looks like a man in the same way a photograph of one does. But there is something underneath, something that is *not* a man. Sophie is scared of this thing, she thinks of the faces of the tribe in the jungle, the hungry looks they had given her. She thinks this thing is just as hungry.

She sits down with it. Too scared to do anything else. When it tells her to close her eyes she closes them. At least now she does not have to look at it, this is good.

"Listen to me," it says. She will try, she does not always manage to listen to everything people say but she thinks she'll manage now. She is too scared that she will miss something important. Something like

"I am going to eat you now, Sophie" or "If you don't tidy your room now I will kill you, Sophie". She will listen very hard, so that she doesn't get in trouble.

"This house is not like a normal house," the voice is saying, and this is a silly thing, of course the house is not like other houses, she doesn't need someone to tell her that, she is not stupid. It is not even a bit like other houses. It looks like a house in the same way a photograph of one does. "It talks, Sophie, it wants you to understand it. Will you try?"

Sophie nods, though she has actually missed what the creature said, despite promising herself she wouldn't do so.

"Good." It takes gentle hold of her fingertips and as much as she doesn't like the physical contact there is another intrusion that displeases her more: she can feel it touching her thoughts. The Inside Sophie that does all the thinking and feeling and understanding is being touched and nothing should ever be able to do that, *nothing*.

She is about to shout out her displeasure when the Inside Sophie is grabbed, smothered and folded into a small parcel from which it cannot escape. Sophie is now empty.

Tom had been wading for hours and could no longer feel his legs. When he saw the foot of the elevator shaft an extra spurt of energy carried him on, eager to be out of the water. He was not in the least pre-pared for the sight of Elise, whose body had washed up on the farthest edge of the platform. He had hoped she would have been carried far away, never to be seen again. He didn't want to remember her as this bloated thing, eyes robbed by insects in the night.

This was not her. This was what she left behind.

Still, he couldn't bear to have it lying there. He rolled the body into the water, sobbing as he did so, trying not to notice the way the skin slid on the bone as it caught on the concrete. He couldn't bear this. Couldn't bear it at all.

He ran to the elevator, determined to be away from there, but the call button had no intention of working, and the cage was stuck at the top of the shaft. There was no easy way for this to be done but do it he must. He began to climb.

"There must be a way out," said Miles, "if you remember being there…"

"I just don't know any more," Ashe said, "I'm sure this is already different." He rapped his knuckles on the glass. "Stupid of me. If time can be altered then how naïve did I have to be to think that I was the only one that could do it? The bastard wanted me out of the way and he's done a damned good job of it." He closed his eyes, concentrating. "If I try and remember what happened now… it's mixed up, all different…I don't meet myself… Shit!" He kicked at the glass. "I really fucked this up."

"I say!" called Carruthers who had wandered off without the others noticing, strolling around the village to see what he could find. They turned to look and he was pointing at the nose of a vintage car that was emerging from behind the pub. "Anyone know how to drive one of these stupid things?"

"Erm…" Miles shrugged. "Not very well, I mean, I passed my test and everything but I've never driven since… why?"

"I've got an idea!"

The empty Sophie is filled by brick and plank, plaster and paint. Her intestines become corridors, her stomach a kitchen, her heart a playroom, her head a library… she is becoming the house and the house is becoming her. The prisoner's captors may well have considered it a perfect solution, ensuring the house could perpetuate itself through humans. A never-ending supply of neuroses and nightmares, imaginations to imprison and terrify. They did not, however, consider what the house might do when presented with a mind like Sophie's.

Wrong. All wrong. This is a Very Strange House.

"Yes, very wrong," the man who is not even a man is saying, "and what do we need to do to make it right?"

When something is always wrong then wrong becomes right.

The prisoner has not anticipated this and for the first time he is wrong-footed. "What are you talking about? The house should be neat and ordered, perfect little boxes, one two three!"

Not this house. In this house that would be wrong.

The prisoner cannot believe that this – the most simple element of its plan – is going awry. Sophie's

logic is turning against him. He needs to think of another way around the problem. A solution occurs:
"If you can get inside somewhere you should be able
to get out again," he says.

Yes.

"And here you can get in from lots of places, any
time you like, any location. So it makes sense that
there must be a way to travel from here to to all of
those places, yes?"

There is silence and he wonders if Sophie has been
listening. He tries again.

"Somewhere in the house there must be a way to
travel in the opposite direction." He makes it a statement this time rather than a question. "A place
like…" he is trying to think of something a human
could relate to "…a place like…"

Sophie has been thinking of somewhere she once
visited with her mother.

A train station.

"Yes!" The prisoner is relieved. "A train station that
can take you to all the places in the world you want
to go, all the different time periods."

A train station to everywhere.

"Yes." He can sense that she understands. Quietly,
and with the sort of feigned, casual gentility that always surrounds the really important questions in
life, he whispers: "Let's go there."

Yes, let's go there.

The house shifts around them, the corridor
falling apart like unravelled origami, walls falling
back to reveal space, the ceiling lifting and

breaking away, replaced by arched roofs of glass and iron.

"That's it!" the prisoner shouts. "That's it!"

In the greenhouse, Stefania's tribe were more in disarray than ever. Their cavern reeked of burned fabric and skin, and black swathes of soot were painted across the walls. Stefania sat and darned her skirt, determined to ignore the sobbing and whining of her people. They were a pitiful lot. Many were the times she had been tempted to walk out on them and never return. Perhaps one day she would. Brave the hole in their world as the old man and his child had done, and see if there wasn't somewhere better to spend her days.

"He's not coming back, is he?"

She looked up to see Lauren (Oxford, 1989, housebound one year), twin tracks leading from her eyes where tears had swept away dirt.

"If you mean that idiot Whitstable, then no, I don't expect he is." Stefania threw her darning on to a table in disgust. "I always knew he was unreliable."

"He used to be so nice," muttered Lauren, "soft, gentlemanly. Talked a lot about his wife."

"Well, now he's an idiot," Stefania replied. "A dead one."

Lauren began to cry and Stefania took a deep breath, ready to hurl insults. Before she could speak, a rumbling noise distracted her. It was like the advance of heavy plant machinery, a rolling and pounding that trembled through the earth.

"What's happening?" someone shouted, as always looking to someone else to do their thinking for them.

Stefania ran outside, aware the tribe would follow.

The jungle thrashed as if in a storm, the leaves of the trees whipping to and fro. The disturbance wasn't in the air though: there was no wind. Stefania could feel it beneath her bare feet. The ground was rippling. There was a crack as a nearby palm was uprooted, pushed up from below and sent toppling.

"Keep back!" Stefania shouted.

"Is it the creatures in the walls?" someone asked.

Stefania had no patience to answer, stumbling forward as the grass beneath her feet rose up. She landed on all fours, immediately furious at having been rendered foolish in front of the tribe.

"It's the end of the world!" someone else chimed in.

With a roar of exasperation she pulled herself to her feet and turned to face her people. "Don't be so ridiculous!" she shouted, "it's just an earth tremor, no reason to start squealing like babies. God!" She was shaking now, her pent-up frustrations pouring out. "What are you for? Pathetic sheep! The minute something happens it's tears and begging. You sicken me, the lot of you. There's nothing to worry about, it'll settle in a minute. Now get on with your work!"

The jungle had little but contempt for her, taking her words as a cue for greater carnage. The ground shook again, this time knocking all to the floor. The trees thrashed with greater frenzy. The air was filled with the squeals and shrieks of wildlife as it stampeded, directionless with panic.

"I will not have it!" Stefania screamed, determined to have her authority returned. "I will not."

There was a deep cracking noise that she couldn't place, a whistle of wind. She looked up towards the sky and wondered why the light seemed to move. It was the last thought in her mind before the section of roof glass embedded itself in her, from temple to hip.

Some of the tribe squealed at that; some were far too concerned about their own safety even to have noticed.

"What are we going to do?" someone asked Lauren. She stared at their bisected leader as the undergrowth turned crimson.

"We stay under cover and hope the tremors die down," she replied. "Not much else we can do, is there?" She began to turn towards the cavern when a thought struck her. "Hang on, let's bring Stefania's body. If we're all to die then let's do so with a full belly. It's what she would have wanted."

Hawkins and his crew had been reluctant to stay near the plughole after Alan and Sophie had disappeared. Alan's certainty that it was the way out was the only thing to give Hawkins pause. The wraith had seemingly vanished with its prey – it was hard to tell because you couldn't see the damn thing.

Ryan, ever fearless, had been the first to look over the rim into the dark pipe below.

"No sign of them," he said, to nobody's great surprise.

"Course there ain't," said Barnabas, "poor bastards will be smeared like soup at the bottom of the pipework."

"If you've nothing better to say," Hawkins muttered, "perhaps it's best you say nothing at all."

Barnabas grumbled at that but thought better than to challenge his captain.

They waited for a few minutes. Hawkins paced around the plughole, weighing up their options.

"What's the alternative?" his wife asked him. "March all the way to shore? Not as if we don't know what lies that way, is it?"

"True."

Just as he was deciding to lower some ropes and make the climb there was a rumbling from above them. Looking up, they could see clouds beginning to gather, dark and weighty with the promise of rain.

"Looks like a storm," said Jonah.

"And here's us with lots of shelter," moaned Barnabas.

Lightning pulsed in the building gloom, a heartbeat of electric blue in the dark grey of the roof.

The ground shook. A spray of plaster rained down across the wet tiles. Thunder churned above them, rain and tiles falling side by side. They cowered, packs over their heads, as the bathroom broke up around them.

• • •

"That's it!" the prisoner shouted, "that's it!"

Sophie can feel the damage around her, the cracking and the crumbling of all the perfect boxes that keep the madness in. She is trying to build not break, she does not understand why the house cannot see this.

Build not break. She insists. *Build not break.*

The damage was felt everywhere. Pictures shook on walls, their subjects screaming and digging oil-paint nails into the canvas in an effort to hold on. The gas lamps alternately flared and died, their flames moving from amber to red like malfunctioning traffic lights. Statuary writhed on its pedestals. The wallpaper rippled like a field of barley in a storm. The carpet split and unravelled like rotting skin.

In the library, books began flying off the shelves, flapping their covers like lame birds as they collided with one another in mid-air.

The pack of stuffed wolves howled as they ran ahead of an avalanche, the crest of snow building higher and higher as it surged down the mountain.

In the cellars, the living sea began to crash against the walls of the tunnels like an animal in confinement. It could feel the storm heading its way and wanted nothing more than to surge away.

In the dark spaces, the wraiths chased their own tails, spinning faster and faster as the devastation around them made them hunger for more.

The house was coming apart and nothing would please it more than to take everyone else with it.

● ● ●

Tom fought to hold on as the shaft vibrated around him, unbuckling and re-forming even as he reached for the base of the elevator, hoping to pull himself inside. Below him the flood water surged, forced away by an unseen hand. The cellars darkened into a single circle of black that receded as his hands pedalled at the air. Everything around him blurred as if viewed from a speeding car. That wasn't right, surely? How come he was still moving forward? The blur resolved and he was freaked to find himself on his hands and knees riding an escalator.

"When you shout, 'I've got an idea!'" said Miles, having to bellow over the roar of the house's shaking walls, "that tends to make everyone assume something really cunning is about to happen. Something that will save the day and have us all home by teatime."

"I'm not a miracle-worker," complained Carruthers, trying to get comfortable on the passenger side of the Morgan Tourer, "and I'm open to suggestions if you can think of another way around the situation."

"You know I can't," sighed Miles. "If I could I would hardly be sitting here, would I?" He tried to figure out how to start the engine.

"You two in?" Carruthers called over his shoulder.

"Yes," Ashe replied, "though I'm far from convinced about this either."

"It'll be fine," said Penelope, squeezing Miles' shoulder. "I have every faith in you."

"That's the spirit!" said Carruthers. "Though if Miles is correct as to the limitations of his driving ability…"

"And he is," Miles mumbled, finally finding the manual choke.

"…then you would do well to hold on tight," Carruthers continued.

The Morgan roared and Miles tried to stop swearing under his breath.

"Ready, old chap?" Carruthers asked.

"I suppose so…" Miles put the car in first, lifted the handbrake and pressed the accelerator to the floor. The Morgan leaped forward with enough force to throw them all back in their seats.

"Open your eyes!" Carruthers shouted to Miles, "you can hardly drive blind!"

"I can hardly drive at all!"

The car hit the glass just as the re-formation of the house reached their section of the wall. It burst forth in a shower of crystal shards as the bricks fell away. The view through the windows was nothing the eye could fix on, shifting shapes and flashes of colour as the house rebuilt itself. It solidified in time for the tyres to hit the ground, the wheels screeching against a polished stone floor as the car went into a skid. Miles didn't have the first idea how to deal with that. "Feathering the brakes!" he shouted, if only to reassure everyone else he was doing something.

"Only you know, darling!" Penelope shouted.

The car spun until it smashed into a newsstand and came to a safe, if rather noisy, halt in a pile of London *Standards*.

"I recognise this," said Miles, peering through the windscreen. "We're in Saint Pancras Station!"

"The train now approaching platform 18,672 is the 10.14 to 1978, calling at Brussels, New York, Lyons and Bournemouth, terminating in the front room of the Thompson family residence, just in time for lunch."

The house had seen minor changes in its time, was in fact in a constant state of flux, yet never before had something so drastic affected its geography. With the resources of mankind's subconscious to hand, however, the alteration was quick to take hold. Not just that, it was elaborated on. The world's dreamers took the concept and fleshed it out, adding detail and colour. The coffeeshops began to wake with the sounds of hammered coffee-scoops and hissing milk-steamers; the amusement arcade flashed lights and top scores in a hail of bleeps and fanfares; pigeons fluttered in the eaves, or scoured the concourse beneath them for scraps of left-over panini or smeared chocolate wrappers. Passengers appeared, ethereal figures staring up at the impossibly long announcement board or dashing towards listless guards who took pleasure in stringing out the process of clicking ticket stubs just long enough for them to board their train with only seconds to spare.

"This is a customer service announcement: the 10.15 to 1934 is delayed due to a breakdown in causality affecting all routes to to the 1930s. Passengers are advised to take the 10.34 to 1929 and make their own arrangements from there."

The announcement board was a never-ending flutter of signage, times and destinations altering almost at random as it tried to keep track of the traffic to and from the infinite line of platforms. An aged ghost of a man stood vacantly behind his bucket of wilting blooms, perpetually working his way along a stick-thin roll-up cigarette. The newspaper seller, unfazed by the presence of a 1937 Morgan Tourer amongst the day's news, hollered headlines from history as his placard switched from one event to another: "Elvis Presley found dead, full story inside!", "Archduke Ferdinand assassinated, fears of war loom!", "Fog in channel, Continent isolated!" A pair of prostitutes eyed each other's fishnets for ladders and touched up their make-up in the reflective surface of a bakery window while the guards looked on and wondered if they might get a staff discount. The queues at the ticket office grew longer and longer, Japanese students shunting their suitcases in front of them like reluctant children as they read their travel guides and plotted the day's photo opportunities.

In the middle of it all, the prisoner stretched his borrowed skin and savoured the feeling of freedom. Nearly there, he thought to himself, nearly there.

Whitstable had been thrashing around in a wardrobe when the change came, convinced he had heard the sound of a child's voice within. There was nothing to be found but spare bedlinen and mothballs but he took his anger out on them anyway, only stopping as he felt the house shift as if hit by an earthquake. The wardrobe doors banged shut behind him and sent him face first into a pile of woollen blankets. Before he had time to slash holes in them with the piece of broken mirror, the wardrobe altered around him, light flooding the confined space. When he regained his vision it was to find himself revolving on the plastic stool inside a photo-booth. The flashing camera took four shots of his angry forehead as he tried to get his balance. He peeled aside the bright orange curtain and then immediately dropped it back into place while he thought about what he had seen. The station – bar its surrealistic touches – was all too familiar from the days when he had commuted for work, but that didn't make its sudden presence right next to him any less alarming.

He took another look, saw the translucent passengers as they hurried past his booth, took in the impossibly large announcement board and the old-fashioned car parked on the opposite side of the concourse. Then his eyes fell on something familiar, something that made him realise today would be a good day indeed.

"Fucking *kill* you!" he chuckled.

"I always was good at emergency stops," said Miles. "All of my test examiners said so."

"We need to get over there!" insisted Ashe, pushing against Miles' seat to hurry him along.

Miles and Carruthers got out of the car and lifted forward their seats to release the other two. Ashe immediately began running, knowing there were only moments left.

Around him the destruction had far from ceased. The station, so fresh and new, was corrupting already. Metal supports creaked over his head. The plate-glass window of a creperie shattered and poured itself on to the trembling floor tiles. "Faster, faster, faster!" he shouted, angry at himself for getting so damned old.

"Fucking *kill* you!" Whitstable screamed, tearing out of the photo booth on the opposite arm of the concourse, his makeshift knife held high above his head as he sprinted towards Sophie, eager to plunge its sharp point into her stupid face. He delighted in the sound of breaking glass and grinding metal; to him it was a round of applause, an appreciative cheer as he charged towards the stupid little bitch. "Fucking *kill* you!"

Sophie was still sitting cross-legged on the floor, her eyes closed and her thoughts elsewhere. If she was at all aware of the changes occurring around them she gave no sign, gently humming as she continued to talk to the house. Whitstable was only feet away, Alan still vacant and unable to move, Chester slumped at his feet.

The prisoner had no intention of helping; he was happy simply to watch, one final little game before he took his leave.

Ashe ignored the stab of pain in his ribs, a stitch threatening to slow him down even as Whitstable was only feet away. He remembered the future so clearly: the parting of skin, the arc of arterial blood, the end of anything worth a shit. He had to do this, had to. He realised he was roaring at them, as he forced his legs to move faster and faster.

Whitstable grabbed Sophie's hair, yanking her head back to expose her throat, and was slashing down with the glass as two shots rang out. The first hit him in the shoulder, making him drop the knife. The second removed a couple of inches from the right-hand side of his head. A red spray of bone and meat painted itself across a bank of ATMs behind him. He dropped to the ground and thrashed like a beached fish, arms and legs slapping the ground as his brain misfired. One more shot made him lie still. Sophie lay whimpering on the floor.

Ashe stared at his handiwork for a moment, aware that he should feel some emotion at having shot a man. He felt nothing. Perhaps this wasn't his first time...

"Excellent shot, sir!" said the prisoner. "And with that, the final round of our game is done."

EPILOGUE

The prisoner reached into his pocket, pulled out the wooden box and threw it to Ashe. Ashe caught it and, almost as an afterthought, emptied the rest of the bullets into the prisoner's chest. "Yes…" said the prisoner, glancing down at the holes in his tank top, "that was a bit pointless, wasn't it?"

"Can't blame a guy for trying."

"I suppose not."

"Well, as long as it's out of your system now I'll give you your orders."

"I knew it!" said Penelope as the rest of them caught up, "he's working for him."

"I certainly am not," Ashe replied, looking at the prisoner. "What the hell makes you think I'll follow any orders from you?'

"From what you said earlier I rather think he can make us do whatever he wishes," said Carruthers.

"Well," said Miles, stepping protectively in front of Penelope, "we'll see about that."

The prisoner shrugged. "Your man has a point, though in the spirit of fairness I should say that my abilities are somewhat limited at the moment. Give me a little time and a proper reality to sink my teeth into and… well, I imagine I could whip up an apocalypse in no time, but right now…"

"Bastard!" Tom appeared from behind them, pushed past Ashe and dived on to the unconscious Chester. He put his hands around his throat and began to squeeze.

"I'd stop him if I were you," said the prisoner to Ashe, "unless you fancy winking out of existence in a few seconds' time – something that would be catastrophic for all of you, I hasten to add."

Ashe grabbed Tom and, with Miles' help, they pulled him off the unresponsive Chester.

"Motherfucker killed Elise and Pablo!" Tom shouted. "*Motherfucker!*"

The prisoner smiled. "Young love," he sighed and, with a wink, sent Tom to sleep in Miles' arms.

"Right," the prisoner said, looking around, "anyone else? Any last-minute rescues or attempts at revenge? No? Excellent, I have a train to catch." He turned back to Ashe. "All of you are now utterly tied into this chronology," he said, "so I advise you to hear me out before attempting any more pointless acts of heroism."

In the far corner of the concourse there was a rumbling noise followed by a shower of glass as a section of the roof fell in.

"Hmm," said the prisoner, "the house really is

suffering, isn't it?" He turned back to his audience. "No matter, I'm sure you'll manage to stabilise things."

"We'll manage?" asked Penelope.

"Yes, my dear, it's up to you now to get everything back on track. Any reality can take a few paradoxes as a tap on the chin, but this one needs stabilising as fast as you can before the whole lot comes crumbling down. And as much as that may seem an attractive proposition, I should make clear that if this place goes it'll take the human race with it. The connection runs both ways, you see. This place feeds off them and they in turn are connected to it. You know how the events in the library extended into 'the real world' – just look at poor Alan here, his head's screwed more than a dockyard hooker when the Navy's home."

"Nice," said Miles.

"One tries." The prisoner pointed at Ashe. "You will agree that if it were not for your timely intervention then Sophie would be dead?"

"Yeah," said Ashe, looking at the body of Whitstable, "I guess that's true."

"Then you need to take that box and make sure it gets to the right people. Without the help of young Tom and the sadly departed Pablo and Elise, you would have died in the cellars of this house. You need to ensure their past selves receive the box and use it, otherwise you will cease to exist. Alongside you will go Sophie and..." he looked at Miles, Penelope and Carruthers "...correct me if I'm wrong but wasn't there some bit of ghastliness with a polar bear?"

"Yes," said Carruthers, "Ashe shot it, otherwise it would have most certainly killed one, maybe all of us."

"But without Ashe we would never have been there in the first place," said Miles. "He was the one who found the doorway through to that room."

"Causality, eh?" said the prisoner. "It's a bitch."

"Forgive me for speaking on everyone's behalf here," said Carruthers, "but what effect in real terms would our deaths actually cause? Don't get me wrong, I'm rather fond of my continued existence, but even I'm not so frightful an egomaniac as to think the survival of everything depends on it."

"But it does!" the prisoner beamed. "So feel proud. There are countless people who have appeared here…" he turned to Ashe, a point suddenly occurring to him "…and mark that you return the box somewhere suitably useful in order for them to always have done so – but you were the key players," he continued to the rest of them, "all of you. You interacted with Alan here and throughly embedded yourselves into the chain of events that leads us to this point. Now you just need to travel these lines… " – he gestured over his shoulder at the platforms – "and ensure that everything occurs as it should.

"If you don't, this place will breathe its last and the rest of your species with it. And none of us want that. Not even me. If humanity is to be wiped out then I wish to get my hands dirty doing so. And that said…" He pulled a mackintosh and trilby out of the air, put them on and tipped his hat at a suitably jolly angle. "I must catch my train."

He flipped Chester up on to his shoulder as if the man weighed nothing more than a small holdall and marched towards one of the platforms.

"Don't worry about this one," he called behind him, "I'll get him to his destination for you. Never let it be said I don't do my bit." And with that he vanished from sight, a hail of crumbling plaster raining down in his wake as a section of the platform wall gave way.

"We can't just let him go, surely?" asked Miles.

"Darling," said Penelope, "if you have the superhuman abilities it would take to stop him then feel free to give chase, otherwise I can't see we have much choice."

"She's right," said Ashe. "We're all bound into this now, and he's left us with our hands full." He looked up at the cracking roof. "So let's get to work."

WORK WILL RESUME ON THE WORLD HOUSE IN

RESTORATION

BY GUY ADAMS

COMING SOON FROM ANGRY ROBOT

ABOUT THE AUTHOR

Guy Adams trained and worked as an actor for twelve years before becoming a full-time writer. If nothing else this proves he has no concept of a sensible career. He mugged someone on *Emmerdale*, performed a dance routine as Hitler, and spent eighteen months touring his own comedy material around clubs and theatres.

He is the author of the best-selling *Rules of Modern Policing: 1973 Edition*, a spoof police manual "written by" DCI Gene Hunt of *Life on Mars*. Guy has also written a two-volume series companion to the show; a Torchwood novel, *The House That Jack Built*; and *The Case Notes of Sherlock Holmes*, a fictional facsimile of a scrapbook kept by Doctor John Watson. He is the current chair of the British Fantasy Society.

www.guy-adams.com

Psssst! Get
advance
intelligence on

Angry Robot's
nefarious plans for
world domination.
Also, free stuff.
Sign up to our
Robot Legion at
**angryrobotbooks.
com/legion**
This is how we
roll.